LEAVING HOME

The basement flat that Martin and Terry had vacated was small and dark. While they ate, Clare told Eve about the district. 'You'll love it here. There's so much to do,' she said.

But Eve wasn't so sure. Her first sight of the multitudinous grey houses with their tiny back gardens and the tall, redbrick terraced houses jammed together made her realise that London would take some getting used to.

Eve could imagine the intensity with which Clare cultivated the friends who pursued a career in music and shared the same interests as she did. Suddenly she was doubtful that this world into which Clare had plunged so wholeheartedly would provide her with the same stimulus . . .

Leaving Home

Joan O'Neill

CORONET BOOKS
Hodder and Stoughton

First published in Great Britain in 1997
by Hodder and Stoughton
A division of Hodder Headline PLC

First published in paperback in 1997
by Hodder and Stoughton

A Coronet Paperback

10 9 8 7 6 5

British Library Cataloguing in Publication Data

O'Neill, Joan
Leaving home
1. Irish - England - Fiction 2. Domestic fiction
I. Title
823.9'14 [F]

ISBN 0 340 69496 3

Typeset by Avon Dataset Ltd, Bidford-on-Avon, Warks
Printed and bound in Great Britain by
Mackays of Chatham PLC, Chatham, Kent

Hodder and Stoughton
A division of Hodder Headline PLC
338 Euston Road, London NW1 3BH

To my daughters: Elizabeth O'Neill and Laura O'Neill, who are a constant source of joy and inspiration to me.

Acknowledgements

I would like to thank my family and friends for their patience and support during the writing of this book.

I am deeply indebted to my husband, John O'Neill, and my son, Robert O'Neill for their patience and help. Trevor Gray was generous with his technical expertise and advice when printing the final draft. Eoghan O'Donnell and Annette O'Connor gave me invaluable help. June Flanagan and Mary Rose Callaghan read the book in draft form and made very helpful comments. Anne Cooper, Jackie Dempsey, Mary Kirby, Maureen Keenan, Rita Stafford and all my friends in our literary group were always there for me. Renata Aherns-Kramer, Sheila Barnett, Alison Dye, Cecilia McGovern, Catherine Phil McCarthy and Julie Parsons gave continued support. Caroline O'Toole listened. John and Kathleen Bird gave me valuable information on the tea-importing business and their time unstintingly. Betty Burton has always been encouraging and generous of spirit. Joan Anne Lloyd and her staff at Deansgrange Library were most helpful with research.

My deepest gratitude to Jonathan Lloyd, whose encouragement, belief and guidance helped me meet this challenge and to my editor, Carolyn Caughey, whose gentle encouragement, suggestions and practical advice made all the difference.

My thanks to Martin Neild and all the staff at Hodder and Stoughton for extending me such a warm welcome, and to Breda Perdue who had faith in me.

Thanks also to A. P. Watt Ltd on behalf of Michael Yeats for permission to reprint "Two Years Later" taken from *The Collected Poems of W. B. Yeats*. The extract on page 95 is from "The Holy City" by F. E. Weatherly.

Two Years Later

Has no one said those daring
Kind eyes should be more learn'd?
Or warned you how despairing
The moths are when they are burned?
I could have warned you; but you are young,
So we speak a different tongue.

O you will take whatever's offered
And dream that all the world's a friend,
Suffer as your mother suffered,
Be as broken in the end.
But I am old and you are young,
And I speak a barbarous tongue.

W. B. Yeats

Chapter One

Glencove, 1968

They sat in deck chairs on the green, in front of the bandstand, to get the best view. The parade always ended at the bandstand in Glencove, a small town on the east coast, twenty miles from Dublin City. Eve Freeman's mother, Dorothy, and Clare Dolan's mother, Agnes, were in the front row, headscarves tied in a knot, winged sunglasses tipped towards the sun, lips pursed in anticipation. Dorothy was wearing a pastel pink suit and white cotton gloves to match her white handbag. She always carried three gloves, 'two to wear and one to wag', a habit inherited from her mother. Eve's grandfather, James Freeman, stayed back a few rows out of the east wind to watch the long parade, undisturbed by the noise and confusion.

The sun shone, the air smelt of sweets and ice-cream. The pounding of drums and the blare of cornets and trumpets heralded the arrival of the Garda number-one band. They swung into view: clarinets, horns, trombones. A symphony of gold and silver against the navy uniforms.

The first green banner, announcing 'Cead Mile Failte', was held by Eve Freeman and her friend Clare Dolan, who came behind them. Hornpipe shoes tip-tapping on the pavement, bare legs lifting to the beat, the rest of their classmates half danced, half marched, keeping perfect time. All local girls, who went to the same school

1

as Eve, Clare, and Eve's younger sister, Sarah.

They moved into the sunlight, arms swinging, smiling and waving. Main Street had been quiet this Easter Sunday until the marchers arrived, resembling a flowing river of green. Soldiers from the Curragh Camp followed the ceili dancers, their uniforms too heavy, their guns in the crook of their arms. The Boy Scouts, with their yellow neckties, looked small and young against the mature grey and red of the St John's Ambulance Brigade.

Pauline Quirk, watching from the doorway of Kinsella's Select Bar, was glad she didn't have to wear a silly green dance costume any more and prance around the streets. She wasn't deceived by Eve and Clare's brittle smiles or the medals on their chests, knowing that they, too, considered the parade childish. Yet from the dark recess of the doorway Pauline couldn't help envying their close friendship, bound by the confines of the school routine that she had abandoned along with the rest of her childhood. Suddenly she felt isolated in her new freedom and, for one solitary moment, she bitterly regretted her decision to leave school.

On the stone steps of the library boys stood, tall and gangly in men's suits, hair sleeked back, with an air of defiance. Clem Rogers was there, his guitar under his arm, and Martin Dolan, Clare's brother, just arrived from England, never having missed a commemoration of the 1916 Easter Rising. Others were strangers, sneering at the girls behind cupped nicotined fingers.

The marching stopped when they reached the green and the band broke into a dance tune. Girls grouped together, hornpipes hammering the pavement, the red and gold Celtic designs of their green costumes merging in the sun.

The crowds cheered, the pace quickened. Glinting instruments dipped and dived as the baton cut the air. Sweat bubbled on brows hidden under bobbing flat hats. Trombones lifted high and tubas swung. Behind the shining brass the big drums marched in time with the chimes. Then a horn played, sad and low.

Eve watched her next-door neighbour, David Furlong, from under her eyelids, as he manned a float marked Furlong Merchant Bankers. Clare's eyes were on Henry Joyce, who was chatting to David. Henry was her childhood friend. His father's farm backed on to the row of cottages behind the railway where Clare lived with her mother.

All at once the band launched into a medley of wild jazz numbers, zigzagging upwards, faltering to a finale as an enormous shuddering trailer, bedecked with laughing girls dressed in green, white and yellow costumes, inched along Main Street. Eve's sister, Sarah, sat with other girls from her class in the next float, scattering petals. Her long blonde hair flowed down her back and her new blue dress was rucked around her.

'Isn't she a picture?' Agnes Dolan said to Dorothy Freeman as they went to meet Sarah.

Agnes was Dorothy's housekeeper-companion, partly because of their shared childhood in Wexford and mostly because Agnes was Dorothy's most trusted friend.

Sarah waved to them but her smile was full of fatigue. Dorothy realised that her younger daughter was so tired that she couldn't wait for the parade to end.

'You're flushed,' Dorothy said, removing Sarah's veil and loosening the buttons of her dress.

'It went on too long,' Sarah yawned.

'Come on. I'll buy you an ice-cream.'

As the band dispersed Eve and Clare slipped away down the main street of Glencove. It had always attracted them: on the left side were Dillon's hardware shop and Reilly's, the butcher's. The right housed their favourites. The pawn-broker's was divided into two parts: the public section, where diamond rings glittered in the window, and the private part, at the back, filled with shelves of dusty boxes and racks of old clothes, through which on cold winter days Mr Rosen, the owner, would let them rummage. Once, they had found a feather boa and cocktail hat for their dressing-up collection. The newsagents on the corner, next to St Canice's parish church, was owned by Mrs Rogers, mother of Clem who played the guitar in a band. Marty O'Brien had rows of glorious Italian shoes in his window at the far side of the church, next to Trish Lynam's Ladies' Fashions. Free-man's Tea Importers, the five-storey building at the end of the town, was Eve's grandfather's business, founded by him in 1922 and now run by her father, Ron.

Eve and Clare skipped down the Harbour Road, past Hilda's Chipper and the tantalising smell of fish and chips, on down the narrow street between the library and dwindling smaller shops that fell away to a sandy path and the harbour. By the time they reached it, the sound of soft, dreamy violins was fading over the water. People walked up and down or leaned against the railing to inspect the sailing boats.

They hastened their steps, past the sailing club and the row of harbourside houses, and sat on the low wall to catch their breath and listen to the waves breaking on the shore. Gulls hovered over the darkening green waters, their white wings tipped towards the setting sun, and fishing boats appeared on the horizon, slowly sailing home.

Eve and Clare were best friends. Both were seventeen, both tall and slender. Eve had large, quiet eyes, and hair the colour of sand warmed by the sun – just dark enough to allow her escape the tag 'dumb blonde'. Clare's gold-flecked eyes, clear and steady, gazed from under a shock of fiery curls, and gave her otherwise plain face a hint of suppressed excitement that threatened to erupt at any moment.

They had known each other since their first day in primary school when they had been sent together to Sister Virginia, the headmistress, to give their names for enrolment. Eve, who had been until then a solitary little girl, was glad to have a friend with whom to share her daydreams. Dreams of Cuchulain, the great legendary warrior, springing her into his chariot, struggling to subdue his mad-whinnying, long-maned steeds as they swooped over the face of a cliff, or rushed like the wind through a dense forest where bandits lurked. Clare recognised in her a kindred spirit. Clare, who lived in a crammed household of high expectation where her mother's volatile temperament could cause instant chaos, with raised voices and slamming doors, found comfort in Eve's spacious house, and ease in Dorothy's coolness.

Clare reached out for her cardigan, which lay on the wall beside her, and began to search the pockets. 'Damn. I thought I had more than that,' she said, looking at the only cigarette in the crushed packet. 'I'll have to get some more somewhere. God, it's hopeless. Can't even afford a smoke.'

'Poison,' Eve said.

Ignoring her, Clare put the cigarette between her

lips and fumbled for her matches. 'I need a job.' She lit up and inhaled deeply.

'You'll have to finish school first.'

'It's unbearable.'

'Not all the time.'

'Maybe not for you – bowing and scraping to the nuns. Yes, Sister, no, Sister, three bags full, Sister, as if they were saints or something. You're a pain in the neck and your da's rich.'

'I can't help that.'

For a long time they sat in silence watching the mail boat in the distance leaving Dun Laoghaire harbour, and thinking their own separate thoughts. Eventually Clare said, 'I wish I was on that boat.'

Eve's eyes followed it. 'You will be when you win the music scholarship,' she said.

'Greta Crawley's better than me. She'll win it,' Clare said. She drew deeply on her cigarette, then trod it out.

'Rubbish,' Eve said. 'You're Sister Aquinas's pet, too.'

'No, I'm not,' Clare protested. 'What you don't seem to realise, Eve, is what it's like for me coming home to an empty house day in day out, now that Daddy's gone chasing after Martin somewhere and Mother's over in your house all the time.'

'Your daddy'll be back,' Eve said. 'And you can come home with me in the evenings if you want to.'

'I've homework to do and Mother doesn't want me hanging around her while she's working.' Clare stood up. 'I have to get cooked ham for tea from Mr Grimes so I'd better go,' she said.

'Ham, jam, anything you want, Mam,' Eve chanted.

They gathered up their cardigans and made their way back along the towpath that ran by the railway track to the town.

'I'll call for you in the morning for school,' Eve said, when they got to the shops.

'Yes.' Clare made a face and looked away.

'Cheer up, it's our last term.'

'I suppose.' Clare waved and was gone, walking away quickly as the church clock struck four.

Eve passed the railway station where the train to Dublin waited at the platform for Tim Reilly to change the signal for it to go. The path was quiet, sheltered by gardens on one side and a bank of grass and nettles on the other. Manus Corrigan, the family solicitor, was crossing the towbridge as Eve approached. 'Eve, my dear,' he greeted her, standing back to let her pass.

'Hello, Mr Corrigan.'

'How are you? Did you enjoy the parade?'

'Yes, thank you.'

'How's your mother?' He tried to sound casual but Eve knew that this was the reason he had stopped to talk to her. Years ago he had been engaged to Dorothy before Ron Freeman had returned from India, flaunting his exotic lifestyle, sports car and expensive presents.

Manus was a handsome man, who lived in the big red-brick house on the hill outside the town. It had casement windows and a solid oak door, and it was reputed to have been built by Edward VII for his favourite mistress. Manus himself was of noble blood, descended from the High Kings of Ireland, and looked distinguished in his tailored, pin-striped suits and red satin waistcoats. His legal practice was in the town, but he worked from home sometimes and sailed with Eve's grandfather at weekends.

'Tell your mother I'll drop in to see her,' Manus said.

'She'd like that.' Eve smiled.

They stood together, looking over the bridge at the

dark water that flowed by the side of Kinsella's Select Bar.

'I believe your father's still abroad,' Manus said in a neutral voice.

'Yes.'

'When's he due home?'

'I don't know, Mr Corrigan.'

'Soon, I hope,' Manus said, under his breath, as they walked on past Kinsella's where Madge Kinsella, the owner, was sluicing an outside drain with a bucket of Jeyes Fluid. Her skirt was so short that, as she bent over, they could see the elastic of her pink interlock knickers.

'Hello, Mr Corrigan.' She straightened herself and pulled down her skirt with her free hand. 'Did you enjoy the parade?'

When Madge was in trouble with the law, over fines for after hours' drinking or had difficulties with her land, she consulted Manus.

'Good afternoon, Madge.' Manus bowed condescendingly. 'I did indeed enjoy the parade. It was splendid. How is your good self?'

'Sure there's no use complainin', is there?' Madge said.

'Getting ready for the rush hour?' Manus enquired. 'They'll be in any minute with a terrible thirst on them.'

As he spoke Martin Dolan rounded the corner, walking quickly, head down, and almost collided with Madge and her bucket of dirty water.

'Howayah, Martin?' Madge said, side-stepping him.

'All right, thanks, Madge.' He paused and gave an all-encompassing smile.

'Comin' in for a drink?' Madge persisted.

'Another time,' Martin said, raising his hand in salute and walking on.

'He's in a shockin' hurry,' Madge said.

'I didn't know he was back,' Manus Corrigan mused, his suspicious eyes following the retreating figure.

'It's a terrible t'ing when you have to cajole the customers in.' Dermy McQuaid, the porter at the new Glencove Hotel, snorted from the far side of the street.

'Mind your own business,' Madge retorted.

Eve sniggered.

Clare's house was in a row of cottages tucked neatly behind the railway station, facing the sea. It was shabby with peeling paint and the front garden was neglected, but the windows sparkled in the evening sunshine and the net curtains behind them were crisp and white.

When Clare got home Martin Dolan was sitting at the kitchen table. His hair was longer and he was growing a beard. He wore an Aran sweater and faded jeans.

'Hi,' Clare said in surprise. 'I didn't know you were coming home.'

'You didn't think I'd miss the parade, did you?'

'I suppose not.'

Not knowing what to say next, she sat down opposite him. 'How's Terry?' she asked.

'Terry's fine.'

'Is she pleased that you've moved over there?'

'Ecstatic.'

'I think I'll have a cup of tea. Want one?' Clare asked, jumping up.

'Don't stir.' Martin scraped back his chair. 'I'll make it. It'll give me something to do.'

Clare watched Martin put the kettle on to boil, then rinse out the teapot. His hands were red and callused, his fingernails ingrained with cement.

'How are things in the music world?' he asked, as he filled the teapot.

'Not so bad. Keeping up.'

'You're being modest,' Martin said, as he placed the cups and saucers on the table, then poured the tea.

'Are you in some kind of trouble?' Clare asked suddenly, her eyes trained on her brother.

Martin slammed down his cup on the table. The tea slopped on to the tablecloth. 'For Christ's sake, what's this? An inquisition?'

'No,' Clare said, blushing. 'It's just that Mother's worried about you.'

'Mother's always worried about something,' Martin snapped.

The front door opened and shut. There was the sound of slow footsteps down the hall and Agnes Dolan came into the kitchen, her face red from the exertion of walking up the hill. 'Martin, you're home.'

The look of delight on her face was enhanced by the peck on the cheek Martin gave her.

Agnes was a tall, solid woman, with thick arms and legs. She had the well-scrubbed appearance of someone who relished hard work and maintaining law and order in her own home. Her strength was evident in her face – a strength that was sorely tested by the behaviour of her wayward husband, Jack. The dreary, unremitting work she did for Dorothy had left its mark in the creases of her brow. Clare resented the hours her mother spent at the Freemans', traipsing around after Dorothy, cleaning, cooking, brushing down the stairs, coming home too weary to talk, but she kept it to herself because she knew that Agnes had no choice.

Agnes's pride and joy was her son. It was Martin's photograph that hung in the sitting room over the statue of the Sacred Heart and the picture of John F. Kennedy. Martin was the blue-eyed boy with the brains, the first member of her family to get a place at university. He was going to study agricultural science. There was no doubt about it, she told her cronies, sitting down, arms folded, and explained carefully to them that a year off would do him good. He would return to his studies, she assured them all, as soon as he had the bug out of his system. Agnes would scrub floors to give him the chance to go, seek no reward, save the envy reflected in her neighbours' faces.

When each crisis befell her family Agnes would say 'God is good' and continued to pray every morning at Mass for the grace to put in another day. Sometimes she would allow herself the luxury of a trip to the cinema with Dorothy, a temporary escape from drab reality. Clare prayed for a different reason: she wanted her father home, rid of his faults and wild impossible dreams. Not once did she imagine that the sculptured bleeding Christ to whom she prayed would answer her prayers.

'It's great to see you,' Agnes said to Martin. 'When did you get in?'

'Nine o'clock this morning.'

'Clare, you'll have to get more ham – a chicken, too. We'll need milk and bread,' Agnes said. 'Run down to Clem Rogers.' She reached for her purse in her apron pocket.

'He's shut. I saw him at the parade.'

'Knock on the side door. His mother'll open up for you.'

Martin raised his hand. 'There's no rush. I'm off to bed.' He rose from his chair.

Agnes detained him with her hand. 'But you must be hungry?'

11

Martin shook his head. 'I had something on the boat.'

'I'll make up your bed.'

When Clare returned from the shops Agnes was alone in the kitchen, ironing.

'To think I was expecting Martin to stay at home and go to college,' Agnes said mildly, but the vigour of the iron attacking her good linen sheets indicated her agitation. 'He seems hell bent on settling down in England.'

'I can never figure out what's going on in Martin's head,' Clare said, putting away the groceries. 'Now, I'm off to practise,' she said, leaving the room to avoid having to listen to one of her mother's tortured monologues.

'Might as well.' Agnes thumped the iron on the ironing-board. It hissed in protest.

The sound of piano music filtering in from the sitting room soothed Agnes's nerves. She straightened up and folded the sheets into neat squares to the first tentative notes of Chopin's waltz in E flat minor. Agnes could picture Clare sitting gracefully at the piano, her long fingers sliding over the keys, soft as a butterfly, gradually increasing their pressure as the rhythm of the piece dictated. She turned the iron on its heel and stood listening, eyes half closed, smiling.

The sun beamed a pool of light through the window, highlighting the drab, sweating walls and the cobwebs in the corners of the ceiling. For once Agnes didn't care. As she put the sheets in the hotpress she began to relax. Clare had the music in her. She was remembering the morning Miss Devine had called her into her sitting room after Clare's lesson. 'Your daughter is truly musical,' she had said. 'She should practise for at least an hour a day on a good piano.'

Agnes understood her duty to keep Clare at it, and bought a black ebony concert piano. Steinway, the name of the makers, was inscribed in gold on the inside of the lid. It was a model recommended by Mr Thomson, the man she consulted at Piggot's Musical Instruments, Dawson Street, and had been one of the more expensive in their range. She took a Saturday job at the Swastika Laundry to help with the repayments, and made Clare practise for two hours every day.

'It's too much for her,' Jack Dolan had complained.

'It's a gift,' Agnes defended herself stoutly.

'Nonsense,' he scoffed. 'Putting notions in the girl's head like that. Out playing on the street, she should be.'

'What would you know?' Agnes had retorted. 'All you ever talk about is the Struggle, the Fight for Freedom, the medals your family refused because of the Border.'

Jack Dolan, or 'Fast Jack' as he was known to his friends, was a handsome man still, with clear pale skin and black curly hair. The pouches under his eyes and the folds of flab around his chin had softened his once regular features but there was still the warning flash in his blue eyes that made people wary of him. Jack was a brickie who had worked during the post-war boom on a good many building sites in England and the North of Ireland. Because of his talent for singing and story-telling he was popular among his workmates. He had a rich, tenor voice that owed its sureness to the Christian Brothers, who had trained him for the church choir, and he told stories about the Troubles and the Rising with the skill of a Seanachi. Also he was hard-working and reliable.

In the evenings he would go to the pub with his

pals. Night after night they would ply him with drink while he sang patriot songs, like 'Kevin Barry', and told stories until he was too incoherent to hold his listeners any longer. When he was put out of the pub at closing time he would wander the streets until he eventually found his way home in the early hours of the morning. Agnes would wait and pray, knowing that he would return when he had nowhere else to go. Until one night when he disappeared.

Jack's family had been involved in the Movement – even his aunts took part in the gun-running. Agnes called them tomboys. The first Agnes knew that he was gallivanting round building sites in England in the wake of his son was when he sent home a postal order for ten pounds.

Now, while she bided her time and waited for him to get sense, she turned her disciplinary powers on Clare. Agnes had never been gentle with the girl, possibly because she was afraid that Clare might expect kindness from others in the outside world and would be let down. As the waltz ended on one soft note Agnes admitted to herself reluctantly that she found it impossible to talk to Clare. With a sigh she folded up the ironing-board and put it out in the scullery.

The small kitchen was hot and Agnes wiped a trickle of perspiration from her forehead. She learned to cope with her everyday problems, money mainly, by not looking too far ahead. She believed that if she could manage today, tomorrow would take care of itself. The pile of ironing, neatly folded on the table beside her, ready for Clare to deliver to Dorothy Freeman, would stave off tomorrow's problems as well as today's. Further than that she refused to think.

Chapter Two

'Pst.' Clare's hand was cupped over her mouth as she stood under the big tree in Eve's garden. 'Come down,' she called.

'Hang on a minute.' The branches of the tree shook and Eve jumped to the ground.

'I was avoiding Mummy,' Eve said, as she brushed down her dress. 'She's having one of her fund-raising dos.'

Clare tilted her head conspiratorially, her face ready to burst into laughter. She looked at Eve in a way that Eve had seen often in their shared childhood adventures. It meant trouble.

'Let's go into the shed.'

It was dim and musty in there. Dust swirled in the golden rays cast by the sun through the doorway. Broken pots, discarded paint and old garden furniture lay in a jumble in corners. They pulled out a couple of chairs and sat in them. Clare lit a cigarette.

'Guess what I heard?' she said to Eve.

'What?'

'Pauline Quirk is pregnant.'

'What?' Eve looked at her in astonishment. 'Who told you that?'

'Bernie Power. Her mother heard it from Mrs Browne who works for Madge Kinsella.'

'Who's the father?' Eve asked.

'Seamus Gilfoyle. She's been going with him a while now.'

'But he moved up north'. Eve looked puzzled.

'Apparently he's been back at weekends. Staying in her flat, too. According to Mrs Browne they're practically living together like husband and wife.' Clare's eyes were trained on Eve's face.

'I don't believe it. Pauline Quirk doing a thing like that in holy Catholic Glencove. Remember her in school? Butter wouldn't melt in her mouth,' Eve said.

'She was scared of the nuns,' Clare remembered.

'Bet she's sorry now she left in Inter Cert. If she'd stayed it probably wouldn't have happened,' Eve said.

'She never got over her mother's death. It was so lonely for her living in the country with that awful Aunt Bea.'

'She couldn't fit in at school,' Eve added.

'But I always liked Pauline Quirk. I was sure she was hooked on Martin,' Eve said.

'She never knew where she stood with him. Nobody does,' Clare said.

'When's the baby due?'

Clare shrugged. 'I'm not sure. Let's see. Seamus was there for Christmas. January, February, March.' She was counting on her fingers.

'Look at you,' Eve chided. 'You're a worse gossip than Madge Kinsella. Pauline with a baby in September. It's hard to imagine.' She wrinkled her nose in disbelief.

'Eve?' Dorothy Freeman came into the garden.

'Coming.'

The sun dazzled the girls as they emerged.

'Really, Eve. Isn't it time you grew out of that childish habit of disappearing when you're wanted to help?' Dorothy Freeman's swift glance took in her daughter's dishevelled appearance and the guilty expression on Clare's face.

'Hello, Clare.' Dorothy smiled graciously at her and turned back to Eve. 'It's time you learned that certain obligations are attached to social acceptability and hiding in sheds isn't one of them.'

'Sorry, Mummy.'

'I've tried to inject style and elegance into you but to no avail,' Dorothy continued, ignoring her. 'Go and bring out the glasses. They're ready on the sideboard.' She turned back to Clare. 'You might help too, Clare. I'm giving a tea party for the Church Restoration Fund. Father McCarthy will be here any minute.'

'Yes, Mrs Freeman,' Clare said.

'Hello, Dorothy. Doesn't the garden look glorious?' Already Father McCarthy was marching towards them.

'Hello, Father.' Dorothy inclined her head and went to join him.

'Come on, let's go,' Eve hissed.

It was getting cool as they made their way to the town and a sharp wind snapped at their bare ankles. Outside the Glencove Hotel Dermy McQuaid was lifting luggage out of a parked Humber Hawk. In his neat grey uniform piped with red, grey pill-box hat to match, he looked respectable.

'Hi, Dermy,' Clare called out to him.

'Howayah.' He nodded curtly, then grinned when he saw who it was.

He stood the suitcases down on the pavement and propped himself against the sleek car in an attempt to disguise his limp. 'Busy weekend ahead. We're expecting royalty.'

'Royalty?' Clare laughed.

'It's all hush-hush, but I can assure you if the people of Glencove knew who'll be gracing us with their presence, they'd be astounded.'

'Tell us,' Eve said, taunting.

'Be God 'n' I won't. Me lips is sealed. Suffice to say they're household names all over the world.'

'Then why are they staying in your crummy hotel?' Clare asked, winking at Eve.

'I'll have you know they're travelling incognito.'

'Ah, go on. Tell us who they are. We won't tell a soul.'

'Give us a kiss and I will.' Dermy pursed his lips.

'Drop dead, Dermy McQuaid,' Clare said, with a look of disgust. 'My mother warned me to keep away from you. Come on, Eve.'

Dermy made a run at them, stumbled over the suitcase in his haste and sprawled on the pavement.

'The curse of God on youse,' he shouted, as they ran off laughing, only looking back before they crossed the road, in the hope that he had vanished.

He was walking off with a hoppity-skip and shaking his fist at them.

It was rumoured that Dermy McQuaid was connected in some obscure way to Archbishop John Charles McQuaid, Archbishop of Dublin, but there was no evidence to prove it. The Archbishop enjoyed the wealth of his palace while Dermy lived with his mother in a labourer's cottage at the end of the Sea Road. He had spent his days in the doorway of the betting shop or Kinsella's Select Bar, saluting passers-by with a nod and a wink, his disappointment in life evident only in his sad eyes, until Henrietta Ford Mathews, the new proprietor of the Glencove Hotel, collared him and offered him the job of porter. 'Sure what would I do that for?' he had asked, looking amazed at her suggestion. 'To commence work at this hour of me life would be tantamount to disaster. Could even be injurious to me health, too. And sure who'd mind me mother?' Henrietta persuaded him, with payment of five pounds a week and a brand new uniform, the trousers of which were permanently at half mast, accentuating his limp.

Mrs Reilly, the butcher's wife, in the doorway of her shop, had seen what had happened and stopped the girls.

'Leave the poor creatur alone. Let him get on with his work,' she shouted, baring her crooked teeth at them.

'We didn't touch him. Honest.' Clare looked at her with wide eyes.

'Don't mock the afflicted. You're bad bitches.'

'Excuse us,' Eve said, huffily, as she tried to pass. 'You don't know what he said to us.'

'What did he say?' Mrs Reilly's ferret eyes gleamed at them as she pulled heavily on the cigarette stuck to her lips.

'That's for us to know and for you to find out,' Clare butted in.

'If your mother knew the carry-on of you, Eve Freeman, and she a respectable lady,' Mrs Reilly shouted.

'You'll probably tell her!' Clare yelled back, and they were running off down the street to where a queue was forming outside the Star cinema. Young men leaned against the wall, watching passers-by, motor cars, anything to distract them, while they waited for the doors of the cinema to open.

Clare shivered as the wind struck at her shoulders, which were bare except for the straps of her new sundress. Conscious that their retreating view was being scrutinised and commented upon, she and Eve nudged one another, then broke into a run.

Boys lounged outside Hilda's Chipper with nothing on their minds but to attract passing girls. Eve, who was shy, evaded them, but Clare, safe in her friend's company and unable to control her wicked sense of delight, teased them with her smile and easy grace.

'Hi, lads,' she said, pushing past them with an air of abandon. 'How's tricks?'

Taken aback the boys exchanged glances, looked away, then grinned at her, not knowing what to do next. As Clare pushed through the door, beckoning Eve to follow her, Charlie Mathews caught hold of her arm.

'Coming to the dance Saturday night?' he asked.

'I might be.' Clare tossed back her hair.

'Great.'

'Then again, I might not.'

Charlie's jaw dropped. 'What d'you mean?'

'I haven't made up my mind yet.' Clare winked at him. 'See you,' she said, moving into the middle of the Chipper where young people in groups of three and four were sitting, chatting.

Eve followed and, finding a vacant table, they sat down.

From the juke box in the corner Engelbert Humperdinck was singing 'Am I That Easy To Forget'. His voice was full of heartbreak as he told of love and betrayal. The song stopped and the hum of unintelligible conversation filled the empty space until someone fed money into the juke box again. 'Jumping Jack Flash' changed the atmosphere. Immediately the girls began to click their fingers and sway in their chairs.

Out of the corner of her eye Eve saw David Furlong at the door with Henry Joyce. She nudged Clare. 'Don't look now but guess who's just come in?'

Clare closed her eyes. 'Mick Jagger.'

'Nearly right.'

Clare turned and the boys approached their table. 'Thought we might find you here.' David Furlong, head and shoulders taller than anyone else in the café, came forward.

'Hello,' Eve said.

'Hi.' He leaned towards her.

'I've got tickets for the summer ball. Like to come?' A look of surprise crossed Eve's face. David's blue eyes crinkled at the corners as he laughed. 'Go on, say you will,' he coaxed.

'I'd love to,' she said, blushing.

'Terrific.' He straightened up, brushed back his unruly mop of blond hair, and said, 'I must get back to the office.'

'It's Saturday.' Eve was incredulous

'You know my old man. Flogs me to death.'

'My heart bleeds for you,' Clare piped up. 'With all the money you're making you'll be able to retire to the South of France before you're thirty.'

'*Touché*,' David said, and with a wave he was gone, weaving his way through the tables.

Henry loitered. 'Would you like to come with me, Clare?' he said. 'Make it a foursome.'

Clare said, making her voice as casual as she could, 'Did you win the tickets in a raffle or something?'

'David's father's sponsoring it. Gave me a couple,' Henry said.

'I'd love to come, thanks,' Clare said graciously.

'It'll be a great night,' Henry said. 'Dickie Rock and the Miami Showband are playing.'

'Wow,' Clare said. 'I'd love to see them.'

'I'll see you before then,' Henry said and left.

'I can hardly believe it,' Eve said.

'All our dreams come true.'

Eve murmured, 'I wonder why he asked me?'

'Because he wants to take you.'

'The girl-next-door. I'm convenient.'

'He always fancied you at the parties in his house,' Clare said, quietly.

'He fancied Bernie Power more.'

'She never left him alone.'

'He didn't seem to object.'

'I suppose he was flattered,' Clare said.

'Poor David,' Eve said thoughtfully. 'His father makes sure he doesn't have much time for socialising.'

'Rich David, you mean,' Clare said.

Eve had always admired David Furlong from afar. The Furlongs' house was the last house on the Avenue, with overhanging trees and wider lawns than the Freemans'. Jasper Furlong was the richest man in the town and he firmly believed in displaying his wealth. Every summer he held a party that, for weeks in advance, was the topic of conversation in the town. When Eve and Sarah Freeman had both been too young to go they had leaned out of Eve's bedroom window to watch the striped fabric of the marquee bulge and billow in the wind and listen to the band.

David, four years older than Eve, had been at boarding-school in England for so long that Eve hardly recognised him when he finally returned home to work in his father's merchant bank. He was handsome, outgoing, smart, and his life was full of adventures and excitement beyond Eve's imagination, let alone experience. On the rare occasions she met him, he was either returning from a skiing trip or taking off to the Far East.

It was in her Leaving Certificate year that he had returned home to work in his father's office in Dame Street, Dublin. Eve, watching him play tennis in his whites on the Furlongs' tennis court with his younger brothers, Jason and George, or driving in and out in his two-tone Mini, longed for the freedom he had – and yearned for him. She longed not to be awkward when she met him, to be like the sophisticated girls with whom he drove around. Girls who were sure of themselves and knew where they fitted in. Consequently, she kept her distance, until one warm spring evening she was invited to an impromptu barbecue in his parents' garden with Dorothy and James.

'You look great,' he had said, when he saw her standing to one side in a mini-dress and high-heeled sandals. From then on he went out of his way to talk to her when they met, sometimes stopping his car in the middle of the road and lowering the window to invite her to play in a mixed doubles. She was looking forward to the dance and, perhaps, getting to know him better.

Kinsella's Select Bar was dark and smoky. As Martin Dolan's eyes grew accustomed to the gloom he saw Seamus Gilfoyle sitting at one of the small tables in the snug. He ordered a pint of stout from Madge, then brought his drink over to where Seamus sat and pulled up a chair opposite him. 'You're looking well,' he said, eyeing Seamus up and down.

'Aye,' Seamus said. 'Why did you send for me?'

'I need you to do a bit of business. Nothing strenuous. Just a little surveillance work.' Martin's eyes were on the other man.

'Listen,' Seamus said, in a shrill whisper, 'I don't

mind driving. But nothing else. No guns, nothing like that.'

Martin shrugged. 'This is a small job. I want you to find out the security details of the next big march.'

'If it's what I'm thinking, you're crazy,' Seamus said.

'Let me worry about that. You just get the information.' Martin sipped his pint.

'How?'

'Get down to the RUC station on some pretext. See the lie of the land.'

'But—'

'But fucking nothing. Do what you have to do. Use your imagination.' Martin's eyes glittered.

'I suppose someone has to do the menial tasks.' Seamus sighed.

'You're useful up there in the centre of things. We need people like you.' Martin drank rapidly.

Seamus perked up. 'Same again?' he said, eyeing Martin's near-empty glass.

'Yeah. Why not? As long as you keep your nose clean you'll be all right.'

'Yes, sir.' Seamus rose and bowed in mock-salute. Martin sat back and watched him as he swaggered across to the bar. Undaunted, confident, dapper, his appearance was a bit bright, though, in that red polo-neck and he was over-confident too. Seamus Gilfoyle's mother, a Protestant, had always been eager to get back to the north. But why Seamus Gilfoyle was in the Movement Martin had no idea: Seamus was too fond of his appearance to be a real fighter and too fickle to be committed.

'Thanks,' Martin said, as Seamus put the glass in front of him.

'Don't mention it.' Seamus sat down. 'Well, spill the

rest of the beans,' he said, easing himself back into the recess.

'I need the information quickly, no delays.'

Seamus looked at him.

'Listen,' Martin leaned closer to him, 'I can guarantee protection so long as you don't do anything stupid.'

'OK. I'll do it this once.'

'Good lad. No bungling, mind. I'll leave now. You hang around. Talk to Pauline.'

'Suit yourself.' Seamus concentrated on his pint.

Madge Kinsella was serving a customer when Pauline Quirk came in the side door, apron on, hair tied up in a headscarf, ready to start work.

'Howayah,' Pauline said.

'Feeling any better?' Madge asked, flicking a yellow duster over the counter.

Pauline glanced sideways at her. 'Why? What's up with me?'

Madge blushed. 'Nothing. Only Delia Enright said you weren't looking well.'

'Nosy cow,' Pauline said to herself.

Madge studied her. 'Are you sure you know what you're doing, carrying on with your man over there in the corner?'

'What d'you mean?' Pauline shot a glance in Seamus Gilfoyle's direction.

Madge lowered her voice. 'Rumour has it that that fella of yours is up to no good.'

'Seamus is a nice lad. Good to me.'

'He's flittin' around that much he could be a spy or something,' Madge said.

'Spy!' Pauline was aghast.

'Shhh! Keep your voice down.' Madge gave her a little push. 'Why's he back and forth to Belfast so much?'

'He comes to see me whenever he can.'

'I knew his mother. Very secretive woman. His father wasn't much better. Never went to Mass.' Madge squeezed her mouth into a tight knot of self-righteousness. 'I think meself that he's involved with a criminal organisation.'

'He's no such thing,' Pauline hissed.

'How will it be if you marry him and you're up there in Belfast trying to rear a family among the bombs and bullets? Stab you in the back as quick as look at you, up there.'

'Well, I'm going to marry him. Where we live is another matter.' Pauline moved down the bar to serve a customer.

Since Pauline had started work in Kinsella's Select Bar and snippets about her background had emerged, Madge had become protective, elevating Pauline to a status of dignity and respect in the pub.

Pauline's mother had died when she was eight. Beatrice Connolly, her mother's eldest sister and a spinster, who had inherited their father's farm, had reared her when her father couldn't cope and was so strict and religious that, to get away from her, Pauline had left school early and gone to work in the pub. With her wide eyes and ready smile, Pauline Quirk was good for business. Untouched by the gossip that surrounded her, she shone among the rough diamonds who frequented the bar. She could hold several conversations simultaneously, moving from one customer to another, pouring pints, dark and smooth three-quarters of the way up the glass, topped with a creamy froth. She measured out tots of whiskey with the same expertise. Often she would rest her elbows on the counter, look quizzically at one or other of her customers and say, 'I don't believe you,' just to get their gander up. She had style and created her own 'look' with the latest cosmetics and the clackety-clack of her high heels.

The bar filled up, smoke reached into its crevices, voices and clinking glasses whirled Pauline back and forth in an endless circumnavigation of tables. Looking around at the men, she could not see one who appealed to her, except Seamus Gilfoyle.

'Howayah,' Seamus said, sidling up to her, blowing her a kiss when Madge wasn't looking.

'Grand. Will I see you later?' Pauline asked, dodging the idle remarks from the men at the bar.

'Course you will. I'll be waiting for you.' Seamus winked and left.

Pauline spent the rest of the evening planning her new strategy with Seamus. She would be firmer with him, assuring him nicely of the impossibility of their settling down in Belfast. Her confidence grew with her planning.

Madge Kinsella was distantly related to Pauline's father, Tom Quirk – a labouring farmhand who had married up when he chose Margaret Connolly for his bride – which Beatrice had never let him forget. Madge was a strong, stout woman. Her uniform was a short straight skirt and voluptuous blouse. She had managed her father's farm and could thin mangolds and turnips quicker than any man and pitch hay before a cat could lick his whiskers. She was thrifty and banked her money as soon as she sold a cow or a ton of apples. When her father drank himself into a stupor she lamented the waste and decided to take over his pub and invest her savings in it. After Sonny Kinsella's death, Madge continued to exercise her authority over her younger brothers, Maurice and Phonsie, driving

Maurice to America to escape her dominance. 'You owe it to me to stay,' she had said to Phonsie, when he decided to join his brother.

'Divil a bit,' he had replied. 'That God-forsaken pub is not for me. The smell of porter and fags chokes me lungs. I need fresh air and space.'

'By my song, but you'll be the sorry boy when you're stuck in America and not a soul to give an iota about you. Back with your tail between your legs, you'll be.'

Phonsie didn't return. Madge, alone and lonely, sold the farm and slowly began to build a thriving business.

Next morning Pauline Quirk opened her eyes, stretched and looked out of the window. A weak sun was peeping through a chink in the curtains. Later, in the bar, it would beat against the glass, circling its beams intrusively into the welter of perspiring men and dark, dusty furniture. She nudged Seamus beside her. 'Are you awake?'

'Mmm. I am now,' came the sleepy reply.

'I was wondering—' She stopped.

'Dangerous game, wondering,' Seamus muttered. 'Go back to sleep. It's cheaper.'

'How did you know what I was going to say?'

'Whatever it is, it's going to cost money. I know you.'

'That's not fair.'

'Tell me then and take me out of my misery.'

'I'll have the baby in Holles Street.'

'But you've no one . . .' He paused. 'It's too early for . . . What time is it anyway?' He raised his head and squinted at the travel clock on the chair next to the bed. 'It's only seven o'clock,' he protested.

'Go back to sleep, then,' Pauline sighed. 'I'll talk to you later.'

Seamus gave a sigh of relief and burrowed down into the bedclothes, his breathing already deepening into an even rhythm. Watching him through the haze of early-morning sunshine Pauline realised that she didn't know Seamus very well.

They had met at a local dance. Seamus, sleek-haired, wearing a suit and matching shirt, stood out like a tailor's dummy in contrast to the worn jeans and sloppy jumpers of the others rocking furiously to the roaring music. It was only when she got close to him that Pauline saw how good-looking he was. His eyes were bright blue, his cheekbones as sharp as the crease in his trousers. It was his mouth, with its wide, soft lips, that made her, shamelessly, ask him to dance.

The music had changed to a fast number and, mesmerised with her smile, Seamus could not take his eyes off her. Martin Dolan, standing in a corner, had a brooding expression on his face, a secret island in a sea of jollity. Pauline, tired of his uncertainty, didn't care.

'Thank you,' Seamus had said, when the dance ended.

Later on, he asked her to dance again, throwing Martin a sidelong glance as he did so. Martin turned away and spat on the floor. Pauline stubbed out her cigarette and, suppressing a shiver of fear, gave herself up to the music.

Seamus was a good dancer, and this time made no attempt at conversation but concentrated on the steps. The record ended and the tempo changed again as 'Cinderella Rockafella' was put on the turntable. Excitement thumped through Pauline at the sensuous movements of Seamus's body, in perfect harmony with her own.

Pauline lay back against the pillows, remembering

Joan O'Neill

that evening a few days later when Seamus had come into the bar and had invited her to the pictures to see *Bullitt*.

They had walked home by the harbour, Pauline telling him about the day-to-day drudgery in the bar, and how she had become an expert at fending off the advances of drunks in pursuit of a *coort*. She didn't mention that Madge Kinsella stifled her, and that she was seriously thinking of emigrating to America.

Soon afterwards Seamus told her that his family were moving to Belfast, his father to work there, his mother to return home. He himself was hoping for a more interesting job than the one he was doing as a clerk in the post office, where he spent his days rubber-stamping letters and documents.

Pauline invited him back to her flat for coffee, glad for once that she had weathered the loneliness of moving away from her aunt. When Seamus looked at his watch and said it was time to make tracks, she heard herself say, 'You can stay here. It's late.' He had fallen asleep quickly and comfortably on the sofa, a blanket covering him. The following morning he had slept while she crept around making coffee and toast, boiling eggs. When she nudged him awake his eyes had snapped open in surprise. Yawning, he reached for her. Her shirt fell open and he could see that she was tanned everywhere, from her chest to her midriff, her shoulders. She was laughing as he pulled her to him, her long dark hair falling over her face. 'Seamus. You're terrible!' she gasped, when he began to remove her clothes, but she didn't resist.

He made love to her gracefully, with the self-assurance of a man who knew instinctively how to please a woman. What surprised her most was her own

30

lack of shyness. After he had moved his belongings into her flat they stayed in bed for hours at a time, in the afternoons or on her free evenings. Often they walked along the beach in the middle of the night, took picnics to Avoca, or Glendalough, famous scenic places Pauline had never visited before. Seamus had a banana yellow Mini he had procured in dubious circumstances in the north and he drove her everywhere. They shopped together, bought ice-cream, lemonade, lollipops, silly things that made them laugh as they walked along hand-in-hand.

Pauline was happy. She loved to squat on him, dangle her firm breasts over his face, let her enormous dark nipples graze his lips. Then she would straighten her strong body and, with her knees gripping his sides, she would move to his rhythm.

'Ahh . . .' Seamus would cry out in a strangulated voice, bringing her back to the moment. Quickening her pace, she would come with him, crying out his name and telling him over and over again that she loved him.

Her flat became a mess, with clothes strewn everywhere. Empty bottles lined the kitchen window-sill waiting to be dumped. The place smelled of perfume, sweat and sex. When she couldn't find what she was looking for, she would throw things aside, laugh and say that she didn't care.

'How's he different?' Martin Dolan had asked in the pub, when he discovered that Seamus had moved in.

'Shh.' Pauline made a face at him to be quiet.

'No. Tell me. It's a fair question,' he insisted.

One afternoon Martin had called at Pauline's flat to patch things up between them, not noticing the yellow Mini parked further down the terrace. From outside as he rang the bell he heard Pauline's shrill laughter. She came to the door in a long T-shirt, her legs bare, embarrassed when she saw that it was Martin. 'Sorry, I can't ask you in. The place is a mess,' she said off-handedly.

He had reached out and touched the purple marks on her neck. 'I can smell him off you,' he had said, with a look of disgust.

'Jesus Christ, what is this?' she flared. 'You don't bloody own me!' She spun round and slammed the door in his face.

Afterwards, in the pub, she tried to reason with the persistent Martin, but he enjoyed playing the martyr. He wallowed in his own misery and blamed Seamus for it. Perversely, he liked the hard-done-by feeling that Pauline's transfer of affections gave him, and planning his retaliation made him more alive and animated than he had been for a long time.

When Seamus returned to Belfast Martin called to the flat to invite Pauline out for a drive.

'I don't know,' she said guardedly.

'Just as friends.'

'I shouldn't, but what the heck? As long as you realise that I'm with Seamus and nothing's going to change.'

They drove to Killiney Bay and Pauline, removing her sling-back shoes, went in the sea for a paddle.

'It's lovely,' she said, returning and sitting on a low wall, drying herself out in the warm air. 'Tell me about London,' she went on suddenly. 'I was amazed you decided to go there.'

'It suits my political leanings to be there at the moment,' Martin replied shortly.

'Don't bite me head off. Seamus would never speak to me like that,' Pauline retaliated.

'Want an ice-cream?' Martin was trying to change the subject but Pauline continued to talk about Seamus, loving the mention of his name. As far as Martin was concerned, Seamus Gilfoyle was an unwelcome third party.

'You used to think I was the cheese,' he said.

'I still like you, but it's different with Seamus.'

'Fucking Seamus,' Martin swore, and began to walk back to the car. 'I don't know how you can feel anything for that creep,' he said as Pauline got in.

'He's different.'

'Bleedin' Micky-dazzler.' Martin turned on the ignition and the car's engine roared into life.

'I'm in love with him.' Pauline spoke quietly.

'What does that mean?' Martin looked perplexed.

'I dunno. When I'm with him I'm excited, nervous, happy.'

'You were like that with me.'

'It's not the same,' Pauline said. 'Anyway, you'll find someone else.' She was close to tears.

Martin stopped the car and leaned over towards her, his face close, his voice threatening.

'They don't screw like you do.' His breath was on her face, his voice hoarse.

'Martin.' Pauline gripped the sides of the seat. 'I'm getting out of this fucking car.'

She jumped out, banging the door behind her, and ran off down the road.

Martin didn't follow her. Instead he left for England the next day. Seamus returned regularly and everything went well until the day in the woods behind the cove, when she had said, through a canopy of green leaves, not daring to look him straight in the face, 'I'm pregnant.'

They were walking through the shimmering trees. Seamus let go of her hand and moved on, his hands clasped behind his back. Eventually, when she was beginning to wonder if he had heard her, he said casually, 'How come? Aren't you on this new pill or something?'

She stared at him through the screen of new foliage. 'I must have forgotten.'

He cursed under his breath.

'It's only a baby, no big deal,' she said, her cheeks burning. 'A mistake I thought I'd let you know before I did something about it. Just in case . . .' she hesitated, a sob in her throat, '. . . you wanted to share it with me. So there, I've told you.'

'No big deal.' He turned on her, his face bitter with temper. 'A baby, for Christ's sake, and you stand there saying it's no big deal. Who are you to take the law into your own hands?' He banged his fist against a tree trunk.

Pauline winced even now at the vehemence of his outburst.

'I didn't think, if you want to know. Didn't care either . . . about anything when we were doing it. Did you?' she shouted at him.

'No,' he said, trembling. 'But I don't know what you expect me to say. That it's wonderful news. The greatest news I ever heard in my life.'

'Forget it. I'll manage on my own. I did before I met you.'

She had flounced off, walking along the craggy path as fast as her high heels would allow her.

'Come back,' he roared, running after her, his voice echoing through the stillness.

'Go to hell, Seamus Gilfoyle! It's typical of you!' she

had shouted, shaking his hands off her. 'If something doesn't suit you, you dismiss it.'

'Stop. Listen, Pauline. I'll organise something. You can move to Belfast.'

She shook off his restraining hand. 'I'm not living there! They eat their young there!' She was still shouting.

'You know nothing about it.'

'I know about the fighting and the grimy streets. I've seen the horrible graffiti on the telly.'

'Shut up,' he hissed, and walked away from her, retracing his steps.

Subdued, she followed him. The wind blew, rustling the leaves. Children ran past them, accompanied by a man in tweeds with a dog on a lead. Pauline cast a glance at Seamus, waiting for a word of regret, contempt, anything. Head down, he kept walking, Pauline glancing at him every now and then. The silence around them was filled with unspoken anger. Suddenly it dawned on Pauline how stupid she had been to tell him. Now she would have to relinquish her right to any choice in the matter of her baby. She could see by the resolute expression on Seamus's face that he would make the decisions and, like it or not, she would abide by them.

'Well?' she said, when they reached Goretti Flats.

'Let's drop it for the moment,' Seamus said brusquely. 'I need time to think. I'll get my things and be going.'

He packed his bag and left her, stupefied with worry, lying awake at night recounting every detail of their meetings and conversations. But when he returned he was full of remorse. 'I'm sorry I lost me temper,' he said, without preamble. 'We'll get married soon.'

'Do you really mean that?'

'Course I do.' He had hugged her. 'Come to Belfast next weekend on the train to see the place for yourself. No big deal, only don't tell Madge, the old windbag. She'd try to talk you out of it.'

So far Pauline had avoided going to Belfast and knew she couldn't postpone it for much longer. She sneaked out of bed, so as not to wake Seamus, and went to the bathroom.

After a quick bath she dried herself, then examined her reflection in the full-length mirror, arms above her head, turning to look over her shoulder at her well-muscled body and the strong legs that held her up for hours at a time behind the counter in the pub. Her breasts were beginning to droop, shaped like pears now rather than the apples they had been before she got pregnant. She sucked in her breath and watched their rise and fall and undeniable swell of her stomach.

Pauline's face had taken on a childish roundness that confirmed her youth and pregnancy. It was in keeping with her strong body. She smiled into the glass, ran her tongue over her even white teeth and pouted, blowing kisses to her self in the foggy glass. Tossing back her head she let her lustrous dark hair fall forward over one eye. A lascivious temptress portrayed by great movie stars like Lana Turner, Joan Crawford, Marilyn Monroe. Her hair was the right length. There was something feminine about a woman with long hair. Seamus liked it too. He played with it, ran it through his fingers, curtained his face with it, tossed and tousled it, pulled it teasingly in a surge of playful battle.

Chapter Three

It was four o'clock in the afternoon and the kitchen was stuffy. Agnes was at work and Clare was sitting at the kitchen table, her unfinished essay in front of her, when Martin walked into the house with a small, pretty girl. Clare could never have described to Eve that first feeling of seeing them together, and the curious silence that followed with the switching off of the radio. Martin was clean-shaven and he wore a white shirt and new blue jeans.

'Good to see you, Clare,' he said. 'This is Terry Packer.'

Terry wore a bright green dress and her hair was held up with a chiffon scarf to match. She extended her hand to Clare.

'Pleased to meet you, I'm sure.' She smiled, her round face dimpling.

'Pleased to meet you too.' Clare was unable to think of anything else to say, but went on lamely, 'You look well.'

Agnes came in. 'Back so soon. This is a surprise,' she said to Martin, before commanding him to stand back to let her have a good look at him. 'You're all spruced up, son. Putting on a bit of weight too.' She patted his stomach. 'You'd want to watch that. Do you remember how heavy your father got when—'

'I want you to meet my fiancée, Mother. This is

Terry.' Agnes approached the girl slowly with eyes that missed nothing. 'How do you do?' She gave Terry a peck on the cheek. 'Come and sit down.'

'We can't stay long.' Terry's voice quivered. 'I promised my granny we'd visit her in Galway.'

'You'll have your tea before you go.' Agnes shot her a sarcastic glance.

'Oh yes. I only meant we can't stop as long as we'd hoped. Just the one night,' Terry stuttered.

'That's something to be grateful for.' Agnes sniffed.

As they talked Clare could feel them leaving already, going away together, while she had to stay behind, alone again in the kitchen, writing her essay on Bismarck. 'Excuse me.' She left the room and went upstairs. She put on her best dress to give the impression that she was grown-up enough to be invited to stay with Martin and Terry in London.

When she returned they were talking about the wedding. Terry was describing her parish church in Clapham, with coloured windows, and the bridal gown with the long train.

'You seem to have it all organised.' The jealousy in Agnes's eyes gave them a queer expression.

'What ails you, Mother?' Martin asked.

'What's wrong with your own parish church?' Agnes glared at Terry.

Terry looked beseechingly at Martin.

'Mother, stop fussing. All you have to do is present yourself with Clare. There's nothing more to it.'

'August. London.'

'We'll have a great time, won't we, Clare?' Terry said. 'You look smashing in that dress. All grown-up.'

'A good time, I ask you. What are you going to suggest to me next? How can I have a good time with no husband, no money and not a decent stitch to wear?'

Martin rose and went to her. Putting his arms around her, he said, 'Leave it to me, Ma. Now, stop fretting.'

The four of them sat round the table and Agnes poured tea. She had been cooking all morning and now she served chicken and ham salad, scones and home-made bread, slowly licking her thumb after she wiped the top of the mayonnaise bottle.

'Tuck in.' She waved at the food and watched with pleasure every mouthful her son ate. 'Everything is homemade,' she said.

'Delicious,' said Martin. 'You'll have to show Terry how to bake bread.'

'I would if she were staying long enough,' Agnes rejoined.

'It's tough luck, but I could only get a couple of days off,' Martin said. 'I wanted you to meet Terry and hear our plans.'

'I was looking forward to having you home for a while. Holidays and the like. A wedding was the last thing on my mind.' Agnes was still peeved.

What she really means, Clare was thinking, is that she'd been looking forward to having him all to herself. She closed her eyes and let the name London conjure up dreams of making a recording with the Rolling Stones, playing a duet with Paul McCartney, singing with the Dave Clark Five, or the Bee Gees.

'What do you think, Clare?' Martin asked. 'I was saying you'd probably like the trip to London. We could go shopping. Buy you a new dress.'

'I'd love that.'

'She'll make do with the one she has,' Agnes snapped. 'Can't have Martin frittering away his hard-earned cash.'

'My treat,' Terry said. 'I've got some savings.'

'Oh, really?' Something in Agnes's voice made Clare despair that her mother would ever warm to her prospective daughter-in-law.

After tea Agnes announced that Clare would play them a tune on the piano.

'They don't want to hear me play,' Clare protested.

'Yes, they do,' Agnes insisted.

Clare went into the sitting room, leaving the door open.

'If she doesn't get that scholarship she'll be very disappointed,' Agnes said to Martin.

'She'll get it all right,' Martin said, with conviction.

'I'm not so sure. The competition's very stiff.'

Agnes had high standards of achievement, and her ambition for Clare centred on the piano. Clare had started lessons at the age of four and Agnes, with the encouragement of Miss Devine, Clare's music teacher, assumed that her daughter would one day become a concert pianist. She would stand in the open doorway, her knitting under her arm, insisting that Clare practise her scales over and over again. Later on, when Agnes admonished her for playing jazz, Clare would switch to a sonata, or a concerto, resentfully acknowledging Agnes's authority. Now, with the presence of Martin, there was no holding back. She let her fingers attack the intricacies of 'Black and White Rag', racing with assurance into the jazz detail that had made Winifred Atwell famous. Exhilarated by the sense of freedom that the tumble of chords gave her, she played as if she were crossing a great divide and would somehow arrive in her own place. So keen was her concentration on the keys that the present slipped away, taking with it her listening mother, brother, and his fiancée, and replacing them with scenes from her childhood. Music lessons in Harbour View, Miss Devine's house, the metronome, her own hands too small to reach the octave, her feet barely touching the pedals. In that stuffy room of long ago, where a tallboy with a display of precious ornaments stood in the corner, and two Staffordshire china dogs leered at her from their perches either side of the black marble mantelpiece, she had learned her love of music.

Jazz chords tumbled through the air as she came to a crescendo. She didn't want the piece to end, loving the feeling of power the music gave her, seeing without looking the admiration in Martin's eyes, and the disapproval in her mother's.

'Makes me all jittery.' Terry giggled.

Martin shot her an affectionate look. 'Lovely,' he said, shaking himself back to the moment.

'I thought she'd have played one of her set pieces for the exam,' Agnes said.

Sensing trouble, Martin said, 'I'm taking Terry to the pub. Coming for a drink, Mother?'

'No, thanks. You go ahead, I'll tidy up here.' Agnes left the room and Terry gave Martin a hug.

'That's the best idea you've had in a long time,' she said.

The next evening after Martin and Terry had left, Agnes went to work and Clare went to Eve's house. The sky was lavender as the girls walked on the lawn in the twilight, Clare recounting the details of Martin's visit. 'It's a pity they had to go so soon,' she concluded. 'He seemed to be in a terrible hurry to get away and Terry wants to see her family. Mother's so disappointed. Come to think of it, so am I.'

'Why don't you stay the night like you used to do?' Eve suggested.

'I'm too old for that now.'

'Rubbish. We'll make tomato sandwiches and have a midnight feast. It'll be like when we were children. Do you remember your mother making seventeen sandwiches out of the one tomato?'

Clare laughed. 'Will I ever forget? "Hard times will come no more," she used to say. But I'd better stay with her tonight. She'll need company.'

In the dark, the wood behind Eve's house was purple. Clare was remembering when they could walk around in it acting like grown-up ladies, Sarah in her pushchair beside them – until they got too big and could only stare into the tangle of branches. Sometimes, with the coming of night, their secret arbour hadn't seemed so friendly. They would get afraid and run up to the shelter of Eve's house. Now, passing by it, Clare thought of Sarah and shivered.

Pauline Quirk came towards her.

'Hi, Pauline. You're in an awful hurry,' Clare called out.

'I'm late for work.' Pauline was breathless.

'Martin was home with his fiancée, Terry.'

'His what?' Pauline stopped.

'He's just got engaged to an English girl called Terry Packer. Brought her home to introduce her to us.'

'Didn't take him long,' Pauline said, more to herself than to Clare. 'What does your mother think?'

'She'd probably have preferred a good Catholic Irish girl. How are you keeping?' Clare looked with concern at the dark shadows under Pauline's eyes and her pallor.

'Couldn't be better,' Pauline lied. 'How's school?'

'Dreadful. The pressure's on now since the holidays.'

'Tell all the girls I was asking for them. I never thought I'd miss them but I do,' Pauline said.

'Why don't you call in? They miss you too,' Clare assured her.

'I will.' Pauline was gone, waving as she went.

The light from the kitchen window was reflected in the dark back yard and brought a lump to Clare's throat. Even before she entered it the house seemed lonely.

The next morning Sister Aquinas was waiting in the music room. 'We have no time to waste,' she said, checking her watch as she seated herself beside the piano to watch Clare's hands, her eyes hardening behind her glasses, her back stiff in the chair.

A scale of broken chords slanted across the mid-afternoon quiet. The scale was repeated. A chord was struck. Then a chain of dissonant chords climbed upwards like a flight of birds. Just where the final chord should have come to complete the scale, there was a halt, a fumbling.

'Repeat.'

Clare repeated, stopping at the seventh chord, echoing all of the unfinished scale. Sister Aquinas shook her head and put her hands to her ears. 'Repeat,' she rasped.

Clare struck and struck again.

'Continue.'

Sister Aquinas raised her eyes as the notes climbed higher as if praying to heaven for the scale of clashing dissonance to move upward. When Clare finally reached the highest octave Sister Aquinas's eyes were on the ceiling. As the scale slid effortlessly downward she bowed as though she were in a chapel, her eyes gradually closing, reverently giving thanks for a perfect finish.

'You must spend more time working on those

scales,' Sister Aquinas said. 'How else can you tackle Liszt's études, for instance?'

For the next quarter of an hour Clare played other standard exercises she had practised.

'Now your repertoire.' Sister Aquinas nodded towards the music in front of Clare.

Clare let her hands ease into Haydn's sonata in C, the last movement.

'Stop,' Sister Aquinas said, mid-way through the first section. 'You're not making enough use of the sustained notes. What about registration? Repeat that last movement.'

The bar was repeated, hard and insistent.

'Get the trill on that F into your brain,' Sister Aquinas harped. 'F. F. F.'

'Eff off,' Clare said to herself.

Again she played the piece from the beginning until she could no longer see the music because her eyes were blurred. She wished she was at a Saturday matinée, watching a gangster or a cowboy film. She enjoyed watching the love scenes, when the boys in the front rows whistled so loudly that the usherette flashed her torch on them, threatening them with ejection if they didn't settle down.

When Clare came back to reality Sister Aquinas was saying, in her rasping voice, 'It's a curious thing that the notes are side by side on the piano and yet you miss the full expression every time. Now Chopin's mazurka.'

This time Clare's hands tumbled into the boisterous movement of the dance music, a favourite. Gradually Sister Aquinas eased herself back into her chair, her ill-temper dissipating with the rhythm of the music.

'The best insurance against memory failure is practice,' she said, when Clare finished. 'You'll lose marks for clumsiness or forgetfulness. Practice makes perfect. Now let us give thanks to God for a successful lesson.'

'I've nothing to wear to the summer ball,' Clare said to Eve on their way home from school.

'You can borrow something of mine.'

Clare blushed. 'Everyone would recognise it.'

'Mummy has plenty of dresses. Come and see if anything would be suitable.'

'What would she say?'

'She only wears a thing once or twice, then discards it.'

The twilight was almost white, Clare noticed, as they made their way to Eve's house. Muffled noises came from the neighbouring houses they passed: children calling, a door slamming, dogs barking in the distance. Eve's house seemed enormous, with its front garden, shaded by laurels, and sweeping avenue. Over the darkening woods at the back the sky was turning dull. Rooks gathered in the elms and small birds whirled above the cedars. As they reached the back door the corners of the house were fading into blackness.

Sarah Freeman was in the kitchen, waiting for Eve. She sat so still that only her dress moved slightly when she beckoned them to come in. Her skin was pale and her eyes had a far-off look as though her thoughts were somewhere else.

'Hi,' Eve said to her. 'We're going to find something for Clare to wear to the summer ball.'

Sarah smiled at her. 'I'd love to be going.'

'In another few years,' Eve said. 'Now, let's look upstairs.'

The hall was dark and chilly, except for a beam of

light from the landing window. Eve led the way to her mother's room passing several empty rooms on the way. Dorothy Freeman's bedroom was warm and her fragrance hung in the air. The discarded dresses were kept in a separate section of her Victorian wardrobe. Rows of shoes with pointy toes lay beneath them.

'Try one on,' Eve said.

Clare approached them cautiously and lifted out a midnight blue silk dress with a tight bodice, shoestring straps and a train.

'Shut your eyes till I tell you,' she said to the watching Eve and Sarah. Eve bowed her head and waited. Sarah covered her eyes with her hands.

When she was ready, Clare said, 'Now I want your honest opinion.'

Eve raised her head and when she saw Clare standing there, one hand on her hip, she could not believe her eyes.

'You look so beautiful,' Sarah said, echoing her sister's thoughts.

'You're having me on,' Clare laughed.

'It's true,' Eve said. 'Come and see.'

Clare went to look in the cheval-glass in the corner. 'Is it not too grown-up?'

Eve studied the dress for several minutes. 'We could shorten it, nip it in at the waist, take that fussy bow off the back and that silly train. Wait, I'll get scissors and some pins.'

In a drawer in the delicate rosewood dressing-table she found Dorothy's sewing-box.

'Won't your mother have a fit?' Clare said, taking Dorothy's silver hairbrush from its matching set and stroking her hair gently with it.

'She gives them away,' Sarah said.

Eve cut off the bow and pulled the dress in at the waist, pinning it higher while Clare stood still and Sarah watched, her head tilted to one side. Then, with a warning to Clare to 'hold still', Eve began to slice off the train. Clare screwed up her eyes, hardly daring to breathe. 'Stand back,' Eve said eventually.

'What do you really think?' Clare looked in the mirror again.

'Perfect,' Eve said.

'Gorgeous,' Sarah reiterated.

'Thanks a million,' Clare said, hugging herself in the dress. 'Now I'd better be going. I've lots of practice to do. That fortnight's holiday's made me lazy.'

'We'll call for you in the morning,' Eve said.

'Good night.' Sarah gave Clare a hug.

When Clare got home there was a note from Agnes to say that she had gone to a Legion of Mary meeting. Clare felt sad at being left on her own again. It was true that she and Agnes had never had much in common. But, these days, Clare seemed to be always alone in the house and she hated that. Agnes wasn't interested in her point of view. If Clare tried to explain anything to her, her mother would forestall her by switching on the radio to hear her ration of strikes and disasters. Or she would place the kitchen chairs side by side and take her beads out of their purse in preparation for the evening rosary.

Chapter Four

Through the iron bars of the basement window Pauline Quirk could see a huddled shadow at the hall door before she heard the knock.

'Who's there?' she called.

'It's only me.' Martin Dolan kept his voice friendly. For a moment, Pauline stood transfixed, then turned the lock and opened the door. She stood, dishevelled and blinking, in the light over the door.

'Cold oul' night for standing on the doorstep.' Martin smiled and, passing her as though he was a welcome guest, walked into the front room, leaving Pauline staring after him.

Standing at the fire, buffing his hands, he said pleasantly, 'Come in. Come in. Nice fire you've got here. Where's Seamus?'

'Sleeping.'

'Get him in here,' Martin barked, making Pauline jump.

'Why?' she asked.

'You heard me.'

Without taking her eyes off Martin, Pauline called Seamus. Martin stood with his back to the fire casting an indifferent eye over the dingy sofa and the table in the corner, which was littered with the remains of a meal. Shuffling sounds came from the passage and Seamus entered the room. He looked surprised and petrified to see Martin.

'Howayah,' Martin said.

'Hello,' Seamus said. 'I thought you were in England.' His eyes met Martin's gaze as he hovered on one foot, like a sparrow, poised for flight.

'And I thought you were in Belfast, where you're supposed to be.'

'How did you know I was here?'

'Ah, now, Seamus. That'd be telling.' Martin tapped his nose with his index finger. 'You know better than to ask questions like that.'

'Yes.' Seamus swallowed to disguise the tremor in his voice.

'Relax.' Martin moved to the baldy armchair beside the fire and sat into it. 'This won't take long.'

Seamus heaved his shoulders and stood staring at Martin, waiting.

'Are you here long?'

'Yes . . . eh . . . well–'

Martin leaped out of the chair and grabbed Seamus by the throat, lifting him off the floor. 'Answer me.' He spat the words in the other man's face and let go of him so suddenly that Seamus stumbled and fell. Staggering to his feet, he stood cowering.

'A couple of days. Pauline's . . .' Seamus hesitated. 'She's pregnant.'

'What's going on?' Pauline's face was puckered with shock.

'Shh,' Seamus cautioned, propelling her to the sofa, while he stood, lips pursed, terror in his eyes.

Martin smiled at Pauline. 'Sorry to discommode you. Only I have a bit of business with your man here.'

'It's nothing to do with me, whatever it is,' she said, her mouth tight with agitation, her eyes defiant. 'I didn't even know you were home.'

Seeing the pitiful bulge beneath her tatty nightdress and her bewildered expression at Seamus's fear, Martin believed her. She was strong. Not for her the snivelling antics of that coward Seamus.

'Leave her out of this—' Seamus began.

'Shut up,' Martin growled, raising his hand.

Seamus took a step backwards.

Martin looked at him and said quietly, 'Surely she should know what you're up to.'

'Stop, Martin. For the love of God, I'm not up to anything.' There was a sob in Seamus's voice.

'What are ye on about?' Pauline, bewildered, had shrivelled into the sofa.

'I think she should know what she's mixed up in. It's only fair to tell her. Don't you think so, Seamus?' Martin turned to Pauline and said, with a smile, 'He's been seen up there in the company of members of the Special Branch, would you believe? Very chummy, I'm told. A traitor in the making.'

Martin's eyes were fixed on Pauline, observing the look of astonishment she cast at Seamus. Just as she turned incredulous blue eyes on Martin, her mouth open to form a denial, a choking sound came from the corner. Seamus was slumped against the wall, knees buckling, his head between his hands.

'We suspect it was you who squealed on Tommy Casey,' Martin shouted at him.

'You're wrong.' Pauline was on her feet, pulling her nightdress down over her thighs. 'Seamus wouldn't do that.'

'Believe me, Pauline, Seamus knows what I'm talking about.'

'But I haven't done anything,' Seamus whimpered. 'I was only talking to a couple of friends in the—'

'Shut up. This time I'll let you off with a warning. Call it a favour for old times' sake. Only because we've no definite proof, mind.' Martin paused. 'But if I find a shred of evidence . . .' he warned, shaking his fist.

Seamus breathed a sigh of relief.

Martin saw it and moved quickly, catching him by the throat, his face suddenly dark with rage. The silence was broken by the sickening crunch of splintering bone as he hit Seamus smack on the nose. Seamus slumped by the wall, blood pumping through his fingers and his frothing mouth.

'Martin. For the love of Jasus.' Pauline reeled forward, her voice strangled.

Martin ignored her. Fists clenched, eyes bulging, he said through clenched teeth to the heap on the floor, 'I'm warning you, you snivelling little rat. Get back to Belfast and stay there until you're sent for. You have a job to do. One step out of line and it'll be a different story. Have you got that?'

For a second it seemed as if Martin might hit him again, but he dropped his hands to his sides. Then he said, 'Get up, ye bastard, and look after that good woman, and don't forget, one false move and we'll find you. It's a very small world.' Martin turned to Pauline. 'He'll be all right,' he said reassuringly. 'Keep an eye on him.

She followed Martin as he walked down the passage wiping his blood-spattered hands on his handkerchief. At the hall door he looked at her, a grin of satisfaction on his face. 'I've wanted to hit Seamus Gilfoyle for a long time. Ever since he stole you from me.'

'You bastard!' Pauline shouted, slamming the door in his face.

On her way to the shops Eve met Sergeant Enright walking slowly along the street, the sun warming his back, the town stretched out before him. He was a big man with a square jaw. He bore the look of the country in his florid complexion and ploughman's gait. He had been stationed in Glencove for the last ten years and knew every inch of it. With his wife, Delia, and family, he lived in the barracks. While his children played in the street, Delia kept watch from the door. She knew everyone and their business for miles around. Nothing escaped her shrewd eyes and she would relay her news religiously to her husband in the hope of his gaining promotion back to her native Dublin City.

'Hello, Eve,' he said, stopping in his tracks. 'How's your mother?'

'Fine thank you, Sergeant.'

Madge Kinsella came up the road, a shopping bag in each hand. 'Sergeant Enright, the very man I want to see.'

'What is it, Madge?'

'It's about Pauline Quirk, Sergeant. She's back and forth to Goretti Flats like a scared rabbit. But she won't say what's up.'

Sergeant Enright looked noncommittally in the direction of the railway track and the shimmering heat over Goretti Terrace beyond. 'Eh,' he grunted.

Like his own wife, Madge was addicted to gossip and he was itching to be on his way.

'Were you talking to her, Eve?' Sergeant Enright looked at Eve.

'Not recently, Sergeant,' Eve said.

'Only it's the sort of thing, Sergeant,' Madge continued, 'that if you don't report it you'd be sorry afterwards, if anything were to go wrong, like.'

'Like what, for instance?' Sergeant Enright said, returning his impatient eyes to Madge.

'Well, that Seamus Gilfoyle she's going with is back from Belfast and you know yourself.' Madge shifted from one foot to the other.

'Know what?'

Sergeant Enright was exact to the point of exasperation. Madge said he was thick.

'Martin Dolan is home.'

'And?' Sergeant Enright prompted.

'There's always trouble when they're around the place together. I thought I'd warn ye.'

'I see, faith.' Sergeant Enright chewed his lip.

'Well?' Madge waited.

'Well,' Sergeant Enright said. 'I don't know what you expect me to do about it when I don't know the problem. I can hardly arrest a person for existing, now can I?'

'No, Sergeant. But trouble's trouble all the same.'

He removed his hat and, with his handkerchief, wiped the sweat from the red rim it left on his brow. He said, 'Good day to ye, mam.' Then he replaced his hat and sauntered off down the road, with long strides.

'I should have known,' Madge said, a look of disgust on her face as she stared at his ramrod-straight retreating back.

'What kind of trouble is Pauline in, do you think?' Eve looked at Madge.

'I don't know.' Madge was concerned. 'But there's something up. I warned her to keep away from Seamus Gilfoyle, but would she listen? I phoned her aunt Bea to see if she knew anything, but she wasn't interested. As prickly as a briar, that one.'

'I'll call in to see her,' Eve said. 'She might talk to me.'

'Good girl. See if you can help her.' Madge trudged off and Eve walked on through the town. The blooms of the lilac and forsythia bushes in the formal beds of the presbytery were fading and the buds of the rose bushes were about to burst open.

Summertime, the best time of the year, Eve reflected, as she hastened her steps. Why did people have to be so aggravating? Could they not mind their own business?

Eve was in the summerhouse, waiting for Sarah to return from her ballet lesson so that she could set her hair, a trial run before the summer ball. She had the rollers, hairbrush and long mirror beside her on the seat. The summer ball would be the most exciting event of Eve's life so far. She would wear the new pink satin dress Dorothy had bought for her. David Furlong would love it because it made her look so pretty.

The garden was warm. Along the trellis, roses and clematis vied with one another for space, their waxy purple and pink petals entwined in the lattice. Her grandfather, James Freeman, was further down the garden tending his plants. Shoulders bent, face ruddy with exertion, he worked slowly. James lived now for his garden, growing chrysanthemums for Christmas, strawberries and tomatoes for summer. He had planted the trees at the end all those years ago when Sarah was born.

Sarah came out. Slender, with high cheekbones, flyaway blonde hair, she looked delicate. Sometimes her eyes were strained and her movements quiet and measured, as if any exuberance was too much effort. She was wearing her cardigan around her shoulders making sure her chest and arms were covered.

'What kept you? I've been waiting for you to do my hair,' Eve said.

'I went to the library on my way home. There was a queue.' She opened her bag to show Eve her books.

'Lovely,' Eve said, taking out *Anne of Green Gables* and looking at the cover. 'That was my favourite story.'

Sarah picked up the bag of rollers. 'I'll put them in tight,' she said.

'We'll have to set it again before the dance,' Eve said.

Sarah began to stroke her sister's hair, gentle at first, then pulling it down slowly, sectioning it off to start rolling.

'Won't you get tired of all the dancing?' Sarah asked, while working on the hair. 'All that twirling and those bright lights. So many people.'

'No.'

The rollers were patted into place.

Tom Jones, singing 'Delilah', blared from the radio next door.

'David Furlong's home,' Eve said.

'I wonder if he's as excited as you are about the ball,' Sarah said.

'I don't know but I can't wait.'

'I don't blame you, he's gorgeous,' Sarah said. 'Do you remember the ceilidh dances Mummy made us go to when we were learning Irish dancing?'

'Yes.'

'Will it be like that?'

'Much more genteel. They were a bunch of clod-hoppers.' Eve smiled, remembering the sweaty hands of the boys that had gripped hers for the twirls, and their intent faces.

'You can say that again.' Sarah sectioned off more hair and began to run the comb through it. Quickly she

56

rolled her hands gently up Eve's head.

Dorothy came out. 'Mind you don't catch cold, Sarah. Pull that cardigan around you,' she said.

'OK.' Quickly Sarah pushed a roller into Eve's head.

Eve blinked. 'Ouch.'

'I told you I was doing them tight to last.' Sarah worked hard and fast. Eve, feeling the pull of her sister's hands on her scalp, concentrated on the gaunt expression on Dorothy's face. It made her anxious.

'Done,' Sarah said at last.

Eve picked up the hand mirror. She was gazing at the helmet of pink and purple plastic rollers arranged in neat rows on her head. 'You didn't miss any?'

'Not a strand.'

'Thanks.'

Eve winced. Already her skin felt tight, stretched back from her head by the plastic cylinders. An ache was forming across her drawn eyes.

Just as they finished, James called to Sarah to get ready for the cinema.

'Grandpa's taking me to see *One Hundred and One Dalmatians*,' she said to Eve. 'Now, leave the rollers in for as long as you can and I'll backcomb it for you when I come home.'

'I will.'

When Eve returned from school the next day, Dorothy was waiting for her. 'Eve.'

'Yes.'

'Sarah's ill. She's got a high temperature.'

'Where's Grandpa?'

'Gone to buy her lozenges.'

'Mummy.' The voice from upstairs was urgent.

'Coming. Put the kettle on, Eve.' The serious

expression on her mother's face made her look stern.

After a few minutes Dorothy came running downstairs. 'I think she's delirious. Keep an eye on her while I phone the doctor.'

Her tone frightened Eve. She took the stairs two at a time.

'Sarah?' The room was in semi-darkness. 'Hello.'

Eve's shoes made a tapping sound on the lino as she crossed the room. Slowly she opened the shutters. Sarah lay in bed, sheets pulled up to her shoulders, her features so frail that she looked like a small child. 'It's hot,' she muttered. Her face was flushed and her fair hair was tumbled and damp on the pillow. Eyes luminous with fever looked imploringly at Eve. 'Take off the blankets, please,' she whispered.

'I can't, pet. Not till the doctor comes.' Eve loosened the covers as she spoke.

Sarah tossed her head and the heat radiated from her like a furnace. The room smelled of sickness.

'Have you got a pain?'

Sarah nodded, indicating her forehead.

'I think my head's bursting. Where's Mummy?'

The wind rose. Eve went to the window and stood watching the swaying trees that screened the back garden from the woods beyond. Tall conifers with brown skirts and green waving arms, dancing in the wind. Sentinels rising majestically to hide gutters, chimneys and rooftops. She remembered now that her grandfather had planted the trees when Sarah was born. They had grown up with her and she loved them. Birds sang in them and nested in the clusters of their branches. Eve and Sarah had played house and dolls in among the trees when they were small. They had made jewellery with the cones. Eve was remembering the time they played Cinderella. Draped in her mother's crumpled satin ballgown, a crown of pine cones on her head, she had stood tall in high heels, while Sarah, the prince, had knelt before her in her father's tatty trousers, clutching a slipper. It didn't matter how ridiculous they looked. They were happy.

When the branches of the trees became more dense they had played hide and seek among them. Cowboys and Indians sometimes. They loved sunbathing by the trees in warm weather, chairs placed against them to catch the heat. Their pine smell evoked deep forests – thoughts of Robin Hood and his Merry Men.

Sarah had started secondary school the previous September and had a new uniform, like Eve's. Brown gymslip, cream blouse and thick brown stockings. When she got sick, her mother had said in a tired voice, 'It's always the same. Every time you go back to school you catch something. Did you take your cod-liver oil?'

'Yes,' Sarah had spluttered, her bronchial tubes congested with phlegm.

'How many times do I have to remind you to button up your coat? Now go to bed and I'll bring you up a hot-water bottle.'

Since she had had whooping cough when she was three, Sarah was often ill, catching colds with such regularity that she was almost an invalid. Dorothy insisted on afternoon rests and daily doses of cod-liver oil and Parrish's Food. Sometimes during the harsh winter she would take her daughter out of school and Sarah would fret about missing her lessons.

Returning to the bedroom Dorothy rubbed Vick on Sarah's chest, massaging it in well with strong capable hands. Sarah began to sag down into the bed with weakness. Dorothy placed a hot towel around her neck and put an extra blanket on the bed, ordering her to sweat it out.

Dr Gregory was the family practitioner and always knew what to do. After he had peered into Sarah's eyes with a tiny torch and felt her skin, he took Dorothy to one side. 'Sarah has scarlet fever.'

Immediately Eve felt the dread of its redness seep through her. The very name had frightening connotations of flames. Sarah's eyes seemed to grow brighter as Eve looked at her.

'Plenty of fluids and keep her in an even temperature. If she doesn't improve we'll have to get her into hospital,' Dr Gregory instructed.

Eve had to stay home from school and keep away from her friends. Disinfected sheets were hung over Sarah's door. They were referred to as the Iron Curtain and their pungent smell provoked in Sarah a terrible feeling of isolation. Eve had helped to mind her when she was a baby, had pushed her in her pram, read her stories and, although she had often complained that Sarah was a nuisance, she missed her. Their mother was so preoccupied with her – carrying trays up and down stairs, a surgical mask over her mouth, that she seemed to forget about everything else. During the day Eve spent hours alone on the beach, collecting shells or walking through the woods at the back of their house. Sometimes she went to the park. But the initial thrill of missing school was soon replaced with boredom.

When Pauline called the next day to enquire after Sarah, Eve talked to her from the kitchen window, explaining the contagious nature of the disease.

'I didn't realise it was that bad.' Pauline looked horror-stricken. 'If I stay out here and don't touch anything, will I be all right?'

'I'm sure you will,' Eve said. 'Clare brings the homework over and posts it through the letterbox.'

'What does Dr Gregory say?' Pauline asked.

'He thinks it'll be a slow recovery for Sarah,' Eve said sadly.

Two days later the ambulance men came to take Sarah to hospital. Eve wanted to follow them upstairs, but her mother told her to stay in the kitchen and keep the door closed. She could hear the men's footsteps clumping through the house and their raised voices as they manoeuvred the stretcher down the stairs. When the reached the hall Eve opened the kitchen door a fraction to watch her mother drape a blanket over Sarah before the ambulance men moved forward slowly as they negotiated the front door.

Dorothy followed them. Eve could hear the bang of the ambulance doors and the whine of the siren as it raced down the road.

'It's cold out there,' Dorothy said, closing the front door. 'Cold as the grave.'

Eve went to her and put her arms around her. Dorothy smelled of lavender water and she was crying.

'They'll know what to do in the hospital, Mummy.'

'I hope so. I wouldn't want to live without her.'

'It was always Sarah with you,' Eve blurted. 'I suppose it's because she's the baby.'

'Oh, now, don't start.' Dorothy sighed. 'Sarah was never as robust as you. Besides, you're seventeen years old. You don't need as much attention.' She leaned forward and pushed back a few stray curls from Eve's forehead. Her hands were gentle. 'You're strong and sensible. Look at you. Turning out to be a real beauty, like your aunt Ellen.'

Next day when Eve came home from the park the

house was empty. The disinfected sheets were gone
and everywhere had been thoroughly scrubbed. As she
took out her school books a watery sun seeped through
the window, casting shadows of trees on the far wall.
Head bowed, Eve struggled with her French verbs: je
serai, tu seras, il sera, nous serons, vous serez, ils
seront. Eventually, she put away her books and went
down to the kitchen to make tea for her grandfather
and herself.

James was working in the potting-shed, screened by
trees, obscured from prying eyes. She stood in the
doorway for a moment waiting for her eyes to adjust to
the dimness. 'Grandpa,' she called, breathing in the
mingled smells of fertiliser, peat and creosote.

Her grandfather came forward. His gardening jacket
was covered in dust.

'Is it yourself, my dear? You must have come in on
angel's wings. I didn't hear a sound.' As he smiled his
blue eyes twinkled.

'I brought you some tea and biscuits. Mother said
you'd be hungry.'

'Thank you, love. Put it down over there on the
bench while I wash my hands. Won't be a minute.
You're not in a hurry?'

'No.'

Eve sat down, the tray beside her. The sound of birds
and the drone of a trapped bee broke the silence.

'How's my girl?' her grandfather asked on his return.

'Is Sarah very ill, Grandpa?' Eve asked.

James looked at her, a sad expression on his face.
'I'm afraid so, my dear,' he said.

'Mummy won't talk to me about her.' Eve hung her
head.

'Your mother thinks of you as a child still, and

children don't have to be consulted or have a say in anything.' His voice was gentle and reasonable.

'Perhaps it's my fault.'

'How could it be?'

'Maybe I didn't look after her properly. Let her stay in the water too long when we went swimming. I often forgot to tell her to put on her cardigan.'

'Nonsense. Stop blaming yourself. It's nobody's fault. It's something that happened and it couldn't be helped. Besides, there's the possibility that Sarah will get better.'

Eve found that the rough, blue-veined hand that took hers was comforting. Her grandfather said things sometimes, not because they were true but because he thought they ought to be. Eve wanted to cry and turned away so that he wouldn't notice.

'The trouble is,' he was saying, 'it's an insidious illness. The doctors don't always know for certain if it's completely gone. Just when they think they've licked it, it can flare up again. It isn't anyone's fault.'

How was it, Eve wondered, that he was the only one who had time to listen to her and explain things?

Chapter Five

From her hiding place in the tree, Eve watched her grandfather slowly, methodically, turning his flower-beds. Tucked into the bower, her spine curved against a branch, she leaned back and let the sound of Dorothy and Agnes's voices, and the rattle of cups, soothe her. So many hours of her childhood had been spent curled up in the tree reading, with only the rustle of leaves and the caw of crows to disturb her. Or playing cards with Sarah when they had both been small enough to fit together into its hollow. Eve would deal slowly, licking her thumb when the cards stuck together. Watching each card as it was laid down, her face screwed up in concentration, her bony knees jutting into Eve's side, Sarah would call, 'Snap,' whenever it occurred to her. Eve would get angry. Now, wedged into the small space, legs dangling through the foliage, Eve realised that the security of her childhood world was coming to an end. Womanhood loomed, and while part of her yearned for freedom, another part dreaded the responsibility of independence. She closed her eyes and let the sun's flickering rays dance on her face.

The chimes of the town-hall clock brought memories of playing in the woods, of Clare and her hurrying home when the clock struck six, sleepless nights when Sarah was ill, listening to the striking of the hour, waiting for the dawn, and for Sarah to be well again.

The clock had been a steady, regular beat in her secure world.

Eve wished she was a child again, playing in the garden with Sarah. She had been a good child but her mother didn't love her the way she loved Sarah. Perhaps it wasn't just Sarah's illness. Perhaps it was the difference between Eve and her mother. Dorothy was practical and liked to take her time. Eve was quick to make decisions, quick with her gestures. Eve loved her mother and wished she could tell her that. She loved the way Dorothy could make people laugh when she was in a good humour. The feel of her mother's hand in hers, guiding her along busy streets, was fresh in her memory too, as was the rapid movement of Dorothy's skirt.

'We must face reality,' Agnes Dolan said.

Eve craned her neck to look out over the branches and caught sight of her mother and Agnes, walking down the garden path towards her.

'Supposing Sarah doesn't get better?' she continued. There it was. The cruel and careless truth delivered with authority from Agnes Dolan. Through slitted eyes Eve saw the horror on her mother's strong face and watched her eyes scan the trees as if she was looking for someone. Eve shrank back, feeling too big for the tree as she tried to hunch down.

Agnes tucked her hand into the crook of Dorothy's arm. 'She's not getting better, Dorothy,' she said. 'She's not even trying to.'

'Rubbish,' came Dorothy's quick denial.

'Come on. Let's go inside, it's getting cool out here.'

'Where's Eve?' Dorothy's voice was impatient.

'Reading somewhere, I expect,' Agnes said.

'It's time she grew out of this habit of disappearing

for hours at a time. In fact, it's time she grew up. She's intent on holding on to her childhood for as long as possible, if you ask me.'

'What harm is that?' came Agnes's terse reply.

'She's never here when I need her,' Dorothy whined.

With a sigh of relief Eve saw her mother turn towards the house, Agnes following her.

Eve's eyes moved over the garden with its well-cut lawn, scented roses, hedged trimmed to perfection, sweet-smelling phlox, and, of course, the trees. Without Sarah, none of it meant anything.

Stretching her legs and catching hold of a branch, she swung herself down. Her muscles ached as she brushed bits of twigs from her frock and smoothed back her hair with her hands.

Then she ran – out of the garden by the side of the house, along the avenue, through Main Street and down to the sea. When she stopped for breath her head was pounding and the air caught in her throat, making her gulp. As the sun vanished a cold breeze came off the sea. The receding tide had left the new-washed sand shining and deserted in the evening sun. Gulls flew over it, their harsh cries heralding the day's end. Only a scattering of visitors, staying in boarding houses, sat in shelters or walked along by the harbour wall, wrapped up against the east wind.

Eve stared straight ahead at the desolate strand, eyes unfocused. She stood still and held in her breath, willing herself to feel nothing, to think nothing, to be nothing. She could hear the sound of the receding tide, and people talking in the distance. But she was removed from it all. For a few blissful moments she detached herself from everything, including her pain. She shut her eyes and cried. Shuddering sobs that shook her body. Kneeling down by the sea wall she ground her fingers into the wet sand. She hated it all. Hated the thought of her grandfather's bewildered face, and her mother's anxious one. The worst part was thinking of Sarah being so ill. She could hardly bear it.

'Damn,' she swore. 'Damn, damn, damn.'

With both hands she packed handfuls of sand into balls and flung them at the sea. I wish I could do something to stop it . . . anything. Her greatest sadness was her feeling of uselessness.

Everybody enquired as to how Sarah was progressing: the nuns, the girls at school, Tom the milkman, Dessie the window-cleaner. Some of the nuns sent prayers and little gifts. Agnes knitted her a bedjacket in pink angora wool and spent any spare time she had at the hospital. Sarah was patient and uncomplaining, except during fits of fever when she would hallucinate, tearing off the bedclothes and imploring her mother, in a hoarse whisper, to take her home. Sometimes when the fever fits were at their worst, she didn't recognise Dorothy.

When the fits receded and she began to improve, Eve was allowed to visit her. She cycled to the hospital. Pauline and Clare took it in turns to accompany her there, and waited outside during the visit. It took twenty minutes cycling through the town. Day after day they would go along the green, past the big red-brick houses owned by Dr Gregory and Manus Corrigan, and the modern semi-detached ones, where Gus Lawlor, the headmaster of the primary school lived. The girls inspected the gardens, called to the children and planned the forthcoming dance to keep themselves jolly.

One sunny afternoon, when the streets were full of

the noise of children, Eve climbed the stairs and went along a corridor. Sarah's bed was at the end of a row and had screens all around it.

When Sarah saw her she opened her eyes wide. 'Eve.'

'Are you feeling any better?'

Pain flickered across Sarah's eyes. 'I have a headache.'

'Shall I call the nurse?' Eve asked anxiously.

'I'll be all right in a minute.' As the pain receded, a smile spread over Sarah's face.

'Would you like a drink of lemonade?'

'No, thanks. Are you on your way home from school?'

'It's Saturday,' Eve reminded her.

'I wrote to Daddy.'

'That's good.'

'How's Clare?' Sarah asked.

'Fine. She was asking for you. So was Pauline.'

'That was nice of them.' Sarah's voice was getting weak.

'In my letter I asked Daddy to come home.' Sarah leaned forward. 'Eve, do you believe in God?' she asked earnestly.

The unexpected question took Eve by surprise. 'Yes, I suppose so.'

'Do you know who He is?'

'He's our Father in Heaven. Why?'

'Do you think He loves us?' Sarah's eyes were intent.

'He loves all creatures.'

'That's what Sister Pauline says, but does He love me?'

Eve took her hand and held it. 'Of course He loves you. Everybody loves you,' she reassured her.

'I know everyone here does, but Heaven seems so far away. Eve, I'm frightened.' Sarah's face puckered and her eyes filled with tears.

'There's no need to be. Heaven is all around us and God is always near.'

Sarah sank back into her pillows, exhausted. 'Sister Pauline says that too. I love Sister Pauline.' Sarah's eyes began to close.

'Have a little sleep now. I'll stay with you,' Eve said gently.

Sarah's smile blossomed and spread all over her face. As she closed her eyes and slept, her expression became vacant and her hands lay quietly on the quilt. She looked so peaceful that Eve began to relax. Sitting there, watching over her little sister, Eve knew that Sarah was going to get better.

Eve was doing her homework when she heard the front door open. She ran down the first flight of stairs. 'Daddy!' she cried.

'Eve.' Ron Freeman came towards his daughter. He was a tall, dignified man, with black wavy hair, flecked with grey, and handsome features.

Sizing him up Eve decided that a kiss would be too intimate a gesture after such a long separation, so she hugged him instead. 'I'm glad you're home,' she said.

'Let me look at you.' Gently he pushed her away from him. 'You've grown taller, more beautiful,' he said.

'I'm almost eighteen.'

'A young lady.' There was surprise in his eyes as he looked at Dorothy, who was standing to one side. 'You didn't tell me that our elder daughter is such a beauty.'

'You should have been here to see for yourself,' Dorothy snapped.

'Indeed.'

Even in the dim light of the hall Eve could see the strained expression creeping across her father's jovial face. Suddenly she remembered all the evenings she had waited expectantly as a child, sitting on the monk's chair in the hall, seeing the dark figure through the stained-glass window of the door. She would run to greet him and smother him with kisses. 'Let me take your coat, Daddy,' she said.

'Thank you, love.' Ron shook himself out of it and handed it to her.

'Grandpa's waiting in the drawing room.'

Dorothy led the way into a cheerful room with a log fire that reflected its bright warmth on the brass fire-irons and the gilt overmantel. From his armchair by the fire James Freeman rose to greet his son.

'Good journey?' he asked, as they shook hands.

'Excellent. Those aeroplanes are getting faster all the time. Less bumpy, too. How are you, Father?'

'Can't complain.' James smiled.

'Splendid. Eve's so grown-up,' Ron said. 'Look at her. My little girl has turned into a young lady.'

'Yes, indeed,' James said handing him a tumbler of whiskey and soda. 'You don't notice it so much when you see someone every day.'

'I suppose not. How time flies. Suddenly they're grown-up and gone. You wonder what it was all about.' Ron finished his whiskey and went to pour himself another.

'Did you see Sarah?' James asked.

'We called in for a few minutes on the way home,' Dorothy said. 'She was thrilled to see Ron. The nurses were fussing, though, afraid the excitement might be too much for her.'

'I'll bet,' James agreed.

'Poor little mite.' Ron stared into the bottom of his glass.

Perking himself up, he said, 'Are you looking forward to going to university, Eve?'

'I'd much rather go to London with Clare, if she wins the music scholarship.'

'London would certainly knock the corners off you.' Ron laughed. 'Change of scenery, meeting people.'

'I want her to continue her studies,' Dorothy said sharply. 'She'll meet plenty of her own kind of people when she goes to UCD.'

'Perhaps it wouldn't do her any harm to see a bit of the world first. Have some fun.' Ron sat back in his armchair and sipped his drink.

'She'll need a career. Something to fall back on,' Dorothy said sharply.

'Spread her wings. Can't see the harm. This country's stagnant,' Ron continued, as if Dorothy hadn't spoken.

'Mr Lemass has done wonders for the economy. Standards of living are rising. We're catching up,' James said.

'More Catholics than ever are applying to Trinity College. You might consider it, Dorothy,' Ron said.

'Eve is going to have a university education whether she goes to Trinity College or the National University.' Dorothy was emphatic.

'Don't I have any say in it?' Eve enquired.

'Travel will give you an education too, Eve, before you get married and settle down,' Ron said.

'What if marriage doesn't appeal to her?' Dorothy asked.

'All girls want to get married,' Ron said, 'Unless, of course, they enter a convent.' He looked at Eve. 'Don't tell me . . .' He began to laugh.

'I certainly don't want to be a nun, Daddy,' Eve assured him.

'And you're going to college,' Dorothy insisted, before leaving the room to see about dinner.

Hot sun and heavy rain burst open blossoms as summer danced into full swing, bringing with it the Leaving Certificate and Clare's music-scholarship examinations. Lupins arched with gladioli and lilies hung their graceful curling heads among the roses.

Clare and Eve went to school in summer frocks, their hair trailing in the light wind, their lunches in empty satchels, the knowledge now in their heads. It was the summer of their last days at school and, thrilled and nervous all at once, they were dreaming of their final escape.

Sister Mildred seemed impervious to their fears. In religion class, with her voice barely above a whisper, she emphasised the values of poverty, chastity and obedience. 'I know at least one of you will be coming back in September to enter, no matter how much you try to deny His calling.' Her eyes glowed with an interior light as she looked directly at Eve. Eve gazed at the chalk dust, dancing in the rays of the sunlight, and smiled.

But in the French class it was a different matter. When she realised that Clare did not know her grammar, Sister Mildred lost her temper and made her leave the classroom, telling her that she was a disgrace.

'Dragon,' Clare said. 'Asking me to stand up and make a spectacle of myself.'

'She's getting some peculiar pleasure from making you suffer,' Eve said.

'If you ask me she's got a screw loose,' Clare said.

With the forthcoming examinations, studying intensified.

Sister Mildred crammed French grammar into her

class, asking them questions wherever she met them, either in the convent or in the garden. She prayed continually to the Holy Spirit to guide them.

The evening before the exams started the whole school was lined up outside St Canice's church for a special Mass. Sister Aquinas clapped her fleshy hands and the choir filed in first through the church doors and took their places in front of the altar, between the high stone columns. Sister Camilla, the sacristan, was lighting the candles on either side of the altar, illuminating the copy of Botticelli's 'Madonna and Child' that stood behind it. Light fell on the compassionate face of the Mother, and the upturned face of the Child. The rest of the church was gloomy with the dull brown of the girls' uniforms and the nuns' hooded heads bowed in prayer. Sister Aquinas raised her baton, a look of pride in her florid face. 'One, two, three.'

'*Ave verum . . .*'

The sweet sound of twenty young girls' voices flowed, pure and high, above the columns into the eaves. The nuns held a reverent silence. Father McCarthy, flanked by his altar boys, stared ahead stony-faced in concentration. Clare poked Eve. 'Definitely the last time for us,' she whispered.

'What?'

The dark Gothic seats, the dim lighting, or perhaps the smell of candle grease and wax, were making Clare feel sick. 'We won't be doing this again, thank God,' she whispered.

Eve glanced at her. There was an expression of secret joy on her friend's face. Her mouth, open to deliver the hymn, was smiling, hinting at some inner knowledge that she was not about to impart. Eve waited for the chant to finish then gazed at her. Tall, more graceful than the rest of the girls, Clare looked infuriatingly happy. The Mass concluded with the choir singing the finale. There was the scraping of feet as the congregation knelt for Father McCarthy's blessing.

Outside the church, Father McCarthy said, 'Thank you, girls. Excellent as usual.' He bowed in Sister Aquinas's direction.

The next day the supervisor came with a locked trunk full of examination papers. Quaking, each sixth-year student took the desk allocated to her in the assembly hall. Sister Mildred said the prayer and they sat down to commence their exams. The supervisor sat on the podium, eyes darting in all directions. As the day wore on the windows steamed up and the air became stale. Sister Mildred was waiting when they emerged, several hours later, flushed and nervous.

'I think I got most of them right,' Eve told her.

'I hope so.' Sister Mildred shot her an affectionate glance and, under her breath, she said, 'This community will welcome you with open arms, regardless.'

Hearing this remark, Clare threw her eyes heavenwards. 'I bet,' she said, as Eve and she walked home together.

The girls knew something of the nuns' routine: that they rose at dawn to prostrate themselves before the Blessed Sacrament, ate plain food, and that long before daybreak they chanted their submission to God, imploring him to hasten the day when they could be with him for all eternity. Contrary to Sister Mildred's hope, none of it appealed to either of them.

In an effort to memorise everything she had learned in the last two years, Eve became panic-stricken, while Clare feigned a calmness that belied the turmoil in her head.

Joan O'Neill

'What will you do when it's over, Sister?' Eve asked Sister Mildred, one evening after school.

'I'll take a holiday with my brother in Kerry and pray that you make the right decision.'

'Yes, Sister,' Eve said, and left the school quickly. In the carefree afternoons, their heads crammed with the day's heaviness, they made their leisurely way home along the green, or sometimes wandered down to the sea, searching for mischief. They knew where the boys would be: ripping the air with shouts of victory on the tennis courts of the caravan park, their broad backs bare, their sinewy legs bronze in white shorts, or swimming at the cove.

Eve and Clare spent much of their free time at the cove, sunbathing on the secluded beach, their gymslips tucked into their knickers. At weekends they swam in the new bathing suits that Ron had brought them from India, lapping up the admiring glances their slender, tanned bodies drew from the young men.

In that mood, during the first weekend of the exams, they put on their best frocks, sponged Creme Puff on their faces, applied their lipstick sparingly, and went down to the cove. Running up the grassy slopes, tripping over roots of trees on dirt paths that led into the interior of the wood, they came to a spot where they could see the boys swimming in the sunlit water below. Tired, their dresses sticking to their bodies, they flung themselves under the shade of the tall trees high above the sea and waited for their panting wildness to subside, hopeful that the boys would come upon them suddenly on their way to fetch their clothes.

Eve, reclining against a tree trunk, squinted through the arc of her elbow at the silvery sea, and worried that the boys might not find them. Clare lay still in the cool

76

place, examining the daisies scattered through the long grass. Birds sang and butterflies darted among the wild roses. She shut her eyes and waited for the shiver of high notes that she had played earlier that day, now tightening in a band around her head, to subside.

'Shh. Someone's coming.' Clare sat up and pointed to the figures in the distance, running through the trees. Finally they came, racing one another, up the hill, their shouts echoing through the woods. Clare jumped to her feet and called, 'Hi, there.'

Eve froze. 'You shouldn't have done that,' she said, in an undertone at the same instant that Henry Joyce and David Furlong stopped and came over to them.

'If it isn't the little Dominican girls,' David called out to Henry.

'Buried treasure,' Henry laughed.

'Crikey,' David said. 'All my birthdays have come at once.'

Clare's eyes were on Henry, his sleek hair and shining body creating a pleasant discomfort somewhere in the vicinity of her stomach.

Henry knew. 'Coming in for a swim?' he asked her.

'We haven't brought our togs.' Clare looked regretfully at the sea below. 'Anyway, it must be very cold.'

'It's lovely once you're in,' David said, regarding Eve from under his mop of dripping hair.

'Suit yourselves.' Henry kicked at the twigs and walked away.

Clare looked after him. There was defiance in his unyielding back and the toss of his head. 'Hey, wait a minute.' She followed him.

David stood stiffly upright, wearing a self-conscious expression. 'How are the exams going?' he asked.

'Not very well.' Eve folded her arms and tried to

think of something to say to keep him there.

'How's business?' she asked, in as mature a voice as she could muster.

David spluttered. 'I'm sure you're not interested in my business, but since you asked, we're doing very well, thank you.' When he didn't make a move to go Eve realised that he was staying there of his own accord and she didn't have to think of anything clever to say any more. 'Of course, working for a parent has its pitfalls. One has to toe the line,' he informed her.

'I'm sure there are compensations,' Eve said. 'You get sent off to exciting destinations.'

'Part of my training.'

'You're always on the move,' she said.

'I love exotic places. Seeing different cultures. Learning new things.'

'You'll be off again soon.'

'Not before the dance.'

'I'm really looking forward to it,' Eve said.

'So am I,' David said. 'By the way, how's Sarah?' he asked, his face suddenly serious.

'She's improving. Still gets awful headaches, though.'

'Let's hope she gets better soon,' he said.

'Yes.'

The wind hummed through the trees. David shivered. 'I'd better get dressed,' he said.

She watched him running through the woods, head down against the rising wind.

Clare returned, her face ready to burst into laughter. 'Hey, guess what?' she said.

'What?' Reluctantly Eve turned her concentration to Clare.

'Henry has asked me to go for a picnic with him on Saturday.'

'Great.' Eve's eyes were on the spot in the woods where David had disappeared. 'Looks as if David'll be off on his travels again soon,' she said, with a sigh of regret.

'What's new?' Clare said.

Chapter Six

On 26 June Clare came into the nuns' parlour with her music case and stood listening to the familiar tune coming from next door. As she removed the music from her case she noticed that her fingers were quivering. The sight heightened her growing fear.

'Now we'll close our eyes and pray together to our patron saint of music, St Cecilia.'

In the silence Clare watched her. How well she knew Sister Aquinas. How often she had looked into the sharp eyes now closed, the fresh face narrowed by the starched wimple, and the bloodless lips mouthing the prayer. It seemed to her at that moment that she had spent a great deal of her young life with Sister Aquinas. But that would not be for much longer.

'Not much longer.' Sister Aquinas was looking at her watch.

Clare listened to the hum of indistinct voices in the next room and wished it was all over. The palms of her hands were sticky and she hoped that she would not crumple in a heap over the piano.

'Chin up. Shoulders back.' Sister Aquinas was the only person who could make her feel big and awkward.

Clare watched the door open and Greta Crawley emerge, red-faced and smiling.

Sister Aquinas went to meet her. 'Good girl,' she said, taking her arm before Greta had time to utter a word.

Clare went into the parlour. A small man was sitting behind a desk, writing. 'Good morning,' he said, with a distracted air. 'Clare Dolan?' His bushy eyebrows were raised in a question mark as he replaced the lid of his pen.

Clare nodded.

'Please be seated.'

She sat down. The keys of the piano blurred before her.

'Scales and chords to begin, pleez.'

He went to stand at the window to listen to her play the scales he called out at random. The notes she had memorised for so long soared quickly and precisely, then fell gracefully from the tips of her fingers, like the sound of a waterfall. The ear tests came next and the sight-reading.

'Now Bach-Busoni Chaconne, pleez.'

Clare began the simple harsh chords and quickly lost herself in the music, remembering the notations, drawing out everything that was there. The notes rose and swelled, circling the room, diminishing as the piece ended. She sat still, her head buzzing, her body tense.

The examiner came to stand beside her. 'Chopin's G minor Ballade, pleez.'

She played clearly and from memory, only glancing at the music from time to time. He stood watching her hands, the long thin fingers stretched over the octaves.

When she had finished she stayed seated while he went to his desk and made notes.

'That is all,' he said finally. 'You may go.' He shook hands with her, his eyes crinkling in a smile. 'Thank you.'

Clare left to report to Sister Aquinas.

The following Saturday morning was bright and sunny when Henry called for her.

'I've organised the picnic,' he said, tapping the canvas bag strapped to his back carrier. 'Got your togs?'

'Yes, and I made sandwiches too.'

'We'll have enough to feed an army.' He laughed.

'Who wants an army along?' Clare asked.

They cycled along the coast road, the breeze blowing into them, bringing with it the smell of the sea and the threat of rain. Clare's hair blew around her face. She raked it back with her fingers.

'We'll stop in the village. Get some drinks,' Henry said.

'Great.' Clare was breathless.

They propped up their bicycles and went into the dark little shop on the corner. The shelves were stacked with tins and jars of all kinds.

'Would you like Coke or lemonade?' Henry asked.

'Coke, please.'

The man behind the counter got four bottles from a tall fridge. 'Headin' for the hills?' he asked, as he took the money from Henry's outstretched hand.

'Indeed we are.'

'Oo've a great day for it. Haven't had weather like this since thirty-two. Oo wouldn't remember thirty-two, I s'pose?'

''Fraid not.' Henry smiled apologetically and backed away.

'I remember thirty-two. T'Oocharistic Congress. Swarms of people from all over the world went to hear the singer John McCormack in the Phoenix Park. Sweltering it was. Mighty it was. Sure oo'd think it was the great Caruso himself was among us.'

Outside the shop Henry opened one of the bottles

and handed it to Clare. She took a long sip, letting the cool taste linger on her tongue. 'That feels good.'

The muscles in her legs ached so she sat down on the low wall outside the shop. Henry drank fast and threw his empty bottle into the bin at the side door of the shop. 'It's the most refreshing drink of them all, isn't it?' he said.

'You sound like an advertisement.'

'I do, don't I? Ready to go?' He looked at her.

Clare nodded.

She leaned forward as they pedalled slowly uphill in low gear. When the road rose steeply they got off and pushed their bicycles. At the cliffs they stood to admire the sweep of the bay from Bray to Killiney to Dalkey, and across to Howth. The tarmac was rutted on the cliff path and the left verge fell away towards the sea. They cycled slowly on either side of a grass channel until they reached a sign, which said private, written big, and was attached to a fence. The woods to the right of it were dark and quiet, the smell of the pine trees sharp in the air.

'Here we are,' Henry said, as he dismounted.

'Good,' Clare said.

Propping their bicycles against the wire fence they clambered over it.

The thick heather and bracken made their progress slow. Half-way down the slopes, above the railway track, they found a clearing. The sea spread out before them, blue and calm against a paler sky. There was no sound except for the swish of the waves around grey, gleaming rocks.

'Isn't it beautiful?' Clare said.

'The water looks terrific. Let's get in,' Henry said, walking further down the path and going behind a clump of bushes to put on his trunks.

Clare slipped off her dress. In her swimsuit, she felt conscious suddenly of their isolation and her bare white legs.

'Hey, come on in.' Henry's call reverberated through the woods and brought Clare running to the water's edge in time to see him surface. Head down, he swam away from the shore, with strong, even strokes. He turned and swam back. His hair was sleek and his body glistened in the sun.

'Come on in. It's lovely.'

Clare edged her way in. The cold water sent shock waves through her but she kept swimming until her body grew accustomed to it. They swam together for a few minutes, with Henry showing off his skills. Clare was first to get out. She ran to the spot where they had left their clothes. Henry followed. He looked almost naked in his wet trunks.

'You're covered in goose pimples.' She laughed, teeth chattering, as they stood looking at one another, both embarrassed. 'We'll get dressed and have our picnic.'

She spread out her towel on the grassy slope and placed the sandwiches on it.

Henry opened more Coke. 'There's chicken, home-cooked beetroot in jelly, salad.' He let his hand linger on Clare's arm as she handed them to him.

He took one and bit into it. 'Nice,' he commented, chewing rapidly, a mischievous smirk on his face.

They ate without speaking, not wanting to break the delicious sleepy silence of the hot afternoon. When they had finished they lay for a while in the warm grass. Eventually Henry sat up and moved closer to her, leaning on one elbow to look down at her.

'Come here,' he whispered, the longing almost palpable in his voice.

She went into his arms, her face lifted invitingly for a kiss. The silence palpitated around them. Suddenly the rain came, drenching them.

'We'll have to shelter.'

They packed their belongings quickly and hurried to the trees.

'What are we going to do?' Clare was watching the relentless rain form gurgling rivulets in ruts and crevices. A soft mist was blowing in, obscuring the cliffs and the sea.

'It'll pass over in a minute.'

Drops of rain fell from the trees soaking her cardigan. She shivered.

'Let's move into the woods a bit. It's dry in there,' Henry said. It was dark among the trees, except for a shaft of light here and there, and so silent that they felt compelled to walk stealthily. Soon they had to force their way through a tangle of nettles and branches, with Henry leading. Clare liked walking behind him, watching his jeans stretch tight across the muscles of his thighs, seeing the lean length of his legs and the flexing of his calves.

He walked ahead, one foot in front of the other, assured, confident, looking out for branches that might trip them, thorns that would graze her legs or catch in her clothes. Deeper into the woods, the path was overgrown with brambles. Henry stopped now and then to hold a prickly branch to one side for her, or to point out a bird, a squirrel, or a rabbit hole, his face animated.

'This'll do,' he said, seating himself on a carpet of mossy brown pine needles.

Clare sat beside him and leaned back, pillowing her head in her arms. The rain had stopped but shadow eclipsed the sunlight. 'It's so quiet,' she said.

'Primeval.'

'I wonder who owns all this land?'

'The Earl of Meath. Been in his family since the Plantation.' Henry spoke with authority.

'Never heard of him.' Clare laughed.

'He lives in a big estate he inherited called Kilruddery. Over there to the left. Bet he isn't forced to sell any of it off either.'

'Have you heard any more about the sale of your farm?' Clare asked.

Henry shook his head. 'Dad's been putting them off and the bills are piling up.'

'What do you think he'll do?' Clare asked.

'Dunno. The work's too much for him, though I'm helping all I can.'

Clare knew Henry's father. Years ago, he had delivered the milk to Agnes in his horse and cart. He would put the nosebag on the horse before coming to the back doorstep to bellow to Agnes or Jack or whoever was within ear-shot. He was a tall, broad-shouldered man, and he wore a peaked cap. Agnes kept a billycan specially for the milk and Mr Joyce used a tilly to measure it out. His hands were red and lumpy and he always poured a little extra for Clare.

'The best thing for her,' he would say.

On cold winter mornings Agnes insisted on giving him a cup of tea while she searched for her purse. He would drink it standing on the step. Agnes said he was aloof because he was a Protestant.

At Christmas time when he called he would bring a parcel of meat and home-made butter. Jack would persuade him in for a drop of whiskey. They would sit by the range and talk about old times, and before he left he would lift Clare up on his shoulders and twirl her round, telling her that she was growing big and that soon she would be strong enough to help him on his round. In later years he appeared less often, letting Henry deliver the milk for him. Henry was shy and would never take a cup of tea, but always made a point of saying hello to Clare.

'Got any cigarettes?' Clare asked.

He took a packet of Gold Flake from his pocket and lit one for her. She propped herself on one elbow while she smoked. 'I wouldn't mind giving you a hand on the farm if you're badly stuck.'

'Can you milk a cow?' Henry was smiling.

'Yes.'

'You're joking.'

'Auntie Bridie taught me when we went to her farm on holidays.'

Henry looked at her in amazement.

'That shook you. I'm sure there are plenty of other things I could help with too.' She laughed, blowing smoke into his face.

'We've got milking machines now, but there's lots to be done. Dirty work too, mind.'

'I'm not afraid of getting my hands dirty.' Clare prodded him in the ribs.

For a while they lay in the cool shadow, absorbed in its heavy sweetness. The sudden sound of birds rising up out of the trees filled the air with vibrations. Henry leaned forward, squinting up at the sky. Clare watched him, glad of the silence. He caught her looking and, laughing, kissed her. She broke away from him and stood up.

'Come 'ere.' He grabbed her round the waist.

'You're tickling.' She pulled free, giggling.

He tried to grab her again, but she twisted away, still giggling.

'You'll frighten the crows.' He clutched her again and, in her effort to escape she fell forward, gasping for breath, her hair cascading over his face.

They lay motionless for a long time, her body almost covering his.

She could feel his heart pounding against her and he had an erection.

'We'd better get back,' she said.

'What time do you have to be home?'

She shrugged. 'Supper time.'

His lips were warm and moist as he kissed her.

Suddenly he slipped his hand between her legs.

'No, Henry. Please don't.' Mortified, she moved away.

'OK, I won't.' His voice had altered in an effort to control it, but he continued to kiss her, pressing her down into the soft mossy earth.

For a moment she lay there too startled by the depth of her own passion to move. Suddenly she pulled away.

'Clare.'

His hand was on her shoulder, shaking her. She had turned on her side away from him and buried her face in the ground. The smell of damp earth rose to meet her. When she looked back at him he was sitting away from her, his head hunched down into his shoulders.

'I'm sorry.' His voice was shaky. 'I was kissing you and . . . I couldn't stop.'

Clare glanced at him, then looked quickly away. She got to her feet and walked slowly through the thicket. A twig snapped, startling her, as she stooped to inspect clusters of berries on a rowan tree. Droplets of rain hung from them, magnifying their unripe beauty. 'With a crop of berries like that we're bound to have snow next winter.' She turned to find him close to her.

'I love snow,' he said. He took her in his arms and kissed her gently. She felt the warmth of his chest against her.

'It's like we're the only two people in the whole world.' Clare's voice was soft in the deep silence.

'I was thinking,' Henry said. 'You could come and help out at the farm, if you want to.'

'I said I would. Now that the music exam's over I'll have more time.'

They retraced their steps through the thicket and down the slope, occasional drops of rain from the leaves of the trees falling on them as they went to find their bicycles. The sky cleared and they could smell the scent of newly washed earth.

Chapter Seven

The evening sun slanted through the bedroom window as Clare prepared for the summer ball. When she thought about her lovely dress she couldn't wait to wear it. She prepared her bath and languished in it, scrubbing the rough skin from the soles of her feet. Back in her bedroom she put on her nylons carefully so as not to snag them with her frost-painted finger-nails. Slowly she slipped her dress over the white lace brassière her aunt Maud had given her for Christmas. The silk rustled as she checked that her seams were straight. Gently she smoothed the satin skirt.

Finally, gazing into the mirror, the refracted sunlight casting mottled shadows on her face, she put on her makeup. The black lines made her look older, exotic, perhaps even sinister. She finished off with lollipop lipstick and stepped into her new high heels.

Strutting up and down and standing for a long time before the glass of her dressing-table, she half closed her eyes and made sophisticated faces like she'd seen models in magazines do, turning her face this way and that. Would she dance clumsily? Or be pushed into a corner by some over-eager groper?

Poised, hairbrush in hand, she stood in an agony of suspense, a yearning reaching into the marrow of her bones. In the mirror everything looked right, hair not too long, breasts high and enough hip curve to lure

Henry. She felt like Marilyn Monroe. Excitement gripped her with such ferocity that the walls of her bedroom seemed to cave in around her and she couldn't wait for the dance to begin. Deep down she knew that this was going to be a great night.

'You look nice,' Agnes said, gazing at her daughter. 'A bit too sophisticated for my liking, but nice.'

'Do you think my neck is too bare? What about some beads? Pearls? My cross and chain?' Clare's hands fluttered at her neck, then moved nervously to pat her hair.

'You're fine as you are. You don't want to draw too much attention to yourself.'

Henry arrived at Clare's house at eight o'clock sharp. He stood in the hall dressed up in an evening suit, awkward, clean, hair plastered down.

He looked at Clare as if he were seeing her for the first time. 'You look great,' he said shyly.

She knew it wasn't the dress he was referring to: it was the beautiful way her face looked with the makeup on, and her new hairdo.

'Behave yourself, now,' Agnes warned her, coming into the hall. 'Hello, Henry,' she said, eyeing him up and down. 'I'd hardly recognise you. You look terrific.'

'Thanks, Mrs Dolan.' Henry grinned.

'Mind your manners, Clare,' Agnes said.

'You always say that, Mother.'

'I'll take good care of her, Mrs Dolan. She'll be all right with me.'

'I know that, Henry. That's why I'm letting her go. Enjoy yourselves.'

Cars were strewn along the alley near the Glencove Hotel and a queue was forming as they got there. Boys stood in groups, talking and smoking. Walking through

the hotel entrance in her ballgown, Henry Joyce beside
her, Dermy McQuaid holding open the door for her,
Clare felt very grand.

'You look smashin',' Dermy said, as she passed him.

'Thanks,' Clare said, polite to him for the first time.

'Would you like a drink?' Henry asked.

'Yes, please.'

While Henry and David went to buy the drinks, Clare
and Eve slipped into the cloakroom to see if their
friends were there. Tilly Johnson and Maureen White
were standing at the wash basins, facing the mirror.
Tilly was coaxing Maureen's hair into a bouffant style
with a tail comb. She was a trainee hairdresser at
Concepta's Hairdressers, owned by Concepta Taylor.

Tilly said, 'Hello, Clare. Did your mother let you out
at long last?'

Clare ignored her, though she could feel her face
flaming red.

'Ah, don't mind her.' Maureen White smiled at Clare
as she picked up what looked like a dark creepy-crawly
and stuck it to one eyelid. 'She's jealous of your nice
dress.' One eye was thickly fringed, making the other
look bare. 'It's a lovely colour,' she said.

'How much did it cost?' Tilly Johnson asked.

'I don't know. My mother bought it,' Clare lied.

'You bought yours in Trish Lynam's,' she said to Eve.
'I saw it in the window.'

'Thanks,' Eve said.

'Well for you. Plenty of money. Now do you want
me to finish your hair, Maureen White, or what?' Tilly
asked.

'My eyes aren't done yet.' Maureen turned back to
the mirror and concentrated on her other eye, blinking
furiously as she fixed the lashes in place.

People swarmed into the cloakroom. 'I love Dickie Rock,' someone said. 'That's a lovely dress . . .'

Voices swirled around them, soft voices and the louder ones of girls in groups talking about the boys who escorted them.

Eve and Clare slipped out of the cloakroom as the band was tuning up. Henry and David were waiting with their drinks. Plaintive guitar chords mingled with piano notes and the rumble of drums greeted them as they went into the dance. Dickie Rock and the Miami Showband were on stage, wearing blue evening suits, white shirts and black bow ties, the lights around them bright, the music too loud for anyone to hear their ears. Slowly they joined the throng, camouflaged by the rustle of different-coloured skirts, comforted by the noise.

'"From the Candy Store on the Corner",' Dickie began.

Someone shouted, 'Spit on me, Dickie.' Laughter broke out.

Henry took Clare's hand, his smile and the gentle tug on her wrist the only indication that he wished to dance with her. She moved forward, making her way through the dancers. His arm was around her waist, pressing her towards him, so close that she could not see his face, only feel the smoothness of his shoulder against her cheek. He held her cautiously, as if prepared to move away should she show the least sign of resistance.

Leaning back to look up at Henry she caught the shimmer of his blue eyes beneath thick dark lashes. He winked as the number changed to 'Do You Know The Way To San Jose', which was an opportunity to show off by trick-acting with fancy steps. He swung her around in a circle, making her laugh, grabbed her hand and spun her away from him, effortlessly catching her back again just as she felt she was spinning out of control. With the laughter she began to relax.

When the dance ended Clare thanked Henry, went to the cloakroom and splashed her face with cold water, letting her chilled fingertips linger on her forehead. As the cold water touched her skin she realised that she was nervous. She smoothed her hair with her damp hands and applied Creme Puff to her face. What was she afraid of? She looked well in her midnight blue dress. Everybody said so. Henry was with her. Maybe that was it. She'd never danced with Henry before and he looked gorgeous.

Clare's fear had started the previous summer when her father, Jack Dolan, had left. At first she had walked the long way to the town to avoid people. Then she had stayed in, listening to her mother and one or other of her neighbours saying the same things over and over, so that the words became a jumble in her head, making her stomach sick. The summer had lasted a long time and had depressed her. Things she had never noticed before upset her. Once, on waking early, she heard a voice that sounded like her father's.

She held herself rigid, listening, but the voice died away, leaving her wondering what she was going to do without him, and why she had been born in the first place. In school she wore a disguise, being her confident, most boisterous self, but hurried home in the afternoon to make sure her mother was all right.

A few girls burst into the cloakroom, laughing, bringing the blare of the music with them.

'What a night.'

'What a lout you were dancing with.'

'Did you see Dickie throwing shapes? Thinks he's Cliff Richard.'

'I think he's terrific.'

'Princess Margaret is supposed to be in town. She might grace us with her presence.'

They laughed.

Clare couldn't concentrate any more so she made her way back to where she'd left the others, jostling between dancing couples.

A slow waltz compelled David Furlong to pull Eve to him. '"Some day you'll want me too",' Dickie Rock sang in his high-pitched nasal voice. Smiling, eyes closed, David held Eve close as Dickie strained and teased out words of love. David smelt of Old Spice and faintly of beer.

'Hi.' As soon as the dance ended, Charlie Mathews caught Eve round the waist, infuriating her.

'Hello.' Eve moved back.

'Not till I have a dance.'

'Go ahead.' David smiled and went to the bar.

Eve was furious.

Charlie grabbed hold of her and began swaying to the music. Whatever about the spots on his face, he could dance.

Henry and Clare watched, laughing.

After the ball David held out Eve's long black velvet cloak for her and, without touching her, helped her put it on over her pink satin dress. On the way home, while Clare and Henry laughed and joked in the back of the car, David hardly spoke.

'OK?' he asked, when he caught her eyes on him.

'Yes. Fine,' Eve said.

'Did you enjoy yourself?' he asked, taking her hand in his.

'It was terrific,' she said.

'Good.' He let go of her hand and concentrated on the road ahead.

A supper of cold chicken and ham salad, which Agnes had prepared and laid out on the kitchen table, was covered with a white tablecloth. Eve's mouth was dry and, as she ate, she felt awkward and gauche. When David and Henry were leaving she stood apart from them while Clare teased them about their dancing. She felt the door handle brush against her hip as David stood in front of her to say goodnight. As he put on his coat she wondered what she could do that would convey to him what she wanted him to know without her having to say it.

His lips were cool against her cheek.

'It's been great,' he said to her. 'We must do it again some time.'

'That would be lovely' she said, leaning back and watching him leave, letting the door take the weight of her distress.

'I'll see you around,' he said.

'Yes.' He was gone with Henry and Clare, their laughter dying on the cold night air.

On the Saturday morning after the ball the sun, streaming through the window, woke Clare early. She crept downstairs to make herself a pot of tea and some toast, and went out to the back porch to enjoy her breakfast in the sunshine. Martin had returned to England and everything was back to normal. When she finished she rinsed her cup and plate and got ready to take Hughie, the baby she minded on Saturday mornings, for a walk. She combed her hair and noticed that she had to stoop slightly to see her reflection in the dim mirror. She was growing very tall and the few clothes she had didn't fit her comfortably any more.

Outside the air was warm and Clare loosened her cardigan as she hurried through the town. Glencove was Glencove, she reflected, with distaste. It held no surprises for her and she was sick of it. Sick of the dreary shops, the bank, Henrietta Ford Mathews' stupid hotel, with its gossiping Dermy McQuaid in his grey and red uniform permanently stuck in the doorway. Kinsella's Select Bar, its glittering gold lettering declaring 'Finest Whiskey' scraped off here and there. The shops all duplicates of one another, except for Mr Rosen's pawn shop with its filigree and gossamer ballgowns, and glassy-eyed fox furs.

'Hello,' Mrs Browne said, hurrying by on her way to work. The same dull women stood in their doorways exchanging the same dull ideas while their children played in the dull streets.

Clare crossed the road and entered the Crescent where Hughie lived. All of the houses had grey pebble-dash fronts and looked identical. Music blared from an open window. A baby wailed. At the corner a small group of children played hop-scotch on the path. Clare crossed the road and walked up to the last house. She rang the bell. Babs Grimes, Hughie's mother, appeared briefly at an upstairs window, then the front door opened.

'Hello, Clare. Beautiful day.' Babs wore a short denim dress and had leather sandals on her bare feet. A see-through plastic shopping bag was in her hand.

'Hughie's all set. See you lunch time,' she said, and was out of the door, crossing the road and disappearing round the corner before Clare had a chance to say anything.

Clare wheeled the push-chair out of the estate, along

the green, until they came to the building site where her father had been working before he left home. The half-built houses were tall, red-brick, and surrounded by scaffolding, the ground around them littered with rubble. A black dog was rooting in a bin full of empty bottles at the side of one of the houses.

'You wait here,' Clare said to Hughie, parking the push-chair near a wall, while surveying the ladder propped against the gable end of one of the unfinished houses. A few minutes later she was on the roof, looking at the roofs of other houses spread out before her. Houses of different shapes and sizes, some with porches, others with verandas, all set in big gardens. Further to her left St Canice's spire rose amid the shops. The sea shimmered in the distance. Behind her the green fields of Joyce's farm sloped gently upwards towards a narrow road that led off towards trees, more farmland and the mountains beyond. Cows grazed in them. All around the sky was blue with only a few scattered clouds. Everywhere was still.

Clare felt on top of the world. She wanted to fly, spread out her arms and take off across the sea. Visit her father. A dizzy feeling came over her and she had to sit down to calm herself. Her feet were hot and slippery in her plimsolls and she wondered if she would have the same grip on the rungs of the ladder on the way down.

Looking around the estate, she saw that the houses were nearly ready. Soon they would be occupied and the children who pestered the builders by playing dangerous games in and out of them would have to make do with the grassy slopes behind them, which would not be nearly as much fun. She took a crushed cigarette from the pocket of her jacket and smoked it slowly, savouring each puff. Leaning back against the parapet she began to sing a little tune.

There was always some kind of music going on in her mind. Perhaps a piano recital she had recently heard on the radio, or the soft, sad notes of a piece by Debussy that she was practising. She heard a sudden cry. Hughie. She had forgotten all about him. Moving cautiously along the parapet she edged her way to the corner of the roof and, leaning over the gutter, looked down. Hughie was still in his push-chair, his tiny hands clutching the sides, his feet kicking out at the black dog sniffing him.

'It's all right, baby,' she called down to him. 'I'm coming.'

Annoyed that her peace had been shattered, she began the slow climb down the ladder, testing each rung first before putting her full weight on it. As she reached Hughie the dog began to bark frantically. The baby was screaming in breathless frantic bursts.

'Shoo!' Clare shouted at the dog, who sloped off. She undid Hughie's straps and picked him up. His fat little arms went around her neck, his fingers grabbing the soft skin at the nape.

'Don't cry. Doggie gone,' she said, hugging Hughie and showing him the retreating animal. She took a soother from her pocket, licked it and put it into his mouth. He stopped crying but from time to time his body still shuddered involuntarily.

It was hot in the empty house and Clare could smell pine resin from the freshly cut wooden beams that lined the floors and rafters. Standing in the middle of one of the rooms, swivelling Hughie on her hip, Clare imagined that it was her house, and that her piano was placed against the wall opposite the open fireplace for her to compose tunes on whenever she wanted. Tunes for all kinds of orchestral instruments. In her daydream, her daddy was out the back chopping wood for the fire to keep her warm while she worked, and Hughie did not exist.

Henry Joyce was waiting at the gate of his father's farm.

'Hello,' he said, coming to meet her.

'Hello.' She smiled at him. 'Hot, isn't it?'

'Here, come and sit down. I've got some fags. Might have something for Hughie, too, if he's a good boy.'

'He is. Aren't you?' Clare tickled him under his chin and parked the push-chair against a tree trunk. She sat on the grass beside it.

Henry sat beside her and took a packet of white chocolate mice from his pocket. Clare held one out while Hughie sucked and drooled it with his soft moist mouth. The chocolate dribbled down his chin on to his new blue coat.

'I worry about this baby,' Clare said to Henry. 'He could be sucking anything for all the interest he takes.'

'I doubt that.' Henry laughed. 'He's nice and quiet.' He lit two cigarettes and handed one to Clare. 'Did you enjoy the dance?' he asked.

'It was smashing, thank you. Did you?'

'Powerful. I love the Miami Showband.'

Clare nodded. 'I love Dickie Rock. Just thinking about him makes me want to swoon.'

'I see.' Henry looked at her. 'How are the studies going?' he asked, changing the subject.

'Could be better. The piano takes up so much time. You?'

'I think I'll pass.' He nodded as if confirming the point to himself.

'Course you will. You're a born swot. That's the difference between us.'

'No, I'm not. There's so much to be done on the farm.' Henry's voice trailed off. After a while he said, 'Delahunt's, the builders, want to buy us out.'

Clare squinted at the cluster of conifer trees in the distance and the cows lying peacefully beneath them.

'Been in the family for generations,' Henry said.

'Will your father sell it?'

'It may come to that.' Henry was gazing up at the sky.

The harsh brightness of the sun cast his features in shadow, but Clare could detect the worry in his voice. 'It's too much to think about just now. In another few years these fields will all be houses.' Henry sighed. 'I know.'

'And you'll be qualified with a practice in Glencove and lots of patients,' Clare said.

'I suppose that's one way of looking at it.'

'The only way,' Clare said.

Hughie began to whimper, raising his arms to be lifted up. 'He's getting restless,' Clare said. 'I'd better take him home.'

It was a warm day. Eve was lying on an old rug under the sycamore tree in the side garden of the convent. Hidden from the prying eyes of the nuns, and shaded by the winged leaves of the trees, she was concentrating on revising her notes on *Hamlet* for her English paper, her final exam.

> O, that this too too solid flesh would melt,
> Thaw and resolve itself into a dew!
> Or that the Everlasting had not fix'd

His canon 'gainst self-slaughter! O God! God!

Everything around her was still and peaceful, except for the insistent croak of the corncrake. The roses were in bloom, and Clare, some distance away, was already plucking the soft tiny petals to make scent. Her preference would have been to pick the flowers at the height of their bloom or before their final disintegration when, she maintained, their perfume was at its strongest.

They had sneaked out into the garden together, Clare with a newly washed jam-jar hidden in her cardigan, Eve with her notes. Having assured themselves at the entrance that no one was following them, they settled into their separate tasks. When Eve looked up and saw the lush green bushes crushed by Clare's greedy hands she said, with horror, 'Why don't you pick the clematis? It's in full flower.'

'Since when did clematis smell like roses?' Clare called back. 'Here, smell this.'

Eve bent her head to the old familiar fragrance of her favourite flower. 'I suppose you're right,' she said grudgingly, as Clare continued to behead the bushes and stuff her jar with petals.

'I'll let you have some.'

'Yuk.' Eve feigned disgust, although Clare was famous for her perfume, turned back to her notes and continued to study.

A bell rang, faint in the distance. Somewhere in the nearby fuchsia bush a bee droned.

Possess it merely. That it should come to this!
But two months dead! Nay, not so much, not two.
So excellent a king that was to this

Hyperion to a satyr; so loving to my mother . . .

'Eve Freeman.' The shrill voice rent the air.

'Damn.' Eve rose quickly and gathered up her belongings. Clare hid her jar of petals behind one of the rose bushes and began to brush down her gymslip with her hands.

'Eve Freeman.' The voice was shriller, nearer.

'We'd better go,' Clare hissed. 'We'll sneak out the nuns' gate and around the back way.'

Too late.

Bernie Power, the head prefect, jaw jutting, was blocking their path. 'Where do you think you two are going?'

'Answering the call,' Eve said.

'I wouldn't have thought that either of you were one of the chosen ones. You don't act it. These gardens are out of bounds, you know.' Bernie turned to Eve. 'Look at the cut of you. Straighten your tie. Reverend Mother Mary of the Angels wants to see you in her office, immediately.'

Eve's face went white. 'What for? What have I done?'

Bernie sniffed. 'How should I know? Now get along. I've been searching for you for ages.'

Both girls hurried to the convent.

Mother Mary of the Angels came to meet them as they approached the entrance, a big woman, with soft brown eyes.

'Eve,' she said, clasping Eve's hand. 'I thought we'd take a stroll in the gardens. Such a beautiful day.'

'But, Mother—' Eve began.

'Clare, you may go to the study hall.' Ignoring Clare, Mother Mary faced Eve, then draped her cream lace shawl over her shoulders. 'Let's go.'

'Yes, Mother.'

'It's a good place to have a talk, my dear.' Mother Mary led the way, bustling along the path, rosary beads swinging, skirts rustling, Eve in her wake. Was it the Latin verbs again? Or that awful maths paper that she knew she would never be able to fathom if she lived to be a hundred. They were walking along the flagged path of the nuns' rose garden. Mother Mary stopped before the statue of Our Lady and turned to her. 'God gave us these flowers to make us happy,' she said, touching a frail bloom on the rose bush beside her. 'God is good, Eve,' she continued. 'In His infinite Wisdom He gives.'

'Yes, Mother.' Eve shifted her weight from one foot to the other.

'And He takes away.' Mother Mary's eyes were trained on her.

'Yes, Mother.'

'Of course, we are all God's creatures. Only He has the power to give and to take life. If we understand that, then we can accept God's will.' Mother Mary's voice trembled.

Eve looked at her defiantly. 'Is Sarah bad again?' She held her breath.

'I'm afraid so, my dear. Your mother has sent for you to return home immediately. Oh, Eve, I'm so sorry,' she said, coming forward, arms outstretched. 'Such a dear child, Sarah.' Mother Mary's moist eyes were full of compassion.

Eve moved away. Mother Mary looked stricken. 'You're very brave, my child. But you must feel free to cry. Don't bottle it all up for the sake of others. Not now, not any time.'

'I'm all right.' Eve lifted her face and looked at Mother Mary.

'Would you like a cup of tea before you go?'

'No, thank you, Mother.'

'Shall I send Clare out to you?'

Eve nodded.

'Get your things together and go as soon as you feel able, my dear.' Mother Mary left, walking quickly away. Suspended in shock, Eve made her way back to the side garden. Distractedly she picked some roses. The fragrance of the new buds, bunched in her hands, their creamy petals ready to unfurl, flooded her with thoughts of Sarah.

She returned to the sycamore tree, the trail of petals, the hushed garden, to wait for Clare. Everything seemed different, though nothing had visibly changed. Removing her cardigan she put it under the tree and lay down. Everywhere was still. Heat cast a shimmer on the newly cut lawn. Images of her mother came into her mind: tall, erect, heartbroken. Her grandfather, too, busily sweeping the paths, tying up stray branches, digging, weeding and clearing away, his shoulders bent with the weight of loss, his heart full of sorrow.

The house was empty when they got there, the breakfast things still on the kitchen table. They sat down, Eve conscious of the vacant chairs, the stillness in the room. When she heard the hall door opening, she jumped to her feet, her heart pounding. Dorothy came slowly into the hall, helped by Agnes Dolan.

'Eve.' Her eyes were transfixed as if she were sleep-walking. 'Oh, Eve. What are we going to do?' Her voice, barely audible, was uncharacteristically gentle, as was her grip on her elder daughter's shoulders.

'Is she going to die?' Eve's voice trailed away as she tried to control her shaking body.

'She's dead.' Dorothy burst into sobs

Eve looked from her mother to Agnes in disbelief.

'Come on, sit down,' Agnes said, helping Dorothy into a chair.

Dorothy sank down and buried her head in her hands. Eve gulped back her tears and sat beside her, holding her while her shuddering sobs reverberated around the house.

As the bells of St Canice's rang out, Glencove came to a halt. Cars lined the streets near the church and the blurry faces of neighbours waiting at its big gates swam into view. Eve looked, and looked away.

'It'll be all right.' Ron Freeman's hand closed over Eve's, comforting, reassuring, as they walked past the hearse and the women. 'I'm here.'

His face was a mask.

Dorothy Freeman walked slightly apart, impervious to her husband's gentle concern, her proud head held high in an elegant black chiffon hat. Inside the church the sun beamed shafts of light through the rose window behind the altar, patterning the black coats of the mourners as they took their places in the front row. The organ played softly. Father McCarthy, dressed in purple robes, stood before them.

'Jesus said,' he began in a croaky voice, '"Do not let your hearts be troubled. Trust in God: trust also in me. In my father's house are many rooms; if it were not so, I would have told you."'

Eve surveyed the early summer flowers on Sarah's white coffin, and the sheaves of lilies spread out on the red carpet at the foot of the altar, and wished that she, too, was dead.

Last night I lay a sleeping,
There came a dream so fair.

The choir of the Dominican convent, Glencove, sang the clear notes, liquid gold voices filling the church as the Mass came to an end.

I hear the children singing,
And ever as they sang.

At the graveside the cold struck them all. Eve looked at her mother's downcast head and her father's arms restraining her as the white coffin was lowered into the ground. She put her hands to her ears to block out the clatter of shovel and thud of earth. She wanted to shout at the gravediggers that they were suffocating Sarah. Her mouth opened, but no sound came out. Nor did she cry.

'The day thou gavest, Lord, has ended.' Father McCarthy blessed the mound of earth that covered the coffin. Dorothy knelt and kissed the ground at the edge of the grave. Ron helped her to her feet and led her and Eve away.

Back at the house, relatives and neighbours came to pay their respects. Ron poured whiskey for men silenced by compassion and grief. Women with drawn faces murmured their consolation between sips of sherry and cups of tea. Eve and Clare stood to one side, in stunned silence.

Later, when the guests had left, Pauline Quirk called to the front door. 'I wanted to say how sorry I am,' she said, shaking Dorothy's hand.

'That's very kind of you, Pauline,' Dorothy said. 'Eve is in her bedroom, if you want to go up to her. I'm sure she'd be glad to see you.'

'Hello, Pauline,' Eve said, barely able to breathe with grief.

Pauline waited while she cried. 'I'm so sorry,' she said. 'Sarah was such a nice child.'

'She was a nuisance sometimes when she was little,' Eve said. 'Hanging around when we all wanted to go off and play, remember?'

'She wasn't really. Only when she was sick. And sure she couldn't help that,' Pauline reassured her.

'The times I used to wish that Mummy would take her with her.' Eve's voice broke.

'Stop crucifying yourself, Eve. You were great to her, so you were. She loved being with you.'

'How are you, Pauline?' Eve asked, in an attempt to staunch her tears.

'Not bad,' Pauline said, and added, 'Considering I'm six months gone.'

'How's Seamus?'

'Smashing, thanks. We're getting married as soon as I can make the trip to Belfast. He wants the wedding there.'

'That's great. When are you going?'

'As soon as I pluck up the courage. I'm not mad about Belfast or his mother for that matter,' Pauline said.

'At least you don't have exams like the rest of us.'

'I wish I'd stayed on in school.' Pauline sighed. 'This would never have happened to me.'

'You'll be all right. Seamus is crazy about you.'

'That's true. There's no turning back the clock now.'

'No.' Eve shuddered.

As the days went by the weather turned cold. Clouds hung low in the sky and gloom pervaded the Freemans' house. Eve dreaded the desolate evenings when

Dorothy, dry-eyed and vacant, would set a place for Sarah at the table in a bitter attempt to lapse back into everyday life as it had been before she died.

'How was school today?' she would ask, as they began to eat. But half-way through the meal the veil would drop and she would wail. With sinking heart, Eve would wait for the sobs to subside. As Ron Freeman gently coaxed Dorothy up to bed, Eve wished she could run away and hide in a small space. Small enough to contain her grief, yet big enough for her to think.

The tree was that place. Her hands would grasp an outstretched branch. Once inside, she would sink into its smooth, familiar bark. Its centre would cradle her and its foliage would give her the protection she craved from the chaos around her. When the leaves stirred in the breeze she thought of her mother's endless berating of God for the cruelty He had turned on her in death.

As first Eve had regarded Dorothy's behaviour as undignified and unfitting to Sarah's memory. But gradually it dawned on her that her mother had had to take that stand. The finality of such heartbreak was so unacceptable that the agony it brought had to be demonstrated with outrage. Day after day the tree held Eve, its leaves blew tiny breaths on her swollen face, its familiar green smell enveloped her, and curtained her tears. Slowly she cried out her heartbreak, beating her fists against her chest, drumming up her own sad song. Little by little she began to feel better.

Chapter Eight

The families of the class of '68 were gathered there to celebrate the graduation of their daughters. Dorothy, in a black chiffon dress, a wide-brimmed black straw hat, long gloves, black nylon stockings and high-heeled court shoes, sat beside Ron, who wore his sombre dark-grey suit and his trilby hat. They watched the proceedings with an air of detached melancholy. Agnes, in her best Sunday frock and hat, sat a few rows behind them, waiting with anticipation, feeling out of place.

Clare was recalling how hard her mother had worked all the years to see her child receive the education that she herself had been denied. An education that might have been her passport through all the frontiers she had never crossed and now never would. Clare was passing into another world, which bore no relationship to the one Agnes occupied and most probably they would be alienated.

The remainder of the main hall was filled with girls, from first years in the front to seniors at the back, all dressed neatly in their brown gymslips, short-sleeved cream shirts, and brown knee socks.

Eve and Clare sat in the back row among the sixth years. Eve sat upright, her eyes focused on the flowers at the foot of the podium. Clare let her mind wander to the glorious freedom of the summer holiday and

Martin's forthcoming wedding. The thought of Eve and herself rampaging through the streets of London, dancing the night away in some smoke-filled seedy nightclub, filled her with such joyful anticipation that she didn't realise that Reverend Mother Mary of the Angels had entered the hall with Father McCarthy, a procession of nuns following them. They took their places around the podium and Father McCarthy began the proceedings with a prayer.

'Now the prize-giving.' Sister Mildred took her stand at the microphone to explain the various awards.

'The Highest Achievement Award goes to Eve Freeman, not just academically but for her strength in what has been a difficult year for her.'

Eve stood up, surprised. She walked up the aisle to the loud cheering of the whole school.

'Finally,' Mother Mary concluded as the noise died down, 'we entered two of our most promising piano students for a scholarship to the prestigious Royal Academy in London.'

There was a hush.

'It gives me great pleasure to announce to you all that Clare Dolan has won this year's scholarship, to be taken up on the first of September.'

The cheering broke out again, raising the roof. Clare could feel Eve's arms around her propelling her upwards. 'Go on.'

She scrambled to her feet, head spinning, knees trembling, and walked up the aisle to a burst of chords from the piano, struck out by Sister Aquinas. Sister Mildred beckoned Agnes to come and stand beside her daughter as each nun in the community congratulated her in turn.

Agnes, dignified yet half apologetic, held Clare's arm

as they listened to Mother Mary of the Angels praise Clare's great achievement.

Afterwards Clare said to Eve, 'I can't believe it. I was sure Greta Crawley stood a better chance than me.'

'I knew you'd walk off with it.' Eve gave her a nudge.

It was a damp Wednesday morning a week after the exams and Clare was walking to Joyce's farm. The rain had eased but menacing clouds, low on the horizon, obscured the cliffs and cove, and hinted at more to come. She was wearing a mac and Agnes's old wellingtons, and stopped on the rutted lane that led to the farm. Tilting her face upwards she let the soft, fine rain of a summer shower drench her. She walked on, breathing in the fresh air.

As soon as she rounded the corner of the Haggard, the smell of cows wafted on the breeze and hurried her on past the fruit trees and a new crop of vegetables to the hedges of fuchsia and sweet-smelling woodbine that bordered the garden of the squat, thatched farmhouse, and its sprawling outbuildings.

Henry appeared at the side gate of the yard, carrying a galvanised bucket. 'Top of the morning to you,' he called. 'Just in time to feed the chickens.' He opened the gate. 'That yard's muddy. Watch your step.'

A sheepdog barked behind a wire fence, pigs snorted and horses neighed as Clare picked her steps across the slippery yard.

'It's dirty work, this,' Henry said, passing her the bucket. 'Gets in under your skin.'

'Doesn't bother me,' Clare laughed.

She took the bucket, balanced it on one knee to get a good grip, then slowly scattered the meal as she walked along calling, 'Chuck, chuck, chuck. Here, chuckie-chuck,' the way her auntie Bridie did on their farm in Wexford. Squawking chickens came from all directions, racing after her with frenzied pecking before the mixture had fallen to the ground. When the bucket was empty she found Henry, some distance away, thinning onions in the vegetable patch.

'You can pick some of them if you like,' he said, pointing to peas toppling from their stalks. Clare knelt down, and moving slowly along the row, began to fill the pail Henry had given her. When she finally stood up the front of her jeans was muddy and damp from the wet soil.

'You've done well,' he said.

'Not too bad. What'll you do with this lot?'

'Sell them to the shops.'

They continued weeding, pulling great dandelions and dock leaves from between the vegetables, shaking the damp, clinging soil from the roots. As the morning progressed the breeze got stronger, bringing with it a strong smell of manure and heavy rain. Eventually they were forced to move into the dairy.

'This is my responsibility,' Henry said, with a sweep of his hand.

The dairy, which comprised the milking parlour and separating room, formed the outbuilding at the end of the yard. Rain hammered on the corrugated roof and bounced off the concrete as Henry began to scour the milking machines, too busy to explain things or even to talk much. Clare, spotting a broom in the corner, started to sweep the floor, continuing on into the adjoining shed, which contained sacks of meal, potatoes, onions, mangolds. They worked all morning without stopping.

'Ready for a cuppa?' Henry called, when he saw her

leaning against the wall, her hand on her back.

She nodded.

In the dim porch Clare removed her wellingtons before entering the bright, clean kitchen. Crockery and cooking pots lined the shelves along one wall to the right of the Aga. A dresser, cluttered with willow-pattern plates and an assortment of china, bills and prayer leaflets, stood on the other side. Clare hung her jacket on the back of a chair and sat down. Henry put the kettle on and took the earthenware teapot from the side of the range.

'I'll have to wash my hands,' Clare said, examining the caked mud under her fingernails.

'The bathroom's upstairs. One thing that's plentiful is soap and water.'

'I'll feel better if I have a wash.' Clare went upstairs.

When she returned to the kitchen Henry was busy making ham sandwiches.

'The tea's drawn,' he said, rattling cups and saucers and plates as he set the table.

They ate in silence, too hungry to talk. Afterwards, Clare washed up, leaving the Delft to drain. Because she didn't know what to do next she sat down at the table again.

'Tired?' Henry asked, passing her a lighted cigarette.

'Thank you,' Clare said, taking the cigarette and sitting back in the chair. 'Yes, I'm tired,' she said, blowing smoke into the air. 'I've enjoyed myself, though. It's good to keep busy. Otherwise I think about Sarah all the time.'

'That's only natural.'

'No matter how hard I try I can't get her out of my mind.'

Henry leaned forward and gently brushed her hair

back from her face. 'Why don't you have a rest while I finish up in the yard? Go into the sitting room if you like. Have a snooze.'

'Are you sure?'

Henry nodded with a smile.

The sitting room was dark and stuffy. Clare pulled back the curtains and forced open the top window, then lay back on the couch, hands clasped behind her head, to examine the room. The glare of the emerging sun gave the heavy furniture a faded splendour and picked out the specks of dust that coated the bookcase and sparkled on the stained floorboards surrounding the faded carpet.

Henry woke her with a mug of steaming tea.

'What time is it?' she said, sitting up.

'Half past four. You fell asleep.'

'It's restful in here,' Clare said, looking around.

'This room's seen better days,' Henry said, his eyes following hers. 'We used to have hoolies in here before the family emigrated. Aunts, uncles, all singing round the piano, my granny playing it for all her worth.'

'What did she play?'

'All the old songs. "Silver Threads Among the Gold", "Come Back Paddy Reilly To Ballyjamesduff". Everything. The place was full of life.'

'What was she like, your granny?' Clare asked.

'A hearty woman. Always working outdoors. I used to help her a lot.'

'You were a good little boy.' Clare reached out to tickle his ribcage.

'You've asked for it now,' he said, taking the cup from her hand and bunching her arms and legs together in his arms while easing her on to the floor, tickling her.

She screeched with laughter, begging him to stop.

'I like it when you laugh. You're so pretty.' Henry's voice was low.

They turned to one another at the same time, so close that she could feel him trembling. Instead she kept her hands rigid against her sides.

'Oh, God, Clare. You're gorgeous.' He was peering along the length of her body.

She didn't answer or move when he leaned over her but stayed perfectly still, her toes curling. He kissed her, long and hard, his fingers sliding down her neck, lingering on her shoulders, thumbs reaching over her breasts to make slow circles, down along her spine, caressing her hips, inching inside her jeans. As he pressed his weight against her she had a sudden vision of Sister Mildred. Clenching her fists tight, she pushed him with all her might, feeling his hardness through the denim of his jeans. He grabbed her wrists and held her up, face to face, his eyes consuming the sight.

'Oh God.' He groaned, raising the flat of his hand against her cheek, holding her, kissing her, pulling her to him until their bodies were merged together, her arms around him, her breasts pressed into his chest. The sound of the zipper of her jeans, rough material sliding against her skin, and the sudden feel of him inside her, made her gasp. Impaled, her head became disconnected from her body as she struggled with him or against him, she wasn't sure which. Half dressed, she rolled away from him and lay facing the wall.

'Clare, I'm sorry. I thought you wanted to—' He moved towards her.

'No. Please don't. I mean—'

'Clare. We've got to talk.'

She placed her hands over her ears and counted to ten.

Henry was tucking his shirt into his trousers. His hair was dishevelled and tears were running down his cheeks. 'I'm sorry, Clare,' he said. 'I wanted you. I won't deny that.' He wiped away the tears with the back of his hand. 'It's all I've been thinking about since we . . . I thought about it all morning when we were out there together, working.'

'Stop talking like this, Henry. You're making it worse.'

'But we've got to talk. It's all my fault. I'm older than you. A medical student, for God's sake.'

'I'm not a child,' Clare protested.

For a few minutes neither of them spoke. 'Supposing you get—' Henry began.

Clare looked at him. His face was mottled and his lips were white and trembling. But it was his bewildered eyes that frightened her. She got to her feet. 'Shut up, Henry. Don't say it. Forget this ever happened.'

He was beside her. 'How can I? It did happen. There's no going back and I'm scared.'

'Scared of what?'

'Scared . . . for you.'

'Don't be. I can take care of myself.'

Clare looked at him: his streaked face, his red eyes. 'I'd better go,' she said.

'Clare, I'm sorry.'

She was so withdrawn from him that she didn't seem to hear him. He caught her at the door and took her hand. 'I didn't mean to harm you,' he said, putting his arms around her in an effort to reassure her – reassure himself. 'We need to talk.'

'Listen, Henry, we don't have to crucify each other because of this.'

'If you're . . . you know what . . . I'll stand by you,' Henry stuttered.

Clare felt the colour drain from her face. 'We have our whole lives in front of us. Things to do. Ambitions. Pregnancy and marriage are the last things on my mind. Forget about it. Now I really must go.'

Outside the clouds were gathering again. Henry stood at the gate, his face expressionless. 'You will tell me if . . . you need to talk?' he said.

'Yes, I will.'

As she walked home Clare felt tired. Her eyes ached with unshed tears and there was a heaviness between her legs. Suddenly she felt very grown-up and she wasn't sure if she wanted to be. In all her imaginings she had never expected it to hurt her. No one had told her it would, nor had she read it anywhere.

At home, in the bathroom, she turned on the geyser and put the plug in the big bath that sat on tiny legs in the middle of the stained-wood floor. It was speckled here and there with enamel chips, and yellowing in places. But it was clean. She waited a few minutes then turned on the taps. The geyser knocked and thrummed while the water gushed in, chipping off more of the enamel. She didn't care. For once she would be extravagant and lose herself in a hot bath even though it was only a week night. She poured in some of Agnes's bubblebath, stripped off her clothes and slid down into the warm bubbles. The water rose to the rim and splashed over the sides on to the good mat.

Clare scrubbed herself thoroughly with the loofah, desperate to erase the guilt and shame of what she had done with Henry. Why had she let it happen? Was it because she craved love and affection, longed for someone to hug and hold her? Her daddy had loved her and, until the day he walked out, had never let her down.

Oh, for her daddy to return. To hear his key in the

latch and his rough voice calling her name. Closing her eyes she could hear the reproach in his voice when he spoke to Agnes. 'Leave her alone. She's doing no harm. You'll kill her with all that practising.'

'I'm getting out of Glencove,' she said to herself. 'It's all right for Eve. She's got everything. Anyway, she's a fool. Trying to explain to her how I feel is like talking to the wall. I tell her, and will she listen?'

A thought came to her. She would stay in London after the wedding. Martin wouldn't mind. Clare went quiet, thinking of London. It was what she had wanted to do for a long time. She imagined Martin and Terry there and all the shops and the people thrown into relief behind them. 'I'll stay with them and get a job.' She had always loved Martin and had felt cheated when he left home.

Meantime, she would have to confess her sin to Father McCarthy. She could picture his big face turning puce behind the grid. He'd give her a lecture about self-control and a rosary for penance. There would be a long queue of nosy neighbours waiting for her to come out. Madge Kinsella and Delia Enright among them. Nothing escaped their notice. Her mother often said they made a religion out of gossiping and would lift a stone for a story. Henry was now what Sister Mildred referred to as an occasion of sin. If she continued to meet him it would happen again. Maybe not immediately. The shame of it made her face burn.

She got out of the bath and, wrapping herself in a worn towel, went to look in her mother's mirror to see if it was possible to tell by her face that she had committed a mortal sin and, worse, had lost her virginity. The eyes that gazed back at her were big and anxious. But she wasn't sure.

Downstairs, she stood in the hallway and watched Agnes, who had just come in, through the frame of the kitchen door, drying dishes. In the yellow light Agnes's face looked tired but her hair was neatly combed and she was wearing the smart black dress she kept for Sundays. Clare went into the kitchen quietly, expecting to be stared at.

'So you finally got out of the bath.' Agnes didn't even look round.

'Yes.' Clare sat down.

'Why did you have a bath?'

'I was helping out at Joyce's farm.'

'Good reason. Are you hungry?'

'No.'

In bed that night Clare lay awake in the dark running her fingers through her rosary beads, praying that she wasn't pregnant. A queer feeling came over her. It was as if the walls were closing in. When she fell asleep she dreamed that the house was tumbling down around her and she was being slowly buried beneath the rubble. The tightness in her chest woke her. Her arms and legs were stiff and she was afraid to move. She made up her mind there and then to forget all about Henry. If she thought of something else every time he came into her head she would eventually stop thinking about him altogether.

Clare couldn't stay still. She had to be on the move all the time. Going somewhere, doing something. She spent a great deal of time at Eve's, or in Hilda's Chipper, always making sure to be with somebody in case she bumped into Henry. She practised the piano, but in a restless way, helped with the garden, vacuumed and polished without being asked to. Anything to keep her mind occupied. If she let herself think serious thoughts she became afraid. Walking along she would have to drum up a tune in her head, something fast and care-free so as not to have to think.

She smoked constantly, in the shed in Eve's garden, mostly. Concentrating on Martin's wedding and the time when she would be able to get away was her only consolation. Perhaps she might travel further afield someday, America, Canada. See the world.

'You all right?' Eve said to her one afternoon, when they were drinking Coca-Cola in Hilda's Chipper.

'I'm worried about the exams. How are you?'

Eve shrugged. 'I'm still waiting for Sarah to walk in the door. I can't believe she's dead.'

'It'll take a while.'

Eve nodded. 'How did you get on at the farm?'

'We . . .' Clare hesitated. 'It was awful.'

'Did you two have a row?'

'Worse.' Clare lowered her voice. 'We did it.'

There was silence while Clare's words sank in. 'Oh, God,' Eve said finally. 'What was it like?'

'Shh.' Clare made a face. 'It was horrible. I don't know which was worse. Doing it or confessing it.'

'You went to Father McCarthy?' Eve was stunned. 'Did he ask you if you'd taken pleasure in it?'

'He said, "Why did you let it go so far?"' Clare mimicked Father McCarthy's accent.

'What did you say?'

'I said, "Have you ever tried stopping a bull jumping over a fence, Father?"'

'You didn't.' Eve was shocked.

In spite of herself, Clare laughed.

The weather had changed and an east wind blew,

changing the weather from hot to cold. The house seemed empty and hollow as Clare sat at the piano letting her hand fall on the notes. The creeper outside touched the window, filling the room with dancing shadows. A flock of birds flew overhead and Clare went to get a closer look. The day was perfumed with the scent of the last climbing roses on the outside wall, and the leaves of the maple tree in the garden next door shook lightly in the wind. She returned to the piano and played 'Amazing Grace' with one hand the way Sarah used to play it. She played it again, giving the resonant, full tone to the ordinary notes. She could picture Eve and herself as small children going to music lessons with Agnes. When Sarah had started some years later she was fearful of the huge instrument and the stern Miss Devine and treated the notes with caution. Struggling to sight-read she repeated each note until it was perfect. Eve gave up protesting to her mother that she hated it. Soon afterwards Sarah stopped going.

Clare has persisted, developing the emphasis, the timing, her fingers racing up and down the piano as she practised her variations of scales. She was full of music, always working towards a true note. Playing the familiar run of single notes, adding the trills, the ribbons of scales, the flood of proud, vibrant sounds, she was magically transported across the sea to the Royal Academy of Music in London. If only Eve could go with her. She would try to persuade her.

It began to rain as she made her way to Eve's house, clear, fine rain that would soon be soaked up by the sun. When no one answered the bell, Clare went round to the back door. James Freeman, busy in his potting-shed with his plants, called out to her, 'They've gone shopping.'

'Hello, Mr Freeman.' Clare went in his shed. 'What are you doing?' she asked, perching herself on a stool near him, watching his strong fingers press down into a pot of clay.

'Getting these chrysanthemums ready for Christmas,' he said.

'Seems like hard work to me,' Clare said.

James straightened his back. 'A job worth doing is worth doing well.' His face was red from exertion. 'Especially as we'll have the benefit of these magnificent blooms in winter.'

'I'm afraid I won't be here to see them.'

'I heard you won the scholarship to the Royal Academy.' James regarded Clare critically. 'By Jove, girl, that's marvellous. Congratulations. I'd shake your hand if mine weren't covered in soil.'

'Thank you,' Clare said.

'Good old England,' James continued. 'Always could rely on England for work. Churchill did a good job during the war, I'll grant him that. Macmillan didn't believe in unemployment. Now all this sudden affluence is bound to have repercussions, of course. Britain has been good to us where unemployment is concerned. Trouble is, they don't understand our need for freedom. We had to shoot them in my time and we'll have to do it again, unfortunately. They never seem to get the message.' He looked at her sharply. 'Do you know, Clare, people would rather have their freedom than all the money in the world?'

Clare nodded.

'You could find London daunting, you know.'

'It's a bit stifling here at times, too,' Clare told him.

'I'll grant you that.'

'Do you think it's selfish of me to want to break away

124

and do something for myself, Mr Freeman?'

'It's human nature,' James said, plunging his hands once more into the rich soil. 'What gets us going in the first place. And we've all been through the mill recently with Sarah's . . . death. I ask myself over and over again why God didn't take me instead and I can't find the answer.' He stopped to clear his throat.

Not knowing what to say Clare remained silent.

'Life goes on,' he continued, looking around him at the stacks of pots in the corner, the rows of plants, the discarded tools and paint-brushes, all testament to years of accumulated effort. 'I suppose a break might be the very thing we all need.' James left his potting-shed and moved into the sunlight to look at his flowers.

Clare followed him. Tall, dignified, he leaned against the wall, lighting his pipe and gazing at the last of the roses.

'They're beautiful,' Clare said, sniffing their fragrance.

'Do you really think so?' James seemed surprised at the compliment. 'The rain brings out their fragrance, you know.'

He held one of the crimson blooms gently between thumb and forefinger. 'Look at the texture of those petals, Clare.'

'Velvet,' she said.

'Velvet indeed,' he repeated, his ability to draw her into his own endeavour evident at he spoke. It was the essence of what made her seek him out time and again for solace and approval.

Clare wasn't sorry to say goodbye to Glencove as she passed through the checkpoint at Dun Laoghaire with her suitcase, ready to get on the mailboat with Agnes for the journey to Martin's wedding. The night before,

Henry had stood at her front door with a bunch of roses and a box of chocolates, looking as though his world had come to an end. 'If only you had given us a chance,' he had said mournfully. 'You've changed since you got that scholarship. I'm not good enough for you any more. You think you can do better in England.'

'That's not true' Clare said defensively.

'You'll become a snob.'

'No, I won't.'

'Prove it, then,' Henry insisted. 'Come back to me.'

'OK, I will.'

They had sat up most of the night planning Clare's return after she had completed her scholarship.

'We'll get married,' Henry had said.

'We'll see.' Clare feigned an optimism she didn't feel, knowing that Henry's plan was unlikely to be fulfilled.

The mailboat left the harbour at half past six that hot August evening. Clare sat beside her mother, watching the receding town fade to a sliver under a pale sky.

At Holyhead they took the train and for a long time passed fields of endless blackness and occasional cities of dark, skeletal buildings and glaring lights. Cities with strange-sounding names like Llandudno, Chester and Crewe. Agnes poured tea from a flask and gave Clare some ham sandwiches. Then Clare slept.

'We're here.' Agnes's voice woke her.

Clare was refreshed and excited beyond her wildest dreams to see a city. Although London was sleeping, Clare knew from the liveliness of the neon lights that they passed in a red bus and the screech of constant traffic that it was huge. Dublin was only a town by comparison. The bus left them close to Terry's parents' home in Clapham. Quietly, Clare followed Agnes up the steps of the large brick house.

Mrs Packer, Terry's mother, answered the door. She wore a black dress and kissed them both. 'You're very welcome,' she said. 'Did you have a good crossing?' The folds under her chin wobbled as she spoke.

'Yes, thank you,' Agnes assured her.

'I'm sure you're tired. Some refreshment?'

'A cup of tea would be lovely. If it's not too much trouble.'

Agnes and Clare followed her into a sitting room where a bowl of plastic roses shone on a polished table beside a silver tray of iced cakes and a silver teapot.

'Make yourselves comfortable while I wet the tea.' Mrs Packer smiled at Clare. 'Would you prefer lemonade, dear?'

'Yes, please.' Clare smiled back.

'Won't be long.'

She returned with the teapot, lemonade and a glass. Mr Packer, a small man with apple cheeks, followed her into the room. He greeted Agnes with a warm handshake and asked Clare if she had enjoyed 'the voyage'.

'Yes, thank you,' Clare said.

'And how are things in Ireland?' he asked.

'Improving by all accounts,' Agnes replied. 'Though personally I haven't seen much of this affluence they're all talking about. Higher wages and all.'

'It'll come. I've great time for the oul' sod. And what are you doing with yourself?' he asked Clare.

'I've just finished school,' she told him, with great delight.

'So you'll be looking for a job. If you want something to tide you over I might be able to help. I'm head porter at the Savoy Hotel. They're always looking for waitresses and chambermaids. Could put in a word for you.'

'Great,' Clare thanked him.

Mrs Packer was talking about the wedding to Agnes, and about the bride and groom, not once referring to them by their names. Clare drank her lemonade slowly and ate a pink-iced cake, careful not to let any crumbs fall on the floor. She kept wishing that Martin and Terry would arrive.

Finally Agnes said, 'We'd better go to bed. We've a busy day tomorrow.'

They slept quietly together in a high bed with plump pillows and crisp sheets. The next day Terry and two of her friends brought Clare shopping. They wandered from shop to shop among the crowds, looking at beautiful gowns and dresses, settling on a pink broderie-anglaise dress for Clare.

On the morning of the wedding Martin, Agnes and Clare sat in a café. As he drank his tea Martin's sharp blue eyes were fixed on Marble Arch.

'Well, something's gone wrong,' Agnes said, wiping her mouth with her paper napkin. 'Very wrong, according to Father McCarthy,' she added, with a grimace.

Martin's gaze shifted to meet his mother's. 'Why so?' he asked.

Draining the last mouthful, Agnes replaced her cup on her saucer and said, 'He called in to see me before we left. He says young Gilfoyle is up to his tricks again.'

Martin flicked his gaze back to Marble Arch. Agnes lifted her shoulders huffily. 'Needless to say I haven't a clue what it's all about but it probably makes sense to you,' she continued. 'Anyway, I'm only passing on the message. More tea?'

Martin lifted his empty cup absently towards the teapot. Agnes poured and, lowering her voice, said,

'Father McCarthy knows he can trust me. Like the confessional I am.'

'Mm,' Martin grunted, his eyes fixed on the plate of Chelsea buns in front of him.

'By the way, Gus Lawlor said to tell you to get in touch with him. He looked worried too. What'll I tell him?'

'Tell him I'll sort out that matter.' Martin bit into a bun and chewed vigorously.

'You know me. Never one to interfere. But sure you can talk to Father McCarthy yourself. He'll be here this afternoon.'

'What?'

'Didn't Terry tell you? He offered to assist the parish priest. Thought we should have a representative from our side on the altar. He's attached to the family, as you know.' She lowered her voice again.

'You're behind this, Mother. You asked him to come.'

'So what if I did? Didn't it ever occur to you that I need a bit of support too?'

Martin glowered into his cup. 'He's an oul' woman.' He spat the words out. 'Should mind his own business.'

'Ah, now, Martin. The harsh word for the poor priest. He's only doing it for my sake. Don't forget we grew up together. He knows I'm finding it hard on my own.'

'Well, then.' Martin slurped his tea. 'Let him get on with his prayers and leave the important jobs to the likes of me. I know what I'm doing.'

'God save us,' Agnes blessed herself, 'but you're a hard man.'

'Shh, here's Terry.'

Agnes bristled. 'You're in something big, son. But, then, if Father McCarthy is in on it too, it must be all right.'

Terry came bouncing into the restaurant followed by her entourage of giggling friends. Her round face was childish with happiness.

'What are the solemn looks for?' she said to Martin, glancing at Agnes then at him. 'Anyone would think it was a funeral you were going to.'

'Might as well be,' Clare said, under her breath. Martin turned to say something to Terry and caught sight of the scowling Agnes as she eyed the shopping bags Terry was shoving under the next table. He stood up, muttering, 'I'll leave you girls to it. Must go and collect the monkey-suits.'

'Morning suits,' Agnes corrected.

He whispered something to Terry, flashed his charming smile at them all and left. As he reached the door Clare caught the look that passed between him and Agnes.

As soon as he had gone they all began talking at once. Terry wanted to know if Agnes had managed to get a hat and if she thought the rain would hold off a bit longer. Agnes enquired about their purchases, stopping to remind Clare to sit up straight at the table and saying that she hoped Clare's new dress was suitable.

Clare said, 'Yes,' to everything and tried to speak to Terry but she couldn't get a word in over the babble of voices. Agnes ordered a fresh pot of tea and cream cakes and presided over the teapot when it arrived, her disapproval evident in her pleated brow.

At midday Clare stood in her new dress to one side of the landing in the Packers' house while Terry's friends helped Terry to get ready in her bedroom. When she emerged, flanked on either side by her bridesmaids, her face was remote behind her veil. She looked so magnificent in her long white dress that Clare was stunned into silence.

St Margaret's parish church in Clapham was filled with family and neighbours, and scented with the blooms of roses and carnations. The congregation got to its feet as the organ began Mendelssohn's Wedding March. Hat brims fluttered as heads turned to catch sight of Terry entering on her father's arm. Agnes and Clare stood side by side in the front pew close to Martin, who waited in the aisle with John Scully, his best man. His head turned to watch his bride approach. Agnes turned, too, her solemn profile barely visible under the sweeping brim of her hat as she stared at Terry. The organ stopped playing as Terry and her father reached Martin's side. Mr Packer gave his daughter's hand to Martin, and went to kneel beside his wife in the pew opposite.

The parish priest came down from the altar, with his assistant, Father McCarthy, and three altar boys, to greet the bride and groom. During the ceremony Clare sat, hands joined, gazing at the magnificent stained-glass window, the high altar decked with flowers between rows of lighted candles dipping and dancing in the gentle draught from the vestry door.

'Do you, Martin Dolan, take Terry Packer to be your lawful wedded wife, to have and to hold from this day forward for better for worse, in sickness and in health, till death do you part?' the parish priest boomed.

'I do,' Martin said in a resolute voice, his eyes never leaving Terry's face.

The priest turned to Terry and repeated the same words, substituting the names. Terry said, 'I do,' in a giggling, trembling voice. Clare wondered what Pauline would make of it all and wished that it was Pauline who was standing there beside Martin instead of Terry. She glanced at Agnes, who gazed ahead of her, chin up, her demeanour giving nothing away. Clare stayed in her place listening to the organist playing a Bach prelude in C sharp while Martin and Terry, their parents and attendants moved into the vestry for the signing of the register. It was a beautiful piece of music that made Clare's heart soar at the prospect of her new life in London and the opportunities it would provide.

Martin and Terry emerged to a triumphant fanfare of organ chords. Terry's veil was turned back from her pretty, smiling face. Her eyes danced as she walked slowly towards the crowded pews clinging to her new husband's arm. Clare could see by the proud tilt of her head that she was thrilled with herself. Martin's charming smile gave no indication as to what he was thinking. It was as if he took it all in his stride. They proceeded slowly, followed by the best man with the chief bridesmaid, Debbie, her pale green silk dress sweeping the ground, her hair entwined with flowers. Terry's other friend, Sandra, followed closely with Terry's cousin Tom, a thin-faced young man.

The pealing church bells filled the summer air as the wedding group stood in the circle of gravel outside to pose for photographs. Agnes swept forward and clasped Martin's free hand with her gloved one, tears in her eyes, her face a mixture of pride and sorrow.

'You have to put Father McCarthy in the picture,' she insisted. 'Come on, Father, over here.' She beckoned to him.

'To be sure, to be sure.' Father McCarthy bustled forward, rubbing his hands together, and stood beside Martin, beaming at the photographer. Father McCarthy was in his early fifties, a big fleshy man with a bulge to his stomach, and a red complexion from an excess of altar wine, some said. He was broad-shouldered and had a thick neck. His wide forehead denoted his brains and gave him a look of strength. Father McCarthy and Agnes Dolan were great friends. He would call to see her on his way home from a walk sometimes and would sit by the fire giving recitals on his favourite topic: the waste of our natural resources, forestry and fisheries. He was a well-meaning man and full of kindness.

'Enough.' Martin raised his hand to the photographer and led Terry to the waiting sleek black car, decked in white ribbon. He tucked in the swathes of her train before getting in himself. They drove amid cheering and laughter, Agnes watching them, a large white handkerchief in her hand. Slowly she moved to another waiting car, Clare in her wake, to drive to the hotel for the wedding breakfast.

'Are you all right?' Clare asked her mother as they drove off.

'Of course I am,' Agnes said.

'Terry looked lovely,' Clare said.

'Yes,' Agnes replied, lost in her own thoughts.

The wedding breakfast, for close members of the family, was held in the dining room of the Red Lion Hotel, Clapham. The tables were set to accommodate thirty people. Silver and crystal shone and the guests took their places, facing the head table with Martin and Terry at its centre. Terry sat in her dress and veil, her face glowing, while she talked to her mother, father, and various members of her family. Mrs Packer, in a dark blue linen suit, sat beside the priest at one end of the table. Agnes sat calm and stately at the other, next to Mr Packer, pretending that she was enjoying it all while Mr Packer inspected the darting waiters and waitresses, a scowl on his face. 'They go too fast for my liking,' he said to Agnes, eyeing one of the waiters. 'It's not like at the Savoy. Everything is precision timing there.'

'I'm quite sure,' Agnes agreed.

Clare sat beside her mother, smoothing her dress.

Mr Packer leaned forward. 'You look very pretty, Clare,' he said.

'Thank you.' Clare said, surprised that he had noticed and glad that she had not let Martin down.

A waiter placed a bowl of soup in front of her while another poured wine into her glass. Then slowly, deliberately she ate chicken and ham and listened to the speeches, sipping her wine whenever Agnes was distracted by something Mr Packer was telling her.

As soon as the reception was over, the tables were cleared for dancing. Clare watched the fiddlers take their places around the piano in the corner. When the dancing was in full swing and the atmosphere charged with gaiety, Clare and Martin danced the hornpipe together. As the clapping died down Clare saw her father out of the corner of her eye. He stood hovering inside the door, leaning against one of the supporting pillars.

'Daddy.' She ran to meet him, smothering him with kisses.

'Dad.' Martin shook his hand. 'Glad you made it.'

'Jack.' Agnes's voice was faint as he came to greet her.

He was wearing an old grey suit, but his shirt was snow-white and his hear nearly combed. 'Hello,' he said, and sat down.

Avoiding Agnes's eyes, he nodded to Mr Packer and said to Terry, 'Sorry I'm late.'

Martin put a glass of beer in his hand. 'Give us a song, Dad,' he said.

Without speaking Jack went to the piano. 'Clare will accompany me,' he said, into the microphone. 'I hear she's coming on great.'

A cheer went up as Clare came forward. Everyone started talking at once. Clare began 'Danny Boy', Jack's favourite melody. His eyes looked heavy as she played. He began to sing: '"O Danny boy, the pipes the pipes are call-ing."'

'Beautiful,' Martin said, clapping when his father finished.

'"T would bring tears from a stone,' agreed Mr Packer.

'What about "Kevin Barry"?' Martin said.

Jack sang with feeling, the words obviously dear to him. When he had finished he dropped his head and waited for the applause to subside, like he'd been taught at school.

As soon as he sat down Agnes rounded on him. 'Where did you come from?' She frowned.

He glared back at her. 'Can't you let me in the door, woman, before you start the inquisition?'

'You're late.'

'I'm lucky to be here. I haven't been well.'

'Typical,' Agnes said.

'For the love of God, let's act like Christians in public, woman.'

Agnes threw up her head as if she were butting something. 'By all means,' she scoffed. 'We'll act like a happily married couple if you want.'

'Good.' He turned away.

Clare was breathless with excitement.

'How did you get here, Daddy?' she asked.

'Bus. I'm working in Knightsbridge.'

'Do you live there?' she asked.

'Not far from it.' Jack sipped his beer.

'I'm going to be living over here.'

'I know. Martin told me.'

When Agnes wasn't looking Jack took a ten-pound note from his pocket and slipped it into her hand. 'Good girl,' he said, 'I'm proud of you.'

'Thanks.' Clare kissed his cheek and, lowering her voice, said, 'Can I come and stay with you?'

'I've only got a bedsitter. But I'm sure I could find you a place. Sure there's plenty of time yet.' Dancers twirled and mingled with waiters. Terry waltzed in Martin's arms, and Agnes danced with Mr Packer. 'I'd better ask Mrs Packer to dance.' Jack put down his glass and walked over to the table where Mrs Packer sat talking to her friend.

'May I have this dance?' Tom was standing beside Clare.

'Certainly,' she said, and waltzed off with him to the strains of 'The Blue Danube'.

Suddenly Martin and Terry were at the top of the staircase in the hall and everybody was summoned to say goodbye. Terry was dressed in a lavender silk dress and jacket, with a matching pillbox hat. Agnes clung to Martin until the very last minute. As they drove away Clare swallowed hard to prevent herself from crying and began to form her plans for a different kind of escape.

That night when Agnes was snoring softly she tiptoed downstairs, careful not to bump her suitcase against the banisters. For a few minutes she stood listening in the darkness of the hall, afraid to breathe. Quietly, she moved to the front door and opened it slowly. A light snapped on as she was about to shut it and Mr Packer's voice called out, 'Who's down there?'

Clare froze. Then she pulled the door quickly behind her, and ran until she reached the corner of the road. Looking back she saw the lights in the house go on, one after another. If he wakes Mother, she thought, she'll miss me. She began to run again, her suitcase bumping against her legs, slowing her down. At the end of the next street she stopped and looked back again. No one was chasing her. All of a sudden she realised that she had no idea where she was going. She checked the pocket of her coat to make sure that the ten-pound note her father had given her at the wedding was still there. Reassured, she began walking again.

The streets were silent and lonely, the lights from the sodium lamps casting a greenish haze over them. Clare walked close to the wall as she left one gloomy street to enter another. The sky was pitch black and she was scared. Finally, she came to a wider street. A car came driving towards her, creeping along the kerb. She shrank back close to the wall in case it was Mr Packer or one of his neighbours searching for her. A man walking further along the street whistled tunelessly to himself as he went. Clare wondered if she should call out to him, 'Hey, I'm lost,' or something like that. Thinking about it made her scared that she might alert the driver of the car. He might stop and get out. Her heart beat in her chest like a drum. As the car passed she saw the driver, saw the whites of his eyes looking through the windscreen. Not moving a muscle she waited in the shadow of the wall until he continued on, stopping further along to call to a woman who appeared from nowhere.

'Chrissie or Missie,' he called out.

'Hey, man,' she answered, tottering on high heels to the passenger door, her hair a halo around her head, silhouetted against a paling sky. The car drove off. Shaking, Clare wondered if she should go back to the safety of the Packer house. If she did, Agnes would never again let her out of her sight. Should she press on? It would be bright soon and the task of finding her father would not seem so daunting. He had said he worked for Wimpey's on a site near Knightsbridge. She'd get a bus. His name would be registered with the builders. She had seen a huge hoarding with an advertisement for Wimpey's somewhere. Hurrying along, her confidence growing, she convinced herself that she would soon be with her father, and that he would be delighted to see her.

Further into the heart of the city the shops were barred against robbers and vandals with steel doors. Winking lights from neon signs reflected their bright colours on the oily pavement, giving splashes of brightness to the wide street, and a false sense of gaiety. The sound of quarrelling came from a doorway, then running footsteps. Fear sprang up inside Clare. She wished she had someone with her. Anyone. She must find her father and soon. She leaned against the wall, too scared either to go on or to turn back, and thought of him.

Cars and buses driving past woke her. It was daylight. She asked a woman passer-by the way to Knightsbridge and was shown the bus stop. Clare took the bus to the Embankment and kept walking until she came to an enormous building site on the corner of Knightsbridge. Jack was sitting down for his early-morning break with the other men, his back against a wall, when Clare came towards him, her battered suitcase in her hand.

'Hello, Daddy,' she said, when she was standing in front of him.

'Holy Mother of Divine God.' Jack scrambled to his feet.

'I told you I'd be coming to stay with you. I'm not going back.' Clare was breathless.

'Does your mother know?' Jack's voice was tight with anxiety.

'No,' Clare answered.

'Sweet Christ, there'll be ructions.'

He looked at his daughter's untidy hair, her sleepy eyes. 'Come on, we'd better let her know. The cops are probably scouring London for you this very minute.'

'I left a note.'

'Then they'll be here any moment. Hey, Larry,' Jack called to one of the men, 'I'm going to make a phone call and sort out this daughter of mine. Tell the foreman I'll be back later.'

'Right,' Larry called back, winking at Clare.

'Let's go, before your mother goes mad altogether.' Jack took the suitcase and Clare followed him to a phone box.

Jack's alarm clock woke Clare with the feeling that she had slept too much and was late. She reached out and she switched on the light. It was half past six in the evening. Lying motionless, she began to recollect the events of the day. The phone call to Agnes, Jack wringing his hands trying to pacify her, telling her that Clare would be all right with him for a while and that she needed a bit of a break. Agnes's tinny voice calling instructions to him down the line while Clare moved away, determined not to listen. Jack had brought her

back to his bedsitter, a large, high-ceilinged room with
two windows facing out on to the street. It was sparsely
furnished, with a bed, table, chairs, a desk where he
kept his writing materials and a shelf full of books along
one wall.

She got up and dressed herself slowly, gazing into
her father's shaving mirror at her bleary eyes, then put
the kettle on in the kitchenette to make herself a cup of
coffee. Certain recollections of the previous night
scared her so she began to hum a little tune to try to
forget about it.

When she was ready she went out.

She had to stand still for a few minutes before she
could remember where she was. She started walking
down the deserted street, feeling strange. The newsagent behind the counter in his shop was leaning on
the cash register when she went in to buy cigarettes.

'Evening,' he said.

'Twenty cigarettes, please,' Clare said.

'Weights?' the newsagent asked.

'Yes,' Clare said, beginning to relax.

She walked slowly back to the house, smoking a
cigarette and browsed through Jack's books while she
waited for him to come home from work. When she
heard his key in the lock she put the kettle on.

'How's work?' she asked.

'Not bad,' he said, putting a bag of groceries on the
table and taking off his coat. 'Did you sleep well?'

'Never stirred until six.'

'Good. I bought bacon and sausages and eggs for
tea.'

'I'll help you cook them.'

'You can set the table. The knives and forks are in
that drawer over there.'

During the meal Jack said, 'I spoke to the landlady. She won't hear of you staying here indefinitely.'

'I'll start looking for a job tomorrow,' Clare said. 'Then I should be able to afford a bedsitter of my own.'

'We'll check the evening papers,' Jack said.

It was during her stay with him that Clare understood things about her father that she had never known before. What struck her most was that he was a separate person, a loner. He would leave his digs before daylight every morning and be gone all day. At night, when he wasn't at his local pub, he slumped over a little table reading Shakespeare's plays or biographies about important people he was interested in, like Daniel O'Connell and Charles Stuart Parnell. He would put his book to one side, wanting to talk to her but not always knowing what to say or even how to begin the conversation.

'How's work?' Clare asked the same question every evening.

'Not bad,' came the reply.

'If I only had time to do more reading I'd be happier,' Jack said one evening. 'I'm slowing down. Not as sprightly.'

Another thing that dawned on Clare was that, because as children Martin and she had always relied on Agnes, Jack had felt cut off.

Towards the end of the week she got a job as a waitress at the Savoy Hotel, procured for her by Mr Packer. To her amazement Clare began to like the atmosphere of London. The incessant noise and movement of the traffic excited her, and within a week she felt part of it. The route to work on her first day took her through some of London's most fashionable streets. She rose early and sauntered along a thoroughfare, stopping to gaze at the latest styles and fashions displayed elegantly in expensive shop windows. The tiny waists and varying hemlines of the Mary Quant dresses amused her. Leaving the busy streets she turned into a side walk that took her through the shaded grove of a garden square, past pavement artists and newspaper vendors to the entrance of the Savoy Hotel with its uniformed doormen hailing cabs, feverishly running in all directions. It frightened her. A perspiring Mr Packer came to meet her.

'Everyone's so busy.' Clare looked bewildered as they walked up the red-carpeted steps.

'You'll get used to the hustle and bustle. Don't let it put you off.' Taking her arm Mr Packer walked her through the vast, glittering lobby, with its deep comfortable sofas, its occasional tables and writing desks. At the dining room entrance he introduced her to an agitated Clive, the head waiter, and left, promising to return later to see how she was coping.

In the first days of her employment, the dining room seemed a forbidding place, with its endless white-starched tablecloths and elegant décor. It was full of people older and richer than Clare could ever have imagined. All the girls carried wide, piled-high trays, carefully balancing the weight from shoulder to arms to hands.

Clive would check the appearance of each one at the entrance before they sailed past, heads held high, to serve at their assigned tables. They wore black blouses, white frilly aprons over black skirts, black nylons and black shoes. The nylons made Clare's legs feel clammy with sweat. But she liked working in the dining room, especially when it was busy. She loved the soothing hum of voices over the hidden, boisterous

142

and often frenzied activity in the kitchen.

'I want to learn everything,' she had said to Clive, the day she started.

Her eagerness and the way she practised the silver-service at every opportunity pleased him. The diners ate with relish and talked intently as she moved quietly from table to table, serving, clearing, resetting. When she wasn't busy she stood near the door, sometimes smoothing her black skirt, waiting to replenish glasses or water jugs.

The ambience and the happy diners sent waves of elation through her. This is me, she thought. I'm able to do this job. Clive is pleased with me. That's all that matters. Sometimes she was homesick. When she thought of her mother a tight, bursting feeling would grab her in the pit of her stomach. In the sticky heat of the dining room, Clare often wished she was at the beach, the water lapping over her hot body, cooling it. Everything about London excited her. She couldn't wait to get up in the morning and never wanted the day to end. One evening, Jack said to her, 'Martin is moving to Belfast,' a note of anxiety in his voice.

'But they've only just settled down. How does Terry feel about that?'

'She refuses point blank to go with him, so he's going on his own.'

'Why?'

'He's got a job as a salesman with Rover. Much more money than he was getting on the building site and he'll be indoors in their nice plush showrooms.'

'What's Terry going to do?'

'Stay with her mother for the moment. Their basement flat will be up for grabs, if you want it.'

'Won't it be very expensive?' Clare asked.

'Not if you get someone to share it with you.'
Clare wrote to Eve that night telling her all about it.

Chapter Nine

The only noise in Pauline Quirk's flat came from the back bedroom where Seamus lay snoring. Pauline closed the front door behind her, called 'Seamus, I'm home,' and went into the kitchen to put away her shopping.

He came down the passage in his shirt sleeves, fastening his trousers and squinting at the clock. 'Is that the time? Jees, I must'a slept it out.'

'It's roasting and the queues will be endless if you don't hurry up – or have you forgotten it's the last night of the carnival? The Cadets are playing.' Pauline's voice had an edge to it.

'No. No. 'Course I haven't.'

'Well, don't take all evening. The kettle's on for your shave.'

Pauline realised, as she spoke, that asking Seamus to hurry was like asking for the moon. He liked to take a long time to wash himself, check his appearance and put his wavy hair in place with Brylcreem.

'Will I do?' he said, giving her a kiss on the cheek.

'Come 'ere.' Smiling, she reached out her arms and grabbed him in a tight embrace. Laughing, her open mouth devoured him.

'Wow, wow, hold on there.' Seamus extricated himself, legs buckling. 'You'll crease me good suit,' he said, straightening his jacket.

'You peacock, Seamus Gilfoyle. You think all the girls will be giving you the eye.' Pauline laughed.

'I don't think it, I know it,' Seamus said, rubbing a rag over his shiny black shoes.

They walked down Goretti Terrace and the Sea Road to the harbour, arms linked, until the carnival came into view. The marquee was bright and colourful. Bunting fluttered from its swooping roof and sloping sides, and lanterns danced and swung in the sea breeze. The smell of chips and seaweed wafted in the air and the sun bounced off the instruments of the band as they grouped together. From inside the marquee there was the sound of a piano running through a snatch of song, a violin tuning up. Concepta Taylor, standing beside Madge Kinsella, glanced at Seamus with flirty eyes as they approached. Pauline nudged him to keep moving. Not heeding her, he stopped.

'Howayah, Seamus,' Concepta said. 'Back again?'

Seamus hovered. 'Hell-o.' He grinned, throwing his eyes from her beehive hair-do to her spiky high heels.

'Isn't it a scorcher?' she went on, giving the sleeves of her off-the-shoulder blouse a quick tug downwards and glancing a smile off Pauline at the same time.

'You're telling me,' Seamus agreed.

'I didn't expect to see you here.' Concepta spoke to Pauline's bulge.

'I'm not sick or anything. Not even that big,' Pauline said, looking down.

'All the same, you should be taking it easy,' Concepta advised.

'You weren't up north for long,' Madge chimed in.

'Ah, sure it's you lovely ladies, you know,' Seamus said, with a grin. 'Can't keep away.'

'That's the rock you'll perish on,' Madge Kinsella

said sourly, her permed head going up and down like the nodding donkey in the back of Seamus's Mini.

Seamus blushed. Pauline walked on, then turned back. 'Come on, Seamus,' she said in a low, controlled voice. 'Don't make free with them.'

'You're a bit too soft on the women for your own good,' Madge continued.

'Can't think of better company.' Concepta giggled.

'You've notions of yourself, Seamus Gilfoyle, and the women are only jeering at you.' Madge was relentless, looking straight through him as she spoke.

'Don't be talking.' Seamus refused to be insulted, shaking his head as if mesmerised at the burden of it all.

Pauline came and jerked his sleeve. He waved goodbye, his eyes on Concepta's bare shoulders.

Inside the marquee Pauline rooted in her bag for the tickets to the dance, Seamus beside her, his fingers tapping on the grid.

'Eileen Reid and the Cadets,' Seamus said. 'Great singer, great band.'

Suddenly Gus Lawlor was beside him. 'Hello, sir.' Seamus jumped to attention.

Gus caught Seamus by the arm and pulled him to one side. His eyes flicked over him. 'I didn't expect to see you here,' Gus said. 'Another holiday?'

'Bit of a break, that's all, sir,' Seamus hedged.

With a sudden grip on Seamus's arm and looking squarely at him, Gus said softly, 'You'd best be on your way back, son. For your own sake. You were told to stay there till you got the job done.'

'Hello, Mr Lawlor,' Pauline said.

'Good day to you, Pauline.' Gus released Seamus quickly, tipped the brim of his hat and was gone.

Turning up the collar of his jacket and putting his hands in his pockets, Seamus said, 'I think we'll go.'

'But we've only just got here,' Pauline protested.

'I know, but still.' Seamus looked around nervously. 'It's not really my scene.'

'What's up?' Pauline asked. 'What did Mr Lawlor say?'

'Nothing.' He shivered as they moved into the blazing sunshine.

'Waltzing Matilda, waltzing Matilda,' the band blared out.

'You hang on here for a little while. I've got a bit of business to attend to. See you back at the flat.'

'But, Seamus—' Pauline started.

He was gone, slipping through the jostling crowd, his eyes darting from one face to another, as if seeking out the purveyors of rough justice among the crowd. Exasperated and tired in the heat, Pauline walked slowly home.

When she got in Seamus was packing the last of his things hurriedly into a bag. 'What's up?' she asked in alarm.

'I have to go.'

'But I thought you were staying for the weekend.' Pauline was on the verge of tears.

'There's no time to explain. Get my stuff out of the bathroom like a good girl.'

'Has anyone said anything to you?' she asked.

'Yes.'

'You're not taking them seriously, are you?'

Seamus sighed. 'I think they mean business this time.'

'Who is it?' Pauline asked.

'Doesn't matter. There's more to it than meets the eye. They think I'm dangerous.'

'You?' Pauline sniggered. 'That's a joke.'

'I'd better get going all the same.'

'Where can you go at this hour of the night?'

'There's the goods train to Wexford.'

'That's not till midnight.'

'I'll wait at the station.'

'I wish you didn't have to go.' Pauline put her arms around him.

'So do I.' Seamus hugged her.

'I'll get the rest of your things.'

When she returned Seamus handed her a five-pound note. 'Get to Belfast as soon as you can. I'll be waiting for you. We'll get married.'

'You make it sound urgent.'

'It is urgent. I wouldn't want any harm to come to you or the baby. Not for the world. You know that. Anyway, look at the state of you. You should be married.'

'I was trying to save up a bit of money first,' Pauline said, gazing into the mirror. 'I'm not too big.'

'You're lovely and neat.' Seamus put his hand on her bump. 'All the same, it's not right for the baby not to have a proper father. Now, I'll have to go.'

'I'll come as far as the station with you.'

'Better not,' Seamus cautioned. 'Stay here, it's safer.'

'It's nearly dark. No one will see us.'

Seamus picked up his bag. 'You're a very stubborn girl,' he said, putting his arms round her and kissing her.

They banged the door shut behind them.

'It's turned cold.' Pauline moved close to him and clutched his arm as they walked along, heads down against the wind.

The station was dark and full of shadows.

'I'll wait here with you.'

'No, it's too cold. Go on home. You keep out of harm's way.'

'Mind yourself,' she said, clinging to him.

'Go on now, go.' Seamus released her suddenly and moved further into the shadow of the platform.

'I'll drop you a line before I come up,' she called out to him.

'Shh. Just get there.' His voice was barely audible. Suddenly two men in balaclavas stepped out of the shadows and grabbed Seamus.

'No!' Pauline screamed. 'Let him go!'

A hand was clamped over her mouth. She struggled, trying to pull herself free.

'Get her out of here,' a voice hissed. 'Hurry.' Another man in a balaclava appeared from nowhere. She felt herself being dragged along the street. Arms flailing, legs kicking, she tried to last out but they were too strong for her. Suddenly she felt herself being pushed into the back of a car.

'Lie down,' a man's voice snapped.

She lay along the back seat.

The two men in balaclavas got into the front. As the car drove off, she buried her face into the cold seat. Her arms and legs were bruised and sore from the rough grip on her.

The car stopped outside the town. One of the men got out, opened the back door and lifted her out. She stumbled as she tried to straighten up.

'Where are you taking Seamus?' Her voice was unrecognisable even to herself.

'Never you mind. He'll be taken care of,' a muffled voice said. 'Be a good girl and go on home and not a word to anyone. You'll have him back before you know it, if you keep your mouth shut.'

The man got back into the car and it sped off into the darkness. Pauline was left, looking after it. Slowly she made her way back to the flat and went to bed, listening for the sound of the car that would deliver Seamus to her.

When she woke up the wind was blowing. The water pipes knocked and thrummed through the house. Someone upstairs was having a bath. Reeling at the normality of it all, Pauline fell asleep again.

Next morning she went to work, hoping that Seamus might walk into the pub or that somebody would say something about the events of the previous night.

Madge Kinsella was hovering at the door. 'It looks like rain,' she said, as Pauline approached.

'Oh,' Pauline said.

'The builders are starting the extension next week. I was hoping the rain would hold off. There'd be a terrible mess.'

'I'm sure it will,' Pauline said, reassuringly.

'Where's Seamus?' Madge asked, as she removed the covers from the pumps.

Pauline felt herself go weak at the knees. 'I don't know.' The words nearly choked her.

'You don't know?' Madge looked perplexed. 'Has he gone back to the North?'

'Sorry. I wasn't listening. Yes. He left early this morning.' Pauline took a tray and began to clear glasses from the tables.

'What's wrong with me?' she said to herself. 'I ought to say something. Cry or something. Ask a question. Pinch myself.' If she started crying now she wouldn't be able to stop and Madge would know that something was wrong. For the rest of the morning she kept her eyes downcast so that Madge wouldn't see the extent of her anguish. She polished the bar counter, and shone the brass railings and the optics until they gleamed, her eyes never leaving the door.

That night she sat up in bed, drenched in sweat. She switched on the bedside lamp and checked her watch. Two o'clock in the morning. No sign of Seamus. She went into the kitchen, made a cup of tea, pulled back the curtain and sat in the dark, staring at the sky. As soon as it was daylight she would go down to the station and look for him. That thought cheered her up.

When dawn broke, paling the edges of the sky, she dressed quickly and made her way along the railway track, her earlier euphoria diminishing with each step. In the hall of the station she waited. There was no movement inside the booking office. She peeped through the glass partition. The room beyond was empty. On the platform she stood where Seamus had stood. It was so quiet that the clickety-click of her high heels resounded as she walked to the spot where she had last seen him. She knelt down to examine the cement for traces of blood, signs of a scuffle. There was no evidence that anything unusual had taken place. She felt empty. As she made her way back to the hall she couldn't feel him anywhere and that alarmed her.

'Hey. What are you doing here at this hour?' Tim Reilly, the signalman, came out of the booking office, a perplexed look on his face. 'There's no train for ages yet.'

Pauline jumped back, embarrassed. The early-morning haze was beginning to lift, giving way to a watery sunshine. Through the door of the station she could see the sea and the wet sand. There was the smell of iodine and the freshness of the morning. 'I was just–' Pauline stopped, trying desperately to think what to say.

'Lost something?'

'Me bracelet. Anyone hand it in?'

'Might be inside. Come and have a look.'

She followed him through the small waiting room to the office. He moved about, pulling out drawers, checking through a pile of papers on the big desk.

'It was me mother's,' she explained. 'Sentimental.'

'No sign of it. Have a cup of tea. I've just made one for meself. It'll warm you up. You look as if you could do with it.'

He took two mugs from a shelf and poured the tea out of a large brown earthenware teapot. Pauline took her mug and put milk and sugar in it.

'Thanks,' she said, wrapping her hands around it. 'Anything strange?' she asked, keeping her voice even.

Tim Reilly gave her a bewildered look. 'Sure what'd be strange around here? Nothing ever happens.'

Pauline felt herself flush. 'Just wondered.'

'Your daddy used to bring you up to the signal box when you were small. Remember?'

'Yes.'

'How is your daddy?'

'Grand, thanks.'

'I haven't seen him for ages. Tell him I was asking for him.'

'I will.'

'You were terrified of heights when you were a child,' Tim said.

'Heights.' Pauline feigned laughter. 'You'd hardly call that high up,' she said, looking at the signal box.

'You were very small, then. Drink up and I'll show you the improvements we've made to it,' Tim said enthusiastically.

They went up the steps to the signal box. Pauline stood on the little platform, looking over the station and the sleeping countryside beyond. The window-frames, doors and railings were all freshly painted and gleamed in the early-morning sun. Beyond it the hills sloped to the distant sea. A lone fishing boat trawled in the calm waters. She wondered if Seamus could be a prisoner on it, gagged and bound, then warned herself not to let her imagination run away with her. Everywhere was peaceful.

'All spick and span,' Tim was saying, gesturing to the polished wood and gleaming brass.

'It's beautiful. A credit to you. But I mustn't keep you from your work.' Pauline made for the iron staircase.

'You're all jittery. What's up?'

'Nothing. Thanks for the tea.' She went as quickly as she could down the steps and out of the station.

At the corner she saw Martin coming up the road, his broad shoulders swinging. She stood blocking his path. He stopped and leaned against the railings, a smile on his face.

'Well, well. What brings you out at this unearthly hour?' he asked.

'I didn't know you were back. Have you seen Seamus anywhere?' Pauline was more nervous than she had imagined.

Martin's blue eyes focused on her and he smiled, a twisted, narrow smile that reflected the growing unease between them. 'Now, where would I see Seamus?' He moved from one foot to the other.

'I can't find him.' Pauline tried to sound casual. 'Have you . . .' Her heart beat faster and faster.

'What? Have I what?' Martin looked patiently at her.

154

She cleared her throat to dislodge the frog in it. Martin's eyes, full of insolence, flicked over her. 'You should be taking things easy,' he said, raising his eyebrows quizzically, letting her flounder.

'I thought you might—' Pauline stopped.

'Might what?'

'Have seen him, for Christ's sake.' She spat out the words.

'He's run out on you, has he?'

'No,' she almost shrieked, but silenced herself in the nick of time.

'Only not everyone would be inclined to trust our Seamus,' Martin said. 'Personally speaking, he's a bit dodgy for my liking.' He quivered his hand in an insinuating gesture.

'What are you implying?' Pauline stared at him.

Martin shifted his gaze. 'Watch your step. Don't poke your nose in where it doesn't belong or you might find yourself in serious trouble.'

'I am in serious trouble. Seamus is my boyfriend. We're getting married.'

'Well, good luck to the pair of you. I hope you'll both be very happy.'

The silence between them grew. 'I'd best be off.' Martin smiled, a wide, generous smile of relief.

Pauline caught hold of the sleeve of his jacket. 'I witnessed something last night, didn't I?' Her voice was so strained that Martin had to lean forward to hear what she was saying. He fixed her with a blank stare. She took a step backwards, nearly falling off the pavement. 'Didn't I?' she repeated.

The expression on his face changed to one of calculated indifference. 'You saw nothing. Absolutely nothing. Do you hear?' He paused for breath. 'I know

Seamus means a lot to you, Pauline, but hysteria won't do you any good.'

'He's in trouble,' she said, in a low voice.

'That fella is trouble.'

Pauline advanced on him, grabbed the collar of his jacket and shook it. Martin took a step backwards, smiling and raising his hands in a supplicatory gesture. She let go. 'You should have listened to me in the first place, Pauline. You've only got yourself to blame for getting mixed up with him.'

'You bastard!' she shouted.

'You've had a lucky escape, if you ask me,' he said, ignoring the insult.

'I suppose I've got you to thank for that.'

'Listen, Pauline, go back to your flat where you'll be out of harm's way. I'll keep an eye open and an ear to the ground. Let you know if I hear anything.' His lustful eyes roamed her body, from her tight sweater to the tips of her high heels. 'I'd hate to see you come to any harm.'

Pauline was crying, wiping away the tears with her fist, hating herself for her display of weakness in front of him.

'You bastard!' Her voice hit the sky and bounced off the pavement.

'Come 'ere, love. Come on now,' Martin cajoled. 'Like I said, you're hysterical.' He reached out for her.

'It was you. I saw you with my own eyes.'

He grabbed her.

'Let me go!' she shouted.

'Shut your fucking mouth, do you hear me? You saw nothing,' he hissed, pulling her to him and kissing her mouth, stifling her outpourings. She struggled against him, her arms throbbing from his vice grip. 'I've always wanted you, you know that,' he whispered into her ear.

'Get away from me. What'll they do to him?'

'Ssh. If you promise you'll go straight home I'll find out for you.'

Pauline looked at him. 'I'll go home,' she said, her voice barely audible. He stood watching her until she turned the corner.

She let herself in and went straight to the bathroom, ran water into the bath and undressed, flinging her clothes into the laundry basket. While the bath filled up she brushed her teeth. In the mirror, her eyes were bright with tears, her face swollen. First she washed her hair, then scrubbed the rest of her body with a loofah, before giving herself a good soak. When Seamus returned she would be ready, clean, untarnished.

Eventually, she fell into a troubled sleep curled up in the big bed. The soft click of the door woke her up.

'Seamus?' She sat bolt upright.

Dermy McQuaid stood in the doorway. 'Don't stir yourself,' he said, with a smirk. 'It's only me. I've a message from Martin.'

He took an envelope from his pocket.

Pauline stared at him blankly. 'How did you get in?' she asked.

'The door wasn't locked. You should be more careful. These are quare times we're living in. Here, I've got to be off.' Dermy handed her the envelope and made for the door. She read, in Martin's sprawling handwriting:

> *Take a few days off, Pauline. Stay out of the way and get a grip on yourself. Be in touch.*
> *Martin.*

Pauline made herself tea and toast and wandered around, tidying the flat, wondering what she would do with herself for the next few days. If she didn't hear some news of Seamus she would go mad.

Since Sarah's death the atmosphere in the Freemans' house had been strange and sad. Dorothy's constant crying made it a terrible time for Eve. Her parents were either unaware of one another or argued all the time. Ron Freeman seemed to have relinquished his business interests. His ambition spent, he was no longer prepared to exert himself to procure the trappings of wealth that had once been so important to them both. All those years away from home, drinking, card games, his bachelor existence, had taken their toll. He had come to a halt, unwilling or unable to continue.

Dorothy had given up any plans of her own and Ron had ceased actively resisting her. Eve was affected by the lonely atmosphere and her exclusion from her parents' separate, grieving worlds. She missed Clare and shunned her other school friends, unwilling when she bumped into them to invite them home in case her house appeared as desolate to them as it did to her.

From her bedroom window she watched David Furlong sunbathing or playing cricket in his garden and privately wished for the ease and comfort of his life. He drove in and out of his gates, waving and smiling when he saw Eve, but because he was busy with his job she saw little of him. One stifling summer evening, Eve opened her bedroom window and leaned out to get some fresh air. The cool sweet strains of Louis Armstrong's 'Wonderful World' floated up to her in the twilight. A quick movement in the Furlongs' garden caught her eyes, and she leaned further out not knowing or thinking what she expected to see. On the terrace David Furlong was dancing with a girl. In the dim light from the drawing room their entwined forms, moving slowly, became a blurred, silvery outline. Eve reeled back from the shock. The record ended and Eve heard David's voice and the responsive tinkly laughter of Bernie Power. She closed the window and went to bed, but the vision lingered for a long time, stretching her imagination almost beyond her endurance, before she finally fell asleep.

When Clare's letter arrived, Eve made up her mind to join her in London. Dorothy's anger at her decision knew no bounds.

'You'll lose your place in UCD,' she shouted.

'I've decided not to go until next year,' Eve said.

'Over my dead body,' Dorothy cried. 'Wait till your father gets home. We'll see what he has to say about it.'

Ron was in full agreement with Eve. 'It'll do you good. A break with Clare should be fun. God knows, you need a bit of fun.'

'What about me? I need her here!' Dorothy yelled.

'We'll manage. Eve is young. She needs to get away from this lonely place.'

Dorothy stormed off, so furious with Eve that she refused to speak to her. Eve wrote to Clare to notify her of her arrival and began to pack.

The morning of her departure, she went up to Sarah's bedroom to have a last look round. It was empty and cold. Sarah's teddy bear lay on her pillow, his only eye staring out of his bald despondent face.

'Ready?' James called up the stairs. He was driving her to the boat.

'Coming,' Eve called back.

On impulse she grabbed the teddy bear and stuffed

him into her grip bag. 'I'm going away, Sarah,' she said to the empty room. 'It's so lonely without you. But I'll be back. Wait for me.'

'Got your ticket?' James was wearing his good coat and his grey trilby, beneath which his face looked lined and old.

Dorothy kissed her daughter's cheek coldly, and watched while James lifted Eve's suitcase into the boot of the car. She stood at the front door, waving until they were out of sight.

At Dun Laoghaire crowds of people, waiting to embark, began to move slowly towards the ramp. James carried Eve's case as far as the checkpoint. People were shouting to one another up and down the queue.

'Don't worry about her, sir,' the man in uniform at the checkpoint said. 'We'll keep an eye on her.'

Then it was time to part.

'Well you'd better go.' James's voice was gruff.

'I'll write to you, Grandpa.'

'Do that. As soon as you can.' He hugged her.

Eve wished she could think of something to say to alleviate his sadness at her going. He had mapped out her route, marking in red biro the change of trains at Crewe for London. Now that it was time to say goodbye she held on to his tense shoulders, unable to part with him.

'Goodbye, darling Grandpa. Don't worry about me,' she said finally.

'You take care of yourself,' he said.

She waved, and kept turning to wave as she went up the gangplank. From the deck she could see her grandfather, standing apart, staring at the ship. She wished he would go home.

At last the horn hooted and the boat slowly slipped

out of the harbour. Eve waited until James vanished from sight. As the boat tilted gently from side to side, pulling away from the fading landscape, Eve recalled the claustrophobic atmosphere that bound her family together and threatened to destroy them. By now James would be at home sitting in his armchair, reading his newspaper, or out in the garden examining the lawn, a stern expression on his kind face. Ron would be having a nightcap in the drawing room. Dorothy, in bed reading by now, would be incapable of comforting either of them. A stab of pity pierced Eve. She stared down at the ribbons of foam that trailed in the wake of the boat. The sky had darkened and light appeared, spread out across the horizon. Gradually, thoughts of Clare, London and the various adventures she anticipated, without the strictures of home, took hold, stirring such excitement in her that it shortened the long journey. As the boat chugged its way to Holyhead she stayed up on deck, thinking back on her life and looking forward to her new one.

After a long train journey, the sprawling suburbs of London came into view, jammed with repetitive rows of small houses, tiny back gardens, businesses and industries. Eve went to look out of the window. A surplus of turrets and chimneys, over-intricate rooftops, obliterated the leaden sky. As the train pulled into Euston station people of different nationalities were moving in all directions, all speaking different languages. Thinking her lungs would burst, Eve longed for the green fields of home.

The basement flat that Martin and Terry had vacated was small and dark. Jack had managed to swap their double bed for two single ones. Eve's was against the wall, Clare's under the window. In the kitchen they ate a supper of ham salad and pineapple rings from a tin, all previously prepared by Clare. While they ate, Clare told Eve about the district, mentioning places of interest, like Portobello Road and the flea market, with a certain importance.

'You'll love it here. There's so much to do,' she said. But Eve wasn't so sure. Her first sight of the multitudinous grey houses, with their tiny back gardens, and the tall, red-brick terraced houses jammed together made her realise that London would take some getting used to.

'What's the job you've got me like?' she asked.

'Hard work, but you'll manage.' Clare's expression was dismissive. 'I've got complimentary tickets for *Giselle* in the Royal Festival Hall and there'll be a season of opera coming up soon which I'll be expected to attend.'

'I'm not crazy about opera.' Eve sounded miserable.

'It tends to grow on you. I could even be lucky enough to get tickets for the theatre too.'

'Where will you get them all from?'

'When I start at the Academy,' Clare said importantly. Eve could imagine the intensity with which Clare cultivated the friends who pursued a career in music and shared the same interests as she did. Suddenly she was doubtful that this world into which Clare was about to plunge so wholeheartedly would provide her with the same stimulus.

They talked well into the night, Eve relaying all the local news.

'Pauline only has another month to go before she has the baby,' she told Clare.

'It must be awful for her in this heat.'

'Madge is clucking around her like an old mother

hen, but she won't be able to work for much longer.'

'At Martin's wedding I was wishing it was Pauline he was getting married to, not Terry. I'd have had the sister I always wanted.'

'Terry not friendly?'

'With Martin in Belfast she doesn't feel she has to keep in touch with us. Whereas if Pauline were here we'd have a laugh.'

'She'd have us dancing at the Hammersmith Palais. She loved dancing,' Eve said.

'Leaving school early makes you much more grown-up, I always think,' Clare said.

'I suppose.'

After her first night of troubled sleep, Eve awoke to a faint light coming through the shutters. She got out of bed in the dark and bumped into a chest of drawers before she found the door. There was a note from Clare to say she was gone shopping and would return at midday. Eve washed and dressed and examined every detail of the flat before preparing a breakfast of tea and toast.

The next day was Sunday. In the afternoon they went to Hyde Park. Newspaper sellers lined the paths outside the gates, shouting cheerily to potential customers. London sweltered in its late August heat as they stood listening to one of the speakers at Speaker's Corner, a man who seemed unconscious of his tatty appearance, but was driven with vitality at his own political pronouncements. They walked slowly among the trees and along the pathways of the green parkland that surrounded the curving stretch of shimmering lake known as the Serpentine.

At the pavilion they drank iced lemonade, their tongues lingering on the ice to cool themselves. Clare pointed in the direction of the Tower of London and London Bridge, squinting in the golden brightness of the afternoon sun.

'There's so much to see. Madame Tussaud's, the wax museum—'

'Any nice fellows on the horizon?' Eve asked.

'Is that all you can think of?' Clare looked disgusted.

'Yes,' Eve said.

They roared.

'There'll be some dishy blokes at the Academy,' Clare mused.

'What about Henry?' Eve asked. 'Aren't you going to keep yourself for him?'

'Henry is history,' Clare said flatly.

'Don't you fancy him any more?'

'Not really. He's seeing Martha Dunne now, I hear.'

'Mummy heard that his parents are thinking of sending him abroad to study co-operative farming or something.'

'But he wants to be a doctor,' Clare protested.

'I don't think they can afford the university fees,' Eve said.

'They should sell their farm, if it's that bad,' Clare said.

'Maybe they're afraid he'll get stuck with horseface Martha.' Clare's infectious laughter caught Eve unawares and she began to chuckle.

'He really fancied you, and you treated him rotten,' Eve told her.

'No, I didn't. Well nothing more than he deserved,' Clare said.

'Stop pretending.'

'All right,' Clare admitted. 'I got sick of all that groping and fumbling. He hadn't a clue, you know. I want a man who knows what he's doing. Especially if I don't.'

They laughed.

'Anyway, how are your folks?'

'Strange,' Eve said. 'Getting stranger. Mummy makes me nervous and Daddy seems to have let the business slide.' Sitting with her legs tucked under her, her face sheened with dampness, she went quiet.

'Have you seen David Furlong?' Clare asked.

'In the distance,' Eve said. 'I blew my chances with him – not sophisticated enough.'

Clare touched her hand. 'You'll learn here, don't fret.'

'I feel a bit homesick.' Eve said it with surprise.

'I did too at first,' Clare said. 'Suddenly one day I thought to myself, What's there to miss, for Christ's sake?'

'To tell you the truth, Clare, I don't think I should have left them to cope on their own. What do you think?' Since childhood Eve had done what was expected of her, which had rendered her almost incapable of thinking for herself.

'A break from them won't do you any harm. Even if I hadn't won the scholarship I'd have had to get away from my family.'

For the first time since Sarah's death Eve talked about her father and mother and the disparity that existed between them, about her detachment from them all, except her grandfather, and the guilt she felt because of it. Clare was a suitable recipient for the confidences. Eve finished by saying, 'I'll never get over Sarah's death, you know.'

'You will in time.'

'That would be disloyal to Sarah.'

Eve looked so sad that Clare wanted to hug her. 'No,

it wouldn't. Sarah wouldn't want you to be miserable.'

'Sister Mildred wrote to me. She said she was sure that Sarah was happy in heaven. That our spiritual faith will prevail. As far as I'm concerned it's a load of rubbish.'

'What?' Clare exclaimed. 'Have you lost your faith?'

'Never had much of it in the first place.'

'And Sister Mildred thought you were going to be a nun.'

'Oh, I tried to believe all that mumbo-jumbo they drilled into us. I really did. But I was never convinced. Still, I'd like to think that Sarah's happy, wherever she is.'

'I'm sure she is. She was always a happy little soul. We should be happy for her.'

'I know. But to you, Clare, life is like a fairy-tale. You live in a fantasy world. Some day you'll be disillusioned.'

'I won't,' Clare protested. 'Because I intend to realise all my dreams.'

'See what I mean?' Eve laughed.

Vaguely, in reaching out to Clare for comfort, Eve felt conscious of a shift in their relationship. Clare, lively and passionate, was desperate to experience life all in one go. Eve was content to take things more slowly and question everything.

Sitting there in the sunshine, shaded by trees, they looked at one another. Clare's newly acquired knowledge of London and the resourceful way in which she pursued her own interests gave Eve the strength she needed to carry on. They were together again, comfortable in one another's presence, and safe enough to be daring.

'Let's go window shopping. You won't believe your

eyes when you see the shops. Come on.' Clare's
enthusiasm made Eve laugh.

They stood up to go, never as close again as they
were at that moment. Oxford Street was crowded.
Several times they lost sight of one another in the busy
streets, then Eve would spot the splash of Clare's yellow
dress, her confident stride, and call to her, 'Hey, look at
this. Look!'

Clare would come and stare with surprised pleasure
in the enormous shop windows, at a display of crystal
or a row of porcelain dolls.

Sometimes, when she had an evening off, Clare went
to visit Jack. She would tell him stories about the
customers she served at the Savoy Hotel. He talked
mostly about how things could have been if he had
managed better, if the drink hadn't taken hold and
scalded the heart out of him. Tears would come into
his eyes as he reminisced and he would brush them
away with his shirt sleeve.

'I'm not getting any younger,' he said one evening.
'Not much use to anybody now. That divil Martin taking
himself off to Belfast has done me no good at all. Left
me high and dry.'

'You should go home, Daddy,' Clare said. 'London is
no place for you.'

'And face herself, is it? She'd tear strips off me. I
have me pride, I hope you know.'

'Mother would welcome you with open arms. She's
been waiting for you to go back ever since you left.'

'What makes you so sure?' Jack said, in surprise.

'I know my own mother. She's lonely and she misses
you.'

'Be God. That's a good one.' Jack shook his head in
disbelief.

* * *

Clare walked down the corridor, listening to the procession of sounds from the studios she passed. A violin being tuned, voices harmonising, piano chords being struck over and over again, the sounds merging into a distorted clashing noise. A young man with a guitar slung over his shoulder showed her Professor Vittorio Fellini's studio.

Inside it, she could hear talking, a deep, throaty male voice, and the quieter tones of a younger one. Clare waited a few minutes, then knocked on the door. Footsteps crossed the room, the door opened, and she was looking into the face of her tutor, Professor Vittorio Fellini, a tall, elegant man, with olive skin, dark eyes and a disciplined mouth. His black hair hung loose around his narrow face.

'You're a little early,' he said, stepping back to let her pass. 'We're just finishing. Come in.'

Clare stood uncertain, inside the door.

'This is Joshua. He's also a new pupil.'

'Hello.' Joshua, a skinny young man, stood holding his violin with his fingers placed over the strings, ready to play.

'If you would like to sit over there you can listen for a few minutes.' Professor Vittorio gestured with his hands to the window seat.

As she sat down Clare could feel her heart thumping with nervousness. Joshua raised his bow. Professor Vittorio sat at the piano, his back taut and muscular. He struck a chord and the bow slid over the strings in a flurry of violent notes, see-sawed crazily to the accompaniment of the piano, finally soaring to a climax with Joshua raising his bow and bowing his head.

'Bravo,' the professor said. 'We'll put you in the first violins this term. Our poor little orchestra needs fresh talent.'

'Thank you.' Joshua packed his bow and violin in their case and went towards the door, waving goodbye to Clare.

'Now we'll begin,' the professor said, shutting the door and returning to the piano without wasting any time. 'I'd like to hear you play something before we talk.'

'Yes, Professor.'

'Call me Vittorio. Everyone does.'

Clare could feel herself tremble. Vittorio came to stand beside her. His athlete's body made him seem out of place next to the piano.

'Don't be nervous. I'm not a schoolmaster. I won't bite you.' He smiled at her.

Clare shook her head. 'I'm not nervous. Honest.'

'Here, try this Bach fugue in A minor from book one. You should know it.'

Vittorio set up the music in front of her. As she struck the first note she put her foot hard on the loud pedal, easing it gradually as the piece became more familiar to her. When she finished and turned to him, tension had made her face blotchy.

Vittorio waited for the sound of the music to die into silence before he spoke. 'You have the touch, the sureness of note,' he said.

'Well, I got through it.' Clare looked delighted.

'You did better than that. It was good. I'm impressed with the rapidity of your sight-reading and the dexterity of your hands also impresses me.'

Clare clasped them together with delight. 'Sister Aquinas was a stickler for the hands,' she said.

'Perhaps. But you held on to that pedal for far too long.'

'Oh, that ruddy pedal. I forget all about it when I'm nervous.'

'Try again. This time without the pedal,' Vittorio instructed.

Clare turned back to the keyboard and stared at the music. Tiny beads of perspiration dotted her brow as she tucked her feet beneath the piano stool and began again. Without the blur of the pedal her mistakes were more obvious. But her earnestness and desperation to impress him carried her through.

'Good. We have plenty to work on,' Vittorio said, writing in a notebook. 'You are untutored in the skills of piano decorum.' He came to stand beside her and ran his finger across her back. 'You sit with your back stiff and your arms rigid, no expression of the music in your body.'

'Oh.'

'Tell me,' he continued, 'what do you know about piano literature?'

'What?' Clare stared at him.

'Composition, orchestra, symphonies.'

'Not much.'

'How can you play so well and be so ignorant at the same time? Have you any concept of what is involved in becoming a concert pianist?' By now Vittorio was pacing up and down, his face flushed, his eyes fiery. 'You have a great deal to accomplish pianistically, but there's something there. It is our responsibility, here at the Academy, to develop it.' As he spoke his hands were gesticulating in a language of their own, expressing his ideas and passions where words were inadequate. 'Are you prepared for the hard work?' He looked keenly at her.

'I'll do anything.' Clare's voice was timid.

'Don't worry,' Vittorio said. 'It's not all your fault. It's that backward country you come from.' He was shaking his head, as if in disbelief.

'I'm willing to learn.' Clare looked miserable.

'The quality of your musicianship compensates for your lack of knowledge and, after all,' he smiled, 'you are here to learn. I expect to see a great improvement over the coming months.'

From that moment on Clare took each hurdle headlong with a force of spirit that he admired. She never grumbled or complained about the preparation he gave her, or the repetition of practice that he insisted upon. Her own lack of fear and the forceful way in which she attacked her weaknesses impressed him. Sometimes an hour went by before she got to the end of the opening bars of an étude or a prelude. The knock on the door would remind them both that her time was up and he would say, with regret, that they had not got as far as he would have liked. Sometimes before she left he would play a piece for her to let her hear the way he wanted it learned for the next session. As she listened, she knew it would take her weeks to master it to his satisfaction.

'The marks of expression are not necessarily those of the composer. Fingering, phrasing or pedal marks are given only for guidance and are not comprehensive or obligatory.'

'But Sister Aquinas said I must stick rigidly—'

'It's time to forget about Sister Aquinas,' Vittorio said, amused.

Occasionally he played something by Debussy, his favourite composer, demonstrating his musical mystery and the incredible beauty of his sounds and perceptions.

'Beethoven is probably the greatest composer who ever lived,' he told her, 'but Debussy's depth and spirituality often escape the performer. Be careful with him.'

Clare practised by day, worked in the Savoy at night, and was so exhausted when she got back to her flat that she often went straight to bed, too tired to eat any supper. A couple of times she fell asleep when she got home from the Academy and missed work altogether. This meant that she had less money to live on for that week. Often she was so short of money that she had to walk everywhere. She would remember it afterwards as a time of great endurance and a change in the routine of learning. Knowledge was given fast and she never had enough time for preparation for her next lesson.

'Trills have many meanings,' Vittorio explained to her. 'They are not merely adornments to a work, but have expressive purpose. Some are fast, some are slow, some loud or soft.'

He would position her at the piano, advising her that her arms should be like snakes and her wrists loose to keep the flow of movement and to ensure fluid, effortless playing. She took in everything he told her. He taught her the value of virtuosity, and the meaning of music and its interpretation.

'Put your personality into it,' he emphasised. 'You're a determined young woman and a passionate one.'

Clare was astonished. 'How do you know?'

'I see the fire in your eyes. Now try again. Head up, shoulders back.'

On their day off, at the gates of Buckingham Palace with Eve, Clare watched the marching soldiers, sunlight flashing off their boots, heads weighted down under the tall black busbies. Their disciplined movements reminded Clare of her routine at the Academy. It was always the same: scales first, then the Rachmaninoff concerto and a brief indulgence in jazz before finishing, if the lesson had gone well and Vittorio was pleased with her. She was still raw, still unable to identify the different composers, except perhaps Schubert and Chopin, her favourites. Her professor controlled the notes that flowed from her fingers, teaching her the passionate pulse of the first phrase, the subtle changes in emphasis and meaning when a phrase is repeated.

'Make the music talk,' he would say.

Relating all this to Eve, Clare summed up the lessons in one phrase. 'I love them.'

What she purposely omitted to say was that the force of Vittorio's presence stirred in her in that small dark room. There was nothing she wouldn't do to extract a smile of approval from him.

Chapter Ten

It was a wet afternoon in September. In the artificial light the flat looked shabbier than ever and the mirror into which Eve was looking had a web of cracks in the left-hand corner that distorted her face. 'I look grotesque,' she said to Clare.

Clare looked into that part of the mirror with her. 'You're falling apart.' She laughed. 'Serious, though, you need taking out of yourself,' she diagnosed. 'I have a date tonight. Will you come along?'

'I don't like playing gooseberry.'

'It's only Gaston. He won't mind.'

'No, thanks.'

'Tell you what. We'll have a dinner party. Invite a couple of blokes from the Academy. Let's see. Chris is nice. You'd like him. He has a smashing sports car.'

'You're the one who wants a boyfriend with a sports car.'

'Yes, but Chris is more your type.'

'Still carrying a torch for Henry, I suspect,' Eve said, with a smile.

Clare ignored that remark. 'We haven't enough plates or glasses,' she said.

'We'll go to Portobello Road and get some,' Eve said.

'With what?'

'Grandpa sent me some money. This place could do

with a bit of improving.' Eve looked around. 'There's nothing homely about it.'

The stalls along Portobello Road were laden with oddments of Delft and china, gold, silver and brass; lampshades, rugs, ornaments and kitchen utensils.

'Like to buy something?' called a heavy-set woman, wrapped in an old fur coat, a red hat covering her unruly black hair.

They bought white china cups and saucers with gold rims, a small jug and sugar bowl to match, an assortment of glasses, soup bowls, dinner plates, dessert dishes and a big china teapot.

Exhilarated by their purchases and thinking about what they would serve for the party they marched up the road. All around them traders tended stalls, calling out their bargains into the cold air. Laughter rang out, vendors shouted obscenities to one another as vans, loaded with treasures, pulled up to stalls to deliver. A fat man in a duffel coat stood behind the fruit and vegetable stall on the corner. 'Ripe oranges, ripe bananas, ripe ladies. What can I get you?' he said to them as they stood inspecting the array of fat oranges wrapped in blue tissue paper, melons, pears, grapes, figs, dates and nuts.

'A bunch of grapes, please. Half-dozen oranges, and a few bananas,' Eve said.

'What about a couple of melons?' the man said, holding up a melon suggestively in each hand.

'And some apples,' Clare added. 'And we'll need carrots, onions, a twist of herbs.'

Eve counted out her change as the man began filling bags, weighing them, marking the price on each. Finally they bought a large chicken in the butcher's and, heaving their shopping to the bus stop, planned their menu while waiting in the shelter.

In the bus they were already rolling out the pastry, filling it with thinly cut apples, coated in sugar. All the next day they worked, cleaning, polishing, cooking. Eventually when everything was overcooked and the Bee Gees had sung 'I Gotta Get a Message To You' several times on the record player, Chris Winthrop's red Lotus pulled up outside. Chris, tall, aristocratic, with wavy hair tied back in a ponytail, stepped out brandishing a saxophone, followed by his friend, Gaston d'Orléans.

'Lovely to see you,' Chris said, running down the steps and reaching out to grasp Clare's hand. 'Where's your friend Eve?'

'Eve, meet Christopher.'

Eve came forward. 'How do you do, Christopher?' She extended her hand.

Chris put it to his lips. 'Chris to my friends,' he said, looking down his arrogant nose at her. 'Delighted to meet you at last,' he said. 'You're lovelier than I ever dreamed.'

'Thank you.' Eve withdrew her hand gently.

'A foretaste,' he whispered in her ear.

Gaston d'Orléans, a delicate, dark-skinned man in a white shirt and blue Levi's, said, '*Enchanté*,' and walked on ahead.

'What a gorgeous creature,' Chris said, his eyes on Eve as he seated himself in front of the gas fire and tucked his burgundy cravat into his cream silk shirt.

The room was dim, with only the glow from a red lavalamp in the corner and the candlelight on the table.

'Charming,' he continued, looking around. 'Fetch in the beer before you sit down, Gaston.' Taking his car keys from his pocket he threw them into Gaston's lap.

'The others will be along later,' he said, turning to Clare.

'What others?' Clare asked.

'A few friends. Old school-mates. Nice chaps. Good for a lark.'

'There won't be enough food,' Clare protested.

'It's booze they're after and I've brought plenty.' Chris sat back and stretched out his leather-clad legs in front of him. Gaston returned with a crate of beer and deposited it in a corner.

'Care for a cigarette, anyone?' Chris snapped open his gold case and waved it around. Gaston tossed him a bottle of beer.

'I'll get you a glass,' Eve said, coming in from the kitchen.

'No need.' Chris opened the bottle with gleaming white teeth, then, lying back, put it to his lips.

Eve and Clare excused themselves and went to the kitchen to put helpings of casserole on plates.

'Delicious.' Gaston declared, clearing his plate.

Chris opened another bottle of beer.

Around midnight Chris's friends arrived. An assortment of loud-voiced girls, clutching stringy-haired men. Among them was Sue Hope, a large sloppy American girl. Over her tight blouse she wore a rabbit-skin fur coat and her stockings hung loose around her ankles. Her wispy blonde hair kept falling into her eyes. In spite of her appearance she seemed confident in her powers of sexual attraction and as soon as she had removed her coat she wasted no time in telling Eve that her father's chauffeur was crazy with lust for her.

'He drives me to the Academy when I'm running late,' she explained.

'Are you a student there too?' Clare asked, liking her instantly.

'I'm training to be an opera singer. Daddy says with a chest like mine I have a great future in front of me.' She poked Eve in the ribs and they roared. 'I'm only here for a short while,' she said confidently. 'I might as well enjoy myself.'

When Eve said that there wasn't really enough room for everyone Sue Hope suggested opening the back door. 'We do most of our entertaining in our back yard at home in the States.'

'Ours is a bit smaller, I'd imagine,' Eve said apologetically, opening the door.

As soon as she did so some of the guests wandered out into the yard.

Chris began to play his saxophone and Gaston lurched towards Clare. 'Let's dance, pussycat,' he said, rubbing his body rhythmically against hers, assuming that he was giving her as much pleasure as he was giving himself. Everything about him was nauseous, Clare decided, from his smug smile to his gyrating hips. She pushed him away. He reeled back against the wall, his legs buckling.

'Bitch,' he said to Sue, who retrieved him and kept him vertical by dancing with him.

Soon people began to leave. Others arrived and Mrs Cartwright, the landlady, who had come down to complain about the noise, was getting tipsy. Eve made coffee and moved around serving it, chatting to everyone. But as the talk and laughter grew she found herself withdrawing to watch Chris Winthrop. He seemed more startling, more vital each time she looked at him. For a moment she dwelt on a fantasy of him making love to her.

'Dance?' he asked, catching her eye.

'Yes.'

He crossed the room in two strides and was beside her, taking her in his arms. She lowered her eyes to hide her fascination with him. As they danced, he held her close. She felt instinctively drawn to him and vulnerable because of it.

Gaston announced, 'We're going home,' interrupting them by standing before them, rocking backwards and forwards on his feet.

'Not already.' Sue pouted. 'We only just got here.'

'Let's make more coffee,' Clare said.

Eve and Chris followed her into the kitchen where dirty plates and glasses were strewn everywhere.

'I wish they'd all go,' Clare said, putting the kettle on.

'As soon as I have Gaston sobered up, I'll take him off,' Chris said. 'Then the rest of them will leave.'

'He's fallen asleep,' Sue said.

'Don't worry. I'll soon wake him.' Chris went back to the sitting room.

When he had Gaston safely settled in the Lotus, Chris returned and took Eve aside. 'I'd like to see you again,' he said.

'I'd like to see you too.' She smiled at him.

'I'll phone you.'

'We don't have a phone.'

'I'll—'

'Chris. Gaston's trying to get out of the car.'

'Be in touch,' Chris said, and left, taking the basement steps two at a time.

During the lunch hour Eve ran around the restaurant with plates balanced in the crook of her arm, sweat trickling down her back. She was too busy serving large businessmen and their sophisticated women, with bouffant hair and long, painted nails, to take any notice of it. When the lunches were over she served afternoon tea, tall glasses of milk, endless pots of coffee, cakes and baskets of fruit. She and Clare and the other waitresses passed each other regularly, gauging the distance between them expertly, spilling nothing.

When only a few tables were left they slowed down. Clare propped herself on a high stool in a corner of the kitchen, lit a cigarette and said, 'It's getting quiet. I'll be able to nip off to practise soon.'

'It's going to rain.' Eve was gazing up at the sky from a chink of window.

'I don't mind a drop of rain. It's cooling.' Clare blew smoke into the air and watched the gathering clouds. 'It might hold off.'

Before she left Eve put on red lipstick, tracing the outline of her lips with it, and pursing them. She picked up her bag and walked out, moving fast.

'Got a date?' Clive, the head waiter, called out to her as she passed.

'I wish,' Eve responded, and strode off through the revolving doors.

The air was cooler outside, the lights coming on slowly over the city. Eve walked quickly. As she left the tube, dusk fell like a shroud. Her arms and legs were aching after the sweltering day. She was still wearing her uniform, with the skirt that was too tight, and the sleeves rolled up, walking without thinking, when out of the corner of her eye she saw Chris. He was standing near his car, tall, hair almost to his shoulders. She looked away, immediately felt the compulsion to look back and gave a slight nod of recognition as she drew near. He crossed the road to meet her. 'Hello.' He tilted his head, letting his hair fall sideways.

'Hi. What are you doing here?' Eve asked.

'Waiting for you. Heat got to you?'

Eve nodded. 'It's too hot.'

'Beautiful,' Chris said slowly, the word weighted in his mouth, his eyes on her body.

'Yes,' Eve said. 'If you don't have to work in it.'

He smiled. He was towering above her, his height making him seem awkward. 'Thought I'd call and see if you'd like to go for a drive?'

'Now?'

Chris shrugged. 'Why not?'

'Do you drive fast?'

'I do.'

'I like fast cars.' Eve looked at it admiringly.

'Good.' Chris straightened up. 'Where would you like to go?'

'I don't care. As long as you go fast,' Eve said. 'I'll have to change first, though,' she added, looking down at her uniform.

'You look very fetching, if I may say so,' Chris said. Eve saw, by the look of restrained lust in his eyes, that he knew women.

'I need to have a shower and change. I'm tired. I don't sleep very well.'

'Why not?' The whites of Chris's eyes gleamed in the dark. 'No one to keep you company?'

'No.' Eve gave an embarrassed laugh.

Chris looked away, as if storing up this valuable piece of information, then smiled suddenly. 'Hard to believe,' he said, shaking his head.

Eve sensed tension in his voice. 'You? What are you doing out all by yourself?'

'I'm free as a bird. The way I like it,' he said.

A warm breeze blew her hair over her face. He

reached out and flicked it back with his finger. 'When I can't sleep I have a drink to relax me. That's what you need after a hard day's work. Shall I get a bottle from the off-licence? Would you like some?'

'Yes, I would.'

'You go on in, I won't be long.'

He drove off and Eve went into the dark, lifeless flat. She turned on the lights, walked into the kitchen, instinctively filled the kettle. Chris returned in a few minutes with a bottle of Chardonnay.

'This'll cool you down,' he said. 'Got any ice?'

Eve took ice cubes from the freezer section of the fridge and put them in a jug.

'How's work?' Chris asked.

'Boring at times, especially if the customers stay too long after a meal. At least I didn't have to work late tonight.'

'I was counting on that.'

'How did you know?'

'Guessed.'

He opened the bottle and poured the wine into glasses. From the pocket of his jeans he took out a packet of cigarettes and, shaking one loose, offered it to her.

'No thanks. I don't smoke.'

He lit it and went out to the back yard with his glass of wine. 'There's a lovely moon,' he called back to her.

She followed. They stood side by side, sipping their drinks. She watched his glance moving from her to the horizon, to the silver moon and back again, observing her, his patient attention so focused that she felt she was being absorbed into a quietness thick with a sense of danger and a waiting grief. Time belonged to the present. He touched her arm. She looked down and saw that her skin had taken on an unnatural sheen in the white light.

'Beautiful,' he said again.

Intoxicated by the night, the light of the moon, his touch, the wine, Eve didn't move or speak, afraid of breaking the delicious spell. She knew that if she wanted him she was going to have to reach out for him, put her arms around his neck, pull him towards her and kiss his lips. She could do none of those things. Instead, she waited and watched, poised for the right moment. When it came, it took her unawares. As he reached to put his glass on the window-sill behind her, his arms went round her waist, his hands pressed her stomach against his. Suddenly her fingers were in his hair, loving the length of it. His hands slid down her thigh, smooth, knowing, touching her as if he had already possessed her.

Abruptly he stopped kissing her, and moving back, his hands still on her waist, he searched her face, his own questioning.

She was so taken aback with the asking in his eyes that she looked away, unable to meet his gaze, yet knowing that if she didn't respond she might never see him again – unthinkable.

Then he said, 'What about that drive then? Shall we do it tomorrow or another day? Wouldn't you prefer that?'

Guilty, she sprang back. 'Yes. That'd be great,' she said, forcing herself to move briskly indoors, away from his penetrating gaze.

She went to the fridge, Chris following, and took out the wine. She refilled her glass and asked, 'Want some?' then gulped hers to ease the restricted feeling in her throat.

Chris looked at his watch. 'No, thanks. You should rest. I'll see you tomorrow.'

She wanted to call him back, tell him how good life felt suddenly, but instead she went into the bedroom, yanked the curtains shut and pulled off her clothes, which suddenly felt too heavy.

In the bath she closed her eyes conjuring him up before her, the way his hands had felt on her skin, the taste of his lips. She lay there hoping to hear his footstep in the hall. But he didn't return.

As they drove towards the river with the windows down, the air cool on Eve's cheeks, Chris pulled her close to him. 'That's better,' he said. 'Have you been thinking about me?'

'I've thought of nothing else.'

They laughed.

Once out of the traffic the Lotus raced along tree-lined roads, dappled by a weak September sun.

'I thought you might get cold feet. That sort of thing.'

The car swerved round a tight corner and Eve lurched against him, laughing, as it swung dangerously.

''Course not.'

'That's my girl.' He grinned, taking the bends at breathtaking speed.

The trees and woods sped past, giving way to open countryside.

'What time do you have to be back?'

'I'm not working tonight.'

'Great.' Chris took one of Eve's hands in his and kissed her fingers, his other hand steering. 'Some friends of mine are having a party. Trouble is it's a bit of a distance away. Could you stay overnight? Whoops.' He swerved out of the way of an approaching car. 'Damned fool,' he shouted, blowing his horn and increasing his speed.

When they arrived the party was in full swing. Cars were parked in country lanes approaching an enormous house set back from the road. Gaston d'Orléans was waiting to introduce them to everyone. Chris, impatient, pulled Eve into the rowdy revellers.

Eve developed a liking for Chris's lifestyle and his friends. She liked the taste of the champagne with which he plied her and began to experiment with other kinds of drink. Often she spent whole nights at parties, discovering that drink sharpened her senses and made her a more interesting person to Chris and his frivolous friends. Also it made Chris's advances more acceptable. Sober, her reaction to his passionate kisses was a sudden image of Sister Mildred and her warnings about the sins of the flesh. With a few drinks her inhibitions dissolved and the gnawing corrosive homesickness that pervaded her every thought dissipated, giving way to fun and excitement. Eve was enjoying herself and, with her new gaiety, she was discovering that everyone wanted to be her friend.

Dorothy Freeman, reading her daughter's letters, attributed Eve's manic *joie de vivre* to her new-found freedom. Anxiously she wrote back to her daughter advising her to calm down, that the world was more dangerous than she could ever imagine, and urged her to come home for Christmas.

Eve ignored her mother's letters and continued to go to parties with Chris, to dance and flirt with his friends. She began to drink at work, hiding a bottle of wine in the linen cupboard behind the tablecloths and sipping slowly from it whenever there were a few quiet moments for her to take a break. She slept in late each morning and relished her time alone, because she always felt tired.

Chris's persistence began to annoy her and when he called, expecting her to be ready to go places with him, she grew irritated. Her excuses made him more demanding and she found herself squirming away from his attentions, preferring to drink.

'You can't fight me off much longer,' he said to her one evening when, in a flash of temper, she had pushed him away, shouting at him to keep his hands off her. 'You prick-teasing little bitch.' His voice was low and sullen.

He walked out in a temper, his hands raised against her in protest.

'Let's go shopping,' Clare said, when she heard what had happened. 'Buy some new clothes.'

'What with?' Eve asked.

'With our next week's wages, dope. I'll get an advance. It'll cheer us up.'

They went to Knightsbridge and acted like ladies, buying mini-dresses, violet for Eve, peach for Clare. Afterwards they drank coffee in Harrod's coffee bar and ate tiny cakes as they listened to elegant ladies in fur coats discussing Janet Reger underwear and the marvellous new-style furniture in Habitat.

'Want a smoke?' Clare rolled a cigarette and put it to her lips.

Eve shook her head. 'Time you stopped smoking.'

'It's sophisticated.'

'There's nothing sophisticated about messing up the table with bits of dung.'

'I'm going. I've got a lesson at four o'clock.' Clare stood up.

'I'm not due at work until seven.' Eve tilted back in her chair.

'See you later, then.' Clare stubbed out her cigarette in the ashtray and left.

The days went by. Eve slept late and walked through Hyde Park on her afternoons off, always looking for a sight of Chris. Sometimes she went to Harrod's and drank coffee in the sandwich bar, hoping for a glimpse of him. Once she thought she saw him from the back, tall and straight, walking quickly, wearing his navy casual jacket. She ran after him, calling his name, but the man who turned his puzzled face to her was so different that she got a shock. Eve went in late for work and took a couple of days off, sleeping and gazing out of the window into their tiny walled garden. Several weeks went by. Reluctant to admit to herself that she missed Chris and his friends, she busied herself during the day with cleaning the flat, washing down walls, rearranging clothes neatly in cupboards and by working hard at night.

'Anything exciting happening?' Clare asked her, as they lolled in bed one morning.

'Usual sore feet,' Eve said.

'We'll get corns with all the standing in those pointy shoes,' Clare said.

'We'll get a pair of working brogues with next week's wages.'

'We've spent that.'

'Maybe someone'll give us a big tip. They're so bloody rich, some of them.'

'It isn't fair. Would it ever occur to them what kind of lives we lead?' Clare mused.

'Perhaps there's the occasional caring person out there somewhere. Dear Lord, please send him to the Savoy for dinner so we can meet him.'

'Them. One each,' Clare corrected.

'Oh, yes. Them. Thank you, Lord. Amen.'

'Heard from Chris?' Clare asked casually.

'No. I wish he'd get in touch.'

They talked for ages about him, Eve analysing his behaviour, whether he was as interested in her as he seemed to be, or whether he just wanted to get her into bed. 'He's sexy,' she said.

'There's too much of a difference between you,' Clare said.

'In what way?'

'Your backgrounds. He's English, upper class, rich, spoilt and, as far as he's concerned, you're a waitress.'

'Temporarily,' Eve added.

'He doesn't know that. Anyway, what do you propose to do? You've lost your place at university.'

Eve sighed. 'I didn't want to go. I'd rather do something in the business world. Meanwhile, I'm experiencing life.'

'You certainly are,' Clare agreed.

'Hello. It's only me,' Madge Kinsella called through the letter-box of Pauline's flat.

Pauline forced a friendly smile as she let her in.

'I brought you some fresh eggs and brown bread,' Madge said. 'How are you, love?' Without waiting for a reply, she went into the kitchen.

'Much better, thanks,' Pauline said.

'You look dreadful. Have you been for your check-up?'

'Yes. I'm getting near my time, that's all.'

'That's what I came about.' Madge looked at the drab, cracked walls. 'I brought your wages in case you were stuck for cash.'

'They're not due till Thursday.'

'I know. But you might be short. I was thinking, Pauline, that maybe you need a bit of a break from work. Till the baby's born.'

Pauline looked at her but Madge's eyes didn't meet her gaze.

'You mean you'd rather not have me around. Too much gossip, I suppose.'

'Well . . .' Madge hesitated. 'The rumours are rife.' Her eyes were on Pauline's stomach. 'What's keeping you two from getting married?'

'If I could find . . .' Pauline stopped.

'Your lack of responsibility is embarrassing, to say the least.' Madge fumbled in her bag for her cigarettes.

'What you mean is that you think I'm a disgrace in front of your precious God-fearing customers.'

'I couldn't have put it better myself. Your condition is a cause for concern in more ways than one.'

'"Pregnant" is not a dirty word, Madge. Only to the likes of you.'

Madge was pacing up and down. 'There's another thing, Pauline. While we're on the subject of Seamus, I know he's involved in the Provos.'

'Who told you that?' Pauline's face went white.

'Never mind. Why all the secrecy? You should have told me.'

'What do you care about Seamus?' Pauline blazed. 'You're only worried that it might affect yourself and your business.'

'That's not true. I'm very concerned about you and you know that. Pauline, I came here to help you.' Madge's tone was conciliatory.

Pauline burst into tears.

'Where is Seamus?' Madge went on. 'When are you getting married?'

'I don't know.' Pauline crumpled into a chair, sobbing.

'Well, do it soon. For the sake of the child if nothing else. There's nothing to stop you. Seamus is more than willing. Sure he's mad about you.'

Pauline bawled.

'Dry your eyes,' Madge said, passing her a handkerchief from her bag. 'I'll make you some scrambled eggs on toast and we'll talk when you're feeling better.'

The thought of scrambled eggs made Pauline's stomach turn.

That night she went out in the freezing cold, approaching every man that came in sight, stifling the temptation to stop him and ask if he'd seen Seamus.

'Let's get you home before you die of pneumonia,' a voice said.

Pauline jumped. Martin was standing behind her.

'I'm not going home.' She tried to resist as he caught her and frogmarched her down the street but he was too strong for her and she was afraid of damaging the baby. The flat was pitch black. Once inside the door, he relaxed his hold on her arms.

'You should be in your bed,' he said.

'I'm on my way.' Pauline went into her room and shut the door.

She lay in the darkness, shaking. Later, she heard the twist of the doorknob, and felt Martin's presence in the room.

'What do you want?' she said sourly.

'I brought you a mug of tea.' He put the light on.

She sat up, wrapping the sheet around herself.

'Here. Drink it. It'll do you good.' He handed her the steaming mug.

'Any word of Seamus?'

'No. Nothing yet. But I'm sure I'll hear something soon.' Martin's voice was soft, placatory.

'You're lying.'

'Honest to God. Relax, Pauline, drink up your tea. There's a drop of whiskey in it.'

Pauline sipped the tea. Felt the sweet bite of the whiskey warming her veins.

'Seamus was in a mess, Pauline.'

'He was all I ever wanted. The whole world to me,' Pauline sobbed.

'I know. But I had nothing to do with any of it, honest,' Martin said.

'Who did, then?'

'I don't know. I warned him to watch himself, though. You heard me. He got in with the wrong crowd. Wouldn't listen.'

'I think I'm going to be sick.' Pauline jumped out of bed and went to the lavatory, her hand over her mouth. Trembling, hunched over the toilet bowl she waited for the dry retching to stop. Visions of Martin's sneering smile floated up to her. She stayed there for a long time. Finally, when she opened the door Martin was waiting for her.

'I'm going to sleep now,' she said, stifling an overwhelming compulsion to rush for the hall door and run screaming down the road.

'Good girl. I'll stay on the sofa. Keep an eye.'

He brushed her hand with his. She pushed it away and went to her room. Soon she heard the click of the light switch and later the sound of his heavy even breathing as he slept.

Chapter Eleven

Clare sank into her work in the pursuit of good results – and into the hopeless pursuit of her tall, elegant tutor. She found out the times of his classes and would wait around the cold entrance hall just to catch a glimpse of him hurrying by, leaving herself late for other lectures. When he did see her, he would greet her courteously.

Vittorio's austere, dignified personality attracted Clare, and if he noticed her presence a little too often in the vicinity of his rooms he never mentioned it. During class when their eyes met he gave no sign of recognising the passion that must have been obvious in hers. There must have been a reason why he couldn't reciprocate at present. Perhaps he was temporarily involved elsewhere, which he would tell her about in time. He was bound to be a Catholic too, and that would undoubtedly make him feel honour-bound to whatever situation he was in at present. She would bide her time and wait.

Clare's evasiveness with the other students made her seem standoffish. Because of her infatuation with Vittorio, she excluded herself from the dating groups. They seemed too immersed in some form of sexual conformity of their own, a sort of tribal ritual whereby they all hung around together, preening, petting, group-dating, with no time for individuality in their relationships.

She didn't look forward to her practice as she had when she was at home in her own sitting room in Ireland. In those days she had got everything done to her satisfaction. Now that her goals were higher, there seemed an impossibility about her ambitions. She wanted to be able to play an étude like Vittorio's rather than her own basic one. She wanted her success now, not in ten years' time, and her growing impatience filled her with anxiety. Her music absorbed her, everything else seemed unreal and unimportant. There were hours of elation when she was at her best and Vittorio's praise took her to rapturous heights. At other, more frequent times, she was so overwhelmed by it all that she felt crushed. The music was always in her mind, phrases and passages playing a pattern in her head.

Pauline's head pounded as she looked at the old-fashioned stained glass before confronting the knocker on the barracks' door. While she waited, the wind blew her hair around her face and plastered her skirt to her legs. The nightmare and uncertainty of the last few days had finally made her tap on the door, checking that no one was on the street before she did so. Immediately it was opened by Delia Enright, who stood smiling at her, neat in her wrap-over apron and her hair in a turban.

'Well, hello, Pauline. What can I do for you?' she asked.

'I – I'm sorry to disturb you, Mrs Enright. It's Sergeant Enright I'm looking for.'

'You'd better come in, then.' Delia watched Pauline with suspicion as she ushered her into the front room. 'Wait here, I'll get him,' she said, rushing off.

The room, obviously Sergeant Enright's office, was cold, the gable wall preventing the rays of the sun from entering it. It smelled of lavender polish.

Delia went into the hall and called up the stairs. 'Mick.' She watched Pauline through the door.

The wind rattled the window-pane. Pauline shivered.

'Cool for September,' Delia said.

'Yes.' Pauline didn't know what else to say.

Floorboards creaked overhead. The heavy footsteps on the lino of the stairs made Pauline's cheeks flame with fear. Even if she had wanted to make a run for it, Delia Enright was blocking her path.

Sergeant Enright came into the room, the top buttons of his shirt open, his braces around his hips.

'Is it yourself?' The weariness in his eyes belied his friendly smile. 'How are you keeping?'

'Fine, Sergeant I—'

A crashing sound came from above, followed by a roar.

Pauline jumped and Delia flew up the stairs, cursing her stupid children and their silly arguments.

'Delia'll put a stop to that racket,' Sergeant Enright said, confidentially shutting the door on the background commotion. 'Sit down, there.'

He cleared a space in front of the enormous desk.

'What can I do for you, miss?' he asked, his eyes burning into her, an encouraging smile playing on his lips as he seated himself opposite her.

'It's about Seamus Gilfoyle, Sergeant,' Pauline managed to say.

'What about him?' Sergeant Enright hoisted his braces up on his shoulders and studied her intently.

'He was kidnapped.'

'Kidnapped,' Sergeant Enright repeated slowly, looking at Pauline as if she had suddenly grown horns.

'Yes, Sergeant.'

'What evidence do you have to substantiate this allegation?' he asked.

'I saw it happen with my own eyes, Sergeant.'

'You saw it with your own eyes,' Sergeant Enright echoed, as he took a notebook from his breast pocket.

'They took him away,' Pauline said.

'Who did?'

'Two men in balaclavas. At the station last Friday week.'

'Why didn't you report this incident sooner, Miss Quirk?'

'I was warned to keep quiet, Sergeant.'

Sergeant Enright licked the lead of his pencil. 'You'd better begin at the beginning. You're confusing me terribly,' he said bluntly.

As Pauline's story unfolded Sergeant Enright wrote laboriously in his notebook, stopping to look at her as if she were a raving lunatic or to question her.

'He's gone,' Pauline whispered, swallowing hard.

'He couldn't have disappeared into thin air,' Sergeant Enright said, checking his notes and scribbling again.

'He was kidnapped, I told you.' Pauline's face betrayed her mounting frustration.

'He could be in Belfast, you know,' Sergeant Enright said. 'Or America.' His eyes bored into hers.

'He would never have left me like this. We were to be married.' Pauline started to cry.

'Have you any theories of your own as to who these people in balaclavas might have been or what they might have wanted him for?'

'I think Martin Dolan had something to do with it.' Her voice shook.

'Hold on a minute.' Sergeant Enright sat back in his

chair. 'You're making serious allegations here. Be careful what you're saying, now.'

Pauline's mind cautioned her to be calm, plausible, but the words came out in a confused rush. 'He threatened Seamus a while ago.'

'Threatened him. You witnessed that incident also?'

'Yes, Sergeant.'

'I see, faith.' Sergeant Enright wrote again.

After what seemed to her like ages he closed his notebook and scraped back his chair. 'I'll look into the matter,' he said, standing up, a glimmer of a smile on his lips. 'Meantime, I would caution you to keep your mouth shut, especially where Madge Kinsella is concerned.'

'Sergeant, I'm scared,' Pauline whispered.

'Then go back to your aunt in Ballingarret and stay there until your baby is born. You'll be safe with her.'

At the door he looked up and down the street before he let her out.

Once outside Pauline walked away, her head down. The decision to confide in Sergeant Enright had made her feel better. As she neared her own gate she decided to leave the town immediately. She had done her duty, acted responsibly, and she was scared.

In the light of a lamp she flung clothes into a bag, straightened the crumpled bed, took her radio, some jars from the dressing-table, her shoes out of the wardrobe, and packed them. Picking up the letter she had written to Madge, blaming her sudden departure on her aunt Bea's illness, she read it through, put it in an envelope and licked the flap.

In the bathroom she washed herself, combed her hair and checked her reflection in the mirror. With shaking hands she took her tube of make-up and squeezed a little on to her finger. It wouldn't do to look too pale or conspicuous in any way.

She switched off the bathroom light and, taking her bag and coat, she let herself out, pulling the door gently behind her. How lovely it would be to be going home to the safety of her mother, she thought, as she walked quickly along the street. Her mother had been a gentle woman, always letting her have her own way. A dog barked at her from behind a gate, raging as she passed, his sharp teeth bared. Pauline walked faster. There was no time to lose.

One morning the quiet of the flat drove Eve out to the off-licence in the high street to purchase a bottle of vodka which she sipped from the neck, still hidden in its brown paper bag, as she walked slowly home.

'You've made an early start.' Chris Winthrop was standing at the basement door, arms folded, the arrogant expression she hated on his face. Barefaced she opened the bottle, put it to her lips and tilted it back.

'Don't.' He went to take it from her.

Turning away she took another swig from it, eyeing him brazenly from beneath her eyelashes.

'Hardly ladylike behaviour.' Chris looked disgusted.

'Mind your own business,' Eve snarled.

'Charming.'

'You got me started.' She bowed to him in an insulting way, forcing a smile of acceptance from him.

'You've taken to it like a duck to water.'

'It's in the genes.'

'Give me the bottle.' Chris reached out his hand to take it.

'No!' Eve cried, flinging it against the wall.

A deadly silence followed the explosion of glass. The upstairs window cranked up and Mrs Cartwright poked her head out. 'What's going on down there?' she shouted.

'Just a little accident.' Eve giggled as Chris began to pick up the shards of glass.

'Tone it down, will ye. Trev's on nights.' She banged the window shut.

'That's all I need, nosy cow.' Furious, Eve stormed into the flat, followed by Chris. She could feel the lightness in her head as the alcohol began to have its effect.

'I don't know what's come over you, drinking at this hour of the day. Surely whatever it is can't be all that bad,' Chris said, sitting on the bed beside her.

'How would you know?' Eve folded herself up and rolled away from him.

'I know your parents would be disappointed if they knew,' he said quietly.

'Since when did you care about my parents?' Eve asked.

'I care about you,' he said, leaving the room. He returned with a glass of milk. 'Here, drink this,' he coaxed.

Eve sat up and took the glass from him with a shaky hand. Slowly she sipped the cold, clean milk and let it trickle down her throat.

Chris sat watching her. 'Come on. A little more. I bet you haven't had any sustenance for days.'

She shook her head and took another sip, just to please him.

'Good girl. One more,' he said, holding the glass with her while she drank.

From then on he called regularly, bringing dainty

morsels to whet her appetite: grapes, a wedge of brie from Grossman's deli on the corner, fresh roasted coffee beans, a slab of chocolate. Contrary to what she expected, and given his privileged upbringing, he knew how to cook and cooked well, adding slivers of smoked salmon to scrambled eggs, or a twist of lemon to a salmon steak, maple syrup on wafer-thin pancakes. Eve was surprised at his patience and how kind he was to her. Chris was nice to all the women he met, even women he met briefly and had no interest in seducing. Eve had noticed this trait in him early on and it made her curious.

Another thing she noticed was that he did not lecture her any more, or talk down to her, but held genuine conversations with her, encouraging her to tell him things. He listened carefully, sometimes more than he spoke, never asking ridiculous questions about her past, like some other young men of her acquaintance did. Nor did he indulge in boring monologues about his own.

'You're an intelligent girl, Eve,' he said to her one evening.

'I'm not coping,' she said. 'I haven't really coped since Sarah's death.'

'Yes, you have,' he argued 'Considering what you've been through. You're working things out for yourself.'

They were lying side by side on her cramped bed, Eve on her front with her chin resting on her hands, Chris on his side, facing her. She had been telling him about Sarah, what she had been like as a child, the things they had done together. She went quiet, thinking about her sister.

They both lay still for a long time, Eve finding Chris's presence a comfort, and his lazy willingness to share his time, his knowledge, his food, whatever he had, with her. It helped her regain confidence and an interest in life again. When she was half asleep he reached out and caught her. They helped each other to remove their clothes and he lifted her down on him. She swayed gently, high above his smouldering eyes and smiling mouth. He held her hips and moved the full weight of her body on to him. She kept her thoughts focused on his face to stop the spread of the high flood that coursed through her, threatening to erupt.

Passive, still smiling, he lay still as she bent down over him. Crouching, her breasts grazing his chest, her hands grabbing his arms for balance, she began rocking slowly. Holding tight, gradually speeding up the rhythm, her head under his chin, she pressed her mouth into his chest to dam the flood of her high-pitched scream as she rollercoasted to a climax.

Prostrate, she stayed for a long time without moving, the mingled sweat of their bodies making them slippery, then cold, as the realisation dawned on Chris that it had been the first time for her.

On the last day of September a sudden pain in her stomach gripped Pauline, then another in her back almost took her breath away.

'I think I'm going to have to go to the hospital, Aunt Bea,' she said, rising slowly from her chair.

'You don't mean you've started?' Aunt Bea's hands flew to her throat. 'Mother of Jesus, help us.' She ran to the medicine cupboard for the holy water and sprinkled it liberally over Pauline.

'Don't panic,' Pauline gasped. 'Just get me to the hospital,' she said, with a sudden longing for the attention of an efficient doctor or nurse instead of the blustering Aunt Bea. Before there was time for her aunt to run to the post office in Ballingarret, to phone for a hackney car, Pauline was seized with another pain, stronger than the last.

'I don't think there's time,' she wailed.

Aunt Bea grabbed her and pushed her up the stairs shouting to Mary, the dairy-maid, to put the kettle on to boil and to tear up some sheets.

'Merciful Jesus,' Mary exclaimed, not knowing which to do first.

Pauline lay on her bed, perspiration matting her tousled hair, a startled expression on her face.

'If we'd had any warning,' Aunt Bea said. 'But it's the cut of you to go into labour so quick. You got pregnant without letting us know either.'

A shriek from Pauline rent the air.

'Stop that din! It won't relieve the pain and the neighbours will think 'tis the way we're killing you!' Aunt Bea roared.

Mary came up the stairs heaving the pail of boiling water as Pauline gave a terrifying scream.

'Go for Mrs Mulrooney, quick, before the nosy Cahills three fields away come tearing over to know if we're slaughtering.'

Mary ran out of the room and down the stairs.

Pauline stuffed the sheet in her mouth and contented herself with moaning softly, while Aunt Bea fussed around her, alternately mumbling prayers and cursing the tardiness of Mrs Mulrooney, the local midwife.

'Have you thought of a name for the baby?' Aunt Bea asked to distract Pauline.

'Seamus, if it's a boy. Margaret for a girl. After my mother,' Pauline said. Suddenly she gave a terrifying shriek.

'Oh, sweet infant of Prague!' Aunt Bea howled. 'What's keeping that stupid woman!'

A few minutes later Mrs Mulrooney thundered up the wooden stairs, her long black skirts bunched up around her waist, a Gladstone bag in her hand. 'Take it easy,' she said gently to Pauline. 'A bit more patience and it'll be worth it all.'

'Look, there's the head. The shoulders are stuck,' Aunt Bea called hysterically to Mrs Mulrooney, who was washing her hands.

The midwife was beside Pauline in a flash, drying her hands thoroughly on a towel. 'A bit of manoeuvring is all that's required,' she said soothingly. 'You're doing a grand job. We'll have you right as rain in no time.'

Skilfully she eased the shoulders with deft hands and the baby slithered out. A tiny, blue-eyed scrap.

'A fine sturdy boy,' Mrs Mulrooney said, wrapping him in a warm towel and placing him in Pauline's arms.

'He's beautiful,' Pauline whispered, kissing him on the forehead.

'Let me hold him,' Aunt Bea commanded, taking him from her.

From that moment Aunt Bea was so besotted with the baby that although she pretended he was an inconvenience she bustled around making sure that Pauline was properly nourished to take care of him.

For the first few days Pauline was terrified. Looking at her new baby she would break out in a sweat at the thought of rearing him on her own. Then, slowly, it dawned on her what she should do. She would go to Belfast and search for Seamus. She began to make plans, hiding her suitcase out in the barn and adding what little money she was given in gifts for the child to her meagre savings.

* * *

The weeks were flying by and it was winter before they knew it. The sun shone early each morning but a treacherous wind sent people running to work, anywhere for a few hours' warmth. Eve and Clare stood at the bus stop, stamping their feet and waving their arms to try to keep warm. They were going to Sue Hope's flat for supper and then on to a piano recital given by Eileen Joyce in the Royal Albert Hall. The bus was late and when it arrived it was so crowded that they had to fight their way along the aisle in search of a seat. Clare gazed through the smudged, grimy window as the bus started. She didn't want to miss a moment of the recital and she was afraid that Sue would make them late for the opening piece.

Sue Hope's family were rich property owners, but drink had diluted her mother's powers of awareness, rendering her silent and unresponsive. It was her father on whom she depended. He was bear-like in stature, and bawled his comments in his deep drawl around his palatial Buckinghamshire home.

'That's my girl,' he roared in Sue's direction, the first time she had brought Eve and Clare home. 'At least she will be when she loses that flab and gets some decent clothes.' To Sue he had said, 'I keep telling you to go shopping. Get Turner to drive you, if you're too lazy to damn well walk.'

'Sure, honey-bun,' Sue had simpered, undaunted by his rudeness.

Beaming at him she had nudged Eve and Clare to keep quiet until they could slip away to the privacy of her bedroom and their fantasies about men. Her room was pink and white, with a patchwork quilt and photographs of the Beatles on the walls. She paid them the kind of homage usually reserved for royalty.

She had moved into her new flat the week after Eve and Clare's party and, according to her, spent all her spare time preparing her body for sexual encounters, rolling her thin hair in huge rollers, passing hours in the beauty parlour having her legs waxed, even removing her outsize bra before her date arrived. Eve and Clare suspected that her casual, unpressed appearance was designed to give men the impression that she was easy. Life was one big sexual adventure to Sue, who imagined every male she encountered as a potential predator. 'He's after me,' she'd announce, giggling behind her hand when men passed her on the street. Eve, perplexed by her assertions, tried in vain to read the lustful messages in their eyes.

She took up with Joshua, the violinist, claiming that she liked his lanky body and long hair. 'He's romantic and unconventional,' she declared. Soon she was claiming a full sexual relationship, listing the intimate details of their lovemaking to Clare and Eve, showing off bruises on the most delicate parts of her body, and the evidence of love bites on her flabby breasts, which she bared for their inspection. Although Eve and Clare were shocked at Sue's unconventionality, her lack of inhibition entertained them.

Her shabby top-floor flat was in a block at the end of the King's Road, but was more comfortable and convenient than their basement one. A steep staircase at the end of a dark hall led straight to the upper floors. The whole building smelt of cooking and resounded with quarrels.

The father of the large, impoverished family who lived in the ground-floor flat was a big sulky Irishman, shouting, 'I'll mallavogue yis,' with screams from the children when he put his threat into action, which frightened Eve and Clare.

Sue's flat was spacious. She had decorated it to her own taste: potted plants, wall hangings, rugs and cushions scattered casually around the room to take the eye off the dilapidated three-piece suite. She started to entertain, at first inviting students home for supper, then dinner when her confidence grew. She was at the door before they rang the bell. 'I thought you were never coming,' she said.

'Sorry. The bus was late.'

'I'm frozen.' Clare hugged her while Eve took their coats, hats and scarves, to throw on Sue's big double bed.

'Smells delicious. I'm starving,' Clare said.

'Southern fried chicken, traditional hash browns.'

She settled them in their places. A log fire burned brightly in the grate, casting its flickering light on the cutlery and glass. 'First let's have a drink to celebrate.' She went into the kitchen and returned with a bottle of champagne, which she opened ceremoniously.

'To us,' she said.

'To us,' they said in unison, raising their glasses.

'Such elegance,' Eve said, sipping the creamy froth and forgetting all about the heavy rain and the rush-hour traffic.

They ate the delicious chicken, followed by blueberry pie, and talked about the months Clare and Sue had shared at the Academy, and Sue's boyfriend in Vietnam.

'He proposes in every one of his letters,' Sue boasted.

'Wow,' said Eve.

'I'm not waiting around for him,' Sue assured them.

'Not keen on marriage, then?' Eve asked.

'Not yet.'

'Only if you have to.' Clare laughed and, raising her glass again, proposed a toast to 'having fun'.

They guffawed.

'There's so much to do and see in London,' Sue enthused. 'The talent around the college is wonderful.'

'Weirdos,' Clare said.

'Fanciable ones,' Sue agreed. 'Clever, even, cultured some of them. But not to be taken seriously. Don't you agree, Eve?'

Eve shrugged and lowered her eyes. 'Well, I only know Chris.'

'I know lots of them,' Sue said. 'Safety in numbers.'

'I'll drink to that,' Clare said, raising her glass again.

'The only way to avoid getting hurt is to keep away from them,' Eve agreed.

'Well, blow me down! I thought you were in love with Chris,' Sue protested.

'We're just good friends,' Eve said.

'Let's change this boring subject,' Clare said.

'How are your folks, Eve?' Sue asked. 'Still want you home for Christmas?'

'Yes. I dread it.'

'I'll come with you. Keep them sweet,' Sue offered.

'Would you? Really?'

'Sure. I've always wanted to go to Ireland. What are your parents like anyhow?'

Eve produced a photograph of Dorothy and Ron from her bag. It had been taken in their back garden in front of the trees the summer before Sarah died. Sue studied it. 'You know I bet your father has a mistress.'

Eve, who had never considered either of her parents in a sexual context, was shocked. 'A mistress?'

'He's sexy. Women would find his exotic looks irresistible.'

Eve's concept of a mistress, someone sophisticated and knowing, was out of the question. 'Impossible,' she replied. 'He's become a virtual recluse, and my mother denies the very existence of sex.'

'Shame. Your mother's so elegant,' Sue said. 'With those shapely ankles she must look stunning when she's dressed up.'

It was true that when she wore her expensive dresses Dorothy looked impressive. But with the shock of Sarah's death her face had become ravaged by loneliness and loss.

'Coffee, everyone?' Sue asked.

'Yes, please.'

Clare said, between puffs on her cigarette, 'Are you serious about going to Ireland with Eve, Sue?'

''Course I'm serious. I've always had a hankering for Ireland. It's an extraordinary place, I hear. Anyway,' she continued, 'Andy's not going to surprise me with a visit. He'll be in the thick of things out in 'Nam. That's the worst part, waiting to hear what's going to happen next.'

'It was the same with Sarah. The waiting. Convincing yourself that she was invincible. That it could never happen.' Eve shook her head. 'I'd hate anyone to have to go through that.'

'My poor love.' Sue stood up, went to Eve and put her arms around her.

'Look at the time,' Clare said. 'It's nearly seven o'clock and the recital's due to start in less than an hour. Come on.'

They tidied themselves quickly and went out into the crowds.

Although Sue had treated herself to a new suede jacket and frosted lipstick for her night at the Royal Albert Hall, her efforts to look glamorous failed, but the recital was excellent. It was a sellout. The girls sat enraptured in the top tier of the Victorian hall, transported to a world untainted by the humdrum of everyday anxiety. They all joined in at the end, showing their appreciation with thunderous applause as the final notes died away.

'Come on, kid, it's over.' Sue was nudging Clare, who was so absorbed that she found it difficult to come back down to earth. As she followed the others slowly along the aisle towards the foyer and exit, she felt suddenly bereft.

It was growing late when Clare reached the Academy. Dusk edged the yellow street lamps and crept through the main door as it swung to and fro on its hinges. The Academy was dimly lit and more silent than Clare had ever known it.

'Most of the students have gone home for the weekend,' Vittorio said. 'But we must get some work in before your exams. Now I want you to begin with the Beethoven sonata in G, opus 79, please.'

He stood behind her as she played. Clare felt hemmed in by his solid body and the keys of the piano.

'That wasn't right, was it?' he said, when she had finished. 'Technically perfect, but you're not doing enough. The sound should be more open, flowing out to the audience.' He waved his hand outwards in the air. 'You should be concentrating on that sound. Got the idea?'

Clare looked at him and said, bluntly, 'No, I haven't.'

He leaned his heavy shoulders over the long squat

piano as she gathered up her music.

'I'm not doing so well,' she said.

'I wouldn't go that far.'

'There are times when I think it's all too much,' Clare said.

'Nonsense. You're a young healthy girl with lots of talent.'

Vittorio placed a Bach prelude and fugue in C sharp before her.

'You know this piece very well. You studied it for your eighth grade so I expect you to give it your best. Think of it as a flowing river. Let the music swell.'

'I'll try,' Clare said.

She began the discordant yet simple fugue.

Vittorio stood listening. 'Wait,' he said, raising his hand in the air.

Clare stopped playing.

'It's too loud. What does it say there? *Adagio*. Give it volume without banging out the notes. Then *andante*. Begin again.'

Clare began.

'Softly, *pianissimo*, now swell out the sound with some depth. That's right. Play down into the keys. Put all your strength into your fingers to bring out the melody. Yes, come on. More dramatic. Play it as if you mean it. Feel, feel the restraint, feel the sadness.' Vittorio's voice penetrated her head, drowning the sound of the notes.

Clare sat stiff and tense, her face rigid over the keys, the notes falling flat from her fingers before she could put into them the expression she wanted. When she finished the first variation and looked up he was shaking his head. 'Where was the intensity?'

Clare had wanted the deep vibrating sadness to swell

over the keys but her hands had refused to follow her instructions. That morning she had practised for several hours, with only an apple to sustain her. She had worked so hard that by the end of the morning she thought she would cry. The same feeling came over her now. She continued playing, the music urging her on, violently and clumsily to an impossible achievement. When she stopped her hands still twitched, and her body sagged with the sinking feeling she got when she knew she had not played well.

Vittorio's voice was quiet when at last he spoke. 'Let's begin all over again. Take your time. As you know, playing the piano is more than fingers picking out keys. Any idiot can do that.'

Clare could hear the impatience in his tone.

'I will show you how I want you to play this piece,' he said.

Clare stood up to let him sit at the piano. She sat crouched forward, watching his long, slim fingers, their tips rounded on the keys. There was musical feeling in his interpretation. It manifested itself in the ripple of muscles across his broad back and the movement of his arms. If she could reach out and touch him perhaps his skill would pass on to her. As he played his frustration with her diminished and by the time he struck the last notes there was a soft expressiveness in his face.

Vittorio was the eldest son of an Italian *conte* and *contessa*. Before she had married Count Fellini his mother, Maria Varenella, the daughter of the biggest vineyard owner in Tuscany, had been a beautiful girl, and a keen musician. She had abandoned her musical studies during her rebellious teenage years. Determined that Vittorio's talent should not go to waste she sent him to school in Oxford, where he excelled at the piano and was a member of the junior orchestra. After leaving school he attended the Royal Academy, before studying in Paris at the Conservatoire with the famous Sir George Saunders. There he became an experienced concert pianist and played throughout Europe for a brief spell, until an injury to his hand forced him to retire and return to his LRAM exams and a teaching post at the Royal Academy.

'I want you to memorise this piece for the next lesson.' Vittorio closed the lid of the piano.

When Clare returned she could play the Bach fugue by heart. Vittorio was so impressed that he encouraged her to work continuously with more of the Bach repertoire and he began her musicological studies. He took her to organ recitals and entered her for a piano-playing competition at the Royal Albert Hall. Each contestant was required to play a Bach fugue. Clare took a week off work and practised all the time.

On the day of the competition the judges sat at the foot of the stage, waiting. As Clare took her place at the piano she was so frightened that she wished she could disappear. Adjusting her chair she began to play with trembling fingers.

Chapter Twelve

Pauline's love for her baby was spontaneous and vital. Holding his small body sent a pain and love and sadness through her. He was so tiny, so pale, and his eyes, full of awe and wonderment at this strange world he had come to inhabit, had the same sad look as Seamus's. Gazing into them Pauline could see Seamus once more, standing on the platform of the station, frightened and lonely and would start to cry.

'Stop that nonsense,' Aunt Bea would say angrily. 'Acting like a teenager and you a mother. Go and help Mary with the supper.'

As the weeks passed Pauline's ability to irritate her aunt manifested itself in a thousand different ways. When she spoke, when she didn't speak. When she sat hunched over the table nursing Seamie for lengthy periods instead of helping with the chores. All of those things had the power to send Aunt Bea into a rage, flaring the antagonism between them. But it was Pauline's deafness to Aunt Bea's snide remarks that caused the most hurtful and sarcastic comments.

When Pauline's father, Tom Quirk, came to visit her he sat quietly in the corner of her bedroom and let her cry herself out.

'You're fretting too much, Pauline,' he said, 'and you'll have to stop it if you're to have the strength to look after your child.'

'I can't help it,' she said, taking the handkerchief he offered and blowing her nose. 'I hate it here and I hate Aunt Bea.'

'Whist awhile, we'll think of something,' Tom said softly. 'I've a few pounds saved that'll see you on your feet again, and sure you have the whole summer to look around for a place for yourself and the baby. Stop crying now and start making plans.'

Pauline smiled gratefully at him through her tears.

When Clare arrived for her final lesson before the Christmas holidays, Vittorio had her competition results.

'Good marks,' he said, handing her the envelope.

'I was nervous,' Clare said, overwhelmed.

'Understandably.' Vittorio nodded. 'It's all good experience. We will work on your weak points. Now, try the Bach fugue again. In your own time.' He smiled and, propping his elbows on the piano top, waited.

As Clare removed her music from its case Vittorio's face was close, threatening the space between them. Placing her fingers on the piano keys, a row of white tombstones chilling her bones, she began. Vittorio's hands rose rhythmically with the phrases nursing her on, then fell soft and satisfied on the last solitary note. She stood up.

'Good. But more feeling.'

Clare knew exactly what he meant. Knew the inexplicable quality he was searching for in her playing. She kept her face blank to disguise her emotion because the worst possible thing that could happen to her would be to burst into tears.

'Come over here,' he said. 'Let's share a cup of coffee.' He took a Thermos from his cupboard, opened it and poured coffee into its outer lid. The steam rose and the smell permeated the room. 'Here, drink this. You look as if you could do with it,' he said, handing it to her.

'What about yours?'

'There's plenty,' he insisted, lifting the flask to demonstrate.

Seating himself at his desk he cradled his cup in his hands. Clare sat opposite him and drank slowly, letting the warmth of the coffee cup seep through her fingers between mouthfuls.

Vittorio looked at her. 'I know I've been hard on you, Clare, but what really matters is playing the music as it must be played, bringing out what's in you, what's in it.' He stood up and paced the floor. 'I can't stress how important it is to practise. Practise, practise, practise.' There was an urgency in his voice that Clare had never heard before. 'Put everything you've got into the music. That's what makes a star. That quality, that extra dimension. You've got it.' He frowned. 'At least, you had it.' He looked questioningly at her and saw the misery in her face.

What was happening to her? She had worked and worked until she was so exhausted that she wanted to cry. So worn out from trying to get that elusive thing he was talking about into her playing that she wondered if it was all too much.

'Perhaps there is something wrong?' He came to stand beside her, his face looming over her, his eyes fixed intently on her.

'I need more time to practise,' Clare said.

'Yes, you do. Listen, Clare. I know what you're capable of. I want to hear you play at the Royal Albert Hall, the Carnegie Hall. Sit in the audience and watch you with my own eyes. Take you to dinner in your ballgown.'

'I can't think that far ahead.' Clare looked desolate.
'Why not?'

'Because I don't feel I'm making much progress at the moment.'

'You play well when you put your mind to it. Keep trying. Give it everything you've got.'

'I do,' she protested.

He shook his head. 'No, there's more in you than that.' He was leaning towards her, his eyes beseeching her.

Clare could not meet his gaze. She stood up, swallowing hard to prevent the tears that surged from falling. His strong, handsome face blurred. Everything in the room merged and swam before her. She stumbled to the piano, gathered her music together and put it in her case.

'I can't take any more,' she said, pulling her coat and scarf from the hook behind the door and throwing them over her arm.

'Clare.' Vittorio caught her shoulders, turned her around to face him.

'Don't run off like that,' he said.

'You're wrong about me. I've tried and tried.' She was shouting, letting her tears fall unchecked.

'I'm not wrong about you. You, my dear, are a rare specimen.' He took a handkerchief from his breast pocket, wiping her tears with it.

Clare looked doubtfully at him.

'Listen, Clare. I wasn't going to tell you this yet. But I've been thinking about your career. You have it in you to become a concert pianist and, if that's what you want to be, then you should plan your future career in that direction now instead of continuing with your LRAM studies. I had a meeting with the members of

216

the board of examiners. They heard you play at the competition and agree with me that you would benefit by going to Paris to study at the Conservatoire.'

Clare looked at him in amazement.

'I shall make an appointment for you to see a colleague of mine, and my former tutor, Sir George Saunders,' Vittorio said. 'The best virtuoso teacher at the Conservatoire. He's coming to London in a few weeks for a meeting.'

'What?'

'I feel it is time for you to begin working seriously with him, if he agrees to take you on. The selection of the right professor is crucial. There is constant contact between the two institutions and in the past I have got Sir George to take an interest in the development of particularly gifted students long before they were ready to graduate.'

Clare was shocked.

Vittorio came to her and held her gently by the shoulders.

'Believe me, Clare, I have not come to this decision without a great deal of thought. Having got you this far, I feel it's over to Sir George now. I've spoken to him about you and I'm convinced that he is the one who will make a concert pianist out of you. You will spend the next five years in Paris learning a way of life where successful public performance is the principal objective with a level of commitment you have only dreamed of until now.'

Clare shook free of him. 'I don't want to go to Paris,' she exclaimed. 'I don't want to study with this Sir George whoever he is.'

Vittorio ignored her. 'The board is willing to transfer your scholarship to the Conservatoire. Early training is vital to master all that is involved in becoming a performer. You must have no life other than music from now on, if you are to meet the required demands. It won't be difficult for you, you're a natural student.'

'Thanks for speaking up for me, but I'm not going,' Clare said resolutely.

'Clare,' Vittorio said, in a placatory tone, 'you found working with me a big adjustment, but you'll have to let go, in order to find yourself. Your vocation is for the piano but, believe me, I too shall find it very hard to let you go.' He looked at her, then rushed on excitedly, 'Now you'll have to spend the next few weeks practising before you are heard by Sir George.' There was no mistaking the pleading in his voice and the yearning in his eyes.

Her heart flipped and her cheeks burned as he leaned towards her, his breath on her face.

He kissed her gently but firmly on the lips, pressing her to him, his usual reserve and hesitancy submerged in his ardour. Panic streaked through her. Her hands shifted against him.

'Clare,' he whispered.

His mouth was crushing hers, hard, demanding, awakening passions in her that had lain dormant for too long. Trembling with apprehension and excitement she gave herself up to his kiss, warning bells clamouring in her ears, her will to resist diminishing as he continued to kiss her. Her arms crept up his shoulders, around his neck. They stood entwined, oblivious to everything around them.

Suddenly he stopped and moved back. 'I shouldn't have done that. Most unethical. I'm sorry. Forgive me. It mustn't happen again.'

Clare watched his throat move as he swallowed.

Dazed, she looked at him, her face burning.

'Don't stand there,' he barked. 'Go off and spend your Christmas holidays practising and when you return I want to see a mature, intelligent woman, capable of taking criticism, instead of the teasing little schoolgirl that you are.' His eyes glittered with anger.

Stupefied with shock Clare stared at him, unable to believe her ears. 'How dare you speak to me like that?' she exploded. 'My best is never good enough for you. What do you want? My life's blood?'

'I want you to do better because I know you can.'

'Right, I will. But without you.' She swung away from him, hurried out of the room, along the corridor, down the stairs and out into the street, Vittorio following her.

'Clare,' Vittorio called after her, but she stalked off down the street, his voice ringing in her ears.

She kept walking quickly, looking over her shoulder once to find that the inky blackness had swallowed him up. On the tube she let the tears stream unchecked down her face. She felt bereaved and her bereavement brought with it confusion and despair.

When Clare arrived at his flat Jack was packing his suitcase.

'Don't look so surprised,' he said. 'I thought about what you said. I'm going home. You've convinced me.'

'That's great news,' Clare said.

'Come with me.'

'I'd love to, Daddy, but I'm going to stay here and practise every hour God sends over the Christmas holidays.'

'What?'

'Professor Vittorio wants me to go to Paris in the New Year, to study at the Conservatoire there. He says that if I want to become a concert pianist I'll have to skip the exams and start now.'

Jack looked astounded.

'I've made up my mind, Daddy,' Clare continued. 'If I'm to get anywhere I'll have to work very hard and there would be too many distractions at home.'

'It's wonderful news, Clare. But what will your mother think of you not coming home for Christmas?'

'She'll be too pleased about me going to Paris to say anything. Isn't it what she always wanted?'

It was overcast when the boat finally came into view. James Freeman was waiting, stamping his feet, the peak of his cap pulled down over his eyes.

Grandpa!' Eve called, running towards him, Sue following.

'Eve.' He waved to her.

'I'm so glad to see you, Grandpa.' Eve threw her arms around him, knocking his cap sideways.

'Easy.' He laughed. 'Good to see you again, pet. This must be Sue. How do you do, my dear?' he said, extending his hand. 'You're very welcome.'

'I'm pleased to meet you, sir.' Sue grasped his hand and shook it vigorously.

'Let's get you both home. I bet you're tired after that long journey. In such bad weather. I wondered if there was a gale at sea.'

'It was very rough,' Eve said.

James took their suitcases and went to open the car door.

They got into the car while he unlocked the boot, lifted in the cases, then slammed it down hurriedly.

'I'll have you home in no time,' he said, seating himself in the driver's seat and starting the engine.

There was very little traffic in the town. Most people were indoors because of the expected storm. The shops seemed dark and huddled together and the lights from Kinsella's Select Bar were reflected on the opposite wall. Only the corner shop was still open.

'Clem still working all hours?' Eve asked.

'It's the only place you can get anything around here after six o'clock,' James said. 'They say he'll soon be a millionaire with catch-penny trade.'

The avenue was rutted and overhung with dangerous branches. David Furlong's house was plunged in darkness.

'Are the Furlongs away?' Eve asked James.

'Spending Christmas in the West Indies. They don't like the cold weather. David's in New Zealand, I think.'

'It's well for him,' Eve said. 'Missing the cold spell.'

James slowed down and turned sharply to the right through the gates.

'It'll be good to have young people around the place again,' he said. 'Cheer the place up.'

They bumped over potholes, between the overgrown verges of the unkempt drive. The trees were bare except for a few straggly leaves that clung in last-minute desperation before the whipping wind would tear them away. Outside the front door the branches waved, creaking and sighing in the wind. As soon as the car stopped Eve jumped out of the back, Sue behind her, and ran across the gravel, up the steps to the front door as the rain lashed against them.

Dorothy opened the door and embraced Eve. 'What a relief to have you home,' she said, her face taut and unrevealing. 'Look at you, you're soaked.'

'Mummy, this is Sue Hope.'

'How do you do,' Dorothy said, as they shook hands.

'Thank you,' Sue gushed. 'It's just darling to be here,' she went on, shedding her coat. Agnes came up the stairs. She enveloped Eve in her big, fleshy arms.

'Home at last,' she said. 'This must be Sue. I've heard all about you from Clare.'

'Oh, gee. Nothing bad, I hope,' Sue chuckled, her large eyes gazing at the formidable Agnes.

'Not as yet,' Agnes said stiffly. 'Time will tell.'

Sue found Eve's house interesting and unusual but she was hell bent on impressing the men with whom she came into contact. In her first week she invited Manus Corrigan to have a drink with her because, according to her, he undressed her with his eyes every time he saw her in Kinsella's with Eve. Flattered and terrified at her lack of inhibition, he declined. Her *joie de vivre* captivated the people she met. They laughed and became instantly intrigued. Dorothy had disliked her on sight but her inherent qualities as a hostess made her determined to impress Sue with traditional Irish hospitality. She encouraged her to eat plenty and even tried to get her to improve her appearance. Sue listened politely, but in her bedroom, with a sigh of relief, she removed her clothes and wallowed in the undisciplined flesh that emerged around her middle.

Sue began to initiate Eve into what she considered her mature sex life, telling her about the rampant sex maniacs among her friends, who apparently had regular orgies, and drawing ridiculous diagrams of the most outlandish sexual positions imaginable. Dorothy was blissfully ignorant of what was going on. Apart from the usual warnings about getting into trouble, she expected Eve to remain a virgin until she married.

Dorothy held a bridge party once a month. It was an occasion to which her friends looked forward, when they would sit around small tables in the drawing room installed by Agnes specially for the occasion. Agnes always stayed on late to prepare the supper, and deliver it to the table behind the sofa, already laid with the best bone china and cutlery. Half-way through the game, the ladies would adjourn to enjoy the freshly cut sandwiches, Agnes's famous apple cake and the finest blend of Freeman's tea.

On the morning of the bridge party Dorothy, laden with parcels and carrier bags, returned from the shops and began to unpack her groceries with her habitual vagueness. After she had been shopping she would usually make a cup of tea and sit down to read the newspaper but, because of the bridge party, she busied herself around the kitchen, a harassed look on her face. 'My feet are killing me,' she said to Eve. 'All that shopping and everything so expensive.' Dorothy's hair had thinned. It gave her face a false fragility. 'I've got a Fuller's cake,' she said, lifting it out of its bag with her fleshless hands. 'Put the kettle on. We might as well have a cup.' She sat down. The kitchen was airless and Eve opened a window. 'Sue still in bed?'

'Yes.'

'One of life's losers,' Dorothy declared. 'All the effort and money we put into your education and what do you do? Get a job as a waitress in London and take up with the likes of her.'

'Her father's rich,' Eve said, hoping that might impress Dorothy.

'I don't care what he is. Of all the nice, conventional girls you could have brought home you had to choose that spoilt, eccentric one,' she moaned. 'I dread having to introduce her to my bridge friends.'

'She's going out.'

'Where?'

'Clem Rogers is taking her to the pictures,' Eve said.

'He has my sympathy.'

That afternoon a weak sun was fading through the windows highlighting the thin layer of dust on the mantelpiece, and the tops of the dark furniture. Dorothy sat and surveyed the garden. The fruit trees were bare and all the colour in the garden had disappeared with the heavy winter frost.

'How are you?' Agnes came in.

'I'm fine, thanks.'

'I'll stoke up the fire,' she said. 'It's getting chilly and they'll be here soon.'

By the time the first guests arrived a hearty fire was blazing beneath the marble mantelpiece. Myrtle Thompson, the auctioneer's wife, ambitious, talkative, always manoeuvring in the upper echelons and Dorothy's best friend, was first to get there with her daughter, Fran. It was Myrtle who had insisted on introducing Dorothy to Ron, at the Trinity Ball. Fran, a younger version of her mother, wore her make-up so discreetly that it was barely noticeable. She also shared her mother's interest in fashion.

Trish Lynam, who owned the drapery shop, arrived next, jangling her bracelets and leaning forward to greet everyone, amusement in her keen eyes.

The fire crackled and snapped emitting a piny odour and silvering the room with its glow. Lamps had been lit and the blue damask curtains pulled against the night.

'I've decided it's time I updated the shop,' Trish Lynam said, during supper. 'Expanded a bit.'

'You wouldn't like to take on a partner?' Myrtle asked.

'Who do you have in mind?' Trish was cautious.

'Fran here.'

Trish looked at the girl. 'I could do worse, I suppose,' Trish said, her eyes twinkling. 'You're attractive, lively. You know how to create an image.'

'Thanks,' Fran said.

'She's bursting with ideas,' Myrtle said.

'Really?' Trish said.

'This wouldn't have anything to do with my recent inheritance from Uncle Teddy, would it?' Fran asked. 'Mother's dying to spend it for me.'

They all laughed.

'Jokes aside,' Trish said, 'do you have any innovative ideas, Fran?'

'Open a French shop. A boutique.'

'Now that would cause a stir,' Trish said.

'You could sell lingerie.'

'How would you spell that, never mind pronounce it?' asked Agnes, who had come in with a pot of fresh tea.

'Would there be the demand in Glencove?' enquired Dorothy.

'You'd be surprised. There's plenty of well-heeled people here,' Myrtle said. 'Going up to Dublin to spend their money.'

'Dangerous place,' Trish Lynam said, helping herself to a smoked-salmon sandwich. 'Would you believe that Delia Enright had her handbag and her shopping stolen in broad daylight? Left them down for a second in Clery's while she tried on a jumper. When she turned round they were gone.'

'How did she get home?' Fran asked.

'Luckily she was with her cousin who lent her the bus fare.'

'I wouldn't go near the city,' Trish said.

'It's not as bad as all that,' Dorothy said.

'You can get everything you need in Glencove,' Trish informed them. 'With no risk to your personal safety.'

'I'd rather spend my money locally,' Myrtle said. 'Seeing as it's local money in the first place.'

'I might consider that idea of yours, Fran. Hop over to London. See some suppliers,' Trish mused.

'Paris, you mean.' Fran said.

'When is Ron off to India again?' Trish asked. 'He could check out the market there. All that beautiful Indian silk. I'm sure they have some very exotic underwear.'

'That sort of encouragement is all he needs,' Agnes said, under her breath.

Dorothy frowned into her teacup.

Chapter Thirteen

Seated in the chapel in Ballingarret, on Christmas morning, her baby in her arms, Pauline watched the priest placing the china infant Jesus in the crib between Joseph and Mary, before Mass. It was consoling to sit in the chapel surrounded by devotion and prayer and the scent of the flowers banked on a garland of green foliage.

The gold monstrance became a blur of colour as Pauline considered her plight. Seamus hadn't sent a Christmas card and Pauline could only conclude that he was being held prisoner somewhere in Belfast. The previous Christmas he had brought her flowers and chocolates and together they had bought a secondhand engagement ring in The Happy Ring House, in O'Connell Street. Gazing at the crib Pauline decided that she would have to search for Seamus if she was to have a father for her son. To do that she would have to go to Belfast. She felt a deep pang at the thought of being parted from her baby. The choir sang 'Adeste Fideles' and Seamie, woken from his sleep, cried.

'Give him here,' Aunt Bea, sitting next to her, commanded, grabbing him and running out of the church with him as soon as Pauline reluctantly released him.

Pauline, hearing him bawling outside, rose from her seat, genuflected, and tip-toed down the aisle vowing there and then that Aunt Bea wouldn't be the one she would leave Seamie with.

Clare, alone in her flat, studying her notes on counterpoint, was hardly aware of the fact that it was Christmas Day until Mrs Cartwright knocked at her door.

'Come and have your dinner with us,' she said. 'Trev's working but he'll be home at eight.'

'Are you sure?' Clare asked. 'I wouldn't like to intrude.'

''Course I'm sure,' Mrs Cartwright insisted.

Over a meal of roast goose, apple sauce, and dumplings Mr Cartwright regaled Clare with stories of his adventures in the war. Their present to her of a beautiful bottle of 'Joy' perfume, nestling on a cushion of blue satin brought back memories of her childhood Christmases: waking up to a silvery dawn, fumbling in the dark for her bulging stocking at the end of the bed, sneaking downstairs while the house was quiet to see what Santa had left. Usually there was a doll or a doll's tea set, a book, or a pencil case and a bag of sweets. One year Santa left her a pink doll's cot almost the size of a real one. It had probably taken Agnes weeks of skimping and scraping out of the housekeeping money to be able to afford it. That was the same year Martin got a toy gun with his games of snakes and ladders and ludo. Agnes had not approved of the gun.

'I don't want him out playing cops and robbers on the street.'

Jack, full of Christmas cheer, had laughed and said it would be the making of him.

The sun shone in a cold, treacherous sky as Clare went

without her coat to a performance by the London Symphony Orchestra at St Martin-in-the-Fields. She had spent most of the Christmas holidays practising the piano and was giving herself a treat. From where she sat she had full view of the instruments, the lighting, the artists. As they began to play, she was so overwhelmed by the volume of sound that she found it hard to focus her attention on what they were playing. But as the first piece progressed she was back in time to her earliest childhood memories, with a yearning for early morning in Ireland and the softness of the day. The music evoked all things past and present, glorious and despairing, taking her far away then jolting her back as it came to a finale. It ended with Wagner's cold, startling violins and chasing horns, which faded to leave her troubled.

When she came out it was raining. A shrill wind blew around her as she jostled and pushed among hurrying people, oblivious of them and of the congested city. The sweeping wind and the music, still ringing in her ears, rushed her along the sprawling streets. Shivering from the ecstasy in the crash of sound that had risen from the singing violins, the calling trumpets, she boarded the tube back to her flat. She would follow that sound. Do whatever she had to do to get there.

She caught a cold and felt so miserable that for the next few days she was forced to stay in bed. The drawn curtains brought Mrs Cartwright clumping down the stairs to ask what was wrong.

'You're in a state,' she said, looking at Clare's flushed face and swollen eyes. 'I'll fetch the doctor.'

'I don't want a doctor. I'll be all right in a day or two,' Clare protested, but Mrs Cartwright insisted on fetching him.

'You have a touch of pneumonia,' he pronounced. 'You must stay in bed.'

For days Clare lay in her bed, drowsy from the medicine, not knowing or caring whether it was day or night. A letter from Henry arrived. 'Why didn't you come home for Christmas? You are utterly selfish in your own pursuits and so self-absorbed that you don't realise that there's a world out there outside of yourself,' he wrote. 'You are weak giving in to your mother's impossible ambitions for you. No doubt you will find someone suitable for her to boast about. Rich and most likely famous too, like you intend to be. Well, I intend to grab life by the throat and conquer it.'

Clare didn't have the strength to reply. Anyway, what was the point of trying to explain anything to him, because he would never understand it?

Mrs Cartwright changed her sheets, tidied her room and insisted on doing her washing. Clare wouldn't let her stay and talk. She preferred to lie staring at the ceiling, thinking of the Dinley studio where she practised now to avoid Vittorio, and the people she encountered there, Cliff Richard, Diana Ross and the Supremes, all practising like herself, the sound of their singing filtering through the corridors. How long could she go on without working? Mrs Cartwright promised to transfer her to the single attic bedsitter as soon as it became available, and brought her food. Although her appetite was gone she knew she had to eat a little and that she couldn't go on indefinitely relying on Mrs Cartwright's good nature. She was too weak to think about it all.

'Your professor called,' Mrs Cartwright said one morning. 'Asked to see you. I told him you were too ill.'

Clare looked at her in astonishment. 'How did he know I was here?' she asked.

'He said he was expecting you back at the Academy and that you hadn't turned up.'

'What?'

'He said you didn't show up for your lessons.'

Clare sat up in bed. 'Why? What date is it?' she asked.

'It's the tenth.'

'I didn't realise that,' Clare replied.

'Why are you hiding from him, then?'

Clare didn't want to admit that where Vittorio was concerned her deepest sensations were called into play. The day she had run out of his studio she had been in a state of complete upheaval.

Vittorio had been a wonderful basis for her early training. He was genuinely interested in her in artistic terms and was ambitious for her. He had been effective as a teacher in inspiring her imagination by teaching her to think orchestrally at the piano. Also, he had brought out the real feeling of affinity for the piano ensuring that its function became second nature to her. From the outset he had insisted on a strong discipline in preparation for what was to come.

Clare now wondered if she would survive in Paris without the hard-working assistance of Vittorio to balance the visionary aspects of this strong discipline. She had so much admiration for him that he only had to say a few words and she would spend days wondering how to interpret his magnificent utterances. Vittorio had made music her life. Now, for him, it seemed to be a matter of life and death.

Her thoughts kept straying to him. She missed his amusing, charming, irritating, irrational behaviour. He was too important, and too handsome, to be interested in her. Here was a man desired by a great many women. He was much older than her too, she thought, calculating his age at around thirty-five. Yes, she was the most unlikely candidate for a romantic encounter with him. She had her career to think of. Yet from the time she had met him he had elicited a strange mixture of responses in her. His astonishing good looks, his ability to make her feel both wonderful and inadequate, depending on his mood, infuriated her. He was ruthless too. And that kiss. Clare could not forget that kiss, and the ensuing guilt as if she had done something wrong in arousing his passion.

As soon as she felt better she took on extra work at the Savoy to pay for her practice time in the Dinley studios. Apart from her essential groceries she didn't go shopping or sightseeing any more, shunning all the places that she knew would cost money. The surge of excitement she had felt on her first walks through London had vanished. To her it had become a vast wilderness of crowds scrambling through doors, barriers, undergrounds and buses, teeming with rush-hour commuters. The initial consciousness of the brilliant shops had left her. Occasionally she visited art galleries to lose herself in the paintings of Matisse, Cézanne, Picasso, or dally at some ancient sculptures. As she stared at landscapes and seascapes, she began to evaluate her life, listing all the things that she had done so far. Sometimes it occurred to her that she was missing out on a great deal, and also that she should listen and be more willing to take advice, instead of hiding herself away.

As she was leaving the Dinley studios one evening, wondering how she would learn so much in such a short space of time, a familiar voice called her name.

She turned sharply to see Vittorio standing there.

'I've been waiting for you to finish,' he said, buffing his hands together, his eyes intent on her.

'How did you know I was here?' Clare asked.

'Never mind that. Come back to your studies. We have no time to lose.' His eyes shone with vitality as he caught her hand and pulled her along the street. 'We must get in some lessons quickly. Practice on its own is not enough, and Sir George will be here next week. It's an excellent opportunity. There'll be a lot of travelling later on. France, Italy, Germany. You will have to work very, very hard. From time to time you must come and see me. Let me know how you are getting along.'

Clare threw up her hands in a gesture of hopelessness. 'I'm not sure if this is what I want,' she said, looking at the expression on Vittorio's face. 'I'm finding it difficult to make ends meet here in London. How would I ever manage in Paris?'

'Give music lessons. That's what they all do. But you must give it a try. Then I shall be able to say, in time to come, that I did the best I could for you. You are a very lucky girl.'

Seething at his audacity, yet knowing he was right, Clare felt the impact of his life force compelling her along. They hurried to his studio at the Academy, and from the moment her hands touched the keys she lost her nervousness, playing with more confidence than she ever had before.

'Bravo,' he said, clapping when she finished. 'You have worked hard. Cup of coffee?'

'No, thank you,' Clare said, calmly gathering up her music. 'I must go. I'll see you next week.'

She left a stunned Vittorio gazing after her.

* * *

The polished woodwork and brasses gleamed in the quiet restful drawing room where an enormous Christmas tree decorated with fairy lights and beautifully wrapped gifts dominated one corner. James sat by the fire reading the newspaper removed from the frenzy in the kitchen where Agnes was preparing for the Christmas feast. Her arms ached from cleaning the fruit, candied peel and cherries for the cakes, beating over a dozen eggs, preparing apple tarts, jellies.

Glencove, decorated in fairy lights and bunting, the shops crammed with plum puddings, slabs of cake, chocolate of all kinds, fizzy drinks, looked festive. Even the hardware shop had toys for sale and holly and ivy leaves clung to the rails of cups and mugs inside the door.

Eve felt excited at the prospect of her father's imminent return from India, the first trip he had felt able to make since Sarah's death. She wished her mother was looking forward to seeing him too. Before she went to meet him, she examined herself carefully in Dorothy's mirror. Would he see a difference in her since she had left for London? That she was more sophisticated, perhaps?

'Anyone would think it was a boyfriend not a father you were going to meet,' Sue said, 'the way you're preening yourself.'

'He sets great store by appearance,' Eve said, hoping that Sue would tidy herself up a bit so that he would not think her a joke.

Dressed in his black overcoat and hat, Ron looked as dignified as ever, but his shoulders had a slight stoop.

'He looks like Cary Grant,' Sue exclaimed, as he approached. 'You never told me he was so handsome.

'Mr Freeman. May I call you Ron?' she asked, quivering with excitement, wisps of hair escaping from her pony-tail, her bosom spilling out of her black silk shirt.

'Certainly.' He beamed as Sue kissed his cheek. Eve was astonished to see a look of reciprocal excitement in his eyes.

In the Shamrock lounge in the airport they drank cocktails, Eve assessing her father from Sue's point of view. Suddenly he seemed like a glamorous stranger and Eve wanted to say something funny to get his attention, to please him and make up to him for her mother's hostility. She wanted to contain his restless spirit with scintillating conversation, but he had eyes only for Sue, studying her with undisguised interest. Sue stared back at him. They seemed to be conducting an exploration of each other, or reading some coded message visible only to themselves.

From the moment Sue met Ron Freeman she set out to make him fall in love with her. The first time she had sneaked off to meet him, her skimpy dress billowing, hair flying, she walked as if she bore with great difficulty the weight of her enormous breasts.

Dermy McQuaid had said to Clem Rogers, eyeing her chest as she passed by, 'They're as big as today and tomorrow.'

'The whole weekend if you ask me,' Clem joked.

'Where is that rampant carthorse gone now?' Dorothy asked, gazing out of the window, a look of disgust on her face.

'She has a date with Clem,' Eve said, assuming that that was where Sue was going.

On Christmas morning while the ham was simmering

in the big black pot on the range and the turkey was browning nicely in the oven Eve and Sue went to mass with Ron. In the church they could feel the excitement of Christmas as people crowded in. The organ boomed and voices were raised in unison, glorifying the birth of Christ. Sue gazed at the altar in rapt attention and pronounced the Irish people to be a nation of religious maniacs.

The table in the dining room was decorated with Christmas crackers, paper hats, and streamers. During the meal Ron smiled sheepishly at Sue, pressed her to have another helping of everything, even winked at her when he thought no one was looking. She was remote and dreamy.

'Enjoyed yourself?' Dorothy asked her.

'Yes, thank you,' Sue replied, blushing and dizzy. Eve, relieved that Sue was having a good time, didn't notice. Ron was his usual noncommittal self. A few days later, Sue, her bosom protruding from her low-cut crushed-velvet dress, returned from town with the train timetable and brochures on sightseeing trips. She was going to kiss the Blarney Stone. Would Eve, Ron and Dorothy like to come too? It would take them out of themselves. Ron, exhilarated and flattered, agreed, Dorothy refused to go, saying that she had a cold. Ron drove, Sue beside him, lust pulsating from every pore of her body. Alone in the back of the car, Eve was confused by the mounting hysteria between them and the shared privacy of their jokes.

The first time they made love would be the only time. That was what they agreed.

'Once more,' Ron said, desperate for her.

Sue had set out to do whatever he wanted so that he would fall in love with her. It hadn't been her fault that she had found him irresistible, she explained to Eve a long time afterwards. 'What would you like to do to me now?' she would coax him in her little-girl voice.

They spent as much time together as they could, in all sorts of secret locations. 'This is the very last time,' Ron would vow each time. 'I'm too old for you. I'd ruin your life.'

'It's only a little fun. Relax,' Sue would say. Relieved that they hadn't been caught, they promised to keep away from each other for the rest of her visit, but neither of them could endure it.

'We'll have to stop now,' Ron said. 'If Dorothy were to find out, there'd be hell to pay.'

'You think I care about Dorothy?' Sue stormed. 'My life is good because I make it exciting. You're just fucking around the edges of yours. You're married to the silliest bitch in Christendom and you don't even know how to free yourself of her. Well, fuck you, I'm not hanging around.'

'I have to leave early,' she told Eve, coming into the house, running up the stairs, stuffing her outlandish garments into her suitcase. 'My mother has been taken ill.'

When Ron returned to the house that evening, Eve informed him that Sue had gone. Disbelieving her he went upstairs to Sue's bedroom. There were no scattered clothes tumbling out of half-open drawers, no wild laughter. Only silence and a hint of her musk perfume that sent him wild with longing. To hell with Dorothy, he would find her. He went to his study and with the feverish anguish of an adolescent he telephoned her parents. Her father told him that Sue wasn't there but that he would get her to phone when she arrived. When Ron and Sue were finally connected, the warm rush of her voice sent such a pang of loneliness through him that he began to weep on the line as he presented her with his plans.

'Fine,' she kept saying. 'That'll be fine.'

When he replaced the receiver he thought about her for a long time. He wasn't sure that he liked her but his nearly out-of-control passion for her overpowered him. He liked the sense of freedom she oozed with her 'liberated woman' tab and he knew that she had slept with a lot of men. But he wanted her. When he was with her he forgot everything else: all the nagging doubts and irrefutable claims about his business. Even the arguments with his father over the way the company was being run were driven from his mind. He was getting tired of the way James came, unannounced, into the office these days, pestering him about the business.

Dorothy's expectations of him were too high, but Sarah's death had been the final straw. It had destroyed their fragile love for one another. It had been Sarah's pure unconditional love, pure need, that had called him home so often in the past. Now that she was gone, nothing made sense any more.

When Sarah died, Dorothy's rage had been directed at Ron. She would wake up in the night, screaming at him, tearing her hair out. One day on his return from work he had found her dispassionately breaking dishes and glasses, laughing with pleasure as they smashed on the floor.

Her voice from the hall door made him sit up quickly. 'I'm home.' The high-pitched call brought him down to earth.

He winced as he heard the thump of her bag on the monk's chair. Before going down the stairs to confront her he examined his face in the dressing-table mirror for the familiar tug of dislike he felt for his wife.

He felt sick as he watched her moving backwards and forwards in the kitchen, grace and elegance at every turn. Not knowing what to say he switched on the radio, wishing with all his heart that he didn't have to hurt her.

Dorothy said, 'Fran Lynam is getting engaged.'

'Who's the lucky man?' Ron asked, without interest.

'Ned Griffin. Tom Griffin's son.'

'Something to celebrate, I suppose,' Ron said. Dorothy continued to speak idly with the usual long pauses between remarks.

'I've got a seed catalogue here James asked me for,' Ron said, seizing it and the opportunity to leave the kitchen. 'I'd better bring it out to him.'

'You're so restless,' she said, shaking her head.

Once outdoors he walked slowly, suddenly struck by the freedom he felt at the thought of leaving the stifling Dorothy. He straightened his shoulders and continued on, feeling his step lighter, the yoke finally being lifted, the weight of his marriage falling away.

'He's gone!' Dorothy screamed. 'Gone!' she spluttered. 'Lost to me for ever and I hope you're satisfied. Do you realise what I did for him?' she shrieked. 'Sacrificed everything. Gave him all my inheritance to help expand the business. Slaved to bring up you children, alone, when he was away overspending in his over-staffed offices in India. All the sacrifices I had to make. Still have to make. For what? For that freak to take my husband away from me! I'll kill him if he ever sets foot in this house again.'

Ron had left, saying he had urgent business in Hong Kong, and no one would have been any the wiser had

Sue's father not telephoned a few days later asking to speak to her. That precipitated hours of hysterical calls between him and Dorothy in their hunt for Sue and their tracking her down in Hong Kong. With Ron.

Eve got the blame. 'Have I ever done anything right in your eyes?' was all she said, in heartbreak and exasperation.

'No!' Dorothy shouted back. 'You were born into the best social structure, given the best opportunities, the best education money could buy, and you wasted it. Mixing with the lower elements and misfits. You're gullible, you trust people, believe what they say, when all the time you're being used. You don't appreciate what's done for you. You'll never get anywhere at the rate you're going and you've ruined my marriage and my life.'

There hadn't been many sacrifices, Eve was thinking, but dared not say so. The expensive cars were still in the driveway, Agnes came over every day to clean the house and cooked enough food for a large family.

James, who had founded the business, had worked hard and, in his retirement, preferred to absorb himself in his garden. He had been an industrious and caring employer, ploughing back the profits into expanding the business and employing more people. But Ron preferred to spend his time travelling, ostensibly to get in orders, staying in expensive hotels, finding one excuse after another not to return home.

Eve was remembering how one rainy day over the Christmas holiday she had gone searching for her father, calling him. Rain was hammering on the roof of the shed, overflowing along the gutters, the sound like the rush of an endless river. Through the arch of the trees she had seen him and Sue together, crouched behind

the fronds, the rain hardly touching them. They were
laughing. She had called to them, beckoning to Ron to
come to the phone. They had waved back gaily and
come running up the path. How could she have been
so stupid?

'Someday you'll wake up to reality. Know who your
real friends are. I hope, by then, it won't be too late,'
Dorothy said.

In Dorothy's eyes Eve was a fool and now also an
enemy. She made Eve feel as if the reason for her
existence had been to deprive her mother of her husband and her marriage. Dorothy's assessment of Sue
was proving right too, but Eve, living in her dream
world, had not recognised it.

Eve had noticed a change in Sue's attitude the minute
she had set eyes on Ron: a look of triumph, and something else – mockery at Eve for not grasping the
situation. Now, in idyllic surroundings, was she enjoying the vision of the havoc she had wrought, and the
consequences she had known it would bring? Was it
possible that when she had seen that photograph of
Ron, the night of the Eileen Joyce recital, that she had
invented a plan to rob Dorothy of her husband, Eve of
her father, and destroy their lives? No matter how hard
she tried, Eve could not find it in her heart to believe
that this was so. All her life Eve had longed for her
mother's approval, even a tiny expression of pride in
something she had done. Now that dream, too, was
destroyed.

Before embarking on her studies with Sir George
Sanders Clare decided to go home for a holiday. She
gave notice to Mrs Cartwright that she would not be
returning to the attic bedsitter into which she had

moved when Eve had not returned. At the time it had been a godsend with a cheaper rent so that she had been able to manage financially.

Jack and Agnes were at the station to meet her, a little distant with each other still but curiously united, like strangers to Clare. Agnes eyed her up and down.

'You've changed,' she said, giving her a kiss on the cheek. 'Something in your expression and your manner.'

'Oh, be the hokey, but you're a real lady,' Jack said, with great satisfaction in his voice.

'Yes, you're coming on fine,' Agnes agreed, 'but I wish you'd take more care of your health. That skimpy dress can't be good for your chest in cold weather like this.'

'Mother!' Clare groaned.

'I speak as I find,' Agnes affirmed. 'There's too much of you exposed. You should cover yourself up.'

Agnes hadn't changed. There was no nonsense about her. She had no interest in idle chatter.

That evening she prepared a special meal for Clare. Homemade vegetable soup, rack of Wicklow lamb, new potatoes, a choice of vegetables, and rhubarb crumble.

'To think that there are people starving,' Jack remarked, watching the preparation in the kitchen. 'God be with the days when a good plate of bacon and cabbage was a feast.'

'It's a special occasion,' Agnes snapped, stirring the good red wine into the sauce. 'It's not every day a daughter gets first-class honours in her exams and a transfer to Paris.'

'I suppose not.' Jack rubbed his hands in satisfaction.

'Anyway, didn't the Irish starve long enough?' she concluded.

'We deserve to starve with this carry-on,' Jack retorted, but he was in a good mood.

After all the years of conflict, Jack and Agnes seemed to have reached a compromise. He had given up his resistance to her will and she had given up trying to force it. It was as though they had exhausted each other. Clare had the feeling that she was intruding on their private little world.

The following Sunday she accompanied Jack on his favourite walk, a survey of the railway and the various properties he had worked on over the years. 'I should have bought that dilapidated old place after the war, when property was going for a song,' he lamented, as they stood outside a Georgian mansion encased in scaffolding. 'Went for a bucket of money last month. Could turn my hand to anything then. If only I had had the foresight, I'd be worth a fortune today.'

Father McCarthy came cycling up the road and, seeing Clare, wobbled over to the kerb. 'Clare,' he crooned, dismounting, his hand stretched out in front of him. 'Is it yourself?' His watery eyes gazed at her as if she were an apparition of the Blessed Virgin. 'Marvellous, marvellous. Sure 'tis the price of you, little Clare Dolan. Who'd have thought?' He stood shaking his head and hemming and hawing through his nose.

'Thank you, Father,' Clare said, smiling to hide her discomfiture.

Jack gave Father McCarthy a curt nod and stared into the middle distance as if something fascinating had just caught his eye.

'Don't go getting high-falutin' ideas now with all this achievement,' Father McCarthy continued. 'I expect to see you at Mass on Sunday with your mother.' He patted her hand as if they were old friends.

'Yes, Father,' Clare assured him, with a smile, as he mounted his bicycle again.

'Bring your father with you,' he called over his shoulder. With a nod in Jack's direction he was off, wobbling down the road.

'Hypocrite,' Jack spluttered with rage. 'Him and his oul' talk. Excommunicated us in twenty-two. Now they want us back among the flock. Hooligans the lot of them. If only I had me gun back.' His voice was high with rage.

As they continued their walk, harsh reality struck Clare. Things were changing fast in Ireland. The town was becoming fashionable with its boutique and hair salon and smart new supermarket on the corner. Builders were busy turning the lush fields of Joyce's farm into a concrete jungle and television aerials were springing up from the roofs of the new houses, the owners of which were of a new breed and generation: bank clerks, marketing managers and advertising men.

The more time Clare spent with Jack, the more she was forced to listen to his reminiscences of the civil war, a fascinating landscape of memories in his unreliable recollections, the only place where he felt he truly belonged. Jack had changed. He was quieter, content to sit down at the kitchen table to read his newspaper, or listen to the sponsored programmes on the radio while Agnes worked around him.

'He's mellowed,' Agnes remarked to Clare.

Clare was uneasy. Jack had always been long-suffering and uncomplaining about his health, but when she made enquiries about the pain in his back all he said was, 'Nothing that a pint won't cure.'

'What did Dr Gregory say?' Clare asked anxiously, when the pain forced him to go to the surgery.

'Who'd take any notice of him? Bloody blaggard, blaming the cigarettes and the drop of drink. It's an old war wound.'

Agnes, face flushed from the effort of making brawn out of a pig's cheek, sighed deeply and said, 'Dr Gregory's right. He didn't do seven years' training in the Mater Hospital for nothing. Giving up the smokes won't do you any harm. And as for the drink . . .' She threw her eyes up to heaven.

Jack shook his head dismissively and, taking his *Ellery Queen's Mystery Magazine* off the dresser, left the kitchen without another word.

Clare noticed a gradual yellowish tinge to his pallor. He stayed in bed a lot but was still uncomplaining, more concerned about his country than himself. 'The RUC men have invaded the Bogside of Derry,' he read from the *Irish Press* newspaper. 'Batoning men, women and children in the streets and in their homes. A deputation of citizens from the Bogside went to London to protest to Prime Minister Harold Wilson about the behaviour of the RUC and the B Specials.'

'Fat lot of good that'll do,' Agnes said.

'Didn't I always tell you this would happen?' Jack ranted. '"Ian Paisley protesting in London,"' he read. 'Now, that Bernadette Devlin might do something.'

'Who's she?' Clare asked.

'She's an undergraduate at Queen's University and a founder member of the People's Democracy Movement.'

Clare did not share Jack's enthusiasm for what was happening in the North. Hiding the strain of her forthcoming move to Paris and her reunion with Henry was proving too much for her. Henry had called to the house with an enormous bunch of roses. But his new air of affluence had taken Clare by surprise.

'You've changed,' he had said, his eyes darting nervously round the room and returning to her face, drinking in every detail.

'Really?' Clare asked, amused at his expression. 'So have you.'

'You're shining,' he said. 'Full of vitality or something.'

'Thank you,' Clare said.

Henry had acquired a new brashness that did not seem to belong to him. He took her to the Glencove Hotel for dinner, told her that the sale of the farm enabled him to return to medical school and about his ambitions to have a practice of his own some day. As he talked, it dawned on Clare that he had not invited her out to court her, but to make her suffer for having left him. She soon discovered that he was teaching her a lesson, proving to her the mistake she had made in rejecting him, and showing her what she was missing. To the onlooker they were a handsome couple, enjoying themselves, but all Henry was doing was pointing out her weaknesses. 'Maybe your mother did me a favour after all,' he said, when he had stopped talking about himself. 'You're turning into a snob. Too good for any of us. Soon you'll be up there somewhere, closeted and pampered by your adoring public.'

'Do you really think so?' Clare enthused, desperately wanting to hit him across the face.

'Oh, yes. I think you did me a favour, too, by putting your career first.' Raising his glass, he said, 'Here's to you and your dominant mother.'

'It's your own fault,' Agnes said, when Clare confided in her. 'You shouldn't have had anything to do with him after you came back. Since the Joyces got that ridiculous amount of money for their farm they think they're Christ's first cousins. Anyway,' she concluded, 'if you'd really wanted him you'd never have left him.'

Clare opened her mouth to protest and shut it again, realising the futility of anything she might say.

When Martin arrived home Agnes was making bread, kneading the dough with her rough, capable hands.

'I've got a few days off,' he said, licking the mixture, 'but I don't want anyone to know I'm here.'

'What's up now?' Agnes asked, scrutinising him.

'Something I have to sort out,' Martin said cagily.

Agnes continued to work rhythmically, slapping the mixture against the side of the bowl, her whole body concentrated on her task.

'Bernadette Devlin said that if the British troops are sent in she wouldn't like to be either the mother or sister of any unfortunate soldier stationed in the North. I have a feeling that something awful is going to happen,' Agnes said, lifting the bread into the oven, her breathing heavy, her arms smeared in flour.

'I wouldn't dispute that,' Martin said.

'You should get out of Belfast, Martin.' Agnes had a pleading look in her eyes.

'You're an astute woman, Mother.' Martin took a warm fruit scone from a batch that was cooling on a wire tray. He smoothed it over carefully with butter and jam, then bit into it, tearing apart the warm fresh dough. Still chewing, he took another, worrying and teasing it between his fingertips, reducing the carefully constructed dough almost to crumbs. 'You understand the need for freedom,' Martin said. 'I can't abandon the Cause now.'

'The Cause, the Cause. That's all I've ever heard all

my life,' Agnes remonstrated. 'This time the price might be too high, Martin.'

'I would never have taken you for a Me Feiner, Mother. Freedom at any price – isn't that what we always believed?'

'Not if it means loss of life.' Agnes wiped her brow.

That evening they all sat down to dinner, Jack at one end of the table, Agnes at the other, Clare and Martin between them. Agnes blessed herself, stiff and cere-monious in her Sunday dress, and proceeded to say grace, thanking God for his goodness in bringing together the whole family for the first time in months. Clare, sensing Martin's discomfort, closed her eyes and kept them shut until the blessing.

'You were late last night,' Jack said to her.

'I was practising with Clem. We're thinking of doing a concert together for the old-folks' home.'

'That's a nice idea,' Jack said.

'Clem Rogers,' Martin scoffed, furiously stabbing his fork into his meat. 'High-society Clem.'

'There's nothing wrong with Clem Rogers,' Clare said.

'Nothing at all,' Martin agreed. 'If you don't mind gravitating to the lower elements.'

'Clem's from a good family.' Clare straightened her-self and ate with elegance.

'I thought you'd be above all that crowd by now,' Martin said. 'Still, each one to his own.'

'Clem's talented. We need a bit of variety in the concert,' Clare said.

'So speaks the voice of Miss Prima Donna.'

'Yes,' Clare said. 'You probably don't understand the word talent, Martin.'

'Considering it's been shoved down my gob ever since you won that scholarship.'

'Oh, Clare's the girl with the talent,' Jack said, with a conviction that brooked no argument.

'Depending on the way you look at it,' Martin said, a slow insolent smile spreading over his face, intimating that winning the scholarship had more to do with an inherent cunning than any talent she might have.

'The curse of God on you for a begrudger, Martin.' Jack thumped the table, which shook.

'He didn't mean it like that,' Agnes said. 'Now let's have a bit of decorum here.'

The rest of the meal was eaten in silence. As soon as it was over, Jack left the kitchen with the newspaper and Agnes went upstairs.

Clare began stacking the dishes. Martin lifted them over to the sink.

'There was talk of you last night,' Clare said.

Martin shot her a sidelong glance. 'What talk?'

'Somebody said they heard you were involved up North.'

She tilted her head to look at him. His eyes were bright and his jaw set in a decisive line. A pulse throbbed at the corner of his mouth, the only indication of tension in the strong features he had inherited from Agnes.

'Shh,' he hissed. 'Who was talking? Not that snotty-nosed Clem Rogers? You don't choose your company very well, Clare.'

'Are you?' Clare asked.

'Heavily,' Martin replied. 'And proud of it.'

The dishes clattered in the sink.

'Don't say anything to Mother,' he continued. 'She doesn't know the extent of it.'

'What do you hope to achieve?' Clare searched his face, waiting for an answer.

'Understanding. We come from a long line of patriots.'

Clare opened her mouth to say something and stopped, arrested by the chill in Martin's eyes. Eventually, she said, 'I don't understand why anyone would want to put themselves in that kind of danger.'

'Because I care about the poor unfortunate Catholics who can't get a job or a house. I care about freedom and a united Ireland.'

The banging on the front door and the hiss of whispers woke Clare.

'Are you in there, Martin? Martin, come out.'

Clare heard her brother's bedroom door open. 'What the fuck?' His footsteps on the stairs, running down, the bolt on the front door shooting back.

She lay rigid, listening.

'What's up?' she heard him say.

'Molloy's been lifted. Change of plan. Come on.'

'Bastards,' Martin said.

'Got a gun?'

Clare heard him running upstairs and their parents' bedroom door opening.

'What is it? What do they want?' Agnes's voice was an anxious whisper.

'Go back to bed,' Martin muttered.

He was gone, running down the stairs, crashing the front door after him. There was the sound of running footsteps, car doors slamming, the car driving off. Silence.

When she thought it was safe, Clare got out of bed and went to the window. The street was dark and deserted. She opened her bedroom door quietly and stepped onto the landing. Through the wall she could hear the mumble of Jack's voice.

Next morning Agnes was in the kitchen, her face stony, obviously not in the mood for a conversation. 'I think you'd better stay in your room a bit longer. You'll be tired. I'll bring up your breakfast.'

Clare climbed the stairs slowly, her legs heavy as lead. Throughout her childhood her room had been her refuge with her bed snug under the eaves. She stood at the window watching Rita Sampson's young sister Peggy marking out piggy-beds with her friends, to one side of their washing-line. She opened the window to listen to the early-morning noises: pigeons cooing in the woods behind the houses, a thrush singing in a nearby bush. All the familiar sounds of her childhood for which she had been so homesick.

For once, those soothing sounds couldn't shut out the feeling of hostility. Returning to her bed, she buried her face in her pillow to staunch the tears that flowed. For as long as she could remember her little room had wrapped itself around her, a protective shell, holding her as she slept through the night. Often she would lie with her curtains open, staring out at the stars, trying to remember the various formations her father had taught her.

At last she got up and wandered around, tidying up her clothes, making her bed. Catching sight of herself in her mirror she stood before it and studied her face, as she had on the night of the dance. It was the same face but there was a tiny frown between the brows and a slight puckering around the mouth, as if she were about to burst into fresh tears.

Her family were alien to her. Agnes, without saying much about it, would be on Martin's side. Martin, her only brother, whom she had revered, for whom she had always had time and of whom she was proud, was a let-down, his ambitions and ideals meaningless. Now Clare understood that they didn't know one another any more. When Agnes came up with her breakfast she seemed calm, but said nothing about Martin.

That evening Martin was sitting at the kitchen table, eating his fry of bacon and sausages as if nothing had happened, Agnes presiding over him with the teapot.

'They panicked, that's all,' he was saying, when Clare took her place at the table.

'Bad luck to them anyway,' Agnes exclaimed. 'The fright we all got.'

'Couldn't be helped. They're lifting innocent people all the time.'

'Listen, Martin,' Agnes said, her face an inch away from his. 'Lie down with dogs and you get up with fleas. Keep away or God help us all.'

'I nailed my colours to the mast a long time ago, Mother.'

'I hate to see all that trouble starting again. What did your father's shenanigans with that crowd ever bring us but misery?'

'There'll be no peace until the Brits are out of the North.'

'Innocent folk will be killed and maimed,' Agnes said. 'There's nothing heroic about that. Cold-blooded murder if you ask me.'

'I come from a long line of freedom fighters,' Martin said.

Agnes stood up. 'I've heard this for as long as I can remember. All I know is that I don't want you involved in any of it. You have a wife to consider.'

'Terry can take care of herself. She understands.'

'Doesn't care, more like,' Agnes snapped. 'Your personal crusade won't change a thing, Martin – believe me, I know. When nothing's changed in twenty years' time, will you look back and think of the needless bloodshed?'

'Well, I'm off to bed,' Martin said, leaving the room.

'That boy is exhausted. He doesn't know what he's saying,' Agnes said to Clare, getting out her ironing board and erecting it between her daughter and herself, a wall of practicality around her fear and outrage, and a conversation stopper.

'I'm going over to Eve,' Clare said, and left.

Chapter Fourteen

Late one night there was a knock on the side door of the pub. Madge Kinsella peered through a chink in the curtains but could see no one. She went downstairs and called, 'Who's there?' from behind the door.

'It's me . . . Pauline,' came the soft voice.

Slowly Madge opened the door and there stood Pauline in the shadows, her face full of misery, a baby inside her coat.

'Pauline. Come in,' Madge said, astounded. 'You must be frozen.'

In the flat upstairs, over the pub, Pauline huddled into the fire, the baby on her knee, her face withdrawn through fear.

'You'll have to mind him for me, Madge,' she said.

'What?'

'Just for a few days. I'm going to Belfast to look for Seamus.'

'Belfast? Why didn't he contact you since?'

'I think he was kidnapped.'

'What?'

'Sergeant Enright warned me not to tell anyone. He made enquiries and he says he has reason to believe that Seamus is in Belfast.'

For a moment Madge was speechless. Then she said, 'I see.'

'If I leave the baby with Aunt Bea she'll take him

over and I'll never get him back.'

Madge made tea and they talked about Seamus and the dreadful situation in which Pauline found herself at a time when she needed him most.

'You must hide the baby,' Pauline said. 'If Aunt Bea knows he's here she'll come and take him back. She wants to keep him all to herself.'

'She can't do that,' Madge said.

'You don't know her. She can do anything she likes. You'll have to keep him hidden. I've brought a couple of bottles for him and some nappies. He's on Cow and Gate. It tells you how to make up the formula on the back of the tin. You've a warm, safe place, Madge, and no one will come searching up here.' Pauline looked around her, desolate and sad.

'What's his name?' Madge asked.

'Seamie. After his father.'

As if on cue Seamie woke and smiled sleepily at Madge. He was a beautiful baby, with blond cobweb curls thickening over his head and big blue eyes.

'How old is he now exactly?' Madge said, lifting him up into her arms.

'Four months.'

'My, but you're a prime boy for your age,' Madge said, hugging him.

As they discussed feeds and sleeping arrangements, a look of relief spread over Pauline's face.

With Seamie's first whimper Pauline heated his bottle and fed, soothed and burped him, talking to him while Madge got the old oak cot down from the attic. She cleaned it thoroughly, made it up and put two hot-water bottles in it to air the mattress.

That's how Madge came to be in possession of Pauline's baby when Eve called to see her the next day.

'Don't tell a living soul,' Madge warned her. 'Pauline's gone to look for Seamus and she doesn't want her aunt Bea to know. She'll be back in a few days.'

'Bet she's run off,' said Mrs Browne, the cleaner, who was eavesdropping. 'The slut. Unreliable, her sort.' Mrs Browne had worked for Madge since she took over the pub in 1960. She was a sharp-faced, withered little woman with rimless glasses and bright orange hair. Her husband was a farm labourer and, according to her, had helped build up the agricultural industry in the area single-handed.

The first thing she did each morning was make a cup of tea to build up her strength for the day's work ahead. 'Have a cup,' she said to Eve. 'Since that Pauline left there's no one to help out with the chores.' Her nose quivered with indignation. 'Suits herself, that one.'

'She's got a baby to think of, Mrs Browne,' Eve protested. 'Her baby's father. She wants to find him.'

'If he wanted her to know where he was he'd tell her,' Mrs Browne said.

'A little beauty,' Madge said, bringing Seamie into the kitchen for Eve to hold. 'I'll have to go shopping. Pauline only left me one clean Babygro. I'll buy some nice things for him to wear.'

'Huh,' Mrs Browne said. 'I wouldn't be surprised if she never comes back. You watch it or you'll get landed with him for good.'

Mrs Browne took her vacuum cleaner, aerosol sprays and dusters out of the cupboard under the stairs and went into the bar, her hat bobbing in disapproval.

The doorbell rang. Madge peered out of the window. It was Sergeant Enright.

'Get that, Eve. Don't let on about the baby.'

257

'She's having a rest,' Madge heard Eve say. 'Call back later.'

'I'll have to go out some time,' Madge said, when he had gone. 'The baby needs fresh air and more Cow and Gate.'

'I'll get Sarah's pram out of the garage. You can borrow that,' Eve said.

Later, well wrapped up, Madge trudged uphill to the corner shop. She hid the pram behind a clump of trees and made her purchases quickly.

'Awful weather,' said Mrs Rogers, Clem's mother, eyeing the tins of Cow and Gate as she wrapped them. 'Any news?' she asked, folding her arms across her heavy bosom, ready for a chat.

'Divil a bit.' Madge left quickly, crossing the road at the end of the lane when she saw Sergeant Enright coming towards her.

'Madge?' he called.

The pram zigzagged on the muddy, rutted ground as Madge increased her speed. She struggled, breaking into a run, uphill, her legs and arms moving mechanically. Gasping for breath, she reached the door of the pub.

Eve helped her prepare the baby for bed, cooing, comforting, changing his nappy.

Sergeant Enright came into the bar.

'Pauline's aunt has been in touch. She's looking for Pauline. I thought she might be here,' he said.

'I haven't seen sight nor light of her,' Madge lied.

'According to her aunt she's disappeared off the face of the earth and taken her baby with her.'

'If I hear anything, Sergeant, you'll be the first to know,' Madge assured him.

'She won't come back here if there's trouble,' Mrs

Browne said. 'And you're getting too attached to the baby. I can see it happening already.'

'Poor little soul.' Madge sighed. 'I'll run up and see if he's awake.'

'He's not yours and there's no use pretending he is.'

'Shut your trap, Mrs Browne. I'm sick listening to you.'

Pauline unbolted the side gate that Tim had left unlocked. The rusty bolt creaked in protest. As the red signal went up, the train came into the station, its throbbing engine spluttering into the night air. When it stopped, Pauline opened the heavy door and climbed in, closing it carefully behind her. In the signal box Tim pulled a lever and the green signal flashed. The train lurched and bumped forward, crawling its way along the old track, head-lamps pointed towards the city. Pauline relaxed into her seat, the draught from the window cooling her perspiring brow. As the train gathered speed her world dropped away into a dark abyss, the hills and sea of her childhood merging into blackness. Her heart was breaking because she was leaving her baby behind, along with the wasted years of lost opportunities, the shattered dreams, the feeling of belonging.

Once she found Seamus she'd be back home again. There would be no more urgency, no panic. When the bumping ceased and the train ran smoothly along the coast she leaned back, gazing at the dark waters to the left of her. Tim Reilly had been good to her. He had arranged for the non-stop train to stop, had kept watch in his signal box to make sure she was safely aboard. A light from the corridor cast a glimmer on the sea, which was visible only through gaps in the hedge. It lay immense and still, a sphere of darkness.

As the lights of the city came into view Pauline adjusted her slingbacks, straightened her coat and walked the distance that separated one station from the other, glancing over her shoulder now and again, reminding herself that there was no time to lose. She was struck by the lights reflecting off the wet pavement of the Dublin city streets. In the glowing brilliance of Kingsbridge station she was conscious of her blotchy face, her untidy hair, and glad that no one was waiting to meet her. As the train rattled into the platform she took her place in the queue to board it. Staring at her reflection in the inky black window, she settled into her seat thinking of Seamus, both of them sharing baths in the dilapidated tub in her basement, taking turns to soap each other, singing at the top of their voices 'Needles and Pins' or Millie's ear-splitting 'My Boy Lollipop'. Sometimes they harmonised just to annoy old Miss Cuff, the busybody overhead. If they forgot the words they improvised. It didn't matter if they missed a beat. Seamus had a good strong voice and could raise the roof with it if he wanted to. When she would ask for the facecloth, soap or shampoo, he'd laugh and say, 'When I become an octopus I'll let you know.'

Seamus would dry her slowly, first one arm, then the other. He would linger over her legs and by the time he started on her front, caressing each breast slowly with the towel, kissing her for a long time, they would both be driven mad with desire. He would comb back his wet hair, standing in front of the mirror, dancing as he sang 'Can't Buy Me Love', his body lean, firm, his skin smooth, the towel wrapped round his waist, threatening to fall at any moment.

During the long summer of her pregnancy, Pauline

had sensed Seamus's irritation. She wasn't sure if it was with her for letting herself get pregnant, or for worrying too much about the future, the rent, the bills, or with himself for not having the lifestyle he craved.

As the Belfast train gathered speed, Pauline was remembering the times she went by train to Bray with Seamus. They would sit in the carriage holding hands, laughing, happy together. Passengers would smile at them. What did people see now when they looked at her? A heartbroken, sullen, stringy-haired girl, alone and unloved, whose dreams had been shattered. As her eyes closed involuntarily and sleep caught up with her, giving her some respite from the long, tedious journey, she dreamed about Seamus. That he was coming towards her, smiling.

The cold woke her. By the time Belfast swung into view her feet were freezing. She fumbled in her bag to get her ticket ready, gathered up her belongings and went to stand by the door as the train came to a halt. Once outside the station she stood trying to decide whether to start walking towards a bus stop or to get a hot drink somewhere.

Out of the corner of her eye she spotted a bus with Sandy Row written on the front of it, parked at the corner of the station. The Gilfoyles, Seamus's parents, lived there. She took her notebook from her bag and checked the address. As the bus moved slowly through blocks of burned-out buildings, past ghettos, Pauline felt a frightened sense of exile that she tried not to think about. Cars, even trucks on the two-lane highway, looked different.

In Lisburn Road the bus pulled into a siding and parked. The conductor signalled to her that they had reached their destination. The houses were small, red-brick, terraced, back-to-back, with graffiti painted on the gable ends. 'FREE IRELAND' and 'UP THE REPUBLIC'. Heart pounding, Pauline walked quickly, past police, blockades, barbed wire, advancing further into the warren of streets. All the houses looked the same. Children, playing together, stopped to stare at her. One pointed his index finger straight at her shouting, 'Bang, bang.'

Quickly she walked down one street, up another, checking the numbers on the doors, unable to find number ninety-one. Realising that she was lost she stopped a woman and asked for directions to the Gilfoyles'.

'From the South?' the woman asked.

Pauline nodded.

'Thought so,' she said, eyeing her up and down. 'Two streets further on.'

Pauline ran all the way.

Mrs Gilfoyle answered her knock. 'Pauline!' she said in amazement.

'I'm not here to cause trouble,' Pauline said. 'I had to see you.'

Mrs Gilfoyle opened the door wider and let her in. She was a tall woman with a pinched face and beady eyes that missed nothing. Her hair was mostly dark with a hint of grey and the proud way she lifted her head, even her gesticulations, reminded Pauline of Seamus.

'Come in. How did you get here?' Mrs Gilfoyle said, ushering her into the kitchen.

'Train,' Pauline said.

As Mrs Gilfoyle took out her best china and cut sultana cake, she eyed Pauline. 'I suppose you've come to tell me something about Seamus?' she said.

'No.' Pauline hesitated. 'I thought you might know where he is.'

'My son,' Mrs Gilfoyle announced dramatically, wiping her hands on her apron, 'has not let his family down. They were shipbuilders you know, down the docks here. Fought in the wars for their king and country.'

Pauline presumed that Britain was the country she was talking about.

'I know Seamus went off somewhere,' Mrs Gilfoyle continued, 'but we're expecting him home any minute.' Her sharp, defiant eyes dared Pauline to contradict her.

For once Pauline was content to let herself be consoled by the strength of the other woman's conviction. She wanted to tell her everything she knew, but decided against it.

'The policeman who came round making enquiries told me that Seamus was suspected of touting. But sure I know that Seamus would never do such a thing. He's too smart. He'll be back as soon as the dust settles. Mark my words.'

'I'm determined to find him.' Pauline burst into tears.

'Shush,' Mrs Gilfoyle said. 'Let you not get involved. The police'll take care of it.'

It would be pointless to argue with Mrs Gilfoyle, Pauline discovered as they talked. She would put her own interpretation on everything Pauline had to say, constructing her version of events to suit what she could cope with. Pauline understood straight away that Seamus's mother wasn't interested in anything to do with her. The only thing of importance to her was that Seamus was coming back and nothing would shake her belief.

'Don't worry,' she said, leaning towards Pauline, a vindictive look in her eyes 'We'll find him, and if they've touched a hair of his head we'll get the bastards. I mind you that we're not people to be trifled with.'

Pauline believed her.

Mr Gilfoyle called out from the sitting room that the news was on.

'He's a wee bit deaf,' Mrs Gilfoyle said. 'Come on you in and say hello to him.'

Mr Gilfoyle was crouched into a corner, his ear cupped in his hand, glaring at the screen, expecting news of trouble. He nodded in Pauline's direction as if she were a regular visitor, and continued to watch the blaring television. Pauline sat down on the sofa and thought of Seamus. They would emigrate together. Take Seamie with them. Make a new start. It was the only way. She had dreamed of their reunion, both of them so anxious to make things right that they would end up screaming out their rage and bitterness at one another.

What would he look like when he came through the door? Unshaven, his clothes crumpled as if he had slept in them. He would smile at her, walk towards her. She would feel happy and sick all at once.

'You'll be stopping the night?' Mrs Gilfoyle asked.

'If I may,' Pauline said.

'Just the one night,' Mrs Gilfoyle said. 'There's a lot of tension. People are getting very edgy. You must be away tomorrow. It's dangerous times we're living in.'

Pauline nodded, glad she had not mentioned her baby.

The next morning Pauline decided to call to the depot where Seamus worked to see if anyone there knew his whereabouts. On her way down the Falls Road she heard quick, light footsteps behind her. Her first impression was that the person who approached was decisive, fast, determined.

'Howayah?' Martin stood in front of her, blocking her path. 'You don't look delighted to see me.' He smiled.

'How did you get here?' Pauline gasped.

'Surprised?'

'I wouldn't be surprised if you stuck a knife in me this minute.' Pauline looked away disgusted. 'You were following me, weren't you?'

'Ah, come on, Pauline. Don't talk like that.' Martin caught hold of her elbow and propelled her across the street.

'Where are you taking me?'

'Friends of mine. Nice guys. You'll get on well with them.'

'I'm sure that concerns you.' Pauline glanced at him.

'You should be glad to have someone you know to escort you in a strange city,' Martin replied.

'I don't trust you,' Pauline retorted.

'Let's not argue. Get in.'

Before she knew what was happening she was being pushed into the passenger seat of a van and Martin was installed beside her. He flashed her a brilliant smile that seemed to exude a tremendous energy as he started the engine.

'Don't fret. You're safe with me,' he said, as they drove through the city, Pauline hunched in her seat.

'Are you kidnapping me, too?' she asked.

'Only trying to protect you. It's dangerous for a good-looking woman to be on her own in a place like this.'

Pauline gazed out of the window.

'Now don't go feeling sorry for yourself, Pauline.' Martin took her hand

'I don't indulge in self-pity,' she said, snatching it back.

They drove through stretches of sturdy houses and tower blocks. Pauline was shocked by the downtrodden area, where buildings were shuttered and deserted. There were signs up, neon lights sometimes, but no affluent hotels or restaurants that she could see.

Martin stopped the van at the corner of a huge block of flats. 'Here we are,' he said, jumping out and running round to her side to open the passenger door for her.

At the lifts they faced one another. There was a serious expression on Martin's face as he hesitated before pressing the button. The lift clanked down. Stepping into it, Pauline shivered.

'Don't be scared,' Martin said, brushing the hair away from her face and pressing the button marked eight.

The door of the flat was opened by a squat young man with broad shoulders and a crew-cut. His face was white and drawn, as though it had not seen daylight for a long time.

'This is Scully,' Martin said. 'Scully, this is Pauline, a friend of mine.'

'Hi,' Scully said, standing back to let her in. She walked past him into a sparsely furnished room, assessing it the way people do when they enter unfamiliar territory. A glass door opened out on to a balcony, which circled around in front of the other apartments, giving a view of wasteground below.

Pauline opened it and went out, stiffening instantly against the cold wind. She returned quickly, closing the door behind her.

'I'll get you a cup of tea,' Scully said, and disappeared as Pauline seated herself on a high-backed chair.

'How did you know where I was?' she asked Martin suddenly.

'No great mystery,' he said. 'The Gilfoyles. They know that I'm looking for Seamus too.'

There was silence. Martin seemed lost for words. Pauline said, 'I thought you'd have been safely banged up by now.'

'I haven't done anything wrong.' He grinned.

'You mean you haven't been caught yet.'

'You're a terrible girl, Pauline. Do you know that?' Martin smiled indulgently at her.

She looked away. Not asking him any questions seemed proof, if he needed proof, that her interest in him stretched no further than someone with whom to kill a few hours before she was on her way to look for Seamus. Maybe she should be nice to him, reach out in the hope that he would soften and give her some information. He seemed so different from his usual enthusiastic self: unsure of what to say, what to do, another person. Scully returned with two mugs of tea.

'Thanks,' Martin said, dismissing him with a nod towards the door and handing Pauline one of the mugs.

'I'll leave you to it, then.' Scully hesitated a moment and left.

When they were alone Martin said, in a voice that sounded sincere, 'You know I think the world of you, Pauline.'

She concentrated on the mug she was holding in an effort not to cry.

'I'd hate it if anything were to happen to you,' he said.

'I only came here to find Seamus. I promised him a long time ago that I'd come to Belfast. But I never dreamt it would be like this,' Pauline said.

'Look for him all you want. But you'll need protection.' Martin stood up.

'Will you help me find him?'

Martin nodded.

'Thanks.' Pauline smiled gratefully at him, but the
chill in the marrow of her bones belied her smile.
'Martin?'

'Yes?'

'There's something I have to tell you,' she said.

'What?'

'I . . . I went to see Sergeant Enright.'

'You what?' Martin blazed,

'I was frightened.' The words were choking her.
'Maybe I shouldn't have.'

Martin grabbed her shoulders, lifting her out of her
chair. 'What did you tell him?' His eyes bored into hers,
sharp, vivid all of a sudden.

'Let me go!' she shouted.

He loosened his grip.

'I told him that Seamus was missing. That you
threatened him.'

'Oh, Christ! You little fool.' Martin slumped into a
chair. 'Now he'll start interfering. Why the fuck did
you do it? I told you not to go to the cops.'

'Because when Seamus didn't come back I got
worried.' Pauline was wringing her hands. 'I couldn't
bear to think of him tied up in a cellar or something.'

'Your imagination is too vivid.'

'I was terrified.'

'You'll be more terrified if anyone in the organisation
finds out that you spoke to Sergeant Enright.'

'How will they?'

'When he starts agitating, asking awkward questions.
That's how. Then we'll all be up to our necks in it.'

'You are already,' Pauline said.

Martin looked at her, shaking his head in disbelief. 'What in the name of Jesus were you thinking of, Pauline? You know there's collusion between the cops north and south of the border.'

'How would I know that?' Pauline said defensively. 'Anyway, I have a right to know what happened to Seamus. He's the father of my child.'

'You've put us all in danger,' Martin said quietly. 'Why do you think I left Glencove in the first place? Went to England? Why do you think I'm here?' He looked at her. 'I've business up here, Pauline, and you're jeopardising it.'

'I know nothing about your business.'

There was another silence.

'I don't even know how involved Seamus was,' Pauline said.

'Not much. A few messages here and there. Bits of information.'

'How involved are you?'

'Plenty.' Martin lit a cigarette and spat out a thread of tobacco. 'I'll be behind bars if Sergeant Enright co-operates with the crowd up here. And it'll be all your fault.'

His accusatory look frightened Pauline. For a moment she thought he was going to lose his temper.

'The best thing is for you to stay here for a while. Talk to no one. When we do find Seamus you'll be here waiting for him.'

Chapter Fifteen

It was a glorious day. The sun was shining and Dorothy was sitting at the window in the drawing room, absorbed in D.H. Lawrence's *Sons and Lovers*. After the initial shock, her reaction to Ron's departure had come as a complete surprise. She seemed to need to fill every minute and hour of the day with trips out to visit friends or to the shops to buy clothes, jewellery, hats. Anything that cost money. Her compulsion to spend gave her some sort of release. Suddenly she looked young again and was more energetic.

When James Freeman gently reminded her that the cash to meet her bills might not always be available, all she said was, 'We'll be dead long enough.'

The frantic ringing of the doorbell disrupted her pleasure in her book and brought Agnes flying up from the kitchen to see if the house was on fire.

'Eve's not here,' Dorothy said, to the attractive stranger Agnes escorted to the garden.

'My name's Chris Winthrop. I'm a friend of hers.' He smiled at Dorothy.

'Would you like to wait?' Dorothy asked, detecting that his accent was English. 'She won't be long. She's babysitting for a friend.'

While he waited Chris flattered Dorothy, telling her that she looked far too young to be Eve's mother, and invited her to join Eve and himself for dinner as soon as Eve arrived home.

Far from being impressed, Dorothy was deeply suspicious of his intentions and scornful of his choice of profession.

'He looks a very presentable young man to me,' Agnes said, in the privacy of the kitchen.

'A saxophone player, I ask you?' Dorothy said. 'I don't trust him. Too suave. What does he want with Eve?'

Agnes threw up her arms in a gesture of hopelessness and left the room.

Dorothy's hostility diminished slightly when she saw Eve's delight at seeing Chris again. 'What are you doing here?' Eve exclaimed, coming into the drawing room.

'I missed you,' he said.

Later, when they were alone, he said, 'Come and live with me.' The suggestion was posed as if he understood that she worshipped him and was so sexually in thrall to him that she was incapable of saying no.

'How can I?' she said, aghast. 'Mother would have a fit.'

'I'll have a word with her,' Chris said confidently.

Eve looked at him in astonishment. 'She'd have a ginnet if you came out with that mouthful.'

'Well, I'll marry you then, if it's the only solution. I must warn you, though, that I don't believe in the institution.' He gave her a hug. 'I'm willing to make a concession. I'll tell your mother we're getting engaged. Will that do?'

Eve was doubtful.

'Under no circumstances!' Dorothy raged. 'How dare you even consider it?'

Calming down, she proceeded to quiz Chris about his background, his parents, his education, his income.

None of his answers impressed her. Not even the fact that his father was a well-known banker whose name appeared regularly in the *Financial Times*, or his family's connections in the City of London.

'Obviously your mother doesn't approve,' Chris said to Eve, when they were alone again.

'She's hard to please,' Eve said.

'We'll run away. Get married in Gretna Green.'

'What?' Eve gasped. 'I can't do that.'

But the more her mother grilled Chris, the more determined Eve became to marry him. Apart from the newly awakened lust she felt for Chris, which must have been obvious to the shrewd Dorothy, Eve wanted to get away from her mother.

Next morning, as Dorothy checked the deaths in the newspaper, Chris said to her, 'I think you should know that Eve and I have decided to get married.'

'Married?' Dorothy said the word as if she had never heard it before.

'Yes.' The enthusiasm in Chris's voice weakened as his eyes met Dorothy's cold stare.

'It's all arranged,' Chris said.

'I don't understand.' Dorothy looked baffled.

'We've made an appointment to see Father McCarthy,' he said, puffing a cigarette, enjoying Dorothy's dilemma.

'Are you crazy?' Dorothy's voice rose. 'Do you honestly think I would consider you a suitable candidate for my daughter?'

'Your daughter has agreed to be my wife.'

'We'll see about that.' Dorothy threw down the newspaper and stormed out of the kitchen.

Eve, too polite to answer her mother back and not having the strength to fight her, persuaded Chris to return to London with a promise to send her the money to elope with him as soon as he acquired it.

'Do you really think you'll be able to put this elopement plan into action?' Clare asked.

Eve was thoughtful. 'It depends on whether Chris sends the fare or not. I haven't got a bean.'

'You really think it's a good idea?' Clare looked doubtful.

'Yes, I do,' Eve enthused. 'The only thing is that there won't be a wedding reception and all the trimmings.'

She stopped for a moment, reflecting on the wedding she had always imagined for herself. A beautiful dress, her favourite roses, happy voices, photographs on the lawn against the trees. A pang of longing shot through her for something that would now never be.

'You're mad,' Clare said. 'But if that's what you want, I salute you.' She raised her glass. 'God knows, we've had enough warnings and lectures about the pitfalls of marriage.'

'Mother'd have a seizure and Grandpa . . . I don't know. He doesn't say much.'

'One of nature's gentlemen,' Clare said. 'He'll probably think you're right to take your chance at happiness. So do I, in a way.'

'Do you?'

Clare nodded. 'We don't get many chances in life.'

'What about you? Have you met anyone yet that you'd like to spend your life with?' Eve asked.

The question took Clare by surprise. She sat up and leaned forward, her face intent. 'I keep falling for the wrong type,' she said. 'I don't seem to be interested in Mr Nice Guy or Mr Available.'

'So there is someone?'

'I thought you'd have guessed by now.' Clare laughed.

'Not Vittorio.'

The name brought silence.

'He's too old.'

'He's thirty-five.' Clare looked at Eve. 'It strikes me sometimes that I'm incapable of love. I don't give the right signals, respond. Can't seem to give or take, for that matter.'

'You play your music with such passion, you can't be cold. You need the right man to bring it out.'

'Vittorio,' Clare said, and they both laughed. 'Anyway, good luck with your adventure. Let me know what happens.'

With a wave she was gone, running down the steps across the lawn, taking the short cut home.

Dorothy listened intently to the report on the radio news bulletin about the bombings in the north, then switched it off with a quick, angry movement. Since Chris's outburst she had been full of outrage. She remained tight-lipped and scowling.

When Eve reported this to him on the telephone, Chris said, 'She's jealous. She wants to be the centre of attention with you running around after her all the time.'

'It's all a game to him,' Dorothy said. 'He'll dump you the minute he meets someone else. What kind of a husband will he make, anyway? One-night stands everywhere. Playing the saxophone is no way to make a living.'

Eve went into Sarah's bedroom and sat in the chair beside the bed. She picked up Sarah's Cinderella book from the locker. Cinderella in a frothy pink dress stepping into her carriage, the Prince arriving at the ball, searching for her among the crowd. She could see Chris's face looking for her in the crowd at Euston station. She would not let him down.

There were two long weeks of waiting for Chris's letter, during which time Eve convinced herself that it was never going to arrive. When it did, she set off early one morning, after breakfast, duffel bag over her shoulder, ostensibly for a walk and to do some shopping, but really to take the boat to Holyhead.

At Dun Laoghaire harbour she watched the swarming throngs for the mailboat. Seagulls swooned and dipped above the blue sea, glistening in the sun. Eve found a quiet place up on deck and settled down to consult her guidebook, preoccupied with thoughts of her mother's reaction to her disappearance. As she sat there her uneasiness grew. What would her mother say when the neighbours found out? They would be less than charitable about the motives for her hasty wedding.

Chris was not at Euston. Thinking that he had changed his mind, Eve stood waiting, not knowing what to do. Suddenly a hand reached out and caught hers. She turned to see him beside her. The sight of him made her heart somersault.

'Come on.' He grabbed her hand and they ran out of the station. 'Bet you thought I wasn't coming,' he said, as they got into his sports car.

The sound of the engine exploded into the air and the heat vibrated around them. The wind caught in her throat making her choke and laugh all at once. They tore northwards through the flat, quiet, country roads of the Midlands and rugged forests further up, the road curving towards the horizon. A rush of pleasure raced through Eve's body as the speedometer pushed past a hundred. Nearer to the border Chris said, 'I'm hungry,' and parked outside a small town Wimpy bar. As they stepped inside Eve felt that all eyes were on her. The customers looked up as the waitress came towards them.

'Table for two?' She directed them with a smile to a quiet corner.

Chris, casual in a yellow cashmere sweater and jeans, and Eve, in a pink jacket, jeans and white high-heeled sandals, could have been any happy couple. They ordered Wimpys and milkshakes. Seeing the food made Eve hungry. She took a huge bite of her hamburger, the grease smearing her lips, the ketchup oozing around her mouth

Chris laughed. 'I own the whole world,' he said, his arm going around her waist.

All Eve knew was that she had shed her old life, was bursting upon a new one, no questions to be asked, no point asking them. Everything she wanted was there at that minute. They continued their journey, Chris describing the tiny flat in Chelsea his mother had leased for them for a year. Eventually he parked outside the Robbie Burns Hotel and, her hand tight in his, led her into the bar, the Scottish night air cold on their faces.

They were greeted by a cheerful landlady and a roaring fire. 'I was beginning to wonder if you'd got cold feet,' she said, shaking hands with Chris and kissing Eve.

'Not cold feet but cold everything else,' Chris said, with a grin.

'Come and get warm . Would you like a drink?' she asked, steering them to the fireside. 'You must be exhausted. Something to eat?'

'No, thanks,' Eve said. 'I'm too tired.'

'I'll show you to your room when you've finished your drink.'

Before she left the room Chris looked at her for a long moment. 'Good night,' he said eventually. 'I'll see you in the morning.'

His eyes had that expression in them that made her want to ignore everyone in the place and fling her arms around his neck. 'Sleep well,' was all she said, before she went up the stairs.

The sunlight filtering through the curtains woke her. She lay still for a moment, wondering where she was. There was no sound except the faint rattle of cutlery and the distant moo of cattle.

Jumping out of bed she crossed the room and drew the curtains. On one side of the road, ploughed fields stretched as far as the eye could see and on the other green fields, dotted with craggy rocks, swept down to a lake.

When she got downstairs, Chris was in the dining room, finishing his breakfast. 'I wondered when you'd make an appearance,' he said, rising to greet her.

'You should have called me. Am I late?' she asked, giving him a quick kiss.

'There's no such word as late here,' the landlady said, coming into the dining room to serve Eve. 'Did you sleep well?'

'Like a log, thanks,' Eve said.

After breakfast they walked hand in hand along a deserted path at the edge of the woods. New growth was evident in the haze of green that spread through the trees. A stream gurgled alongside them, sloping its way through muddy fields. Daffodils danced in the wind.

Having checked the address of the register office,

Chris led Eve through the run-down entrance. A woman's high-pitched voice drifted down the broad staircase but there was no one in sight. Chris knocked loudly on the first door they came to. It was opened by a stout man with a beard and glasses, dressed in a dark suit.

'What can I do for you?' He looked suspicious as he stared briefly from one to the other.

'We'd like to get married,' Chris said.

The man brought them into his untidy office and went to consult his diary. 'What date did you have in mind?'

'Now.'

'Now,' the man repeated, looking with contempt from him to Eve, as if they had offended him in some way.

Chris explained that they had come all this way and asked if he could make an immediate appointment.

'Do you have any witnesses?' the man asked.

'We were hoping you could supply them.' Chris looked young, vulnerable, out of place and Eve moved out into the corridor, embarrassed. By the time Chris emerged, he looked pale and diminished in some way, as if it were all too much for him.

'What did he say?' Eve asked.

'Tomorrow,' Chris said.

'One more day won't kill us.' She laughed.

'You might change your mind.' Chris looked at her. She stopped and kissed him, burying her face in his shoulder.

'I want to spend the rest of my life with you,' she said solemnly.

The ceremony was short. Eve wore a white lace dress Dorothy had bought her for her birthday. She missed

Clare, her family, church bells, the rush of confetti.

There was a knock on the front door. Agnes looked up nervously.

'I'll get it,' Clare said.

Sergeant Enright was standing on the doorstep, his finger poised on the bell, the badge of his peaked cap glinting in the sunshine.

'Grand day, Miss Dolan,' he said, a smile playing on his lips that belied the severity in his steely eyes.

Clare gaped at him.

'Is it yourself, Sergeant Enright?' Agnes said, coming into the hall and opening wide the door with a sweep of her hand, proof of her courtesy and lawfulness. 'Come in, come in.'

'I'd like a quiet word with Martin,' Sergeant Enright said, in a sham soft voice.

Jack, who knew Sergeant Enright for his tireless law-enforcing rituals, came downstairs and stood to attention as he entered the hall. 'Sergeant?' he asked, almost saluting.

'You'll have a cup of tea, won't you?' Agnes said, rushing for the kettle to conceal her fear. 'Sure it's thirsty weather we're having.'

'No, thanks. I'm in a hurry.'

'Sit down, Sergeant,' Jack suggested.

The policeman seated himself. Agnes left the room. 'Martin's not here,' Jack said.

The genial expression on Sergeant Enright's face disappeared. He faced Jack. 'A complaint has been filed concerning a disturbance in this neighbourhood. Would you know anything about it?'

'No, Sergeant, I'm afraid I don't,' Jack said.

'Didn't see any strangers in the area recently?'

Jack shook his head.

'Your silence is deafening, Jack. Rumour has it that persons unknown from the north, linked to the IRA, are hiding down here. You wouldn't know anything about it, would you?'

'No, Sergeant. I haven't heard a word.'

'Listen to me, Jack, me boyo.' Sergeant Enright stood up, put his arm around Jack's shoulders in an intimate gesture and said, in a low, insinuating voice, 'There's trouble brewing. Take my advice and make sure that your son Martin stays well clear of it. I'm holding you personally responsible.'

Agnes, listening at the door, dipped her finger in the holy-water font in the hall and made the sign of the Cross, her eyes beseeching the ceiling.

'I understand, Sergeant.' Jack nodded ushering Sergeant Enright towards the front door. 'You can rely on me.'

'Good,' Sergeant Enright said.

Next morning Agnes scrubbed the kitchen table until every particle of dough was removed from the bleached grain. 'It's a form of degradation to have the law coming to the door,' she declared to the table, perspiration bubbling on her brow. 'You know I'm terrified of the law.'

'There's no need to be frightened, Mother. Sergeant Enright's chancing his arm, he knows nothing,' Clare said to placate Agnes, uncertain if that was really the case.

Later that day, Clare left quietly and walked through the empty town. It was growing dark and the stars were beginning to appear in the sky. Main Street was quiet, most of the shops closed for the day, the blinds drawn. She walked with her head up, shoulders back, breathing in the tangy salt air. Some boys, involved in a game of cards, called, 'Hello,' to her as she passed by.

'Hello,' she said, recognising Peter Grimes, Hughie's cousin. 'How's Hughie?'

'Grand, thanks,' Peter said.

'Tell Babs I'll call over,' Clare said. As she walked she couldn't stop thinking about the trouble at home. It would be there waiting when she got back, the atmosphere thick with it.

Concepta was sweeping up outside her hair salon when Clare saw her. 'Coming up for a chat?' she called to Clare.

'Hi.' Clare crossed the road.

Concepta Taylor lived in a flat over the salon. Her mother, Mazie Taylor, was seated at the window, gazing out, calling, 'He's coming,' or 'He's going' to no one in particular every time Father McCarthy came out of the church, and biting the head off anyone who disturbed her concentration. There was nothing Father McCarthy did that she wasn't aware of. When he came flying around the corner, heading the Sodality of the Sacred Heart procession, his biretta cocked sideways on his head, the holy-water sprinkler dancing a jig in his hand, she declared to Clare, 'That poor unfortunate man. A saint among a parish of sinners. The divil's own children, the lot of them.'

'Hello, Mrs Taylor,' Clare said.

'See that young Tommy Reilly carrying the thurible? The little git does nothing but curse from morning till night. Oh, a born liar too, like his father. He brought the meat last week and left me short of a pound of mince. Swore blind it was in the parcel.'

Clare looked out of the window but the procession was over, the remaining stragglers heading into the church for confession.

'What ails you, Mother? You're terrible cross,' Concepta said.

Mazie Taylor didn't answer her but remained silent for the rest of the evening, something she did when she was in a sulk or making a sacrifice.

'Come on into the salon,' Concepta said to Clare, and began to sweep up the day's cuttings into a neat pile, her plump chest bouncing as she worked. From her brassy hair to her shiny nylons and high heels she exuded sex. She went to dances in Parnell Square, in Dublin, and was keen on a guard in the city, who, according to her mother, was 'an eejit'.

'Tell us all the news,' she said to Clare. 'Sit down over there.'

'You've done a lovely job,' Clare said, eyeing the new pink wash-basins and the see-through hoods of the dryers.

'We're doing nicely,' Concepta said, stopping to light a cigarette with her nicotine-stained fingers. 'Can't do much without a bit of money, can you?'

'No,' Clare agreed.

'I hear you're doing great over in London. Heading for the big time.'

'I'm working hard,' Clare said. She removed the pins that held her hair piled up on her head, shook it loose, and said, 'Will you cut a bit off this for me?'

'What magnificent hair,' Concepta said admiringly.

'It's too long.' Clare looked at the hairdresser with troubled eyes.

'If that's what you want I'll do it,' Concepta said.

'I'm going to make a fresh start. When I get to Paris I'm going to live and breathe the piano. Cut out everything else in my life.'

'And your hair,' Concepta said.

'Not too short,' Clare said. 'Leave it long enough for me to pin up.'

Concepta snipped the burnished locks. 'Don't be too hard on yourself, Clare,' she said. 'Life is short. You have to enjoy it too.'

'I see so many people stuck in a rut,' Clare said. 'That's not for me.'

'You were always impatient to be off somewhere, doing things,' Concepta said.

'There's nothing here for me.'

Clare was twisting a comb in her long, tapering fingers. Her eyes were fiery as if she were being pursued by some force within. 'Are you in some kind of trouble, Clare?' Concepta asked, her hands on Clare's shoulders, her head to one side, her eyes scrutinising the girl.

'No,' Clare said. 'But I know someone who is and I don't know how to help them.'

'Is it Eve?' Concepta asked, resuming her snipping. 'I haven't seen her around.'

'She's fine,' Clare said.

'What do you think of Pauline Quirk going off like that?' Concepta asked.

'It's very strange. Has Madge not heard from her yet?' Clare asked.

''No. Apparently Pauline's aunt is up the walls. Wants to take the baby from Madge.'

'I can't believe that Pauline would desert her baby,' Clare said.

'Not a line from her. Nothing,' Concepta said. 'Apparently she went up north to Seamus. Madge thinks now that the pair of them might have scarpered off to America or somewhere.'

'Never,' Clare said resolutely. 'Pauline wouldn't do that.'

'Seamus might have persuaded her. He's a bit of a fly-by-night.'

'I hope she's all right,' Clare said. 'Not sick or anything.'

'It's very strange, going off leaving her baby with Madge Kinsella.'

'She'll be back,' Clare said.

'I hope so,' Concepta said. 'Now stand up and let me see the result.'

Clare stood up, tall and elegant.

'It suits you,' Concepta said.

When she got home, the house was quiet. Martin's grip bag was still in the hall, under the clock. In the kitchen Jack was asleep in his chair, snoring quietly. Everywhere was peaceful. Clare wondered if the previous night's disturbance had been a dream. Dermy McQuaid was walking up the path. She opened the door before he knocked, so as not to disturb Jack.

'Clare,' he said, drawing himself up beside her.

'Hi, Dermy,' Clare said. 'How are things?'

'Oh, game ball. Kept busy with one thing or another. I'm collecting Father McCarthy's shoes,' he said, pointing to the bag in his hand.

In his spare time, Dermy McQuaid ran errands for Father McCarthy and swept the paths of the church grounds. In return Father McCarthy gave him his hand-me-down shirts and shoes and the occasional pound note. Dermy was thirty years old but he looked ageless. His legs had been affected by some disease, which had given him the hoppity-skip when he walked. But his mind was crystal clear. 'I have a message for you,' he said, his voice low.

'Me?' Clare looked at him.

'Father McCarthy wants you to call in to see him.'

Clare was aghast. 'What for?'

'A little chat, like. Nothing to worry about. He's in at the moment. Bring Martin's bag.'

As Clare approached the presbytery everywhere was quiet. Somewhere nearby a cat miaowed. In the distance a train rattled into the station. As she knocked on the door a cold breeze came up from the sea.

'Clare,' said Father McCarthy. 'Come in. Come in. Good to see you.'

'Hello, Father. Dermy McQuaid said you were looking for me.'

'I was. I was.'

Clare stood in the middle of the sitting room, surveying the pile of books and papers, Father McCarthy's fiddle. He played well but was too restless to practise, preferring his walks along the roads that led to the sea, his stick under his arm, his Jack Russell, Patch, at his heels.

'Sit down,' he said. 'How are you? Tell me about your studies.'

He pared his tobacco while he listened intently to Clare's account of her progress, his strong face full of interest. 'Ah, the music. Nothing like it,' he said. 'You're a great girl. Off to Paris. Marvellous. Marvellous,' he repeated, filling his pipe and lighting it.

Just then the door opened and Martin came into the room.

'Martin!' Clare jumped up with fright. 'What are you doing here?'

'Keeping out of Sergeant Enright's way,' Martin said. 'He'd hardly think of looking for me here, now would he?'

'To be sure.' Father McCarthy laughed. 'I'll be off to the novena. You two can have your little chat in peace.'

He left the room quietly, pulling the door behind him.

'I'll be going before daylight,' Martin said. 'I want you to give this letter to Madge Kinsella.' He handed it to Clare. 'It's from Pauline.'

'Have you seen her?'

'Yes. Don't look so startled. She's fine.'

'But what's she doing all this time? Why hasn't she come back?'

'She'll be back soon,' Martin said patiently. 'I want you to keep an eye on the parents. I'll be away for a while.'

'How can I do that? I'm going to Paris soon.'

'Just tell them everything's all right when they get nervous, that sort of thing. I'm anxious about Dad. He's not well.'

'Don't I know. They think you're in trouble, with Sergeant Enright calling to the house.'

'That's what I mean,' Martin said. 'Tell them everything's under control.'

'You must think they're a pair of fools,' Clare said, going to the door. 'I don't know what you're scheming but mind yourself and make sure Pauline gets back here. Soon. We don't know what to expect next. It's very distressing.'

'Take it easy,' Martin said. 'Everything will be all right.'

Chapter Sixteen

From the front-room window of the high-rise flats in Belfast Pauline had a bird's-eye view of the city stretching out below her. Rooftops, office buildings, traffic snaking along roads to the South, docks, shipyards, cranes, dirty grey water. She hated it all but she had to stay. Martin said it was the only way to ensure her safety. Who would come looking for her in a top-floor, high-rise flat? Who indeed? She couldn't help wondering sometimes if everyone she had ever known had forgotten about her.

Below her window, two small boys were playing near some parked cars, reminding her of Seamie. He must be getting very big. In another while he'd be out to play like the two little boys below. She missed him. Missed watching the varying expressions on his face, his beautiful smile. At night in bed she cried with longing for him and prayed that Madge was coping.

Leaning over the balcony made her feel dizzy. She needed the fresh air but she was afraid of the height. This was no place to live. While she kept the place neat and tidy and read copies of *True Romance*, she was sure that at night in the front room Martin and his cronies plotted murders. They spent hours at a time poring over maps, checking times, places, people's movements, often meeting in dark alleys to discuss plans and strategies, their secrets intact from wives and girlfriends. The day before a gunman had fired a shot from the roof of the bank, barely missing Martin. He himself had used a hatchet to gain access to a policeman's home, looking for information. Pauline had heard him boasting quietly about it to his friends over a game of cards, sniggering into his beer. Sometimes she listened at the door to snatches of their conversation, the low voices camouflaged by the jabbering television. That's when Martin was there. He was always slipping away. 'Business', he called it. This time he had said he was going to Dublin and would check up on Madge and Seamie. He had no information about Seamus yet, and Pauline was frustrated and doubtful.

She wanted to go back to Glencove, but not without Seamus. She was not going back to Aunt Bea and she couldn't make alternative plans until she found him. If her mother had been alive Pauline would have made a run for it. All her memories were focused on the happy years of her childhood before her mother had died. Her father didn't feature much in her reminiscences. He was always an obscure figure, screened from the comings and goings of the household by his newspaper and the cat curled up on his lap. While her mother cooked dinner, Pauline played skipping on the road with her friends, chanting rhymes, squealing with delight when one of them tripped on the rope and was out.

There was trouble everywhere. Riots in the streets, petrol bombs, burnt-out cars, threats. The city throbbed with a sense of terror. Pauline grew more petrified at every news bulletin.

'I need to get out,' she said to Martin, when he had returned from Glencove and was sitting in the kitchen, legs crossed, reading the newspaper.

'It's risky,' he said.

'Just for a walk down the road. Stretch my legs. This place is getting me down. There's a few things I need to get at the shops.'

'All right,' Martin conceded. 'You can go as far as the High Street tomorrow. But don't delay.'

'I don't like taking orders from you,' she snapped. 'It's a simple request. I remember a time when you thought I was the greatest thing since the sliced pan.'

'So you keep telling me. We had good times together, didn't we?' He came to her, circling her in his arms. 'Listen, they're playing our song.'

From the radio Dusty Springfield sang 'You Don't Have To Say You Love Me' and Martin pulled Pauline close and began to dance. She let him lead her around the room.

'I sent word to Madge that you'll be home soon.'

Pauline's heart leaped. 'Great.'

Martin tightened his grip. 'I gave up too easily,' he said quietly, into her ear. 'I should never have let you go.'

The slow beat, the comfort of being held, soothed her. She let herself be lulled into a cocoon of false security.

'You're still in love with me, Pauline, only you're too stubborn to admit it,' Martin said, turning to kiss her.

'No, I'm not.' She pulled away from him, went out to the balcony and in spite of her fear, stayed looking down at the wasteground and the street beyond, her elbows propped on the rail.

The next day as she walked along the high street the stores increased and became more interesting. There was a café, and a record shop at the precinct on the corner. She wandered around Boots, marvelling at the assortment of shampoos and cosmetics. A large green bottle of 'Herbal Shampoo' caught her eye. 'Vitamin Enriched' was written on the label. 'Extra Shine'. She paid for it with some of the five-pound note Martin had given her. At the counter she took a lipstick from a display stand and some eye shadow and paid for them, courtesy of Martin, too. Fuck him. He was the one who insisted on holding her hostage. Next time she might treat herself to a compact. With her own money she bought an alarm clock, notepaper and stamps to write to Madge to let her know when she was returning.

She walked back slowly, looking in shop windows, thinking of what kind of employment she could get if Seamus didn't turn up. Perhaps a job as barmaid in a hotel, where accommodation would be provided. She didn't mind where she worked as long as she could have her baby with her.

On the strip of wasteground outside the flats a body on the ground was covered with an overcoat. Pauline stood watching as police and B Specials arrived on the scene to divert the gaping pedestrians. A photographer was taking pictures. She walked on, her hands shaking, and ran to the lifts. In her room, she dumped her purchases on her bed, and sat down on the edge, forcing herself to take slow, deep breaths to calm herself. She heard Martin's footsteps outside her door.

'You took your time,' he said. 'I was worried about you.'

Pauline came out. 'You're beginning to sound like an old hen,' she said, walking past him into the kitchen.

'I have your tea ready,' he said, following her. 'What kept you?'

'Did you think I'd gone off with someone?' she asked,

eyeing the fry under the grill and the set table.

'It's always a possibility,' he said. 'Here, sit down and eat this before it goes cold.'

'Do you think I'm so desirable, Martin Dolan, that I can't walk down the street without being ravaged by a B Special?'

'You're an attractive girl, Pauline. I keep telling you it isn't safe out there but you're too headstrong to listen to me.'

'If I listened to you I'd do nothing for the rest of my life except decorate the place with me presence.'

'You can see the trouble for yourself. And it's going to get worse.'

'I know.'

That night Pauline lay awake for hours, watching the moon through the net curtains. She was thinking of Seamus, of the time he had driven her to Bray in his new yellow Mini. She had sat beside him in the passenger seat admiring everything about it. The seafront was quiet, the holiday-makers not yet arrived. They had walked along the promenade, the breeze whipping around them. Pauline had stood at the water's edge, letting the waves break over her feet, the water bearing the black sand and tiny pebbles between her toes, frothing at the edges, making her nervous. The sea pulled back again, taking the gurgling, protesting pebbles with it. When their lips had turned purple from the cold and they were shivering, they had gone into a café and ordered fish and chips and a bottle of Coca-Cola each.

Later, in the arcade, they played the slot machines, drove the dodgems, ate candy-floss and sat in the shelter huddled together, kissing one another until they were out of breath.

'Let's get back to the flat,' Seamus had said.

'Why?' Pauline had asked, looking innocent.

'You know.' He nudged her.

'I hope you don't think I'm easy, Seamus Gilfoyle.'

'No, but—'

'I don't fancy giving Father McCarthy a heart attack in the confessional tonight.'

'You still go to confession?'

'The retreat is on.'

'I hate sins and confession. It's a load of cobblers.'

'Seamus, don't say that.' Pauline was horrified.

'All that idolatry and superstition. Sprinkling holy water and rattling rosary beads. It's not for me. Come on.' Seamus had got to his feet, angry.

'I won't listen to that kind of talk. You can feck off. Easily known your mother is a Protestant.'

Seamus had stood rigid, his hands digging into his pockets, and Pauline had sauntered off in the direction of the railway station. He hadn't followed her. As she waited for the train the rain came down, slowly at first, then it lashed.

Seamus found her huddled into her duffel coat. 'Come on,' he had said. 'You'll get pneumonia if you stay there freezing.'

It had been their first row. They had driven home in silence, both full of anger.

If he came through the door now he would probably say, 'I should have known you'd come looking for me.' He often said, 'You're strong.' He would add, pacing the room, 'I've let you down. Time has gone by. You've probably discovered that you're better off without me.'

'I desperately wanted you to come back,' she would protest. 'Make sure you were all right. It's hard to have been so close to someone the way we've been, know everything about each other, then suddenly, hey presto! it all stops. Anyway if you'd known so much about me, Seamus Gilfoyle, you'd have known how much I loved you and you wouldn't have let me suffer, wondering if you were still alive.'

'I've made a mess of things, Pauline,' Seamus would say.

'We're together. That's all that matters.' Pauline fell asleep, almost believing that she had been talking to Seamus.

Eve Winthrop was enjoying life. Chris played his saxophone in clubs and dance halls, drove his two-seater red Lotus that she now knew he had purchased with his inheritance from his grandmother, and made love to her with tremendous verve and energy. He told her of his dream of forming his own band, that he had every intention of doing so. 'I want to be like Mick Jagger,' he said, strutting up and down with his hand on his hip. 'I'm going to compose my own songs too.'

'You'll be better than Mick Jagger,' Eve assured him enthusiastically.

Eve loved his ambition. Loved it when he turned on the charm, telling her she was beautiful and calling her 'darling' and 'gorgeous', finding his transparency appealing.

'My old man will cough up to get me started,' he said. 'I'll be making the big bucks in no time.'

One evening Chris returned home, calling her from the front door. 'I've got great news,' he said. 'A top rock-band leader has a vacancy coming up. He phoned my agent this morning.' He threw off his jacket and caught her around the waist, lifting her up in the air.

'Wonderful!' Eve said, laughing.

'A good salary with bonuses and extras. It's a chance to get started. Give me experience for when I form my own band.'

When Chris left home to go on his first tour with his new band, Eve's mind was a jumble of emotions. While she was delighted with his success, she was lonely. The days were dull, rain threatening all the time. Unable to sleep, she would toss and turn, wishing the weather would break, that a torrent would pour down from the skies to clear the air and let the sun come out.

Alone in her flat she gazed out at an angry sky, squalling rain sweeping across the grey city. Immediately after Chris's departure she had wallowed in self-pity, crying into the phone when he rang her from a call-box, his words barely audible in the din of background music.

She answered an advertisement for a receptionist in an office near the BBC in Shepherd's Bush and took the tube to work and home every day. Dorothy was furious that her daughter, recently married into a wealthy family, had to work and accused Chris of being parsimonious and unreliable. When Chris returned after a month touring around England, Scotland and Wales, he said, 'I'm off again next week,' and kissed the top of her head.

'Where?' Her voice was edgy.

'Germany.'

'But you've only just got home,' she said, feeling her anger take hold.

'It's my job. What I do,' he said, and told her that she would have to learn to be reasonable and manage without him.

Soon she discovered what being possessive was, rushing home to linger in the bath, standing naked before the mirror, trying to decide what to wear to elicit that hungry whisper: 'I'm crazy for you.'

By the time Chris was packing for his German tour they had been married three months and had spent only five separate weeks of it together.

'Can't I come with you?' Eve asked.

'Nope.' Chris shook his head, pulling the zip of his grip-bag and sitting down on the chair in the hall to extract a cigarette from its packet with his teeth.

Eve felt her temper slipping out of control. 'You've got someone else.'

Leaning back, he blew smoke rings into the air. 'Don't be ridiculous. My career takes up all my time and energy.'

'You can say that again!' Eve shouted, and let out a string of abuse and accusations.

He stood up and walked towards the door, then turned, pointing a finger at her. 'I don't answer to anyone, least of all you. Do you hear?'

Shaking inside, Eve stared at him. 'I'm your wife.'

'Yes, and I wish you'd act like one. Now, I really have to go.'

'Don't.' Eve detested the pleading note in her voice.

Chris muttered, shaking his head as he went to the door. Eve followed him, grabbed the belt of his jeans, stood on his boots, reaching for him, anything to hold on to him. He stood, let himself be kissed, then said, 'I've got to go, the taxi's here.' He moved towards it so fast that she was left looking at an empty space.

She ran after him, bumped into the door as he opened it.

'What the—' he began.

Her mouth was on his before he could say another word. The weight of her made him stagger backwards.

He leaned against the car for balance.

'I can't let you go like this,' she said, devouring his lips. 'I have to have you. Now.'

'Stop, Eve. For God's sake – the neighbours.'

'Take me inside.'

He shrugged, took her by the arm and dragged her into the house, up the stairs, throwing her across the bed. 'If that's what you want,' he said, removing his belt.

He made love to her with such intensity that she cried out, begging him to slow down. He only laughed and said that he had to go.

She prepared for his return by buying a fuchsia silk dress that slid over her hips, and tied back her hair with a matching clip. Their flat was sparkling, with a new sheepskin rug in front of the fire and net curtains drawn against prying eyes. When he finally arrived home, two days later than expected, she turned away from him when he kissed her.

'Where were you?' she asked, her voice cool, her face reserved, in contrast to the cosy atmosphere of the flat.

Chris stepped back and blinked. 'Why?' he asked. 'What difference does a couple of days make?'

'All the difference.'

He left the room without another word, went upstairs and locked himself in the bathroom.

'Chris?' Eve's voice was drowned by the gushing water.

Finally he emerged, wrapped in a fresh white towel, his body gleaming and tanned.

Eve was pouring vodka into a glass. 'Dinner's ruined,' she said, sulkily.

'I'll get a takeaway.' He went to the phone in the hall.

'I had a letter from Grandpa,' Eve said. 'I think I'll go home for the summer.'

Chris looked at her wide-eyed. 'There'll be hell to pay with your mother.'

'Grandpa says they'd be delighted to have me any time.' She sipped her drink.

'I doubt that,' Chris said.

'I know,' Eve said, as if to herself.

'Still, I suppose you'll have to make it up with her sooner or later. You can't go on hating each other just because of one silly mistake.'

'Mistake? Is that what you consider our marriage to be?'

'Well.' Chris paused. 'Perhaps we rushed things a bit. But there's no harm in you going home for a while. You'll have company while I'm in the States.'

'I could come with you. I've always wanted to go to America.'

Chris shook his head. 'It isn't as if we're going any place interesting. One-horse towns in the back of nowhere. You'd be a liability.'

'That's a nice thing to call your wife!' Eve shouted.

'It's the truth. With your nagging and drinking, you're getting tiresome.'

'Perhaps you'd like me to go home for good.'

Chris brightened. 'Yes,' he said. 'I think I would. Now, I'm off to bed. Coming?'

'No. I need a drink.'

Ignoring her, Chris left the room, closing the door behind him. Eve poured herself some vodka, added lemonade to it and drank it quickly. When it was finished, she helped herself to more. As soon as the glass was empty, she hurled it at the closed door. What was happening to her? What was she doing? Where was she going?

In her haste to marry Chris her life had been turned

upside down. Her elopement, an act of bravado and a response to her mother's anger, had backfired, leaving her feeling empty and lonely. What she had thought was going to be a wonderful experience had proved nothing but a disappointment. Chris had made it no secret that he was disillusioned with her, and after the first flush of ardour, she had found his lovemaking mechanical. To Chris she was another conquest, something for which he had use only occasionally, when it suited him. Her resentment made her pour herself another drink.

Sir George Saunders was an elderly gentleman who wore starched white collars and shone with cleanliness. While Clare played, he paced the room, checking her roughly, sometimes hammering points home to her with a ruler or the top of a pen on her shoulder.

'The emotional concept of what you are playing must be in your head and your heart,' he said, as she went through her virtuoso pieces. 'Show your utmost understanding of the composer's intent, especially if it's Bach, Mozart, Schubert, or Beethoven. You should lose all consciousness of technique at this stage,' he said to her. 'When technique ceases to rule your thoughts, art takes over.'

Sir George's rooms were situated in a small square off the rue Saint-Honoré. His studio was small and airless. Clare was bombarded ceaselessly with noises from other instruments and traffic. Sir George seemed unaffected by it. 'I shall turn you into an inspired musician,' he told her. 'Your spirit will shine through the notes.'

Sometimes, when her lectures were over, Clare would sit with her French grammar in her hand and try to master the language.

At the end of June, after five months' study with Sir George, he said to Clare, 'You play with all the authority of an experienced concert artist but without the millions of tiny details that go into the making of a concert pianist.'

'What shall I do?' The old feeling of frustration, which had been there so often at the beginning of her studies with Vittorio, was back.

'Relax,' Sir George said. 'The best way to learn to be a performer is to become one. I shall put you on stage by entering you for the Chopin Competition here next month. Soon you will be giving recitals to the other participating students.'

Gradually patiently, he advised her to follow her imagination. 'Your aim is to achieve the best possible results with the least possible exertion. You must not play for an audience for six months so that you can practise scales and exercises very slowly for a considerable period.'

Clare continued her lessons every morning, and spent the afternoons practising or discovering the magic of Paris. The minute she set eyes on the city she fell in love with it. She loved to peer in shop windows, walk along the banks of the Seine, gaze at the Eiffel Tower. She stayed in a flat owned by the Friends of the Symphony. People came and went. Sometimes several people were staying there; at others she was alone.

One night, when she was on her own, she was woken by a tapping at the window. Her heart jumped with fright.

She crept downstairs and called to the shadow through the glass door, 'Who's there?'

'Martin.'

'Martin!' Clare pulled back the bolt. He came in. His

hair was tousled and he shivered with cold. 'What are you doing here?'

'Someone was following me at the airport. So I came here to distract them.' He smiled at her. 'Visiting my sister is quite legitimate, isn't it?'

'Certainly is.' She bolted the door behind him.

'I've got to meet a bloke in Montmartre to discuss an operation with him. He's French and, as I don't understand the lingo, having you along would be a great advantage. Will you come?'

'What's it in connection with?'

'We're making arrangements for an arms shipment.'

Horror-stricken, Clare looked at him. 'Martin, what are you getting yourself into?' she asked.

Martin laughed. 'Don't look so shocked. What do you expect us to use for guns? Hurley sticks?'

In spite of his bravado Martin was anxious, chain-smoking. 'It's taking too long,' he complained. 'The dealers are getting fussy about the currency now. Don't want Irish money.'

'What will you do?'

'Collect the rest of the down payment in francs.'

'For God's sake, Martin, get out of it before you get yourself into serious trouble.'

Martin gave a brittle laugh. Clare looked at his hunched shoulders. He was strung out, wrecked.

'I'm *in* serious trouble, Clare, and I need your help. Do this one favour for me. Come with me.'

'No!' Clare shouted, losing the last tenuous hold on her self-control. She let rip with a string of expletives and recriminations, finishing off by saying, 'I'm sick of you and your Cause. Upsetting Mother, making Daddy ill. I want nothing to do with it.'

Martin shielded himself with the palms of his hands,

outstretched in supplication. 'Clare. Stop.'

'No, Martin. I've had enough. You'd better leave now.' She opened the door and waited, head down, until he walked past her. Then she banged it shut after him.

When Dorothy opened the door to Eve's knock, it was difficult to tell which of the two was more disconcerted. Dorothy, in her dressing-gown, her hair wrapped in a towel, looked blankly at her daughter.

'I didn't expect . . .' she began

Eve waited, unsure if Dorothy would let her in. Dorothy, full of the shame and resentment that still pressed into her stomach at the thought of Eve's elopement, returned her look, the pain as sharp as a fresh wound. They faced each other, Dorothy's nostrils flaring. Her monstrous love twisted and knotted around Eve, thick as bindweed, threatening to break loose and destroy her.

Eve said, 'Grandpa wrote. Thought I should come home.'

'You might have phoned to let us know your plans.' Dorothy's words were brusque as she stood to one side to let her daughter in. Cautiously Eve stepped into the hall and watched an unsmiling Dorothy shut the front door behind her. She followed her into the kitchen, her heart pounding.

After a moment's hesitation, Dorothy said, 'You must be hungry.'

'Yes.' Eve sat down at the table.

There was silence while Dorothy fussed with the teacups and saucers.

'If you'd rather I didn't stay . . .' Eve stopped, baffled as to the next move she should make. Suddenly she felt like a child again, anxious to please her mother.

'I think we'd better talk.' The foreboding note in Dorothy's voice made her sound harsh.

Eve sat forward and stared at her mother, as if waiting for the next blow to be delivered. As soon as Eve had left the full responsibility of the household had hit Dorothy. No more glorious shopping days, no cheques in the post from Ron. She had taken a job in Lynam's boutique, leaving early sometimes to prepare dinner for James.

As they sipped their tea, each waiting for the other to begin, Eve felt awkward.

Finally, in desperation to break the silence, Dorothy said, 'He seems fine. Back at the office these days. He hides behind that genial nature of his but I don't think he's liking it.'

Eve nodded.

· Silence again.

Eve took a deep breath. 'I don't think I'll be going back to Chris,' she said.

'I'm not surprised,' Dorothy countered. 'Always going off on tour.'

'Yes,' Eve said, in painful honesty. 'I seem to have made a mess of everything. This is the punishment. I'm sorry.' She began to cry.

'No.' Dorothy was out of her chair, the towel slipping from her head, beside her daughter, her arms around her shoulders. 'It's not all your fault. I've wanted to tell you that for a long time. Didn't know how.' Dorothy gestured helplessly in the air. 'I was childish to blame you for that dreadful girl's behaviour. He wouldn't have gone if he hadn't wanted to. It's been happening all our married lives, only not under my nose. Grandpa made me realise that I was driving you away. You're not a child any more, Eve. You know what it is to love someone enough to want to cover up for them. And you're old enough to choose your partner in life. I should have welcomed the news.' She turned away so that Eve couldn't see her tears. 'I'll never forget what your father did. But I don't blame you.'

'Thank you,' Eve said, not knowing what else to say. The tension between them eased.

In the weeks that followed Eve could hardly believe how much she resented other people's happiness. A couple walking in the street, talking, laughing, holding hands, would bring on an attack of such deep desolation that she would feel ill. She found an ally in her grandfather, who persuaded Dorothy to leave her alone.

In the warm summer weather Eve wandered around the garden, sat by the sea, and whiled away the hours reading or watching James absorbed in tending his roses or watering his tomatoes.

She had spent such a short time with Chris. How had it gone so wrong? Alone, she would think about, examine, question every aspect of their three-month marriage. His eagerness to marry her, in defiance of Dorothy's outrage, had amazed Eve as had his sudden loss of interest in her as soon as he got the job with the band.

'You should try to eat a little more,' James said. 'We can't have you looking so thin and pale.'

'Food makes me feel ill,' Eve protested. 'I'll be fine in a few days' time.'

James extended his hand in a gesture of love. Eve grasped his fingers. 'Do me one favour, Eve,' he said. 'Go and see Dr Gregory. He's good, you know. You look very tired.'

Dr Gregory examined Eve thoroughly. 'Nothing the matter at all,' he said. 'How's married life treating you?'

'Chris doesn't want me,' Eve said, lifting her dark, empty eyes to meet his.

'Oh, I'm sure that can't be the case. You may be feeling a bit depressed at the moment. Marriage is a big step. It's all so strange at the beginning.'

'Yes.'

'You rushed into it, Eve. Give yourself time to absorb everything that has happened. In a few weeks you'll feel differently.'

'Yes, Doctor.'

'Meanwhile, you owe it to yourself to rest and relax as much as you can.'

For the next few days Eve lay in bed, listening to Agnes singing as she moved around the house, and feeling a gradual return of her interest in everything around her. Life had to go on and she was still part of it, regardless of Chris. She began talking about him to Agnes, laughing at the way he had stormed into her life, then breaking down and weeping at the recollected pain.

'It's not the end of the world.' Agnes was busy knitting a blue angora cardigan for Clare's birthday and encouraged Eve to talk, listening quietly to what she had to say. While Agnes polished and cleaned she told Eve stories of her own childhood, about her country upbringing, meeting Jack, the difficulties of their courtship. 'As a child I never minded the hard work,' Agnes said one morning, when she was cleaning the drawing room. 'It was shared out among us. My job was the Monday washing. It went on all day. What I did resent was not being allowed to further my education. Had I taken up the scholarship I won to the Munster and

Leinster Institute when I was eighteen, I'd have been a domestic economy teacher and I'd have some standing in the community. But my father needed me to help on the farm. Then I married Jack. He left me countless times, you know,' she said to Eve, her face crimson from the exertion of polishing the brasses. 'Oh, yes. You're not the first to be treated like this and you won't be the last. Often I had no idea where he was. Even after we were married and had a family. They were hard times but happy too.' Agnes regarded her handiwork. 'You can see your face in them,' she said, replacing the fire irons on the hearth.

Martin was out and Scully was talking on the phone when Pauline realised that the front door was unlocked. She grabbed her purse from its hiding place under the wardrobe and left quickly. The light was ebbing outside as she walked down the street and caught a bus to Sandy Row. She was confused by the enormous buildings *en route*, and it took her a while to find her bearings. She went to the Gilfoyles'. There was no one in so in the dark she caught a city-centre bus. She kept looking over her shoulder. The woman in the seat behind her blew cigarette smoke into her face. Pauline coughed. The woman stared out of the window, unconcerned.

As she passed a chip shop in the city, she noticed a man behind the counter in white overalls shovelling golden-brown chips from one place to another, vigorously shaking the basket as sweat trickled down his face from the steam. Her mouth watered. She went in and joined the small queue waiting to be served. By the time the man asked what she wanted she was starving.

'Cod and chips, please, and a glass of milk,' she said, deciding to eat her meal there while she planned her next move. When she opened her purse to pay there was only a couple of pounds in a fold at the back. Her savings were gone.

The chips were so hot that she had to blow on them before putting them in her mouth. They tasted delicious. The man at the counter watched her until Pauline, uncomfortable, looked around to see if he was staring at someone else. There was a group of boys and girls too engrossed in their meal and each other to be of interest to anyone. Pauline felt like asking him if there was something he wanted.

As soon as she had finished she left to make her way back to the Gilfoyles' to tell them what had happened to her and ask them for the fare home to Dublin. They were still out and Pauline, wondering desperately what to do next, decided to hitch a lift to Dublin.

She came around the corner unprepared for the four women huddled together, in deep conversation, near the charred ruins of a jeep. She heard the name Gilfoyle mentioned and, from their accusatory looks, she could tell that they were talking about her. Martin had been right. She shouldn't have stayed out so late. The street ahead stretched away, long and deserted. She stayed near the houses, walking slowly so as not to draw attention to herself. In the lights of a pub on the corner she could see her own white, frightened face in the Jameson mirror. She kept walking, humming a little tune. When she heard someone behind her she began to run. Rapid footsteps followed her along the deserted streets and caught up.

It was the four women. They grabbed her, pulled her into a doorway. The blow to her cheek knocked her sideways. She staggered, straightened herself, then slid down again with the next smack. Her cheek stung. Someone clamped a hand over her mouth reducing her scream to a pitiful grunt. 'Don't move,' one warned her as she tried to struggle.

They held her head. She felt their fingers dragging her hair backwards. Scissors cut through it. They said nothing. Clumps of dark curls fell to the ground. As the tears rolled down her cheeks she told herself that it didn't matter. That her hair would grow again. Her captors pressed into her, making sure she couldn't move. One woman's face was so close to Pauline's that she could feel warm breath on her skin.

'Shut your eyes and keep them shut.' The voice was rough.

'Or you'll not see the light of day again.'

Silence.

What scared her most was that she didn't know what they were doing. The smell of the warm, gooey tar overpowered her as it trickled over her head, down her face, into her nostrils and mouth. Coughing and spluttering, she slumped forward under the weight of it. They pulled her up by her shoulders.

'We'll make sure you don't fall,' another voice said reassuringly, as they dragged her to a lamp-post and tied her hands and feet to it.

'Serves the bitch right.'

'Traitor. All the Gilfoyles are traitors.'

'Tout.'

She was found at closing-time by a trickle of stragglers making their way home from the pub.

Pauline walked stiffly along the hospital corridor. Her head ached and she had to stop sometimes and lean against the wall for support. Her arm was in a sling.

'The bruises will wear off,' said the nurse, who had cleaned her up. 'Tar doesn't leave a mark. You're lucky you're strong. And if you rest plenty and try not to worry, everything will be all right. I don't think you should go back to work for a while.'

Pauline's body felt weak and she shook each time she thought of the women. Almost every night she had dreams, in which she saw their faces, leering and distorted. Martin visited her daily. He said he would collect her. That's why she was standing waiting for him, wondering why he had not come sooner.

She limped to the front entrance of the hospital and stood leaning against the door jamb. Whenever she took a deep breath her ribs hurt. What did she want from him anyway? She could manage on her own. Well, not yet, maybe. Her head was bandaged, her arm in a sling, her eye-sockets purple. She could hardly walk.

A policeman had come to the hospital to question her. 'Have you no idea who did this to you?' he had asked.

'No. I don't know anybody,' she had said, her hands clenched as she spoke.

The policeman's brow creased. 'Have you any idea who might be responsible for this? Anyone behind it that you can think of?'

Pauline thought of the Gilfoyles and their mixed religions, Seamus and his alleged touting, Martin and his involvement with the IRA, the women watching from the corner as she passed them to get to the Gilfoyles', their earnest faces full of hatred as their eyes followed her.

'No. I don't know anybody up here at all,' she had said.

'No enemies?' The policeman's eyes were on her bandages.

'No.' She felt herself blush and kept her eyes downcast.

'Are you a member of a political party?'

'No.'

The policeman gave a sigh of exasperation.

'Maybe they thought I was somebody else,' Pauline said, in an effort to seem helpful.

'Maybe, but I'm not convinced about that. There's usually a good reason when someone gets tarred and feathered. Did you know the word "traitor" was written on a notice in front of the lamp-post they tied you to?'

Pauline's face flamed. 'No, I didn't.' Martin hadn't told her.

'So you can't throw any light on this little mystery?'

She shook her head.

'Did you recognise the women's faces?'

'No.'

'We'll find out sooner or later. You're lucky you were discovered within a couple of hours, otherwise you might have died and then we'd be conducting a murder investigation.'

Before he left he wrote down her name, address, age and occupation.

Afterwards she thought about the women who had come to get her. Should she have given him a description of their cruel faces? Told him that, from the hatred in their eyes, she had known there had been no mistake? How much did Martin know? He told her that he had phoned the hospitals when she had not returned and tracked her down to the Royal Infirmary. But he refused to discuss the perpetrators. 'If I told you,'

Martin had said, 'they'd do it to you again, only it'd be worse the next time.'

Pauline heard his voice before she saw him. 'Sorry I'm late. Got caught up in the traffic.' She tried to straighten up but her knees gave way. Martin put his arms around her. 'Take it easy and you'll be all right. Here, lean on me.' They moved slowly together. 'Good girl. A few more steps and we're there.'

'Oh, God,' Pauline gasped, when she reached the car. 'My ribs are killing me. I think I'm going to fall.'

Martin eased her into the passenger seat. When they got back to the tower block, he helped her into the lift. In the flat he laid her gently on the settee. 'I'll make us both a strong drink,' he said.

He went into the kitchen and poured gin into two glasses, adding tonic, ice and lemon.

'Here. Get this down you,' he said, coming back and handing her a glass. 'It'll do you good.'

'Thanks.'

It hurt her to reach out for the glass so he held it to her lips while she drank.

'Did they ask you any more questions?' Martin said.

'No, thank God. I'm sick of bloody questions.'

'What did the doctor say?'

'I'll live.'

'Still, that gash on the side of your head doesn't look too good. I'll change the dressing.'

'Ouch,' Pauline said, as he removed the old one.

'Sorry. I'm being as gentle as I can. Stay still. That's better. Of course, you shouldn't have been out on your own. It can't happen again. Now let's get you into bed.'

'Cluck, cluck,' Pauline scoffed. 'As soon as I'm better I'm going home. I hope you realise that.' She was exhausted.

They were quiet. Then Martin said, 'You shouldn't think about things like that until you're fit and well. Anyway, I'm looking after you.' He lit a cigarette and blew the smoke into the air. 'I'm the only one you have to take care of you.'

'You've got to let me go,' she said. 'I have a baby waiting for me.'

Martin looked at her. 'It took courage for you to come here, Pauline. I admire you for that. Courage is something you were never short of. I remember.'

Pauline blushed.

'Where will it all end?' She sighed, not able to forget the look of admiration in his face, or his kindness.

He shrugged. 'God knows.'

'I'm a bit tired now,' she said.

'It's time you had a good rest.'

'I'll stay here on the sofa. I don't want to be in the bedroom on my own yet.'

While she rested he washed the nightdresses she had brought back from the hospital. There was blood on them and he had to rinse them several times in cold water to get it out. He pegged them on the balcony, checking her several times to make sure she was all right. She lay watching him, thinking about him, his worshipful attention to her, the way he looked at her.

Pauline had to rest a lot because she was always tired and she had backache. Martin had taken to leaving early in the morning, returning after dark and not saying where he had been. Scully never left the flat, and the door was always locked. As time went on she improved. After she had tidied the place each morning, as best she could, she sat in the chair on the balcony where she had a view of the women on the street below, arms folded, heads together, blissfully unaware of their children shouting obscenities and flinging stones at passing police cars. They were like the women in Lisburn Road, who had tarred and feathered her. She wondered if they knew them. Sometimes, after dark, Martin took her for a walk to help her regain her balance and strength. They walked slowly side by side, silent and awkward together, like a married couple. Pauline felt that they were being watched by suspicious men and women everywhere they went. Sometimes they passed the barbed-wire barricades and headed for a pub a bit further along.

'What did you do today?' Martin would ask when the drinks were served.

'Read a book. Did some knitting.' The answer was always the same.

One evening, when they were finishing their drinks before retracing their slow steps home, Pauline said, 'I'm running out of wool.'

'I'll get you some. What colour?'

'Lemon. I'm sick of blue, and I'm sick of being caged in like an animal. I want to go home, Martin.'

'And leave me?' He looked sad.

'I miss Seamie. If I don't get back soon I won't recognise him.'

'You're not well enough to travel. As soon as you are I'll take you.'

'Promise?'

'Promise. You're a restless spirit, Pauline.'

'You're a fine one to talk.' She laughed and drained her glass.

'You wouldn't want me around you all the time, would you?' Martin said, diverting the conversation, knowing that to pursue it would be to embark on dangerous territory.

Pauline grimaced.

'Hungry?'

'Starving.'

'Come on. We'll get a takeaway.'

An explosion made them jump. Martin ran out of the pub. A fleet of police cars was tearing up the street, heading in their direction. Another loud bang followed, then a sound like a crack of thunder. Flames shot up from a building across the street. There was screaming.

'I'll get you back to the flat.'

The street was filled with people running in all directions, fire engines, ambulances, policemen.

When they reached the flat, Martin said, 'I'm going to see what all the commotion's about. Will you be all right for a few minutes?'

'Yes,' Pauline answered.

When he banged the door after him she went to the window. She saw him come out of the flats and disappear round the corner into the thick of the action.

Chapter Seventeen

It was a glorious day in Paris. From the window of her bedroom in the flat, high above the 8th arondissement, Clare gazed at the shafts of sun dazzling the building on the opposite side of the boulevard, merging them into a blur of light. The tops of the trees, too, were tipped with gold, their shadows reflected on the bright pavement. Clare gazed across the familiar stark lines of the taller buildings, set against a clear blue sky. A perfect day in Paris, she reflected, as she closed her window against the cool breeze and returned to finish her lunch of baguette and fresh Brie. She was waiting to hear confirmation of her booking at the Salle Pleyel for that evening where she was to play a recital for the Friends of the Symphony. Restless and animated at the thought of playing in public for the first time, she paced the room, then stood in the sunlight watching the restless preening pigeons pecking at the crumbs of her baguette. She noticed the time on the clock tower in the square below, and synchronised her watch with it.

She telephoned the Salle Pleyel to ask permission to practise on the piano she would be playing, put on her jacket and went out into the sunshine. There was excitement in the air as she walked along, her eyes darting here and there: she half expected to see someone she knew in the surging afternoon crowd.

Since her arrival in Paris she had put her heart and soul into the music. The struggle to master the piano was now over. All her anxiety and discontent had fallen away as music came to her in a more sensuous form. The basic hard work was done and she found a new sustained joy in her playing.

At the Conservatoire she practised for hours, a continuous repetition of beautiful flowing sounds, like a river. Her music enveloped her physically and mentally. It was not just part of her, but the whole of her. Musical phrases took on new meanings and new sensations. There was joy and laughter in the elements of her playing. She kept her life simple, uncluttered, her music the only definite thing. Her playing was improving all the time, with more vitality than ever before, and her understanding of all the interpretations that Vittorio had taught her so ardently clicked suddenly into place and made it all easier and more interesting. She was alive, living through her music and enjoying it.

That evening the members of the orchestra took their places on the lower stand before the crimson curtains. A burst of applause greeted the conductor as he stood on his podium. Clare peeped through the curtains at the rows of people. She was nervous and excited. The conductor faced the audience, bowed, tapped his baton and the music began. As the lights dimmed the orchestra became a great shadowy pit. The violins played the first sweet notes of Handel's prelude in G, from *Seven Pieces*. Slowly, the curtain rose, heightening the sense of anticipation in the hall and making it look cavernous to Clare. She stood, in her long black, crêpe dress, bowing to right and left, before taking her place at the grand piano.

The spotlight picked out the contours of her face as

she joined in with the orchestra. A jewel of sound rose up, every note clear and distinct, every phrase simple and consummate, casting a spell on her audience. In the darkened hush they sat rapt, listening to Handel's fugue, from suite no.4 in E minor, beginning with gentle chords, then the singing voice accompanied by the sombre bass, bringing to mind the beauty of life.

Listening, feeling her concentration, feeling the on-off compression of the pedals, connecting the most magnificent sounds ever heard, Clare took the listeners with her to another world, a world of calling birds, sounds from long ago, an enchanted palace. Clare's music beckoned, her notes burst forth, retreated only to return, triumphant. Sir George sat, his face lifted up, full of pride.

Clare was lost in the music of her favourite composers, Handel, Chopin, Mozart, transported to another world of gaiety and serenity, where Martin, bombs, anxiety did not exist. When it was over she rose and chatted to the conductor, then to Sir George, who came to congratulate her and talk to her about how she had coped for the first time with the backing of a full orchestra.

Afterwards as she was coming out of the side door she heard someone calling her name. She knew the voice before she turned round to look at its owner.

'Vittorio!'

She had imagined meeting him in all sorts of places and situations, but never once had it occurred to her that it would be in Paris. She was staring at him, terrified and joyous all at once. 'I never expected to see you here. How did you—'

Vittorio laughed. 'It's not too difficult. I have been keeping track of you.'

'Oh.'

She had rehearsed the words she would say to him when they met again, but suddenly they were forgotten.

'I wanted to see you. Congratulations. You played beautifully.' He kissed his bunched-up fingers.

'Thank you.' Clare smiled and in the silence that followed she felt jittery: he didn't know what to say either. 'Are you over on business?' she asked.

'A meeting of the Friends of the Symphony.'

'Oh.'

'And you?' Are you enjoying the Conservatoire and Sir George?'

'Very much, thank you.'

Vittorio nodded. 'You have improved enormously,' he said.

As another silence ensued, Clare prayed that he would go but at the same time wished that they were on a desert island so that he couldn't escape and she could study the varying expressions that crossed his face, smell his particular smell.

'I'd better be going,' she said.

'Yes.'

'Goodbye.' She held out her hand.

'Goodbye, Clare.'

She waved as she walked into the night.

'Clare, wait.' Vittorio was back, walking beside her. 'Would you like to have a drink with me? A little celebration?'

'I'd . . . love to. Are you sure?'

'Of course.'

They laughed together as he took her elbow and steered her to a café across the road.

As soon as they were comfortably seated at a corner table and Clare was sipping a glass of wine, he said,

'How have you really been? Tell me everything.'

'I've been working very hard.'

He smiled. 'It shows. I thought about you a lot. Wondered how you were getting along.'

'Sir George is pleased with me.'

'He has every right to be,' Vittorio said proudly.

After another pause, he said, 'I wondered if you were thinking of me, sometimes.'

'Yes. I was,' Clare said.

'May I ask what those thoughts might have been?' He looked teasingly at her. 'Or are they private?'

'I wondered how you were,' she said slowly. 'What you were doing.'

'Yes.' His eyes were intent upon her.

'And I thought about your hands . . . your smile.'

He took a long drink of his beer. 'I thought of you, too.'

'Thank you.'

She was trying to absorb him, his voice, his gestures, the brevity of words, as if they were inessential and pretentious, music the only currency between them. She was recalling the way he moved when he walked or leaned or smoked, even his hesitant silences, all testimony to his eloquence.

'How long are you over for?' she asked.

'A few days. What do you think of being a concert pianist so far?' he asked, gazing at her long, slender tapering fingers, their perfect nails painted the merest shade of pink.

'Nerve-racking.'

'You've grown up while my back was turned.' He shook his head, mesmerised.

Glancing at his watch he said, 'I mustn't keep you. Selfish of me.'

They stood up together and walked to the door. Vittorio hailed a taxi for her. 'Will you have dinner with me tomorrow night?' he asked suddenly.

'That would be lovely,' Clare said.

Outside in the milling crowd he said, 'I'll telephone you tomorrow at the Conservatoire.'

'Lovely,' Clare said.

He helped her into the taxi, inclined his head towards her and stepped back. As the taxi pulled away from the kerb she watched him until the crowd swallowed him up.

It was a hot summer's evening and Clare stepped off the bus. She spotted Vittorio at once, hesitated for a moment before running to greet him, breathless and brimming with laughter.

'Vittorio,' she exclaimed.

'I was getting worried,' he said, catching her arm and holding it. 'You look divine.' He guided her into his hotel and found a table in the corner in the foyer, ordered drinks and sat down beside her. 'I've ordered the meal to be served in my suite. Is that all right or would you prefer . . . ?'

Clare sensed his discomfort, saw it in his eyes.

'I would hate to embarrass you,' he continued.

'That would be lovely,' she said.

When they had finished their drinks Vittorio led her to the lift and swept her away up to the top floor of the hotel. Once inside the suite she was unsure what to do.

'Champagne,' Vittorio said. 'To celebrate.' He removed a magnum from a cooler on the sideboard and poured it into two glasses. 'To your success,' he said, handing her a glass and raising his to meet hers, unconcealed desire flickering in his eyes.

'Thank you.'

'To my stubborn, studious Clare,' he said in a low voice. He removed his jacket, loosened his tie and sat on the sofa. Clare watched the long, expressive fingers that held the glass. 'Congratulations again, Clare.' His voice was quiet. 'On a wonderful performance.'

'I was scared,' she said. 'I hope it didn't show.'

'Not a bit. It was excellent.'

'So it worked. All that pleading of yours for "the passion".'

Amusement made his eyes sparkle. 'I certainly haven't led you astray.'

'I had no idea how difficult it would be or how much I still have to learn.'

'No one said it would be easy either,' Vittorio said. 'You, Clare, have the makings of a great performer. I'm telling you that now.'

Clare bowed her head. The fading sun cast a rosy glow over them.

'Would you like to eat?'

'Yes, please.'

She looked at him as he phoned room service. Everything about him was familiar, every move he made, every gesture. With a shock Clare realised how much she had missed him. He came to her and took her hands in his. They sat like that for a long time. When she could stand the silence no longer, she tilted her head back and looked at him, waiting, sensing his cast-iron control.

'Clare.'

'Yes?' Joy surged through her at the way he said her name.

'Did anyone—'

The knock interrupted him. Two waiters delivered

trays of sumptuous food and served it from the sideboard, lifting the copper lids simultaneously from the plates to reveal prawns packed in slivers of smoked salmon.

When they had left, Vittorio said, 'I hope you're hungry.'

'Starving.'

While they ate Clare could feel his eyes on her. She hardly touched the food on her plate. Now that she was alone with him in this magnificent suite she was terrified of the intimacy and of making a fool of herself.

As they finished their meal of beef Wellington followed by baked alaska, Clare's courage began to drain away.

'You've gone very quiet,' Vittorio said. 'I know I said that it would be all right to come up here, but now I'm . . . You see, I've never been in a situation like this before.'

Her eyes were on his face, beseeching him to understand. He was beside her, drawing her to her feet, taking her fingertips and kissing them, one by one. He kissed her face, her eyes, her forehead and lastly, very gently, her mouth.

'Clare. Oh, Clare.' He pulled her into his arms and held her close to him. 'I would never force you to do anything you didn't want to do.'

'I–' she began.

He hushed her with more kisses, until she lost all power of speech.

'It's not that I don't want to be here,' she said, pulling back to look up into his face.

'I would never do anything to upset you. Not in a million years.' He went to the sideboard and got the bottle of champagne. He refilled their glasses, handed her hers and sat down again.

'Don't be uncomfortable, my beautiful Clare. It was inconsiderate of me to bring you up here. I didn't think. If I have embarrassed you, I'm sorry. Please forgive me.'

Clare looked at him, not knowing how to respond.

'I don't want you to do anything you might regret.' His eyes held hers.

'Oh, Vittorio.' Suddenly she felt foolish and tongue-tied. Speechless, she held out her arms to him, her love for him written all over her face.

He held her gently and kissed her deeply.

'This was meant to be. From the time you walked into my studio, all gauche and shy and brimming with talent, there was something about you. That passion I talked about. I saw it instantly. I loved it. I loved you.'

He lifted her and carried her into the bedroom, laying her carefully on the bed. 'I won't touch a hair of your head unless you want me to,' he whispered. 'But you must tell me, darling.'

'I do want you.'

He moved away and began to undress, his eyes never leaving her face. Gradually, her fear eased as she watched him reveal his broad shoulders, the lean, athletic body. Then he was lying beside her helping her out of her clothes, kissing her with butterfly kisses. Naked she lay in his arms, gazing trustingly at him. He cradled her, and pulled the ribbon that held her hair in place. Her auburn curls cascaded around her shoulders. He laughed at her shyness. 'You're adorable,' he said hoarsely.

Slowly, tantalisingly, he kissed the hollow of her neck, making her shiver. Gently his tongue flicked over her skin, down her throat, between her breasts, teased the tips of her nipples, until every fibre of her was consumed in a flame of desire so strong that all resistance flew from her leaving her in a frenzy of longing.

'Are you sure you want this, Clare?' he asked, his voice shaking.

In answer she arched herself up to meet him and he lifted her on top of him. She was riding, high and weightless, up . . . up . . . and away, floating in a warm, fluid, sunlit space, carried along into a golden glow of intense passion as wave after wave of ecstasy broke over her. She rose higher, frantic, clinging to him.

'Vittorio,' she cried out, desperate to take him with her.

Together they rode the waves and came crashing to earth, spent, entwined, submerged into one another Clare lay still for a long time, her head on his shoulder, peaceful.

Eventually she looked at him shyly, with wonderment, knowing that after this new experience she would never be the same person again.

There was adoration in his eyes and pleasure on his face as he whispered, 'I love you,' his hands caressing her hair, his lips kissing her eyelids.

As she gazed into that face she knew that she had taken possession of his heart in a way no other woman ever had.

'I'll never let you go,' he vowed. 'No matter what happens.'

'Even if I don't become the world's greatest pianist?' she said, laughing.

'Especially if you don't become the world's greatest pianist, but you have a great future, my darling, and I'll be keeping an eye on you every step of the way, wherever you are.'

Their time together was hectic. Nights and days merged in endless hours of passion. They spent all their time making love, venturing out only for fresh air along the banks of the Seine. She adored him and never ceased to tell him, opening her heart in a way she had never believed possible. As Vittorio dropped his guard and let her see into his soul, his boyish charm came to the fore. His devotion made her forget her fears. All doubts and suspicions vanished as she gave herself to him, time and again, without reservation.

On their last evening together Vittorio took Clare to his favourite restaurant, Les Relais, in Montmartre. Quietly, they went over every detail of her performance at the Salle Pleyel. Now, she saw new meaning in his words, his gestures. Afterwards, back in the suite, they made love slowly, exquisitely, and for a long time. 'From now on, you'll be able to face the world, my darling,' he said, looking so sad that Clare reached out and touched his face.

'You'll be with me.' She smiled.

He shook his head. 'I'll follow your every move, but I cannot be with you. You have to make your own way.'

'Without you, none of it would mean anything.'

'You, my little fledgling, are about to take off in your career and fly away. I can only watch and wait and hope for your return.'

'Of course I'll come back.'

'You'll write and tell me about all your adventures?'

'Yes, but I'll see you soon, won't I?'

Taking her hands in his, he held them and said, as if he were talking to himself, 'I love you, Clare. But I can't be with you very much. I'm not free and you have a life of your own to lead.'

'What do you mean, you're not free?' Clare tried to

keep the surprise out of her voice.

He laid his head against their joined hands. 'Darling, this is not the time or the place to tell you.'

'Tell me what?' she urged.

'I have commitments elsewhere.' His voice shook.

'But I thought – I mean, I assumed ... we'd be getting married some time in the future.'

Vittorio looked at her gravely. 'No,' he said. 'I'm afraid not.'

Clare sat bolt upright as if she had been struck by lightning.

'I know you probably thought–' he began.

'Probably!' She rounded on him. 'You invited me up to your room alone ... to ...' She stopped. 'Knowing that you weren't free.' That could only mean one thing. 'You have someone you're going home to.'

'Clare. I had every intention of explaining.'

'No, you didn't. You hoped that I'd be so enthralled with you that I wouldn't ask or care.' She could feel her face flaming as though someone had struck it.

'You've got to listen, Clare. She's ill. Has been for a long time. Her parents are dead. There's no one to look after her. But for that I would have left long ago. You must believe me. You're the one I love. You're the one in my heart and soul. It never occurred to me that someone with your talent and ambition, whose aim to succeed was so strong, would fall in love with me.'

Clare jumped out of bed and began to pull on her clothes.

'Clare, wait. It's not what you think.'

He was out of bed, beside her, holding her arms, pinning her to him, forcing her to listen. 'I knew that if you let me make love to you nothing would keep us apart. That you would be mine regardless. For ever.'

Clare struggled free. 'How arrogant of you!' she shouted. 'What about your wife or mistress or whatever she is?'

'She is not my wife. I told you—'

'Spare me any more details or pathetic excuses. I've read better stories in *True Romance*.'

'Clare, listen!'

'No.' She turned on him. '*You* listen! You made a fool of me. I'm going and I never want to see you again.'

She left his suite with as much dignity as she could muster. Doubts and indecision plagued her. Vittorio had betrayed her and Martin's involvement with the IRA frightened her. This was a turning point. She would never again trust a man.

Chapter Eighteen

In August 1969, British troops arrived in the North. Raids and searches became part of everyday life. People were afraid to go out. A curfew was imposed. Armoured trucks and jeeps roared through the darkened streets, searchlights blazing. When Martin did not return, Pauline lay in bed, terrified, as boots kicked in locked doors in several of the flats.

'Where's he gone to?' she said to Scully, the next day.

'Don't know. But there's a bit of a shindig on tonight at headquarters. He's sure to be at that.'

'Will you take me with you?'

'It's only for members. Unless you're thinking of joining up.'

If that's what it takes to find Seamus, I will, Pauline thought.

They pulled up outside a house in a square and parked alongside a row of trucks, cars, motorbikes and bikes.

'This is it,' Scully said, nodding towards the tenement.

Pauline felt as if she was entering a fortress. Looped barbed wire circled the periphery and some men were hammering together what seemed to be a small platform. There were microphones and speakers on either side of it.

'What's going on?' Pauline asked

'We're expecting a big crowd,' Scully said, as he headed into the house and went straight down the hall. Pauline followed him. A group of people were standing around in a big room at the end of the corridor. When they saw Pauline, they hung back. Nobody said anything. A tall man, with a patch over one eye, kept staring at her. She felt the hair rise on the back of her neck. She said, 'Hello,' as cheerfully as she could to him, trying to show that for her to be there was the most natural thing in the world. Scully seemed disinclined to introduce her. He looked around, then they went straight back outside again. People were beginning to congregate. Several men in jeans and T-shirts were sitting around drinking beer and talking. Thin girls in tight jeans with skimpy T-shirts and stout women in drab dresses stood around talking together, tough-looking as the men.

Catching their stares, Pauline kept looking away. She tried to give the impression that she was not scared by smiling.

Other men arrived and blocked the doorway. They watched Pauline, nodded, exchanged glances.

'I'm looking for Martin. Did you see him?' she said to one, to deflect his curiosity.

'Upstairs.' He inclined his head towards the house.

She pushed her way past them out into the hall. A man with eyes like a bloodhound's stared at her from where he sat on the bottom stair.

'Like a smoke?' He pushed a packet of cigarettes under her nose.

'No thanks. I'm looking for Martin Dolan.'

'Try upstairs.'

She ran up and knocked on a door. When no one answered she opened it slowly and stepped inside. A suitcase lay open in a corner with clothes in it. She wasn't sure if they were Martin's or not. Tense, wary, she headed back downstairs, determined to find him if he was there. People were milling around, moving towards the stage. Someone was testing the loud-speakers. Music blared, then stopped.

A small, sour-looking woman, who'd been watching her, approached her.

Pauline went back inside and opened another door.

'Looking for someone?' asked a tall young woman with long blonde hair and hard eyes.

'Martin Dolan,' Pauline said.

The tall woman looked at her, her mouth twisting into a sarcastic smile. 'If I were you I wouldn't bother, love,' she said, in a confiding voice.

'Why?' Pauline asked.

The woman took a swig of beer from the can she was holding. A microphone whistled in the back-ground, then screeched and stopped abruptly.

'Why?' Pauline asked again.

'Martin's got a lot on his mind. He won't appreciate you adding to it. Get going before the crowd get here, if you've any sense.'

'I have to see him. It's important.' Pauline's look defied the woman to contradict her.

The woman gave a high-pitched laugh. 'That's what they all say,' she remarked. 'Anyway,' she continued, 'away on with you. Martin's too busy to have women chasing him. You have no business here.'

'What is he to you?' Pauline asked.

The woman laughed again, a loud, rasping sound.

'Wouldn't you like to know?' she said.

'Do you know Seamus Gilfoyle?'

'I do. Don't tell me you're looking for him as well. I

think you should go home to your mammy, love. You're asking too many questions. Not healthy.'

There was a knock on the door. 'Greta,' a voice said. 'Are you in there, Greta?'

'What do you want?' The woman was annoyed.

A short, balding man with a moustache put his head round the door. When he saw Pauline his eyes widened with surprise. 'Didn't know you had company,' he said, looking her over.

'I don't. She's just leaving.'

He came into the room. 'Greta,' he said, in a low voice. 'You know you're not supposed to be drinking. The boss'll be here soon. He wouldn't want to find you drunk.'

He reached down to take the can she was holding, but she pulled it into her chest and glared at him. 'Fuck the boss,' she said. 'And fuck you.'

'You've had enough,' he insisted.

'I'll drink Ireland dry, if I want to,' Greta said.

The man shot Pauline a sideways glance. 'I think you should run along now. Your presence won't be welcome here if you're not a member.'

'She was just leaving,' Greta repeated.

'I'm looking for Martin Dolan,' Pauline explained to him.

'He was here earlier. He'll be back I'm sure.'

An explosion rent the air outside. Pauline leaped to the wall, slid down to the floor and squatted, waiting, her hands over her head against the whine of a rocket and the sharp report of bullets, blasting over the roof.

An awful silence followed. The wall was cool against her back. Slowly she straightened and stood up, her knees stiff, then ran down the stairs and out of the door. Smoke stung her eyes and she covered them with her hands against the blinding white flashing light of a fire. The smell of sulphur assaulted her nostrils.

People were running in all directions. The men who had stood in the doorway earlier were taking cover. Flashing blue lights appeared, flames crackled, petrol bombs whistled through the air and exploded in waves. Pauline squinted in the smoke for a glimpse of Martin.

Rahhh . . . A series of sharp reports coming from behind made her leap into the air, a scream rising in her throat. Dear God! she thought. What possessed me to come here? Covering her head with her hands she ran down the path, bullets whistling around her, sparks hissing and sizzling.

A screaming, hysterical woman tried to grab her. When she looked she saw it was Greta. Ducking sideways, she ran. Suddenly she saw Scully moving across the garden, his face streaked with blood and smoke, his hair wild. She ran to meet him.

'Pauline, come on! Cops!' he hissed.

He pulled her to him and, using his body as cover, he pushed her forward down the side of the house.

'Faster!' he said, sprinting past police cars, men in helmets, women screaming, children crying, dragging her with him. They zigzagged away, everything exploding around them.

Gasping for breath Pauline slowed down, the world crashing around her, jagged, fading into blackness. When she came to the noise had stopped. She could hear voices somewhere close by but she decided to stay still and not try to see who was talking. As her eyes adjusted to the light she saw that she was in a small space lying on a mattress. In the distance she heard another explosion. She waited. Time passed. She could still hear the voices but she couldn't make out what was being said. A door creaked open. Someone's face hovered above her. A hand reached out and grabbed her foot. 'You awake?'

It was Scully.

'What happened to me? Where am I?'

'You got a bang on the head.' Scully was bending over her, examining the bruise. 'I think you'll live. Come on.'

Pauline peered up at him. 'I feel dizzy,' she said, as she tried to get up.

'You'll be all right when you get into the fresh air. Hold on to me.' Half carrying, half walking her, he helped her along. She went limp and let him, not wanting to go without Martin, not wanting to stay either.

Harsh sunshine dazzled her.

'Get a move on,' a man said to Scully. 'The cops will be back.'

'Where's Martin?' Scully asked.

'He made a run for it. Someone must have tipped off the cops.'

Pauline wanted to cry but instead she sat down on the path and rubbed her scratched, bleeding legs to get the circulation going.

'Let's get out of here.' Scully looked anxious. 'We'll get you home.'

'Home. That's a laugh.' Pauline's voice was laced with sarcasm.

'Come on.' Scully helped her to her feet, gently pulling her arms.

She walked, keeping her face averted. Pain shot through her legs and she started to sag.

'Lean on me,' he said, kindly. 'The car's only up the road.'

He caught her, his strength propelling her forward. All around them lay smashed glass, charred wood and heaps of debris.

Once in the car, Pauline looked straight ahead. Sirens wailed in the distance as Scully manoeuvred it out of the lane.

'Get your head down,' he hissed. 'There's cops everywhere.'

'I don't care,' Pauline moaned. 'I just want to get away.' Scully drove down back roads, along winding dirt tracks.

Eventually they reached the tower block to find it in darkness. 'You'll manage on your own now for a while,' he said, giving her a key. 'I'd better go and find Martin.'

'So you trust me not to run away?' Pauline looked at him.

'I don't think you'd get far, do you?'

'No.'

'Keep the curtains pulled. Don't answer the doorbell.'

Pauline nodded. 'Thanks. See you later.' She walked towards the lift on rubbery legs.

The key wouldn't turn in the lock.

A man in overalls came up the stairs carrying a bucket.

'Locked out, love?' he asked.

'I can't turn this key,' Pauline said.

He took it from her and gave it a twist in the lock. The door opened. 'There's a knack,' he said.

'Thanks.' Pauline smiled gratefully at him.

The emptiness in the flat gave her a cold feeling. She was sick of the dirty walls, and the bareness of the place. She walked slowly down the hall to Martin's room. The book he was reading, *Cry Freedom*, was on the chair beside the bed with his cigarettes and lighter.

She picked up the lighter and examined his initials engraved on it. She flicked it on. The sudden burst of blue flame took her by surprise and made the corners of the room look dark and menacing. A sudden pang of longing for her baby hit her in the pit of her stomach. She lurched off the bed and went to the kitchen for the comfort of the kettle.

She stood at the window with her cup of coffee staring down at the dull slate rooftops below her, and the lights of this strange, evil city flickering on, line after line of orange street lamps stretching away to the South.

James was sitting in front of the fire, nursing a whiskey. He had returned earlier from his office and announced to Eve that he was changing into his gardening clothes to stake up the roses, pointing to the lop-sided bushes seared by the strong wind. Eve followed him down the garden path. 'Anything the matter, Grandpa?' she asked. 'You don't look very happy.'

'We may have to sell up, Eve,' he said, without preamble.

'Sell here? But why?'

'It might be the only solution. Seems there's nothing left.' He began to hammer a stake into the ground.

'How did things get so bad?'

'Gave too much responsibility to your father, I'm afraid.'

As James spoke Eve was recalling her mother's words: 'He won't stop until the business is totally destroyed.'

'Why didn't Daddy tell you?' Eve was perplexed.

'He hinted at trouble. Pared down the workforce. Realised some assets to keep afloat. What I didn't know was that he was borrowing heavily against the house.'

'Oh, Grandpa.'

'My dear, it's no good blaming him. I should have taken more of an interest myself, instead of pottering around here all the time.'

He leaned against the stake, his face drained of colour. He seemed to drift off, looking into the distance, perhaps thinking of the old days when he had been in charge and business was booming. 'I should have done something about this with the first hint of trouble,' he said, coming back to reality. 'Modernised. Caught up with the competition. But we were doing so well. It didn't seem necessary. Now it looks as if it's too late. Nothing left.' He spoke as if he were talking to himself.

Eve looked at him. 'Perhaps there are alternatives.'

'If there were I'd hardly be worrying your pretty little head,' James said, reaching for her hand.

'Why did Daddy have to go off like that?' Eve said. 'I just don't understand it.'

'That's life. If we understood it all there wouldn't be any mystery.' James was back to his old philosophical self. 'We'll think of something.' Wearily, James handed her a ball of twine to hold for him while he caught up the limp branches in his strong, capable hands. 'We'll battle along. Mightn't be such a bad thing in the long run if we sell up. The place needs repairs, maintenance. Noose around your neck at times.'

'Mummy will rant and rave and give you a hard time,' Eve said.

'Once she gets used to the idea she'll be fine. Deserves better, Dorothy.'

'Couldn't I help out, Grandpa?'

'You're looking after your mother.'

'She's in the boutique most of the time and Agnes still does quite a bit. Mummy doesn't need me. I'm sure I could be useful in the business. I worked as a receptionist in London.'

'Would you like to have a go?'

'I'd love it.'

The next morning Eve swept out the shed for James, arranged his seedling pots into neat rows, tidied string into bundles, and filled sacks with rubbish. Seagulls circled overhead, swooping down from time to time to swipe crumbs from the window-sill. The smell of baking wafted through the open kitchen window and Agnes's voice crackled along with the radio as she clattered her pots and pans. Familiar sounds, all part of Eve's life. She would miss Agnes's company if Agnes had to go. How would Grandpa cope, though? Wasn't he too old for the drastic changes with which he was faced? Might he not pine away if stripped of his home? It was different for her. She had the restlessness in her that welcomes change and the youth to confront life head on and explore it. Optimism, Grandpa called it. But while she looked forward she knew that nothing would ever be the same again if James was forced to sell his house.

'I'm making a pot of tea,' Agnes called out of the window.

'I'll be there in a few minutes,' Eve called back.

The kitchen was stifling. Agnes had filled the sink with scalding suds and had begun to scour the heavy pots. Eve insisted on drying them before they sat down.

'How's Jack?'

'Quiet,' Agnes said. 'Writing long letters to Martin. They're hatching something, the pair of them.'

'As long as it keeps him occupied,' Eve said.

'He comes and goes as usual but he's much quieter,' Agnes said. 'Have you finished cleaning out there?'

'Almost,' Eve said.

'How's Madge getting on with the baby?'

'She adores him. I think she's going to try and adopt him.'

Agnes shook her head. 'It's amazing all the same that Pauline abandoned him,' she said, sipping her tea.

'She wrote to Madge ages ago from Belfast,' Eve said. 'Said she was coming home in a day or two. That was in June.'

'I ask you,' Agnes said. 'What happened to her?'

'Mrs Browne has Madge almost convinced that she met a fella up there.'

Agnes stirred her tea. 'Who'd take any notice of Mrs Browne? The worst word out of her mouth is all you'll ever hear from her.'

'Agnes, what do you think about Grandpa selling up?'

'It's not my place to make anything of it, Eve. But, seeing as you ask, it would be a disaster.'

As she finished the dregs of her tea Agnes gazed out of the window. 'Nice man, your father. But Dorothy could never depend on him,' she said. 'All that travelling in India. As far back as I can remember.' She stood up. 'A gentleman all the same,' she concluded.

'He might be on his way home.' Eve's face brightened. 'To help us sort out this mess.'

'He'd be better off staying where he is a while longer. Your grandfather'll see to things. He's still a powerful man. Highly regarded in these parts, Eve.'

'What a terrible shock for him, though. Poor Grandpa.'

'And what about yourself?' Agnes's eyes were on

Eve's face. 'Any word from Chris?'

'No. I wrote to him and phoned lots of times. I don't know what to do.' Eve shrugged.

'He's on the move. Put your trust in God and go down to the church and say a few prayers. Works wonders. Did Clare write and tell you about her recital?'

'It's marvellous, isn't it?'

'She's talking about coming home soon, too.'

'Great. I'll write to her tomorrow. Now I must get over to Madge to see how Seamie is.'

'Don't you go getting too fond of that child,' Agnes warned.

'He's adorable,' Eve said.

'You'll be getting the longing next.'

Eve started work at Freeman's Tea Importers in September 1969. The quality of the company's blended tea, with its genuine own-label products, packaged on the premises and with delivery guaranteed within twenty-four hours, had set it apart and given it a reputation for excellence.

Freeman's tea blenders were the most skilled in the country: their recipes took into account the quality of the water in each area in which the products were sold. The tea was bought at auction each week from a public warehouse, then delivered to the blending house. The top floor stored the original teas. The tea sales room was where the blend was made up and the quality of the tea depended on the blender. The taster went from one bowl to another along a counter, tasting, never swallowing. Twenty chests of various teas were put into the hopper and fed into the drum on the next floor where the tea was mixed, cut to size and fed into another hopper on the next floor where all the tea-packing machines were located. On the ground floor it was packaged, off-loaded and palleted, ready for distribution. The large accounts had their own packaging and labels. Eve studied the files from the tea sales room, the blenders office, the accounts department and the sales office.

In 1936 James Freeman had returned from a tea plantation in India where he had been superintendent, to set up his own business with the financial help of a number of individuals, including his bank manager, Jasper Furlong. It was a competitive business, with other tea companies like Lipton's, Bewley's and Barry's vying for a share of the market. James operated on a shoestring, instructing his sales manager to give special deals to the larger shops – his bread-and-butter accounts, as he called them.

Eve's first job each morning was to open all the windows and let in the fresh air. She liked to arrive early before the intrusion of the post and telephones. She would spend the time checking files and acquainting herself with the accounts system to which Miss Carver, James's secretary, had introduced her. To get to know the business she had to work her way through it, and she spent several weeks in the tea sales room and the warehouse. She also had to get to know the other major tea companies.

James, meantime, was busy contacting everyone he knew in the trade, drawing on the loyalty of acquaintances and colleagues in India to help in his financial crisis, pleading with banks and finance houses for more time to settle his debt, checking hauliers, cars, delivery vans to find out where costs could be cut. The whole workforce was under threat.

In the evenings Eve would read reports of past

meetings but all the time Chris was never far from her mind. She wished she could stop loving him. His mocking, handsome face was before her everywhere she went and in everything she did. The attraction between them had been so strong that it had been easy to run away with him, and facing the consequences afterwards hadn't even been so bad. What Eve found difficult was contemplating life without him.

One Saturday morning in late September, Eve heard the crunch of tyres on gravel, the sound of brakes, the cough of an engine as it stopped suddenly, then hurried footsteps on the path outside. The bell rang.

Cautiously she opened the door.

'Hello.' Chris stood there in Levi's and leather jacket, his face sun-tanned, his eyes glittering. Looking at him, Eve felt suddenly vulnerable, defenceless – and pale. He was watching her reaction, smiling. His hair was longer, streaked with blond and tied back.

'Hi.' Eve cleared her throat, moved back and almost staggered.

'Hey.' Chris steadied her, held her lightly and looked into her eyes. 'How are you?' he asked.

'I'm fine,' she replied, refusing to meet his gaze. 'Come in.'

The air was thick with silence.

'You're not glad to see me?' He pushed his face close to hers.

'Why should I be glad to see you?' She laughed, a choking, sobbing sound.

'What's so funny?'

'I—' Eve burst into paroxysms of mirth.

'Eve?' Startled he took her wrists and held them, pressing her slowly back against the wall.

'I . . . can't.' She leaned back shaking, the laughter suffocating her words.

'Eve, stop!' he shouted.

Abruptly she was quiet.

The silence closed in around them: she could hear the beat of her own heart. Closing her eyes for a minute she half expected him to disappear but when she opened them again he was still there.

'You're not glad to see me, then?' His voice was low.

'Shocked.' Eve stared at him.

'May I come in?'

Moving back she let him pass, conscious that she was still in her dressing-gown. In the kitchen she put the kettle on to boil and said nothing.

'How are you doing?' Chris asked, taking a cigarette from a packet of Gauloises, the brand he had always smoked, and flicking the gold lighter she had given him for his birthday.

'Can't complain,' she managed as, with shaking fingers, she assembled the coffee-maker.

Several times she started to say, 'It's good to see you,' or 'I'm happy you're here.' But the words stuck in her throat. Finally, all she said was, 'Well, you're here,' in a harsh, accusatory tone.

They sat down opposite each other. Eve was a little out of breath.

'How are you? Really, I mean.' Chris seemed determined to keep things pleasant between them.

'I'm fine. Working in the business with Grandpa.'

'I'm impressed. How did that come about?'

Eve shrugged. 'He needed help. I needed something to do.' She fiddled with the sugar spoon.

Chris raised his hand as though to ward off a blow. 'I know. I know. I neglected you.'

'You certainly did.'

'Well, I'm here now and we're talking.'

'Are we?' Eve looked at him. 'Why did you come?'

'I'm playing a gig in Dublin.' He looked out of the open window at the sunlight making shadows on the lawn. The voices of children playing down the street floated in, their laughter ringing out amid swearing.

'What about us?' Eve said suddenly.

Christ turned back to her. 'I'm not proud of the way I treated you, Eve. But it happened and there isn't much sense in dwelling on past mistakes.'

'No. I suppose not.'

There were so many questions she had wanted to ask him – like Why did you do it? What was I to you that you could dump me so easily? What am I to you now? After a while, she said, 'Why did you come back?'

He continued to gaze out of the window, somehow diminished.

'I . . .' His hands fluttered helplessly as if he had been taken unawares. 'We have to talk. Sort things out.'

'I agree.'

'Come on, then. Let's get out of here. I always found this place stifling.'

'Give me a minute to get ready,' Eve said.

'Sure. Wear something cool. It's hot.'

She ran upstairs, put on her shorts and a T-shirt, brushed her hair into a pony-tail and threw her make-up into her vanity case, scared that if she didn't hurry Chris might leave without her.

'Where are you going?' Agnes was standing in her bedroom doorway, watching her.

'Chris is here.'

'I noticed.'

'He's waiting downstairs. He's taking me out.'

'Are you sure you should be going?'

'No, but I am.' Eve was searching frantically for her purse.

'How long is he here for?' Agnes looked agitated.

'I don't know. I didn't ask,' Eve said.

'What'll I tell your mother?'

Eve stopped and looked at her.

'Do you think it's wise?' Agnes continued. 'I mean, where has he been all this time?'

'I don't know,' Eve said. 'But I'm sure I'll find out.'

Agnes shook her head sadly. 'You'll get hurt again, Eve,' she said.

'I never stopped hurting.'

'Well, you're asking for trouble, my girl.'

'Right. I'm off.' Eve grabbed her bag and made for the door. She stopped and looked back at Agnes. 'Tell Mummy for me when she comes in. Will you?' She gave Agnes a pleading look.

'If you want me to. But she won't understand.'

'I know, but you'll make things all right. You know how. I'll be back later on.'

'You're expecting me to work miracles.'

'You usually do.'

'Best say nothing for the present, if you want my opinion,' Agnes said.

'Not tell her Chris is here?' Eve asked.

'Precisely.'

Eve kissed her cheek and ran down the stairs.

'It's your own business,' Agnes said to the fleeing figure. 'Your own funeral,' she muttered, as she moved to the window to watch Eve jump into the front seat of the waiting Lotus, Chris smug behind the wheel.

'I wanted to see you again,' he said, as they drove off,

his smiling face conveying nothing.

Eve tried to read his expression – amusement, joy, pity? Its blandness puzzled her.

He drove out to the cove. 'I've always loved this spot,' he said, as they got out of the car and walked along the beach.

'Me too,' she agreed.

He told her about his tour of America. How he'd got the wanderlust out of his system and that now he wanted desperately to study at RADA.

Haltingly, Eve told him the bits about her life that she thought might interest him. 'I like working for Grandpa,' she said. 'I've discovered an aptitude for business that I didn't know I possessed.'

They skimmed stones at the water's edge, like they used to do. Chris's stones went further and better, bouncing off the top of the water several times, making tiny whirlpools as they flew along.

'You're winning,' she said.

'Of course.'

They laughed.

Suddenly his arms were round her, his face close to hers. 'And you're coping,' he said, gently. 'I gave you a tough time, Eve. Everything came together at once and it was all too much for me.'

'I thought I'd die of heartbreak. That I wouldn't be able to live without you. But I didn't die. I'm here, living and breathing.'

'You won't die of love,' he said, touching her cheek, then leaning forward and kissing her quickly. 'There are plenty of men out there more worthy of you than me. Men who'll love you properly, the way you deserve to be loved.'

Eve stepped back, stunned. She walked away so that

he wouldn't see the rush of tears to her eyes.

He came after her. 'What have I said now?' he asked.

'Nothing,' she answered, with a sob.

He reached for her shoulder and pulled her round to face him. 'Eve, I was paying you a compliment. It's the truth. I wasn't being offensive. Was I?'

He touched her cheek, cold from the sea breeze, and she lifted up her face to his, willing him to care for her as much as she cared for him. He kissed her, warming her lips with his. Abruptly he released her. She clung to him, thinking that if she didn't she might faint After a moment they walked back down the beach.

Eventually she said, 'I know you think you're much more mature than me, Chris, and that you know more about life than I do. You probably do. But you know nothing about me. You never bothered to find out.'

He looked at her. 'I see,' was all he said before he walked on.

She raised her hand. 'No. Let me finish. You were always too selfish, only interested in what you wanted out of life for yourself, afraid I'd hold you back or something.' She had stopped walking and was standing, arms akimbo, in the middle of the beach. 'This is something I've thought about for a long time,' she continued.

'Obviously,' Chris said.

She waited for him to turn, and when he did, he said, 'You look ridiculous standing there like that with such a serious expression on your face.'

They laughed and the atmosphere between them changed. They continued their walk, smiling at one another, stopping at the harbour wall to gaze into the dull grey sea.

Chris said, 'It isn't fair to expect you to trail along

everywhere after me, Eve. There's more to you than that. You're carving out a niche for yourself now and it would be wrong of me to uproot you again, with no stability to offer you while I'm still on the road.'

'You're not making sense, Chris. All I know is that I'm your wife and we've got to decide what we're going to do, once and for all. I've been living in a kind of limbo since I came back.'

'I agree.' Chris took her hand and led her back to the car.

She wished the world would go right by them and leave them alone, there, in that place, for ever.

When they got back to her house he said, 'I've got to go now.'

'Aren't you staying here?'

'No. I have to get back to the city. We're off to Galway.' He kissed her cheek. 'Sleep well tonight. I'll phone you tomorrow.'

Taken aback she moved towards him, hoping he would kiss her again, but he just smiled, touched her cheek and said, 'See you.'

Chapter Nineteen

By the time Clare arrived home on holiday, early in October, the whole of Glencove was agog at the news that she, Clare Dolan, daughter of Jack and Agnes Dolan and sister of the wayward Martin, was becoming a renowned concert pianist.

At the mention of her name, everyone marvelled at the turn of events that had catapulted her into the limelight. People in sleepy Glencove chuckled delightedly at the change of fortune for their hearty pal Jack, who had always been respected for his patriotism and his abiding loyalty to the Cause.

In spite of Jack's good humour and optimism, though, his health had deteriorated since Clare had last seen him. His skin's yellowish tinge was more pronounced and he was losing weight.

'It's his liver,' Agnes said to Clare. 'Dr Gregory wants him in for tests but he won't go. He's tried to destroy himself with the drink and now he's going to succeed with his own carelessness.'

To Jack she said, 'You can sit around cogitating all you like but you have to do what Dr Gregory said and go into hospital for tests.'

'Rubbish,' Jack said. 'I'm much better and I feel stronger.'

But daily he was growing visibly weaker. His stomach and feet were swollen and when he walked he leaned heavily on his stick. Soon he became confined to his chair by the window, gazing down the road, surveying the passers-by, commenting on everything he noticed.

Where his health was concerned Jack had always been long-suffering and uncomplaining. But Clare realised that he knew more than he said and that he was more concerned about the well-being of his children than he was about himself. 'You look so unhappy,' he said to Clare one evening when Agnes was out.

'What about Vittorio? Have you heard from him?'

'No,' Clare burst out, ashamed and humiliated that the man who declared his love for her so ardently could have been involved elsewhere.

One morning, when Clare came downstairs, Agnes was standing in front of the range in her dressing-gown, her hair untidy, her expression strained, the frying pan in her hand.

'What's the matter?' Clare asked.

Agnes put down the pan and reached for the newspaper. 'Dorothy brought this over earlier,' she said, handing it to Clare.

It was the first British newspaper Clare had ever seen in their home.

> Self-styled paramilitary officer, Martin Dolan, 25, is wanted in connection with the murder of an unarmed constable in Belfast after a riot last Wednesday night.

Clare sat at the kitchen table and read the same words over and over again.

'What are we going to do?' Agnes asked.

'Nothing.' Clare was emphatic. 'We'll do nothing.'

'I'd no idea he was involved in such danger,' Agnes said. 'If I had I'd have stopped him.'

'Mother, Martin wouldn't have listened to a word you said.'

'We were so close, so close. I thought I knew everything about him.'

'Your blue-eyed boy,' Clare said, staring at the newspaper again.

'Why? Oh, why did he get so involved?' When Jack came slowly into the kitchen Agnes was weeping. 'It's all right for you, Jack Dolan,' she sobbed. 'You thrive on all this trouble. Encourage it. I'm not able for it.' Agnes's voice was harsh with tension as she put rashers, sausages, black pudding in the frying pan. The smell was friendly and familiar and, for a moment, it was as if nothing had happened. She made tea and poured it out, handing a cup to Jack.

Silently he took it. After a while he said, 'Martin's doing his bit as he sees it.'

'I'd rather have nothing to do with what Martin's doing,' Agnes retorted. 'I can't find any excuse for one human being killing another. Do you honestly think the world will be a better place just because Martin has killed someone?'

'You're assuming too much, Agnes. They said he's wanted in connection with murder. No one said he did it.'

Agnes wasn't listening. 'We're disgraced, that's what we are. I want no hand, act or part in this. It's uncivilised behaviour.' She was shouting. 'Our lives are ruined!'

'Stop it!'

'I won't stop it! Courage is one thing. Murder is another,' Agnes shrieked.

'I gave up arguing with you a long time ago, Agnes Dolan, and I'm not going to start again now.'

'I'm washing my hands of this whole terrible business,' Agnes said. 'And of Martin.'

'You can't change your feelings and opinions about your country like the weather,' Jack said.

'Yes, I can. And about my own son, too.'

'Turning our backs on him isn't the way. I'm off to find proper legal representation for him,' Jack said, standing up from the table.

'Who has the kind of money he'll need for bail?' Agnes asked.

'You'd be amazed. Friends of the Nationalists, let's call them. Very wealthy, some of them.' Jack took his hat from the hook behind the door and plonked it on his head.

'I hope you know what you're doing,' Agnes cautioned him.

'Just setting the wheels in motion,' Jack said.

'What's going to happen next?' Agnes buried her head in her hands.

Jack went over to her and touched her shoulder. 'Courage, woman. Where's your courage?'

The word 'murder' had a chilling ring to it. Clare could imagine the courtroom: lawyers in black robes mouthing cold, official words, headlines screaming, 'Martin Dolan. Killer.' The distorted photographs of his handsome face that would appear in the papers would upset Agnes. Clare could not imagine Martin bolted behind heavy prison gates. That wouldn't suit him at all. She thought of him roaming around somewhere, carefree, nonchalant.

Two weeks later Jack was admitted to hospital for tests.

'Nothing we can do for him,' said Mr Mulvanney, the specialist. 'I'm afraid his cancer was let go too far.'

'Cancer?' Agnes whispered.

'I'm afraid so.'

Jack said to Clare, 'You have your whole life before you, Clare. You must go back and continue your studies, not sit here and watch me die.'

'You can't leave me all on my own with him,' Agnes said. 'I wouldn't know what to do.'

Jack came home to die. Clare's heartbreak over Vittorio gave way to the terror of losing her father. Jack seemed to shrink a little more each day. His dark, expressive eyes were veiled and his beautiful smooth skin became papery. Gradually he stopped reading his newspaper, ceased to watch television or comment on the trouble in the North. Finally he stayed in bed, disinclined to sit by the window and watch the goings-on in the street, the pain more severe than he would ever admit.

Jack's eyes began to dim, and his breathing became increasingly laboured. Clare sat by his bedside and watched him retreat to somewhere unknown as his pain grew and Dr Gregory increased the doses of morphine. She despaired at her powerlessness to help him and, for the moment, the outside world ceased to exist while Jack's suffering took over her life.

His friends disappeared, too, when politics and reminiscences about the past might have been a distraction for him.

One day, Dermy McQuaid stopped Clare to enquire about him. 'Why don't you call to see him?' she asked, bewildered at the sheepish look he gave her.

'I will to be sure,' he replied, impatient to be off.

Several times Jack was admitted to hospital, where

he lay among rows of shrunken men, in varying degrees of agony, inert, and alone. Agnes and Clare took it in turn to sit by his bed, night after night, praying for his laborious breathing to cease and for his suffering to be over.

The end was near but Agnes strengthened her resolve to provide him with all the material things she wanted him still to enjoy. Washed, his wavy hair combed back, he sat up in bed, propped by his pillows, unable to eat the meals she prepared for him. He was eagerly awaiting Martin's safe arrival home.

Lying on her bed in Martin's dressing-gown, the bruise on her head gone, the scratches on her legs healed, Pauline listened to the sound of the traffic swooshing below on the wet streets. Rigid, watchful, she told herself to calm down and be patient, that soon she would be going home. She fell asleep, waiting for the sound of Martin's key in the door.

The clank of the lift woke her. She recognised Martin's quick, light footsteps crossing the landing outside, and the scrape of his key in the lock. She didn't move. 'Pauline.'

'In here,' she called from her bedroom.

He came down the hall and stood in the doorway. She could barely make out his silhouette as he sat down on the bed beside her.

'You're back,' she said.

'Yeah. You OK?'

'You were gone a long time, this time,' she said. Martin leaned forward and touched her hair. She could smell the beer.

'The cops raided the place. They gave me no choice. I had to make a run for it.'

'You left me stranded. I was scared,' Pauline said, hating to own up to her weakness.

Martin was silent for a minute. Then he said, 'You shouldn't have come to our headquarters, looking for me. That was no place for you to be in.'

'Scully took me.'

'I know. Still, you can't go chasing around after me. I'd better go to bed, I'm tired.'

'No.' Pauline clutched his arm. 'Don't go. I'm frightened. I can't stop shaking since Scully told me that you're wanted by the police.'

'Scully told you that?'

'Yes,' Pauline said.

'He should have kept his mouth shut. I've sent Scully off to sort out another problem. A worse one. He'll be gone a few days. But you needn't be frightened any more. I'm here now. Everything's taken care of,' he slurred, and lay down beside her.

'What's everything?' Pauline asked.

Martin didn't answer. She watched him, waited while he dozed off. When she thought he was sound asleep he suddenly came to and said, 'Business.'

'What sort of business?'

She heard the sound of his breath as he sucked it in. 'You wouldn't understand. It's better that way. Safer for you.'

'You've got plenty to hide,' she said.

From the hall light she could see his eyes glitter. She shuddered. Martin shifted his weight on the bed, tense, uneasy.

'Look, Pauline,' he said, sleepily, 'I care about you. I always have. I'm trying to look after you. If anything were to happen to you I don't know what I'd do. That's why I'm so protective. I love you.'

'Do you really?'

'You know I do. You love me too. Fight it all you like but it's no use. Feelings are feelings. In the end you'll give in.'

'Martin.'

'What?'

'Nothing.'

He moved back next to her. 'I'm here now. I can protect you, don't worry about anything.'

She wanted to beg him to let her go home, but every instinct told her not to. Everything inside her warned her that if she did she would regret it. It was not the time.

Martin stood up, removed his jacket and threw it to one side. He unbuckled the holster that held his gun and let it drop to the floor. The weapon slithered on the bare boards. His shirt followed and then his boots.

They lay quietly for a long time, neither moving. His breathing evened out and Pauline knew that he was sleeping.

Suddenly he wakened, jumped up so swiftly that it made her jump too.

'What's wrong?' she asked.

'Better go.' He moved away, then leaned towards her, reached out his hand and touched her cheek. In the light from the hall his face was a blur of angles; only his profile distinguished him. He saw her watching him, grinned and came closer.

'I know Seamus broke your heart,' he said. 'But life goes on and broken hearts mend. Believe me, Pauline, I'm an expert on broken hearts. I can fix yours for you.'

'What happened to Terry?' Pauline asked.

'She chickened out. A coward like Seamus. He had no balls.'

Pauline cuddled into him, ran her fingers over his chest. 'What did you do with him?' she coaxed, keeping her voice casual.

'He was no good for you, Pauline.' Martin's words were still slurred.

'I realise that now. But, all the same, what did you do with him?'

Martin lay back on the pillow. 'The swamp . . . down by the gas works. You were far too good for him, Pauline.'

'I know.'

His breath was hot on her face, as she leaned further towards him, and felt his lips on her neck.

'I could give you sensations you'd never forget if you'd let me,' he whispered hoarsely, his tongue teasing her ear.

She stayed curled in a tight ball, not moving, but not resisting when he began to remove her nightdress. His hands were soft, caressing.

'You're nervous,' he said.

'Yes.'

'Don't be.' He pulled her closer. 'Come 'ere.'

She didn't push him away but kept her eyes on the narrow space between herself and the open door, her pulse quickening.

In the dark she could feel his eyes on her. She stared ahead, every muscle taut, aching. A tremor ran through her body as he pulled her so close to him that she was wedged between his legs. She felt his weight, smelt the warm scent of him. His breathing quickened, his hands held her wrists, he kissed her, his lips pressing hard into hers. Pulling her against him, he held her firmly with both hands, hoisting her legs up, higher, clamping them around his waist. His thighs, big and muscular,

Joan O'Neill

pressed into hers, imprisoning her.

His jeans were off and as he arched her up to meet his mouth he was inside her, holding her still, possessing her. 'Don't move,' he whispered, as she tensed, gripping him with her thighs.

His eyes were on her, watchful, questioning. Slowly, ever so slowly, he started to move. His sweat dripped on to her hair and face. She licked it off, tasting the thick raw sweetness as he moved deeper into her. With an agonising cry he exploded inside her, releasing her so suddenly that she fell back on the bed. They lay motionless for a long time. After a while he said, 'You can have anything you want, Pauline.'

'I want money. Enough to get to America,' she said. He reached for his jeans and pulled his wallet out of the pocket, removing a wad of grubby notes.

'Here,' he said, peeling some off and handing them to her.

'That's grand,' Pauline said, taking it.

'I have enough for both of us to go,' Martin said, putting away his wallet.

'OK,' Pauline waited.

'We've been through a lot together, Pauline.'

'Yes,' she agreed. 'Too much.'

'But we were meant for each other. You know that now, don't you?'

'Yes.'

'It's no good with anyone else, sure it isn't.' His voice was thick with sleep.

'No.'

'I told you Seamus would never be any use to a girl like you. Never give you what I can give you.'

'I know.'

Sated, he fell asleep, his arm tight around her waist.

She waited, watching his face. Slowly imperceptibly, she reached under the bed, stretching her fingers to reach the gun. She held it carefully for some time, letting her hand get acquainted with its pearl handle. Lovingly, she lifted it up and held it close, fondling it. Gently she coaxed it towards his face, pointing it precisely, pulling back the hammer with her finger, all the time moving it slowly forward until the tip of it was almost pressing against his cheek.

In sleep, his jaw had slackened and, as he snored mildly, she moved the revolver down, closer to his mouth, easing it gradually between his lips. Not liking the taste of the metal he coughed and spluttered. Holding it firmly she jammed it in his mouth. As his eyes flew open she pulled the trigger.

Pauline sat there, trying to think. She was so tired that she just wanted to sleep. Lie down and sleep. But she couldn't do that. 'I have to get out of here before Scully comes back,' she told herself.

She got up and left the room slowly, forcing herself not to look back. Guilt and terror accumulated in her in a rush as it dawned on her what she had done. Through the crack in the door she could see the hall light. She would have to go back into the other room to make sure that Martin was really dead.

From the doorway, she could make out the heap of his body twisted on the bed, his clothes scattered on the floor, a briefcase nearby. She moved nearer, her mind racing frantically over the last few hours. But as she stared at the blood-covered medallion and chain around his neck, she felt only relief. Now she could forgive Martin for what he had done to her – if not for Seamus's death.

She stood, listening intently as she had so often done since coming to this flat, finding the silence comforting. She walked back down the empty corridor, the dark behind her evil and threatening, the flat seeming to grow larger. Hearing voices outside she ran to the balcony to see a group of people in a flat opposite, talking, their voices mingled with laughter. Suddenly she felt lonely and lost. As she gathered together her belongings she tried to understand the mystery of what had brought her here in the first place, and the endless struggle in which she and Martin had found themselves locked. It would take a long time to unravel it all.

Breathless, heart thumping, Pauline realised that she wasn't dressed. Looking down she saw blood spattered over her nightdress, her body, her hands. She washed, dressed and threw some of her belongings in a bag.

Before she left she tossed Martin's dressing-gown over him. Her finger grazed his arm. Already he was cold.

Once outside in the night air she walked briskly, bumping her bag against the wall, staggering sometimes in the dark. She found herself outside a small all-night café. There she sat, eating burgers and chips, feeling free for the first time in years and full of gratitude because of it. She was going home to her baby. As soon as it was daylight she left for the station and home.

Chris didn't phone Eve. She couldn't sleep, couldn't concentrate on her work, couldn't talk about it. She shouted at Dorothy, kept her distance from her grandfather. Agnes, the only one who knew that Chris was back, called him a bastard and said that he had returned to make sure she was still in love with him. A week later, when he finally phoned, asking her to meet him in the apartment where he was staying in the city, Agnes begged her not to go.

'I might as well see him,' Eve said. 'What have I got to lose?'

'Your dignity,' Agnes harped.

Eve wet-plaited her hair, so that when it was dry it combed into Ophelia ripples. She painted her eyes harebell blue and wore a pale blue chiffon dress. She took the bus and walked quickly through the busy streets. The wind blew wildly, whipping a long strand of hair around her face. She climbed the stairs to the apartment to which she had been directed.

A woman answered her knock. 'There's no one in,' she said. 'You'll have to come back later.'

Eve checked the address. 'I have an appointment to meet someone here at four o'clock,' she said.

The woman put on her coat. 'Must have got delayed. I only work here and I'm off duty now. Make yourself at home. I'm sure they won't be long.'

Eve looked around. The place was neat, luxurious and bare, with deep cream sofas, coloured-glass chrome-edged coffee tables, and posters of far-off places expensively framed and hung on the plain white walls.

The kitchen was tiny, the fridge packed with bottles of wine and cans of beer. Eve took a glass from a cupboard and poured herself a glass of white wine, carried it into the sitting room and leafed through a copy of *Time* magazine while she waited. The nervous energy that had given her confidence to go there in the first place began to evaporate. She helped herself to another glass of wine and gulped it down.

By the time Chris arrived she was lying in the middle

of the big soft double bed in the bright front bedroom, naked under the white covers, the empty wine bottle and glass on the floor beside her.

'Hello,' she said, looking up at him, laughing, happy.

He came to her, startled and magnificent. 'I see you made yourself at home,' he said.

'I am your wife and you did invite me.'

'True.'

They made love slowly, tenderly, the way it had been in the beginning, with the last rays of the October sunlight filtering in through the narrow slats of the venetian blinds. As the shadows lengthened, Eve relaxed and became her old familiar self again. She held him for a long time, asked him what he would like. Eager to please him, she aroused him again, touching, tasting, relishing every part of him.

'I can't stay,' she whispered into his ear, when he could hardly stand it a minute longer. 'There'll be a search party out for me if I don't get home soon.'

'Stay, stay,' he begged. 'Phone them.'

After her phone call home, they made love and lost all track of time. It was Chris's turn to please her and, in a trance, she let him do what he liked, when he liked, how he liked, wanting him so much to want her that she would not ask him to stop. They finished only when the last drop of juice had been wrung out of both of them and Eve was raw and swollen inside.

That Chris didn't love her, perhaps never had, was of no consequence to Eve. She would make herself indispensable to him. Of that she was convinced.

At midnight, spent, sated, not an ounce of energy between them, they got up, showered and dressed. Chris took her to the Trocadero for dinner. Her hair was damp, her lips chapped and swollen.

The following evening, they sat across from each other in the apartment sipping champagne. Eve was listening to every word of the conversation as if her life depended on it. Roy Orbison was singing in the background. This was Chris's last evening and neither of them was ready to say goodbye.

'We've had a great time,' Chris said, studying the intricacies of the crystal glass in his hand, 'but,' he hesitated, 'time marches on.'

'You'll be back soon,' Eve said, clinging desperately to the peaceful aftermath that comes only after lovemaking and is so short-lived.

'I'm sure I will. I've grown very fond of Ireland.' He looked at her. 'When is another matter, though.'

'We haven't sorted anything out,' Eve said, keeping her voice calm.

'Look, Eve. I know how much you wanted the perfect marriage, the two children, the happy-ever-after.'

'You wanted it too.' Eve's eyes were defiant.

'Well, I didn't think that far ahead. Anyway, that's not the way it turned out.'

'That's for sure.

Chris laughed mirthlessly. 'I'm hardly a candidate for family life. We know that now. Some time in the distant future, maybe.'

'Spare me,' Eve said. 'We've been through this part. What do you intend to do with me now?'

Chris stood up, frustrated. 'We've had great times. I won't deny that,' he said 'Good fun too. We enjoyed each other.' He turned to her slowly. 'We're prolonging the agony, Eve. I think we both know it's time to split.'

Dumbfounded, Eve sprang to her feet. 'What are you saying? That our marriage is over?'

Chris nodded. 'I thought you understood that in London.'

'Yes, but we were doing something about it, patching it up, these last couple of weeks . . .' Her voice trailed off as she saw Chris's face. Instantly, through the searing pain that coursed through her, she realised that nothing she could do or say would make any difference. 'I'm in love with you, don't you know that?' she cried out.

'You're in love with sex and the idea of love and marriage and everything it involves. But the reality proved different. We're only growing up now, Eve – and face it, we were miserable living together.'

'Well, with you always running off–'

'Would you blame me, with you permanently pissed?' He spat the words at her.

'Let's stop this, now. We'll only start hurting each other again.'

'It won't be that difficult to let go,' he said. 'Not as bad as the first time.'

'What about my family? What will I tell them?'

'That it wasn't meant to be, that's all. Listen, Eve, we can be civilised about this. Be grateful for the good times and forgive each other the rest.' The way he said it made it sound so easy. Already he was withdrawing from her: she could tell by his expression that, as far as he was concerned, the problems, the dramas were hers.

'What did you come back for, Chris?' Eve's gaze was steady on his face.

'A divorce.'

'So, let me get this straight,' Eve said. 'Are we separated now? Do I have to go through some trial time before I start dating again? Explain the next move, Chris, because there is no divorce in Ireland and I have no idea what it entails.'

'Leave it all to me,' he said, missing her sarcasm.

'I suppose your mother will pay to get rid of me the same way she paid for the wedding, the honeymoon and the flat.'

He flinched as if she'd struck him. 'I'll talk to you when you're in a reasonable mood,' he said. 'Now I'll take you home.'

'You pig,' she said, slapping him hard across the face. 'I can find my own way.'

She stormed out of the apartment and marched to the bus stop. On the way home she wondered if he already had someone else lying next to him in their bed in London, doing the things to him that she had done. Her fury with him carried her along. She thought of the girls he had known from wealthy, privileged backgrounds. What had attracted him to her? A waitress, as far as he knew, with nothing to recommend her but her come-day, go-day attitude to life.

It was only after they had married that her possessiveness had got out of control, and with it her drinking. When they fought she took a secret pleasure in drawing blood on his beautiful face with her nails, aware that he wouldn't retaliate. Yet although the hard part was still to come Eve realised that over the last few days she had been clinging only to an idea of him. All that energy had been expended in vain and she hated him.

Chapter Twenty

The ambulance came to take Jack to the hospital to die. Clare flew home again from Paris and spent every moment she could at his bedside, holding his hand. Once or twice he spoke to her to ask for Martin, but mostly he slept or lay peacefully with his eyes closed. One evening in early November he gave up his tremendous struggle and slipped away in his sleep with Agnes and Clare sitting on either side of his bed.

What Clare found incredible was that at eleven o'clock on the morning of the funeral Glencove shut down. Stalls disappeared from outside the fruit and vegetable shop. Blinds were drawn in Kinsella's Select Bar, Reilly's the butcher's, Concepta's hair salon and at Lynam's boutique. Even the new supermarket was closed, the batches of fresh bread untouched on the chrome shelves. The people of Glencove didn't go to work or shop or take their children to school. Instead they buried Jack Dolan.

There was no sign of Martin.

Clare had reminded Father McCarthy of her father's dislike of church services and asked him politely if he would keep his eulogy short.

'Jack had his own brand of religion,' Father McCarthy told the congregation, 'his own set of values. He lived for his country and valued his people. A true patriot and a good man.'

Clare was recalling the father who had always told her that the stars were never brighter than after a shower of rain, who never lost his roguish charm or his extravagance. Jack, who talked to men he knew and men he didn't, all of whom accepted him warmly. Jack the raconteur, who held his audience spellbound by using the end of one story to ignite the beginning of another, pausing only while they lapsed into laughter, or to savour his drink.

The biggest surprise was Agnes's inconsolable grief. She had borne Jack's illness with an air of tolerance, but in the church she broke down and wept loudly. Watching at the graveside, Clare could not believe that it was her daddy who was in the coffin and that he was truly dead. Had he known how much she had loved him? Why had she never told him?

On their return from the graveside, Jack's empty chair sent Agnes into hysterics, while Clare retreated to her bedroom and stayed there. From then on, Agnes's behaviour changed. She seemed to let go, making up for all the years of keeping her own counsel. All her speech was punctuated with talk of Jack. Sometimes she told stories lovingly about where and how they met, the endearments she had bestowed on him when they first fell in love. At other times she railed against his flaws, his patriotism. She took no interest in Clare's plans for the future, her whole life now submerged in her great loss.

For the next few weeks Clare remained with her mother. She felt distant from Agnes and guilty because of it. Sometimes when she came into the house at night, the dark silence overwhelmed her. Everything was still the same, but Jack's bed, his chair, his books, all the objects that had been important to him, were now meaningless.

When Sergeant Enright called with the news of Martin's death, Agnes was out. The stillness took over. There was no life in the sitting room or the kitchen. Martin's room was full of his clothes, his books on Irish nationalism, forestation, the co-operative movement in America. His school drawings were still pasted on to the walls. When Agnes returned Clare was in her room. She heard her mother turn on the radio, and the clank of the pots as they struck the cooker.

She found Agnes peeling potatoes at the sink.

'Sergeant Enright called,' Clare began.

Agnes wheeled around. 'What did he want this time?' she asked abruptly.

'He came to tell us that Martin's ... had ... an accident.'

'What?'

'He's dead,' Clare said, baldly.

Agnes's hands dropped to her sides, suddenly helpless, as tears streamed down her face. Clare went to her, held her, felt the sobs convulse her body. A long time passed before she started to ask questions. Clare recounted Sergeant Enright's story, omitting the detail of the bullet through Martin's mouth.

Clare stood opposite Father McCarthy and concentrated on his deep wrinkled forehead, his kind eyes shaded by thick heavy brows, as he prayed over Martin's coffin. Suddenly it struck her that she would never see Martin again. Neighbours came to her to express their sympathy, not knowing how distant Clare had grown from Martin, how tired she had become of waiting for him, worrying about him. She kept up the semblance of grief but deep down her heart was numb.

Much later when she was alone Clare let herself think about her brother, walking purposefully away, his easy, swinging stride distinct as he turned to say goodbye with a quick wave.

Chapter Twenty-one

Madge and Pauline were alone, talking. Madge was washing glasses, while Pauline wiped down the bar and the sink behind it.

'It's amazing how you get attached to babies,' Madge said, surprise at the power of her feelings towards Seamie in her voice. 'He makes me feel young again,' she said. Her face looked smoother and more youthful, her expression alive and happy. For once she wasn't thinking or caring about the 'rainy day'. 'He's cutting another tooth,' she said proudly. 'Poor little mite.'

'Not so little any more,' Pauline said, watching Madge as she worked with her quick, practised hands.

'He reminds me of my brother when he was small,' Madge continued. 'I used to mind him a lot because my mother was never well. Having Seamie here brings back all those memories.'

Pauline collected more glasses from the tables and stood them on the bar in neat rows, drawing comfort from being in the pub, close to Madge, but fearful that she would ask more questions about her trip away.

Madge glanced over at her. 'It's awful that you missed so much of his babyhood.'

'Worse than you could have imagined,' Pauline said. 'I used to dream about him. That he was near me and I was calling him but he didn't seem to hear me, toddled right by me without stopping. In the dream I chased after him and grabbed him, calling "Seamie, Seamie, it's me," but he didn't recognise me.' Pauline was crying as she spoke. 'I said, "Don't you recognise me, Seamie?" but his eyes were staring straight ahead as if he couldn't hear or see.'

'Well it's all over now.' Madge's tone was soothing. 'And, you're back here with him.'

'I couldn't wait to see him again, talk to him, explain things, even if he doesn't understand them yet.'

'Don't worry, I explained it all to him for you.' Madge laughed. 'Invented reasons for you not turning up.'

Pauline looked at her, eyes streaming.

'Bit late to be crying now,' Madge consoled. 'It's all over.'

'No, it isn't,' Pauline said, through her tears. 'I'll have to be off again.'

'Nonsense. I've room for you and Seamie and there's plenty of work here for you. We could be a proper little family.'

'I know,' Pauline said, 'and I'm grateful, but . . .' She took a deep breath, struggled for a minute but gave in to her misery. She wept, sitting on a stool, leaning against the bar. She wept for the bad things that she had done and seen, for the ugliness that she had witnessed, for the waste. Because she was confused by this mixture of emotions and the rage that burned inside her towards Seamus for being too stupid, and Martin, for causing her so much pain, she couldn't stop crying. And even though she knew that she should keep quiet about all that had happened in Belfast, she thought she would burst if she contained it any longer. Slowly, haltingly, she told Madge everything, and was released at last from her torture and helped in a way she would never have thought possible.

'You'll have to get away,' Madge agreed, white-faced. 'And soon.'

'I'll go to Aunt Mary in Long Island.'

'You'll be taking Seamie with you, I suppose?' Madge asked.

'Yes. But sure you can come out to visit us when we're settled.'

'Wild horses wouldn't stop me,' Madge said. 'But first things first. We'd better make some plans.'

The instant she woke on the morning she was leaving Ireland, Pauline went to look out of her bedroom window in the flat over the pub for the last time. The early mist was clearing over the dull, grey sea, and the sky was already turning blue. Even as Pauline watched a weak sun appeared through the clouds. She would miss the slow pull and suck of the tide, the crashing waves. The sea had been her constant companion when she had lived in Goretti Terrace. Pauline had swum in its depths, walked along its shores, watched it in all its forms of shifting light and shade, from grey to blue to azure. But, most of all, it reminded her of Seamus.

She packed her few possessions into a proper brown suitcase of Madge's, constantly afraid that Sergeant Enright would appear on the doorstep asking questions. Madge paid her nephew, Eamon, to drive Pauline and the baby to the station, and Pauline held Seamie tight as she stepped out into the November morning and waved his little hand to Madge as the car drove off. Madge cried for Seamie, at the sight of him in his blue brushed-wool coat and hat she had bought him. He was so excited to be driving off in the car, taken away, with no idea of where he was going or of what was about to happen to him, and would forget all about the time she had spent with him over the past eleven months.

Pauline spent the journey in tears. Her eyes would fill up at the least thing: if Seamie cried or laughed or said, 'Da da,' or once when the train swayed and Seamie nearly toppled over. She sat like a child herself, letting the tears fall, not bothering to wipe them away. People stared at her but she barely noticed them.

Through her tears she watched the racing fields, the hedgerows and small cottages rising in the distant hills, smoke curling from their chimneys as if she would never get her fill of them. She was desperate to see all she could, to memorise everything as she soaked up the beauty of the Irish countryside rushing by the window.

The sun shone through the carriage window, warm on her face. Pauline embraced it, let it dry her tears. With all her misery, the new sense of freedom prevailed. The Pauline who had left school early to work in Kinsella's Select Bar, who had been involved with Martin Dolan and Seamus Gilfoyle, was gone. She was being left behind in Ireland. She was about to invent another Pauline Quirk, in her new life with Seamie in America. Soon she wouldn't recognise herself.

Eve had trouble sleeping. She would lie awake for hours watching the early dawn light stealing in through the curtains, its long tentative fingers reaching out across the bed, touching the white jug and basin on the wash-stand, the chair. Sometimes she would wake abruptly in the middle of the night and play her music softly or study the notes from her business course, burrowing into her bed, quiet so as not to wake anyone. If she lay in the dark, thinking, all the memories of Chris would intrude, destructive memories of rows and humiliation.

Often she would dream of him, his face so clear that she would jolt up almost seeing him, tranquil beside her in the dark. Even as she yearned to be with him, looking at him, smelling his particular smell, she knew it would never happen. Getting him had not been a challenge for her. Holding on to him was an achievement to which she would no longer aspire.

Often she would stay in her room for hours, finding excuses not go out, until Dorothy would rap on the door to insist that she open a window to let in some fresh air. Sometimes, late at night, when James and Dorothy were asleep, Eve would dress up and sneak out. Taking long strides, her hair flying back in the cold wind, she would make her way to Kinsella's. There she would sit drinking with anyone who cared to join her, leaving only when the lights had been turned off twice and Madge had called, 'Time, please,' several times in her direction.

'Have you no home to go to?' Madge would say in exasperation as she cleared the table. Eve would stand up, unsteadily and stagger to the door. Once outside, she would walk quickly to Hilda's Chipper, or go to someone's house for a game of poker.

One night she went to the Pirate's Den, a brightly lit restaurant in the outskirts of the city, with Tony Coleman, the manager of her grandfather's warehouse, and a couple of his friends. Eve ordered a bottle of wine while the others drank beer.

'Let's go to a nightclub,' Tony suggested, leaning back in his chair, stretching his legs.

It was late when they arrived at Jokers, a dark basement nightclub. The place was full of people drinking and smoking. They ordered beer, and more wine for

Eve. The music blared to the four corners, 'Build Me Up Buttercup'.

They danced in a knot. Through a fog of alcohol Eve noticed the strange face of the man with whom she was dancing. With a thrill of fear she realised he was dancing her towards the door.

'Let's get out of here.' His voice was hoarse.

'No,' she said.'

'You want to fuck. I know you do,' he breathed into her face, and she began to laugh, awareness dawning on her that he was unbuttoning her dress. She stepped back and he lunged at her, grabbing her arm. She pulled away. 'Hey, you're with me,' he said. His laugh was ugly. He grabbed her again, and started to dance with her, lifting her dress, shouting, 'Look here,' to anyone nearby.

'Cut it out,' the barman said, coming across and freeing Eve from the man's grip.

The man threw up his arms and lurched forward.

'Let's get out of here.' Tony took her hand and, like a child, she followed him.

At home, Eve managed to get to her bedroom without making any noise. Once in it she switched off the light and undressed in the dark. The sheets were freezing but she soon fell into a drunken sleep.

She continued to go to work in the daytime and out at night with Tony to get drunk.

In the quiet of her bedroom she drank, too, hiding the empty bottles under the bed and in the dark recesses of the wardrobe. One night she stayed with Tony and woke up to find that he had left for work. She began to stay out regularly, sometimes waking up in a strange room, not knowing how she got there. Gazing frantically around her she would wonder what she had done and with whom.

'I'm concerned about you,' Dorothy said. 'I've arranged for you to see Dr Gregory as you won't listen to anyone.'

Instead of keeping her appointment Eve went to the city, taking James's car, wandering along the streets, gazing at lavish displays in the shop windows of Grafton Street, drinking slowly and quietly in a corner of a bar, enjoying the ambience, the isolation and, most of all, the anonymity.

Sometimes Tony took her to a party. Eve would wear heavy makeup to look older, and would smoke dope, then stay the night to wake up still feeling drugged, unsure of where she was and how to get back home.

'What's going to happen to us?' Tony asked her one evening on the way home from a party.

'Nothing,' Eve said. 'We'll just boogie on down. Enjoy ourselves. It's kind of exciting at the moment. Addictive.'

The car lurched. Eve leaned forward and shrieked with laughter.

'We'll have to calm it, Eve.'

'Why?'

Tony pulled the car into the kerb and turned off the engine. 'I'd do anything for you, Eve. You know that, don't you?' He held her face in his hands.

'Yes.'

'I think you should do something about your drinking. I've eased up on mine.'

'Just because you've decided to be a spoilsport doesn't mean I have to be one too.'

'It's beginning to get me down, that's all. It's false or something. Or else I'm getting old,' Tony said diffidently. 'I'm bored with it all.'

'Does that include me?'

'Of course not. But I think you should slow down before you do yourself some damage. Make a New Year's resolution to give it up.'

'You really mean this, don't you?' Eve looked at him.

'It isn't easy to tell someone you care about that they're on the slippery slope.' Tony looked out of the window. 'That's the reason I'm sticking my neck out. I care about you, Eve. It's awful to watch a lovely girl like you destroying yourself. All because of some pompous ass who couldn't hold a candle to you.'

'I think you should mind your own business!' Eve blazed at him. 'What I do with my life is my business, nobody else's. I'll thank you to remember that.'

'Suit yourself.' Tony shrugged.

Taking a leaflet from his pocket he handed it to her. 'There's an address. Keep it in case you ever feel the need of it.'

Eve took it and, without looking at it, shoved it into the back of her handbag. Calmer now, she saw the genuine concern on his face.

'I'm sorry, Tony,' she said. 'I shouldn't have lost my temper. I know you mean well.'

'That's the trouble,' he said. 'Well-meaning people are the worst kind. Maybe you're right. Maybe I should mind my own business.' As he dropped her outside her house, he said, 'Take good care of yourself.'

It was a clear, cold night as Eve walked through Loughmore to the community centre near the station. The town was empty, with the exception of a few people walking here and there. At the centre two weary-looking women sat together in a room marked PRIVATE, waiting for the place to fill up. Eve checked her watch. It was only seven thirty and the meeting wasn't due to start until eight.

As she crossed the floor her footsteps echoed on the wooden boards. She stayed apart, not wanting to get into a conversation, and sat on a hard plastic chair, her coat collar turned up. She could hear the minute hand of the wall clock tick, and kept her eyes on the NO SMOKING sign in front of her. She wished she hadn't come and promised herself that she could leave whenever she felt like it.

As the room filled up with friendly people, chatting to each other, her tension eased. She stayed in the back row, several rows of others between her and the desk at the front.

At eight o'clock sharp a man came in and sat down at the desk. The meeting began. 'Good evening,' he said. 'My name is Len and I'm an alcoholic.' He talked about his life, his family and his long absences from them when he had been drinking, and his wife who had stayed at home to care for their mentally handicapped child. About a year before he had joined AA, Len continued, he had decided to stop drinking. But he couldn't stand the normality of going home every evening without a drink to look forward to. He was brusque with his wife, dismissive of his child, and he refused to believe what the doctors said – that if he didn't give it up he would die.

His son died and his wife left him. He had been in despair when someone had told him about AA. He went to a meeting the following Monday night in the parish hall, uneasy and wary of its Twelve Step plan. Len recalled the hopeful faces around him, everyone's rapt attention during the meeting as they took in the stories of fellow alcoholics. He went the following week and continued to go because the meetings seemed to lift him, change him, until the next crisis. Over the years he learned the Twelve Steps slowly, with the help of a sponsor, and absorbed them into his daily life. When he had been sober for several years he had become someone else's sponsor.

His listeners clapped when he finished talking. Then others began, taking it in turn to have their say. 'My name is . . . and I'm an alcoholic . . .' There was no reproach, only nodding heads and sympathetic understanding. Eventually when the wall clock indicated that the meeting was drawing to a close, Eve cleared her throat and said, 'Hello, my name is Eve. This is my first meeting and I'm . . . scared.' She felt the constrictive click of her throat as she tried to say the word alcoholic. Weeping, mostly with relief, she kept her eyes unswervingly fixed on the chairman.

'Hello, Eve,' they chorused.

She talked about her family and the anxiety her drinking was causing them. When she spoke of Chris, she was startled by the sudden tender feelings of regret that stirred in her.

At the end of the meeting Eve tried to make her way quickly to the door, but people greeted her, introduced themselves, and invited her to join them in a cup of tea.

All the way home Eve felt she had found something. A secret in herself, pure and solitary. Driving past the bars and restaurants that she usually frequented, she found that she didn't want to go into one. As she turned into the dark driveway of her home, it began to dawn on her that she might have found the peace of mind that she was looking for.

Sir George Saunders made Clare practise scales and exercises for a considerable period before each performance. He taught her to balance her hands for a particular effect, to listen to every note as her fingers came down slowly, and to analyse the sound. 'You have real talent and quality in your playing, Clare. With the right work you will become a fine pianist.'

When Sir George decided that the time was right, Clare gave her first concert at the British Embassy in Paris in March. The ambassador, his wife, and many other notables in the diplomatic service were present, including the Archbishop of Paris, in his red robes.

For her performance she wore a long gold lamé dress and her hair was piled high in curls, studded with marguerites. The room was packed, the audience tense, as Clare walked forward, bowed to the right and left, then took her place at the grand piano. Beethoven's sonata in D minor was graceful and clear, the solemn, elaborate notes creeping in. Then came the Bach fugue in G minor, slow, sombre, the strings muted, growing louder and richer, ending abruptly, leaving the soul bereft and weeping. The understanding and inspiration Clare brought to her playing showed in the expression of her flexible body and the vitality of the music flowing from her fingertips. It was as though she was reassuring her audience that in her music she had found all the answers for which she had been looking. The orchestra moved swiftly into Chopin's impromptu in A flat and Clare broke in, her playing nimble and light. Everything that had happened to her – the death of her father, the death of Martin – had brought her to this depth of feeling, this sweetness of tone. The sudden *adagio*, with its capricious ornaments, was a powerful, stirring melody, evoking the break of dawn, the pealing of church bells. The piano was loud and shrill, drowning the orchestra, the timing effortless as the pace grew faster.

Clare finished with a concerto, the violins quivering on the long D. How many times had she practised that long note in Vittorio's studio, against imaginary violins, without the range of orchestra, space and acoustics?

As the curtain fell, the applause burst upon her ears. She walked to the front of the stage to receive a bouquet of fresh spring flowers from the British Ambassador, the audience clapping as she bowed before them.

At the stage entrance, well-wishers were bunched in little groups, hoping to get a glimpse of her. Smiling graciously, she stopped to sign autographs, then made her way out, chatting a little, here and there, to people who stopped her on the boulevard and at the waiting car. Just as she was about to get in Vittorio stepped out of the shadow.

'Clare.'

'Professor.' She gave him a searching look as if she didn't recognise him.

'Clare, it's me.'

'Vittorio.' Clare was so exhausted that she thought she must be dreaming. 'You're the last person in the world I expected to see.'

'I came to hear you play.'

'Did you think it was good?'

'You were excellent. I know you're tired but come and have a nightcap with me. I have so much to say to you. I won't keep you very long, I promise.' The urgency in his voice made her acquiesce. He took her arm and ushered her towards a hotel.

Once inside Clare sat in an armchair in the lobby and looked at him again. He smiled. 'It has been a long time,' he said, taking her in. 'You were magnificent. A wonderful performance. I wouldn't have missed it for the world.' As he spoke his face was triumphant.

They gazed at one another.

'You look well,' Clare said.

'Thank you.' Vittorio paused. 'I thought it was a good opportunity to see you again, Clare.'

'Did you really enjoy my playing?' She was like a child waiting for parental approval.

'I loved it. What would you like to drink?'

'Tea, please.'

'Tea?'

'I have an early start in the morning. I must keep a clear head. And I really am very tired tonight.'

'Could you spare an hour to have lunch with me tomorrow?'

'I don't think that's a good idea,' she said. It would be better to leave him in the past where he belonged.

'An hour won't do any harm. Give us time to go through your performance.'

'Very well, then. One hour.'

The following morning when Clare woke up the first thing she thought of was Vittorio. Why had he come back into her life? For a long time after he had gone she hadn't been able to eat or sleep. Now, as she prepared her breakfast, she didn't want to think about him. But she owed him so much and she valued his opinion. To have refused to meet him would have been wrong.

The pain she had thought was gone had returned, as acute and vivid as the day she had walked out of his life. She forced herself to concentrate on recalling last night's performance. Had she remembered all the nuances of tone, the musical phrases? During the concert she had drifted into a world of her own and such details had escaped her.

They met in the Jardin du Luxembourg. Vittorio held her at arm's length, admiring her. 'You look wonderful,' he said. 'Your hair, your skin. You're alive, fresh, vital.'

'I was exhausted last night.' She smiled. 'When I first saw you I thought I was dreaming.'

As they walked through the park all the awkwardness of the previous night's meeting vanished. The old harmony and understanding were back, but it was a more self-assured, confident Clare who was beside Vittorio. She took his arm and led him to a nearby seat, under a leafy tree. The park was all light and shade, full of the delicate green of new growth. In the distance, drifts of bluebells and pale cream lilies swayed in the wind.

'Have you seen *Le Monde* this morning?' Vittorio asked.

'Yes. They're very kind.'

'It's not kindness. It's the truth,' he said stoutly. 'And well deserved. Your playing was perfection.'

'Thank you. I thought at one point the violins came in too soon. Perhaps the syncopation didn't quite work in the concerto.'

Vittorio laughed. 'My little perfectionist.' He looked at her indulgently.

They went over the minutiae of her playing as they always had at the end of a lesson. Over and over Vittorio reassured her. Clare looked at him, joyful, beaming, as if the struggle was finally over and it had all been worthwhile. 'Come on, let's go,' she said, getting up quickly and gracefully.

Vittorio walked along with her, animated by her company. 'Let's have lunch somewhere quiet,' he said, steering her out of the park. 'I know the perfect place.' He hailed a taxi.

As they entered the Belle Vue restaurant waiters in red waistcoats and black trousers rushed to greet them.

Quietly they studied the menu, watching the *bateaux mouches* on the Seine. Some were anchored in a line, others sailed up and down the river. Once or twice Clare closed her eyes in an effort to slow time, to retain what she was seeing and what was happening to her. Under her lashes she watched Vittorio. Although he was still lively and vigorous, she detected a subdued air about him, a hint of coolness.

'Have you decided what you would like to eat?' he asked.

'The *foie gras* to start with, please, and the salmon with asparagus.'

Vittorio ordered a bottle of champagne and checked the label before the waiter opened it. 'To your next performance,' he said, raising his glass. 'I have no doubt that you will go from strength to strength.'

They drank, savouring the delicious aroma that permeated the restaurant while they waited for their meal.

'How did you keep so calm?' he asked.

'I kept my mind on practical things to start with and then, once I got a sense of the audience, I drifted off. It's something that seems to happen to me on stage. I can't really explain it. I'm conscious on one level but on another I'm in a different world.'

'Well, it worked,' Vittorio said. 'Here's to your great future.'

Clare inclined her head and, meeting his gaze, blushed.

'How is life otherwise? Outside your music?' Vittorio asked mildly, his face a mixture of the conflicting emotions he seemed unable to hide.

'I don't have one,' Clare said simply.

'Understandable,' he said. 'But a shame too.'

'You warned me in London that I would have to

sacrifice a personal life for the music. I didn't find it difficult.'

'I'm surprised. A beautiful girl like you.'

'If you're wondering whether I've fallen in love, the answer is no.' She saw the quick flash in his eyes and was sorry she'd been so outspoken.

'Do you know what I thought about when you started to play?' he said.

She shook her head.

'I was remembering the time when you were ill and your landlady wouldn't let me see you. I pleaded with her but she was adamant. Did she tell you?'

'She said you had called. I had a high temperature and I had nightmares of you pushing me on to practise, forcing me to go on and on. I woke up screaming your name one night and frightened Mrs Cartwright.' Clare laughed, but her head drooped and tiny creases furrowed her brow.

'I was very hard on you. I'm sorry.' Vittorio looked contrite.

'I wouldn't have missed it for the world,' Clare said resolutely. 'Not a minute. It was all part of my development.'

'Yes, you took it well enough,' Vittorio said. 'Most of the time.'

They ate their meal and sat gazing at the river.

'I have so much to tell you, Clare. But I'm scared you won't want to hear it.'

Clare's eyebrows rose.

'It's hard to know where to begin,' he said. 'Life takes so many twists and turns.' He broke off, too choked to continue, a bitter expression on his face.

Clare said, 'I'm sorry. I don't understand what you're saying.'

Eventually, he said, 'I despise myself, Clare, for the way I wronged you. I should have kept away from you. But when I heard about your first concert,' he raised his arms in a helpless gesture, 'how could I be indifferent?' His hands were held out to her in supplication.

Clare was silent.

'How could I expect you to understand?' he finished, his face close to hers.

Clare said, with composure, 'The past is over. There's no more to be said about it. At the time it was difficult but it showed me how hard life is, the way things really are.'

Vittorio nodded, his head down, shoulders hunched.

'I put my heart and soul into my art,' Clare continued. 'It took me away, somewhere else, where I could cope and, who knows, perhaps it gave me the interpretations in my playing that I have today.'

'No doubt that it did. But I always believed in you, Clare.'

'I know. I carried your teaching with me wherever I went. I owe you so much.'

'You owe me nothing,' Vittorio said sharply. 'You haven't finished yet. There is more in you, Clare, that can only come out with time and maturity. The sky is the limit.'

'I hope so,' Clare said modestly.

They finished their meal and parted outside the restaurant, Clare to return to her practice, Vittorio to go to the airport.

Chapter Twenty-two

The sun streaming through her window woke Eve. She dressed quickly and went downstairs. James was in the kitchen, finishing his breakfast.

'What are you doing up so early on a Saturday morning, Grandpa?'

'I'm off to work. Just for a few hours.' He replaced his cup on the saucer and stood up. 'I've a meeting with the sales manager.'

Eve walked with him to the hall door. As she opened it the postman was there.

'Postcard for you,' he said to Eve. 'Hong Kong must be an exciting place.' The fact that he had cycled all the way up the drive with it seemed to entitle him to know its contents. 'I only got as far as Lisdoonvarna and then Mother sent for me to come home.'

'Why?' Eve asked.

'Thought I'd meet someone entirely unsuitable at the matchmaking festival.'

Eve giggled. 'Better luck next time.'

'She says she's coming with me next year,' he said, mounting his bike and pedalling off.

The postcard read:

This city is impossible. Teeming streets, noise, sirens, horns. No peace, no sleep. Doing good

business but don't like cities. It's not home.
                                        Dad.

Eve handed it to James, who scanned it and passed it back. 'I'll have to write to him to come home,' James said. 'We need him here.'

'Let him rot in hell,' Dorothy said, coming down the stairs.

James left quietly.

'By the way,' Dorothy said to Eve, 'Bernadette Power was asking for you. She's home from the States.'

'Bernie Power asking for me?'

'Called into the shop today. Lovely girl, Bernadette.'

Eve was remembering Bernie's heart-shaped face and her blonde hair. She had been the envy of Eve's class, the one who could engage the boys in conversation. Slim yet curvy, she wore red lipstick, gold stud earrings and wonderful clinging, vivid micro-mini dresses to show off the permanent tan on her shapely legs.

'She'd love to see you,' Dorothy continued.

'I haven't come across her since we left school.'

'She looks terrific. Bought two dresses. You should phone her.'

'What would I have to say to her?' Eve asked. 'We never had much in common at school.'

They had David Furlong in common. The vision of David and Bernie dancing in the twilight, moving stealthily like silvery fish came into Eve's mind.

'She's having a party. Wants you to go.'

'I don't feel like it,' Eve said.

'You could take Tony.'

'I haven't seen him for a while.'

As they returned to the kitchen the silence between them was tense.

'You want to make an effort to meet new people,'
Dorothy said. 'Make a fresh start.'

Eve kept her mouth clamped tight shut to stop herself
from retaliating.

As the door closed behind Dorothy, the house, with
its draughty rooms, was silent and lonely. For the first
time Eve noticed how dingy the walls were, how
warped the windows.

The door of Bernie Power's house opened as soon as
she knocked.

'Eve.' Bernie grabbed her in a tight embrace. Rita
Sampson was standing beside her.

'Rita, good to see you.' Eve felt as if she had been
catapulted back in time as other faces appeared. Tilly,
Maureen, Jean . . . Faces she remembered from her
class.

They all hugged one another.

'What'll you have to drink?' Bernie shouted.

Eve shrugged. 'Whatever's handiest. I'm not fussy.'

'We know.' Rita chortled.

'It's great to see you.' Bernie led her into the drawing
room to a table loaded with bottles and glasses. 'You
look smashing. I hear you're working for your grandfather since your husband—'

'Scarpered,' Eve supplied, taking the glass of wine
she was offered. 'Don't be scared to say it. I'm not.'

Bernie blushed. 'Well, I must say you look terrific.'

'Thanks. So do you.'

Eve was wearing a tight-fitting black polo-neck
jumper, short black skirt, spiky heels, and was conscious
of the effect she was having on the male guests. Bernie,
dressed in a gold lamé trouser suit, was stunning.

'Couldn't have been much fun for you all the same,

though,' Bernie said, pushing her high breasts practically into the face of Charlie Mathews, who leaned in close and whispered something in her ear that made her laugh – that ridiculous tinkling laugh. 'Oh, you are awful,' she said to him.

Eve raised her glass to Charlie and tilted it back, glancing around the room.

'How are you coping?' Bernie was relentless.

'Not a bother.' Eve shifted sideways, but Bernie's eyes were fixed on her.

It occurred to Eve that Bernie probably knew from Dorothy more of the details of Chris's departure than she herself did.

'You must feel betrayed,' Bernie said.

Eve shifted from one foot to the other, unable to stand the other girl's pitying stare. 'There are advantages,' she said. 'I'm free again.'

Bernie looked at her wide-eyed.

'I can help Grandpa.' She took another gulp of wine.

'I'm sure you're a great help.'

Eve wasn't about to explain her new-found liking for business. She studied Bernie, trying to imagine her waitressing at the Savoy, heading into the rush-hour traffic, standing in the tube while London's weirdoes savaged her with their eyes. Bernie was a cosseted, protected little pet.

'What are you doing with yourself?' Eve asked.

'Drama. I got hooked when I was in the States. Now I'm studying at the Gaiety.'

'Good for you. I think I'll have another drink.'

'Help yourself,' Bernie said.

'I will.'

The music blared. The Seekers, singing 'I'll Never Find Another You', thrummed in Eve's ears as she passed the dancers, the pushed-back furniture. It was like the tennis club all over again, girls dancing together, fairy-lights on the walls, boys lolling around, while Eve and her friends pretended it didn't matter, their overpainted faces wreathed in anxious smiles.

As Eve poured herself more wine she was recalling the agonising suspense, the yearning, the dilemma of trying to lure the boys.

Standing there, drinking, watching, Eve had the feeling that little had happened in the time that had passed. Perhaps Chris had been only a dream and her breasts had never grown. Perhaps she had never stopped drinking. Each sip helped her to relax more. She smiled at everyone, Charlie, Clem, who'd just arrived with his guitar. There were faces she knew whose names she couldn't remember.

She returned to the sitting room and stayed at the edge, drinking sometimes, dancing sometimes, happy to keep moving, unselfconscious. Out of the corner of her eye she spotted a tall, fair-haired young man with bright blue eyes and a golden tan. The sight of him hit Eve like a bolt of lightning. He came straight to her, a broad smile on his face. 'Eve?' he said. 'You look stunning.'

'David Furlong. Good to see you. I haven't seen you for so long. How are you?' She noticed as she spoke that her words were slurring slightly.

'I'm just back from New Zealand.'

'Great. Will you be staying?'

The music blared again, drowning his reply. Then he said, close to her, 'Let's dance. This music takes me back. You were a great dancer.'

'Was I?' Eve said.

'I remember.'

Joan O'Neill

'You're looking smashing, David,' Eve said, full of alcoholic benevolence.

'Thanks,' he said. 'So are you.'

Eve felt dizzy. Staggering, she excused herself and manoeuvred her way to the bathroom. Once inside she looked at herself in the mirror. Meeting David Furlong again after all this time had made her dizzy. Why had she had that first drink? It had only been to calm her nerves, steel her against the obnoxious Bernie and her inquisition. Then she had had another to keep her calm and one to make her feel good about herself. That was it. No more. She splashed her face with cold water, repaired her make-up, careful not to smudge the dark kohl pencil she had drawn along her eyelids. When her hair was combed she splashed perfume behind her ears. The rat-tat-tat on the door made her jump.

'Hurry up!' a voice shouted. 'I'm bursting.'

'Hang on,' Eve called back, adjusting her skirt and glancing in the mirror once more.

When she returned to the party everyone was rocking to the music. David was dancing with Bernie Power, steering her among the crowd to the centre where they stood close together, bobbing up and down to the beat.

When the music stopped David put his arm round her, said something to her. She picked up a record and put it on.

He came over to Eve. 'Dance?' he said, as the Supremes began 'I'm Gonna Make You Love Me'.

Eve laughed, floating away from him. 'I was just leaving, David. I've an early start in the morning,' she said, anxious to get away from him.

'I'll take you home.' He followed her to the door. 'It's on my way.'

'But you've only just arrived,' she protested.

'Come on.' He linked her arm.

She stood up straight, collected her bag, went out with him into the dark night.

'I'm parked here.' He took his keys from the pocket of his jeans and opened the passenger door of the Mustang parked under the street lamp.

It was dark outside Eve's house. As she opened the car door the trees creaked and sighed in the wind.

'Spooky,' Eve said.

'I hear you've had a bad time recently,' David said.

'News travels fast,' Eve said.

'I'm sorry,' David said. 'You deserve better than that.'

'I'll survive,' Eve said.

'I'll see you safely to your door.' David jumped out of the car.

'I'm an expert at alighting from sports cars,' she said, but let him help her. 'Thank you,' she said at the front door.

David said, leaning against the porch, his hands in his pockets, 'The last time I stood here with you after the summer ball you were a schoolgirl.'

'So much has happened since then.'

'You look stunning tonight, Eve. The little girl next door is gone. You're a grown woman.'

'A married soon-to-be-divorced one,' Eve responded.

'Incredible. So much.' David was shaking his head.

'You'd better get back to the party. They'll be wondering where you are,' Eve said, thinking of Bernie Power.

'Good night,' he said. 'I'll see you.'

'Yeah.'

The engine of his car leapt into life and, slamming his foot on the accelerator, he roared off.

* * *

David Furlong was seated behind a desk at Freeman's Tea Importers. The jacket of his expensively tailored blue suit was tossed casually in a nearby chair and the sleeves of his hand-made white shirt were rolled up. His eyes were narrowed, his brow furrowed as he examined the figures before him.

'We meet again,' Eve said.

He looked up. 'Eve,' he said, jumping to his feet, scattering the balance sheets in all directions. 'I didn't know you were working here.' He was thunderstruck.

'Just helping out Grandpa. Learning the business. I was asked to bring you these files.'

'Thank you,' he said, tilting his head in her direction gazing at her. 'How are you keeping? You look great.'

'Thanks. I'll see you at the meeting,' she said. 'Grandpa insists on me being there. I think he's expecting trouble from Daddy.'

'I'll look forward to it,' David said, sitting down again and gathering his papers together.

In the boardroom Jasper Furlong, managing director of Furlong Investment Limited, sat next to his son, David, and looked into James Freeman's eyes. 'That's our offer, James,' he said.

James faced him solemnly but Ron glared, leaving Jasper in no doubt as to how angry he was.

'It's daylight robbery,' Ron said, 'and you know it.'

Jasper grinned at him.

'What you're suggesting is unacceptable,' James said quietly. 'We certainly need help but not to the extent of losing all hold on the company and our jobs.'

'We're an investment bank, James,' Jasper said, his blue eyes sharp. 'Not a charity. Our interest in your company is to buy it, not subsidise it. We intend to run it on our terms, with our own staff, and you in an advisory capacity for the next year.'

'Not interested!' Ron shouted, his face red with temper.

'Enough,' James commanded him, losing his composure for the first time since the meeting had begun.

David glanced at Eve.

'Don't worry about me,' she said. 'I've got plans of my own,' and to James, 'You do whatever's best for the company, Grandpa.'

'Our offer is a good one,' Jasper assured them.

'You must understand that my son has no desire to retire from the business,' James said. 'I, on the other hand, am quite willing to step down as managing director.'

'I'm afraid that's not feasible,' Jasper said.

'Then we'd better leave.' Ron grabbed his briefcase and made for the door.

'Let's not be hasty,' Jasper said.

James hesitated. The months of anxiety over the business had taken their toll. His face was weary as he looked imploringly at his son.

After a pause, he loosened his tie. 'Ron's contacts will be essential to you,' he said. 'He has built up valuable business links in the Far East and Hong Kong. You could use him as a consultant.'

'Why do you think I went all the way to that cesspool, sweltered in the heat? It's the only way to make money,' Ron said.

'We'll retain you for six months,' Jasper said. 'If you don't produce the business we expect in that time, you'll be dropped.'

James sat back, relieved. 'I owe it to some of the workers, old friends of mine, to make sure they're looked after properly in the future.'

'We'll put a redundancy package together,' Jasper said.

'I'll show you how to make money.' Ron was packing up his bulging briefcase. 'You wait and see.'

He left without another word to anyone.

James and Jasper walked slowly from the boardroom, discussing the asset-stripping on which David was set to embark, each engrossed in what he was saying to the other. James was tired: the meeting had taken all of his energy.

David put away his files and walked over to Eve. 'I've got to dash,' he said. 'Another meeting to attend. Otherwise I'd ask you to have lunch with me.'

'Slave-driver still, your father?' Eve laughed.

''Fraid so. I'll see you next week.'

'I look forward to it,' Eve said, and watched David walk down the corridor with quick, purposeful strides.

Mario's restaurant in Dublin's dockland near Freeman's warehouse was busy as James ushered Eve into the bar to wait for Jasper and David Furlong.

'What would you like to drink, darling?' James asked, amid the din.

'Orange juice, please, Grandpa,' Eve replied, and admired his fine stature as, head and shoulders above everyone else, he made his way slowly to the bar.

'To us,' he said, when he returned with their drinks.

Eve raised her glass. 'To you, Grandpa.'

Ron's immediate departure, with the warning 'I'll show them' ringing in James's ears, had left him shaken and sad. 'I was afraid that age had blunted my judgement,' James confided. 'But I think I'll get more or less what I want. That young David is razor sharp.'

'It strikes me that they want our company more than they're prepared to say.'

'Naturally,' James said. 'That's business.'

Just then Jasper Furlong came towards them, a broad smile on his face, followed by David.

Eve sat rooted to the spot feeling the strength drain from her legs.

'Good to see you again,' David exclaimed, shaking James's hand. Then he leaned forward, took Eve's hand and held it for a fraction of a second longer than necessary. 'Your grandfather tells me you're thinking of starting your own business,' he said, when James and Jasper were discussing the difficulties of running a business nowadays.

'Yes,' Eve said, and went on to explain how she had discovered in herself an aptitude for business.

'Good luck,' David said.

Shielded by the long menu, she watched him until he sensed her gaze and once more turned his electric blue eyes on her.

Over the stuffed quail, Jasper Furlong said, 'When you retire as managing director, James, you forfeit your right to any power at Freeman's.'

James stiffened. 'I understand that,' he said.

'As part of the negotiation settlement I agree to allow you to retain forty per cent of the shares in your own name. This enables you to attend board meetings, but you will have equal status with the rest of the shareholders.'

James sipped his wine, listening carefully.

'I have arranged for a surveyor to be at your premises tomorrow morning to look the place over, give us some idea of the cost of modernising.'

'All right by me,' James said.

Eve sighed with relief. By retaining some shares James was ensuring that to some extent the business stayed in the family. It wasn't as much as he would have liked but under the circumstances it was the best he could salvage. He needed money to honour his son's debts, keep his home, give Dorothy the security she deserved and have something for Eve when he passed away.

James had lived a full life – a life of position and wealth – but as he had grown older he had longed secretly for the simpler things. The peace and quiet of the garden where he could contemplate nature, his favourite poets, and read his beloved Shakespeare. Now, his internal conflict over, he would retire properly to the quiet he craved. Getting to his feet slowly, he shook Jasper's hand. 'A fair conclusion,' he said, sitting down again and groping in his pocket for his pipe.

'Let's hope the rain holds off so I can spray the roses,' he said.

Eve watched him walk away and was struck by his slow gait and fragility.

'A thorough gentleman,' David said, as he and Eve left the restaurant together.

Eve was on her way to see Mr Cummins, the bank manager.

She was wearing her new pastel pink suit and had decided to put up her hair to make her look older. Walking briskly she passed the premises she had in mind for her coffee shop. It was in a row between the town hall and the church, only five minutes from the station. The deep bay window would take two tables perfectly and the long narrow space that had been the original shop, with its nooks and crannies, would take about ten more, with good spaces between them. With a mixture of nerves and excitement, she knocked on Mr Cummins's door.

'What can I do for you, Miss Freeman?' Mr Cummins asked, when she had sat down.

'I'd like to borrow some money,' Eve said. 'I want to open my own coffee shop. I've seen a place in the centre of town that's ideal and my grandfather will sell me the coffee at a special rate. He's importing it in small quantities and blending it at the factory.'

Mr Cummins steepled his hands and sat back.

'Nothing elaborate,' Eve assured him.

'What sort of clientele would you expect to cater for?' Mr Cummins asked.

'Glencove housewives, passing trade, retired couples. Somewhere friendly where people can get together for a chat.'

'I don't know many housewives who have the time to spare.'

'You'd be surprised,' Eve said.

'Have you any experience in this trade?' Mr Cummins asked.

'No. But I've worked at the Savoy Hotel in London as a waitress. Served plenty of coffee there.' Eve handed him her reference.

'Impressive,' Mr Cummins said. 'Are you prepared to make the sacrifices required?'

'Yes.'

'Who do you have in mind to work for you?'

'Agnes Dolan is going to bake bread and cakes for me. Mrs Walsh, the present owner, will help out when we're busy.'

'You'll need a down payment. Stock, fixtures, and fittings. What can you offer as security against the loan?'

'Two hundred pounds my husband gave me and my grandfather will act as guarantor.'

Mr Cummins regarded her with interest. 'I admire your confidence, Miss Freeman. I'm prepared to lend you a thousand pounds to start off. How does that suit you?'

'Thank you, Mr Cummins.'

'I'll draw up the necessary papers and get you to sign them.'

'You won't regret it,' Eve said.

The concert at the Wigmore Hall was a sell-out, with long queues stretching to the rear of the building. The Italian opera singer Belindi Rampoli was the evening's star billing. Rehearsals had begun at two o'clock in the afternoon and most of the time had been taken up by Rampoli, practising her accompaniment with the Royal Philharmonic Orchestra.

It was a privilege for Clare to play at the Wigmore Hall. She hoped for a good report from the music critics, the chance to promote further concerts and attract the interest of leading agents. As she hurried down the street for her big night, hair streaming in the wind, her new blue voile evening dress in a bag under her arm, Clare was excited to be sharing the dressing room with such a big star.

The concert would begin with the Royal Philharmonic Orchestra playing Beethoven's Leonora Overture No.3. Clare played his piano concerto No.1 in C minor, this arrangement having been decided by Sir George Saunders. It was important for her that her first performance in London be excellent. She would have to be at her best to win over an audience who didn't know her and to do that she had to get them in the right mood.

Vittorio was in the audience by invitation from Clare. As she played the music flowed from her fingertips, sweeping from one sequence to another, blossoming like springtime in the park, recalling childhood, fore-telling love. It rose, exultant, with the unrequited passion in Clare, and gave hope to the listener. She moved with the orchestra to a triumphant final E, *pianissimo*, then silence.

As the curtain fell the audience got to its feet, clamouring for her, until the curtain rose again. Clare walked slowly to the footlights, her eyes sweeping the crowd, then falling on Vittorio, resting on his face for a long moment.

Sir George Saunders and Vittorio were waiting for her in her dressing room.

'Bravo, my child,' Sir George said, extending his hand to shake hers. Clare curtsied to him as a ballerina does to her master. 'This is a big step forward, Clare,' he said. 'You've arrived at a certain point in your career. You are emerging.' Clare was too moved to speak.

Vittorio took her hand and held it.

Well-wishers crowded into the dressing room to shake the hands of the artists, almost suffocating them with their exuberance.

'Come with me,' Vittorio said, steering her to the stage entrance to escape the crowd.

Lights were on all over the city.

'London never looked so beautiful,' Clare said, gazing at the fretwork illuminating the Thames as they drove along the Embankment.

Vittorio sped through quiet streets, not stopping until they reached their destination, the Complete Angler, at Marlow, in Buckinghamshire.

The light from the candles in the restaurant

flickered as they ate and talked. Such was her emotional reaction to the concert that Clare found herself slowly recounting the details of first Jack's death, then Martin's, sobbing her heart out to Vittorio.

He caressed her cheek. 'Cry all you want to,' he said. 'You've bottled it up long enough.'

'I've practised all day and cried myself to sleep every night for six months,' Clare said.

'Why didn't you come to me?' Vittorio asked.

'How could I? You were unavailable to me. You told me so yourself.'

'I never stopped loving you,' he said, very gently.

Clare was shaking her head. 'Don't talk about it. I don't want to spoil this special night.'

'I was foolish,' Vittorio said. 'I should never have let you go but I couldn't see a way out.'

'You did what you had to do,' Clare said.

'I no longer have that commitment,' Vittorio said. 'Since last Christmas I have been free.' He stopped and looked out of the window at the dark sky and the stars over the water.

Clare covered his hand with hers. 'I'm sorry, Vittorio,' she said. 'I know it hasn't been easy for you either.'

'You came into my life at a difficult time for me, Clare, and nurturing you was the challenge I needed. You were a godsend.'

Although he would never admit that Véronique's illness and consequent depression had been a great trial, until her death he hadn't known what peace of mind was. He continued, 'I met Véronique Dubois, a French Canadian, in London, during a European concert tour. She was staying in Prague with friends of my parents, who had asked me to join them for dinner in their apartment.' Vittorio described Véronique as a tall, elegant blonde, self-assured and witty. Her father's indulgence ensured her the best that money could buy, and Vittorio had been impressed with her childish extravagance and generosity. She had loved giving him expensive and beautiful presents, like the gold watch that marked the occasion of his début in Prague, and diamond cuff-links for his birthday. 'I escorted her to the opera, and invited her to attend my concert. She returned night after night, beguiling me with her smouldering dark eyes and her secret smiles, at the same time scorning me for my jealous possession of her.'

Vittorio invited her to meet his parents. Three weeks later he had proposed, heedless of his mother's warning that she was a girl who would want her own way in everything.

They moved into her house in Mayfair, and she continued to spend much of her time shopping extravagantly, while Vittorio continued his concert tours, accepting engagements in faraway places, his growing dislike of Véronique made bearable only by the distance between them.

She enjoyed life without him, amusing herself, during the evenings, at the theatre or dinner. Music was Vittorio's escape and his salvation, until one day Véronique was knocked down by a speeding car and severely injured.

'I felt my freedom was over. I stayed in London and took up a teaching post at the Royal Academy, knowing that, as long as she needed me, I would never leave her.'

Vittorio was watching Clare's face intently as he spoke. 'You captured my heart. I shut you out because I felt you were too young and vulnerable, and that I had nothing to offer you, except what I could teach you musically.'

'I never stopped loving you either,' Clare said.

Vittorio took her hands in his, kissed her gently and said, 'Let's start again.'

Eve stood before the glass cabinet in her coffee shop, checking the display of cakes, the rich dark chocolate sponges, fluffy meringues, mouth-watering almond slices. She was convinced that getting up at six o'clock in the morning to help Agnes would pay off, if business so far was anything to go by.

On the shelves to the right and behind the counter were neat stacks of pickles, chutney, jam, and a variety of exotic crystallised fruits and chocolate in fancy boxes.

'You've got too much there,' Agnes warned her, glancing over the shelves with a critical eye.

'We'll sell it all,' Eve said confidently.

She uncovered her espresso coffee machine and began to prepare for the morning customers. The aroma of blends she mixed wafted on the air, mingling with the delicious smell of cakes and spices.

'Good morning.' Mrs Browne put her head round the door and, seeing Eve behind the counter, hurried in.

'What a delicious smell,' she said, sitting down.

'Coffee?' Eve asked.

'Please, love.'

Eve brought a gleaming white coffee pot, with matching cup, saucer, jug and sugar bowl, to her table.

'You've done a marvellous job here,' Mrs Browne said. 'Considering,' she added, shooting a side-long glance at Mrs Walsh, the former proprietor.

'Thank you.' Eve smiled. 'How are you keeping?'

'Can't complain,' Mrs Browne said. 'Madge had a letter from Pauline Quirk.'

'How is she?'

'She's getting on great. Helping out in her aunt's guest house in Long Island. She falls on her feet every time. Always someone to give her a hand. You'd miss the baby all the same. Madge is lost without him. I warned her, but would she listen?'

'Still, it's great she's doing well,' Eve said.

As the popularity of the coffee shop grew Eve extended her range to include a selection of cheeses and hams. She was in the process of applying for a wine licence when Mr Cummins appeared early one morning.

'Enchanting,' he exclaimed, gazing at the rows of copper pots hanging neatly from hooks on the wall.

Mrs Walsh, demure in a black dress and white frilly apron and cap, handed him a menu.

While he enjoyed his coffee and almond slice, he watched the groups of women and a few men gathered at tables here and there, chatting. 'Impressive,' he said to Eve. 'You're doing well.'

'I'd like to borrow again, Mr Cummins. Perhaps in June when I have the loan cleared. I'm thinking of doing lunches.'

'What about the hotel and the pub?'

'I was thinking of something light and appetising, like quiches, pies and salads. That sort of thing.'

'Should go down well,' Mr Cummins said.

They both laughed at the pun.

Eve attended her AA meetings regularly. All the love and concern that had poured out to her when she first joined was still there. It kept her going at times when she felt a real need for a drink. When she lapsed she rushed back to her meeting more anxious at having let down her new friends than anything else, but there were never any recriminations, only the same loving support. She was reminded regularly that it was always possible to start again.

Meanwhile, she wrote to her friend Tony, giving him a progress report. He had moved to Cork to work in the sales department of Smith's Motors and found this new challenge exciting.

Out in the garden she went to her tree and squeezed herself into the space that had once accommodated her so easily. She looked around at the other great trees, their dropped skirts brushing the grass, at the tiny heads of the first roses peeping through the gap in the hedge, the woods rising up behind them, pale against the bright evening sky.

Eve loved this place, loved the sweet scent of the garden in the night air. This was her home and her sister Sarah's memory came alive in the smell of the trees, the grass, the loamy earth. Eve's eyes scanned the house, its slates gleaming in the twilight. It was falling into disrepair. The cold seeped into the bare rooms, even in summer. The wallpaper was faded and yellowing, the beautiful Regency furniture lacklustre, carpets worn and stained. Since Sarah's death and Ron's departure, it had been neglected. James had struggled to keep things going, remarking on jobs to be done, mumbling about painters and decorators, succeeding only in keeping up the garden. Dorothy had lost interest.

It dawned on Eve as she looked around that since Sarah's death she had endured her home, its rapid decline and Dorothy's animosity. Although she and her mother had called a temporary truce, they had never seen eye to eye and never would. Now that the financial crisis was over, James could afford to refurbish the place, and keep Agnes on. Eve decided that the time had come to move out and start living her own life.

Calmly sitting in her tree, she felt grateful to be getting away from Dorothy. Grateful, too, for the tranquillity of the garden that had afforded her the only truly peaceful times she had ever known.

David Furlong had an uncanny way of making Eve aware of him, whether it was his magnetic smile or the blatant desire in his laughing blue eyes, she wasn't sure. He invited her to Glendalough. On the way there, minute by minute, the time stretched between them, Eve holding her breath, terrified of saying the wrong thing, waiting for him to speak, give a signal that everything was all right. He remained quiet, eyes on the road, his expression brooding. I mustn't make the first move, she told herself, over and over until the words were a rhythm in her head.

In Glendalough they examined the ancient church, David chatty and friendly, recounting the story of how Saint Kevin slept on a stone slab high above the lake for penance.

'I could live in a place like this,' David said, stretching out on the bank of the Upper Lake.

'Wouldn't you miss the buzz of the city, people? Or are you a country boy at heart?' Eve asked.

'Most definitely.' David laughed.

'Where will you go next?'

'I'm staying put. I prefer it here. Ireland's still my favourite country,' he said, rolling on to his back, his face upturned to the sun.

'Won't you get the wanderlust?'

'Nope. Too much to do here. I'm enjoying it. Tell me about your coffee shop.'

'I love the challenge of working for myself.'

'Inherited that from your grandfather,' David said.

'Yes. When I think how hard he worked building up his business, I feel very sad for him.' Eve cleared her throat.

David looked at her. 'You probably see us as the enemy, come to take everything away from you, but James will have quite a nest egg soon. Invested wisely, he should have a comfortable old age.'

'He hated the thought of selling his home,' Eve said.

'Now he won't have to, and he won't have the worry of the business either, but he'll still have a stake in it to keep him ticking over.'

'He deserves it.'

'He's a lucky man to have a beautiful granddaughter like you to care for him.'

His eyes were on her, making her blush. 'Let's go for a walk,' he said, helping her to her feet.

The path edged the lake, whose stillness lulled them into silence. Further uphill, it trailed off into a steep, gritty track. David held out his hand to Eve and she took it, picking her way carefully so as not to stumble on loose stones.

They walked down the far side of the mountain to the tranquil lake, the forest mirrored in its black depths. David stopped near some granite boulders and, to Eve's amazement, stripped down to his underpants and dived in. He swam away then back to her, leaned against a rock smiling, his eyes sweeping over her.

'Come on in,' he called. 'It's freezing.'

She walked in slowly, holding her dress up to her thighs, liking the feel of the cold water on her flesh.

He swam towards her, caught her unawares, and kissed her, his tongue tasting of lake water.

Pressing his cold, near-naked body close to hers, he guided her out of the water to the tiny shore. He lay on the shingle and pulled her down, close to him. She could feel the sun on her back drying her legs as his eyes, deep and fathomless as the lake, roamed her body.

'I've really enjoyed myself today,' he said, kissing her again.

Eve moved back, surveying the water shimmering on his hair. 'We could walk up to St Kevin's bed.'

'Not in this heat.'

The inflection in his voice caught her attention. There was no mistaking the longing in his eyes.

'I'm crazy about you, Eve Freeman. You're driving me mad with temptation. I didn't bargain for this when I went to acquire your grandfather's company,' David said.

She was suddenly shy. It was difficult to believe that David Furlong, man of the world, tough negotiator, wanted her.

'Me neither,' she murmured, as he kissed her, gently at first, then harder, more demanding, pulling her on top of him.

His thigh muscles tensed beneath her, his breathing became laboured.

'We've got to stop,' she said, gently pushing him away.

'Have dinner with me tonight.'

'Come to my flat. I'll cook it for us.'

'Are you sure?'

'I'd love to.'

Pauline was ironing her uncle Tom's shirts in what her

aunt Mary grandly referred to as 'the apartment', a bedroom-kitchenette and small bathroom at the top of the large white clapboard boarding-house in Long Island. Seamie, eighteen months old now, was toddling around the room pointing to the window, calling, 'Park, Mama, park.'

'In a few minutes, love,' Pauline assured him. 'As soon as I've finished these.'

Seamie clapped his chubby hands and chuckled, showing tiny perfect teeth, then continued to waddle around saying, 'Ball' and 'Park,' at suitable intervals. His dancing blue eyes, full of anticipation, reminded Pauline so strongly of Seamus that she found herself putting down the iron and rushing to hug and hold him in spite of his loud protestations.

'All right, all right, have it your own way!' She laughed, let go of him and returned to her ironing-board to finish the last shirt and place it on a hanger.

She wandered between the two rooms tidying up, before lifting Seamie to wipe his face with a wet flannel.

'No, no,' he protested again.

'Yes, yes,' she countered. 'I can't take you out with a dirty face. What would Aunt Mary say, and she a highly respected landlady in the neighbourhood?'

In the hallway, Pauline strapped Seamie into his push-chair, opened the back door and stepped out into the steady afternoon sunlight. A tall, lean young woman, with dark hair cut very short beneath a white baseball cap, and a pretty, open, tanned face, she was dressed in blue jeans and a white short-sleeved shirt. She walked quickly along the street, clutching the handle of the push-chair, her eyes fixed on the traffic lights at the junction where she would turn right for the park. They passed a row of large houses, most of which were hotels or restaurants, all painted gaily in a variety of seaside colours: pink, green, orange, yellow. The streets were empty, except for the line of enormous cars parked along the kerb, their chrome and enamel glittering in the sun.

As they approached the black iron gates of the park, they could hear the shouts and screams of the children in the playground. By the time she released Seamie from his harness he was tumbling out of his push-chair with excitement, his sun-hat askew. He made for the slide but she caught him and held him.

'Slide,' he whimpered, a wild look in his eyes.

'In a minute,' Pauline said, kissing his rumpled hair and replacing his cap.

Pauline looked forward to the trips to the park with the same eager anticipation as Seamie, but Wednesday was special. It was her half-day and they had the afternoon to themselves. 'Careful,' she said, lifting him gingerly on to the slide, holding his plump, wriggling little body while she straightened his legs out in front of him. Letting go of his hand she watched him slide away, his screams of delight rending the air, before she ran round to the front of the slide and watched his descent, his fine blond hair blowing in the breeze, his laughter splitting his face. As he reached the bottom, she opened her arms to scoop him up and hold him. 'Good boy,' she said, carrying him to the end of the queue to await his turn again, impatiently.

Later, at the swings, Pauline pushed Seamie while guardedly watching the other distracted mothers pushing their offspring. The local women were tough, busy, incurious, something for which Pauline was grateful. Since her arrival in Long Island she had remained aloof, conducting her life with an almost frightening coolness, only entertaining the briefest conversations with lodgers and guests.

Although she had settled into her aunt's boarding house with ease and had rapidly made herself indispensable to the business, she lay awake at night, her arms around her baby, terrified that she might one day be unmasked as a murderer. She had written to Eve a couple of times and had sent a note to Clare, with a photograph of Seamie, warning them not to tell anyone of her whereabouts.

As the brilliant sun beat down on them and the azure sky paled on the horizon, Pauline was glad of the shelter of the palm trees. She had been determined to like this bright, extraordinary suburb of Montauk, where fruit ripened and flowers bloomed early, where her love of the beach and her enthusiasm for small adventures could be indulged, and where her taste in movies was well catered for.

When she arrived, it had been a bitterly cold winter which was followed by a slow, wet spring. Pauline had set out deliberately to make herself happy and reviewed her new life while she kept her eyes on her little boy. She began work at six thirty each morning, balancing loaded trays with professional skill as she pushed her way through the swing door between the dining room and kitchen, never spilling or dropping anything. Her charm and energy were evident as she tripped expertly around the tables, smiling, her face brimming with vitality and goodwill in her determination to make an impact on the guests. She had elected to take on the most menial tasks to justify her aunt's kindness in giving her refuge. Instead, Mary Quirk quickly noting Pauline's natural ability to get on with the lodgers, gradually gave her more and more responsibility.

Mary had a long, narrow face and pursed lips, which gave her a severe look. But it was her green eyes and the proud tilt of her head that made Pauline wary of her, even when she smiled her sweetest smile, which was usually directed at Seamie. Although Mary enticed Seamie with candy and lollipops, the baby remained impervious to her charms, accepting her generosity as his birthright. When she indicated to Pauline her willingness to pay for him to attend playschool, Pauline knew that her aunt would recoup the fees in no time with Pauline's hard work.

Like most of the Long Island matrons, Mary Quirk was highly respected in her neighbourhood, both as a property owner and as a pillar of the Catholic community, of which she was a staunch member and regular entertainer of priests, nuns and all visiting clergy.

In the past few months Pauline prepared the bills for the guests on Friday afternoons, did the wages and took charge of the laundry. This was her aunt's way of acknowledging her intelligence and ambition. To Pauline, though, it was a godsend, alleviating the boredom of waiting tables day in, day out.

When Vittorio phoned her from London, Clare had to acknowledge that since he left Paris she had thought of him so much that she simply couldn't bring herself to acknowledge it. She had thought of his hands touching her, his eyes, dark brown and glittering against the blue of his shirt, and his graceful stride. Most of all she had thought of being wrapped in his strong arms, held against his broad shoulders, her lips raised for his kiss. Because she had resisted him for so long, she had difficulty now in accepting that Vittorio was free to be with whom he chose and that he wanted her.

'Hello,' she said, trying to keep her voice steady.

'My darling, have you been thinking of me?'

'You know I have,' she said, discomfited that he could read her thoughts, and that he knew how much she needed him, even if she were never to admit it.

'Working hard?'

'Of course.' Clare tried to remain austere out of sheer force of habit.

Deep down she did not really want to be involved with Vittorio or anybody. But she had succumbed and now she would have to learn to exercise a certain protocol. She would not let him take it for granted that she would allow him to make love to her whenever they met. That would be a mistake, and there was no room in her life for mistakes. She had invested too much of her life in building up her career.

But Vittorio would never let her do anything destructive. He was aware of his natural power over her and had been since they met. Now that they were together he would use it wisely, knowing that without her career Clare was nothing.

They met at a corner near the Eiffel Tower and walked along the bank of the Seine. Vittorio told her what he was doing with his students, how he was hoping for new, exciting talent to come his way in the next year. He said he was writing musical scores and songs but that as yet he had not shown them to anyone. Clare was fascinated to hear these details of his daily life: she imagined him sitting down each day, quietly working on the notes, forming the characters who would sing them.

'Perhaps some day you'll write something for me to play?'

Vittorio laughed. 'By the time I have anything worthwhile ready, you'll be too great a musician.'

Slowly Clare told him about herself and Sir George, what little she thought might interest him since she had seen him last. 'There's to be another concert as soon as Sir George thinks I'm fit to be let loose on the unsuspecting public.'

'Sir George is being cautious. These are only warming-up sessions. You'll be in the big arena before you know it. You'll travel the world and men will fall at your feet crazy with love for you.'

Clare looked at him, feeling again that great void between them that she had felt in the past. It was as if her life would go on independently of him or anyone, rollercoastering on its own track to a finale of its own making. Although Vittorio was walking beside her, smiling at her, his unmistakable love for her in his eyes, she felt as if a chill wind had enveloped her and she was being slowly blown away from him.

She stood still. He came to her and put his arms around her, sensing her sadness. 'What's wrong?' he asked, holding her tight.

She couldn't speak. She had no words to explain her deep sense of aloneness.

'I'm sorry, darling. I don't mean to upset you. But what I'm saying is true. There will be times when you'll have to make great journeys on your own. It will be difficult, of course, but I'll be waiting for you to come home to me from wherever you are. You think you won't manage without me but you will.' He leaned forward and kissed her. Clare's arms were around his neck. 'I missed you' she said, tears in her eyes.

They resumed their walk, arm in arm, towards Notre Dame. Clare felt completely happy. She would have gladly stayed in Paris, in her own little world with

Vittorio and Sir George, for ever. But already Vittorio was talking about her future, what she would need to do to achieve world fame, conjuring up images of her as a virtuoso pianist.

Silently Clare listened, wondering what had become of that skinny, long-legged girl, who had almost lost her nerve so many times so far. At the archway of the church Vittorio stopped and put his hand on her shoulder. She turned to face him.

'Will you marry me?' he asked gently.

Clare lifted her face for his kiss, the tears in her eyes spilling over, unchecked.

Eve had moved into the flat over the coffee shop. It was newly decorated in yellow and white, with a floral cane sofa and two cushion-covered wicker chairs to match. While the meal was cooking she set the table, turned on the lamps and lit the fire.

'Smells good.'

Eve swung round, a dish of steaming new potatoes in her hands. 'David! I didn't hear you knock.'

'I tried the bell and when there was no answer I came on up.' He was dressed in grey cords and a blue cashmere sweater that matched his eyes.

'The bell's not working. Sorry.'

'You look stunning, Eve,' David said, kissing her cheek.

'Thank you. Make yourself at home,' she said, putting down the hot bowl carefully on the table.

'Nice place you've got here,' he said, glancing around.

'I – I don't often get the chance to try out my culinary skills on my friends,' Eve said, putting steaks on to grill, realising how nervous she was.

'Here, let me help you.'

He took several hot dishes from the oven and

arranged them in the centre of the table, stoked up the fire and opened a bottle of red wine, leaving it in the fireplace to breathe.

'You're very domesticated,' Eve said, admiring his handiwork.

'Comes from living alone for far too long,' he answered ruefully. 'What kind of music would you like?' he asked, turning on the record player.

'Whatever you like.'

They listened to Elvis while they ate and washed up, David drying and stacking the dishes.

Lolling in chairs in front of the fire, they talked sporadically as the music played low in the background.

Suddenly, without warning, Louis Armstrong was singing 'Wonderful World', bringing back the memory of David and Bernie Power so vividly that it overwhelmed Eve.

'Would you like to dance?'

'Wouldn't you rather be dancing with Bernie Power?' Eve asked.

David looked at her oddly, and said, 'No. I'd rather be here with you.'

There was silence. He started to say something then stopped. After a minute, he said, 'Eve. I don't know what you want me to say.'

'Nothing. You'd better get your beauty sleep if you want to be fresh for that meeting in the morning.'

'Damn, Eve, what's come over you?' David said hoarsely. He touched her cheek, ran his fingers along her arm.

'What do you want of me, David?' Eve asked, exasperated.

'You know what I want.' He reached up and stroked her hair.

'If it's playing games like before I'm not interested.'

The intensity in her eyes made him step back.

'That was a long time ago, Eve. You were always there, right next door, and I suppose I took you for granted. Now, suddenly, I'm afraid if I say or do the wrong thing you'll disappear.'

Eve drew in her breath.

He kissed her, his mouth soft and cautious against hers. His hands tightened on her shoulders and his mouth became firm. The feeling of being held, touched and kissed by him gave Eve a warm glow. As his sensitive lips pressed into the hollow of her neck, she clung to him, her resolution to keep her distance driven away. His hands were tracing, exploring her spine, her ribcage, the small of her back. 'Eve.'

She opened her eyes and stared into his. 'Please, David,' she said softly. 'I'm not ready to—'

'Shhh.' His lips fastened on hers, stifling her feeble protest, pulling a powerful response from her. She moved against him, feeling the warmth of his breath next to her ear. 'Relax, Eve. Let me love you,' he whispered.

Her arms slid around his neck. Head thrown back, she waited for his kiss on her throat, shuddering as he touched her creamy skin with his lips and with fingers traced the swelling of her breasts. Groaning, Eve clung to him feeling the powerful surge of his desire.

He moved his hand along her midriff, caressing, opening buttons. Suddenly he stopped, sensing her withdrawal. 'What's the matter, darling?' he asked, his voice strained.

She twisted away from him. 'I'm scared, David.'

'Scared of what?'

'That it will all go wrong.'

He held her closer. 'I won't let anything go wrong, I promise. Trust me.'

He lifted her up in his powerful arms and carried her along the passage to the bedroom. She clung to him, her eyes closed, until he had laid her on the bed. There she gazed at him, hardly believing the longing in this beautiful man's face, the blatant desire in his gaze. He waited, tense and still, for a signal from her.

'David.' She opened her mouth to tell him that she wanted him too, but he was kissing her.

Instead of trying to explain her fears to him, her doubts about his past, her own past, she found herself unbuttoning his shirt while he fumbled with the fastening of her skirt. He stopped and let his eyes travel the length of her body, take in every detail. As his hand moved to her breast, a flame of desire shot through her. She turned towards him, touched his face, his broad chest, let her hands move down him. She hadn't been with a man since Chris and she was unprepared for the sudden surge of pain that shot through her with the knowledge that if she let David make love to her she would never stop needing him. She was unprepared to surrender to a life sentence like that again and what it involved. She was crying.

'It's all right,' he whispered. 'Don't be afraid. I'm here.'

She savoured his closeness, his caresses as he held her, his body protective over hers. 'Forgive me,' she said. 'I've spoilt your evening.'

'Ssh,' he said. 'I understand. You need time and I've got all the time in the world to give you. I'm not going anywhere. Let's take it slowly.'

'Thank you,' she said softly.

'Would you like to come with me on a trip to New York?' David asked.

Eve sat upright. 'I'd love to. When?'

'Sometime next month. I'm not sure of the dates yet.'

'That would be wonderful.'

They were in each other's arms, David holding her tight against him, his mouth seeking hers urgently. 'I'm longing for you,' he whispered.

'Let's go to bed,' she said, amazed at her own forwardness.

His hand tantalised her breasts, gliding down over her flat stomach to rest between her thighs. She groaned as he slid downwards, kisses on her stomach, her thighs, finally covering her most secret place with his mouth.

'David,' she gasped, shocked and thrilled at once by his audacity.

'Ssh,' he said. 'Relax. Let me love you properly.'

Her head was reeling as he continued to kiss and stroke every part of her with infinite gentleness, until she was so aroused that she cried out his name. As she was about to climax he moved over her and entered her so powerfully that she cleaved to him, her legs wrapped around his hips, both of them cast adrift on a sea of passion, pounding and thrashing the waves, reaching the shore together, spent, exhausted.

'I love you,' he whispered into her ear as he held her. Eve couldn't believe what she was hearing. She wanted to look at his face to verify his words, but she was afraid to move for fear of breaking the magic spell that seemed to be cast over them.

'I love you too,' she said, feeling the strangeness of the words.

'I never thought you'd say it.' He laughed, hugging her. A new strength came over Eve. She could put the past behind her now and look forward to whatever challenges she should meet.